https://www.brindlebooks.co.uk

RIDERS OF THE THREE KINGDOMS SAGA

BOOK ONE:

BRIDLED BY LOYALTY

BY

LLOYD MORRISON

Brindle Books Ltd

This edition published by
Brindle Books Ltd
Wakefield
United Kingdom

ISBN: 978-1-915631-17-6

CONTENTS

Acknowledgements

I would like to extend my heartfelt thanks to the following individuals for their invaluable contributions:

To Peter Maddison-Greenwell, for his expert insights on classical horsemanship and his thoughtful suggestions for the cover art.

To Rosie Sale and Alan Larsen of the Sealed Knot and Waller's Horse, whose knowledge of period attire and military cavalry greatly enriched this work.

To Mark Turnbull, whose *Cavalier Cast* podcast sparked my initial interest in the period and provided inspiration for many of my historical characters.

To Stuart Peachy, whose historical expertise and knowledge have been a great aid.

To Richard Hinchliffe of Brindle Publishing, for your unwavering guidance and support in bringing this series to publication.

And, last but certainly not least, to my dear family—Jodie, my wife, and Summer and Skye, my daughters—whose patience and understanding have allowed me to spend countless hours absorbed in my writing. You have my deepest gratitude for tolerating my distracted mind and the long evenings spent lost in this world. I thank you the most.

Prologue:

The bitter cold of January 1641 bit deep as William Stephens rode just behind Prince Maurice, who was always one to lead from the front. They skirted the outskirts of Amberg, an Imperial-held city that they were now besieging, another point of contention in the long war ravaging the continent. Their cavalry patrol scouted for enemy movements while a few foragers searched the nearby farms for supplies. Snow crunched beneath the horses' hooves, and breath steamed in the frigid air.

William, an English volunteer serving with the Protestant Swedish forces under Marshal Baner, had learned to keep a keen eye on the terrain. The undulating hills and skeletal trees offered ample cover for an ambush, and his instincts proved true.

A stir of movement caught his attention; a glint of steel to their right, accompanied by the crack of brush. William urged his chestnut gelding forward to reach the prince's side, shouting, "Dragoons right!"

Before his words had fully left his lips, musket shots cracked through the cold air. Three balls found their mark: one glanced off his breastplate, sending a metallic clang ringing in his ears; another struck the crest of his helmet, jarring his head back. But the third struck deep—his horse, Bruce, let out a pained scream as the ball tore into his flank. The mighty steed faltered, staggered, and collapsed beneath him.

William crashed onto the frozen ground, the impact ripping a painful gasp from his lungs. Jagged ice beneath the fresh snow gouged into his cheek as he lay there, tasting blood and the metallic tang of fear. The world spun wildly, a dizzy vortex of white and grey. Just before darkness claimed him, he caught the frantic pounding of hooves and the sharp crack of musket fire.

Suddenly, the air erupted with pistol and carbine shots, steel clashing in violent response. The prince's men, seasoned and battle-hardened, sprang into action with swift precision. In moments, they had decimated the enemy dragoons, shattering the ambush and turning the chaos in their favour.

Prince Maurice dismounted, his expression tight with concern. "Zee to him," he ordered sharply. A pair of soldiers lifted William's limp form, carrying him back to camp where the prince's personal physician awaited. Blood trickled down from a shallow cut on his temple where his helmet had deflected a shot, but miraculously, he was otherwise unharmed.

When he finally stirred, blinking up at the tent's canvas ceiling, standing nearby he saw Owen Jones, his tall, towering groom and friend, a constant presence and quiet strength in William's life. To his shock, the Prince was also there, standing beside Owen. "You saved my life Stephens," Maurice said in fluent English, though his accent carried a distinct Germanic and Dutch flavour—rounded vowels, guttural undertones with a rhythm reminiscent of those languages. "I vill not forget it," added the Prince of Palatinate, his voice genuine with deep gratitude.

William, still groggy but managing a weak smirk, rasped, "I only did my duty, my Highness." The Prince chuckled, clapping him on the shoulder. "Even zo, I think I owe you a horse".

Chapter 1
Late May 1641: Summer days

The summer sun hung high over the rolling fields of Little Sodbury, casting bright golden rays across the patchwork of meadows and hedgerows. The warm air buzzed with the hum of bees and crickets, creating a harmonious symphony, while the sweet scent of wildflowers and rich green grass filled the summer atmosphere.

Fifteen-year-old Benjamin Akins, with windswept light brown hair peeking from beneath his well-worn broad-brimmed hat, wore a mischievous grin as he leaned low over the neck of his large bay horse, Ralph. The powerful animal thundered beneath him, his hooves beating a steady rhythm into the dry earth of the bridleway that skirted the remnants of the old Roman fort to their right.

"Come on, Samson!" shouted Thomas Ward, the new stable hand, his voice carried by the summer breeze. Urging his sturdier horse forward, he called out, "Come on, keep up! Samson can do better than that!" Benjamin laughed over his shoulder, his mirth light and carefree.

With Ralph in the lead, his glossy coat shimmering in the sunlight, Benjamin felt the wind whip across his face and his loose linen shirt flap against his green wool doublet. His heart raced with the sheer joy of being fifteen on a perfect summer day.

They raced neck and neck now, Thomas striving to impress his new master's son as they galloped toward a gentle rise where the field curved to the right, bordered by ancient oak trees. Benjamin knew this route well; as they approached the turn, he anticipated it perfectly. Sitting back in the saddle, he gave a subtle half-halt with the reins, shortening Ralph's stride to navigate the turn with ease.

"I won't let you beat me!" Thomas shouted, glancing at Benjamin, who had slowed to prepare for the turn. With a firm pull on the reins, Samson lifted his head in protest against the heavy pressure on his bit. Nonetheless, the horse quickly adjusted, slowing to make the corner in a canter.

Benjamin shook his head, disapproving of Thomas's horsemanship but amused by his eagerness to prove himself. "We'll see about that!" he replied, giving a gentle squeeze with his thighs to urge Ralph onward, leaving the old fort behind. Ahead lay a final challenge: a broken tree trunk stretched across the path leading into the woods before they reached Portway Lane and home. "Jump ahead and be ready for this!" Benjamin called back to Thomas.

He shortened the reins, tightened his core, and sat deep in the saddle, encouraging Ralph to maintain his speed. The horse locked onto the jump, lifting his head slightly with a snort of excitement. With confidence, Ralph leaped over the large log, and Benjamin moved in perfect harmony with his motion.

As they touched down lightly, Benjamin glanced back to see how Thomas handled the obstacle. He watched as Samson cleared the log with ease, even though Thomas lagged slightly behind, recovering well. "That'll do—well done for keeping up!" Benjamin slowed Ralph to a trot, raising his hand to signal to Thomas that the race was over.

"I almost had you, Master Akins!" Thomas grinned, standing taller and slighter than Benjamin, though a year older. "This horse is incredible—the finest I've ever ridden!" he exclaimed, admiration shining in his eyes. Benjamin smiled, appreciating the compliment.
As their horses settled into a steady walk, the riders eased their reins, allowing the animals to stretch their necks. Benjamin, breathing hard from the ride, noticed the gentle pats Thomas gave Samson.

"Who taught you to ride?" Benjamin asked.

"My father—Old Man Ward's younger brother," Thomas replied. "He was a farrier; he taught me both the trade and how to ride."

"So, you'll be living with your uncle now?" Benjamin observed.

"Aye, Master Akins," Thomas confirmed. "He said he would take me in."

"Where is your father?" Benjamin inquired tentatively.

"He went off to fight the Scots with the King's army and hasn't returned in nearly two years. I haven't heard a word," Thomas explained, a hint of sorrow in his voice. "I've been getting by as a groom, helping to shoe horses and doing whatever I can to earn my keep. My uncle is getting elderly and needs assistance, so he agreed to let me stay in the hut he rents from you. But first, I had to gain your father's approval and prove my worth."

Benjamin hesitated to delve into the topic of his own mother, a subject that always stung after his loss. Instead, he changed the subject. Clearing his throat, he said, "Your riding is commendable, though a bit heavy-handed. These horses are finely trained and have soft mouths, so we don't want to ruin them with rough hands. I'll help you refine your technique. Your leg position is good, and you have a natural balance, which is why you'll be a great help exercising the horses."

"Next time, I'll beat you, Master Akins!" Thomas said with a determined look in his eyes.

Benjamin laughed, patting Ralph's damp neck as Ralph tossed his head proudly.

"In open flat country, Samson might have the edge, as would his brothers. But put some wide hedgerows in the way and Ralph would win every time, he is brave and will jump almost anything you put in front of him." Ralph seemed to understand the compliment, nodding in agreement. "However, to Samson's credit, he's a much smoother ride; if I were travelling long distances, he would be the horse to have." Benjamin reached over to pat Samson.

"Indeed, he's a comfortable ride solid as an oak. I do love his three white socks, though I imagine they're a challenge to keep clean in winter." Thomas Smirked.

Benjamin nodded. "Spoken like a true groom. We have one grey—Mickey, he's the biggest headache to keep clean as you can imagine, he loves to find mud, think he wants to be bay like his half-brothers!

"Yeah its always the greys that find the muddy patches of the field to roll in, can't wait to meet them" Thomas said with genuine excitement.

"You'll meet him and the others later. We've bred and trained these horses; they're all responsive to commands. Ralph even knows a few tricks."

Thomas looked puzzled. "Tricks?"
"I'll show you one day," Benjamin promised with a grin.

"I would love to see that," Thomas replied, smiling.

"Ralph here didn't have the easiest start in life, his mother didn't survive his birth and it was touch and go for a while. I was just a boy but my father and I helped nurse him back to health. He was a gangly youngster but now look at him!" Benjamin exclaimed.

"He is a fine-looking horse," Thomas said with genuine admiration.

"Now that we've shared some merriment, let's return to the yard and see how you handle those tasks that will occupy most of your time. I must warn you, we run a tight ship with the highest standards and my father is a stickler for detail, we are already running behind for the day."

"I fear no hard work, Master Akins; I have laboured hard all my life," Thomas replied resolutely.

Benjamin smiled. "Haven't we all? I'll give you a run-down of our ways once we arrive."

The young men and their steeds welcomed the cool shade beneath the woods, the horses' flanks heaving as they recovered their breath. The air was thick with the sweet, unmistakable aroma of horses – a foamy scent both familiar and difficult to name, intensified by the warmth. Yet, both riders felt the heat, their eyes drawn toward the sun-drenched Portway Road shimmering just ahead.

The horses carefully navigated the cobbled path, their shoes scraping against the worn stones. As they passed, both riders turned towards Little Sodbury Manor, nestled amongst the gentle, honey-stoned slopes of the Cotswold hills. The Stephens family home, built of that same golden stone, radiated comfortable solidity rather than ostentatious display. Its gabled roof, styled after the early Tudors, hinted at alterations to a late medieval core, a testament to generations of quiet prosperity. Prominent chimneys promised warmth, bathed in sunlight that glinted off the leaded, mullioned windows."

Despite the Stephens being gentry, they had become family friends of the Akins in the last couple of years. The ancient walls spoke of stability, resisting time itself.

It was a sight Benjamin knew well—a constant, quiet reminder of the world of gentry, a world to which he felt he would never truly belong. In his heart, it loomed not as a welcoming home, but as an obstacle, a tangible representation of the social divide that threatened to keep him from winning the heart of the girl he secretly adored.

His family owned their own land and a modest yet respectable farmhouse. They had done well in just one generation, rising from servants to yeomanry with help from some benefactors; however, they lacked the connections and prestige of families like the Stephens—breeding and titles that would deem him a suitable match for the Stephens' only daughter. Benjamin understood this, despite the family's fondness for him. Alas, Jane Stephens was far beyond his reach. Even if she felt as he did, which he often suspected, he could not be certain. Yes, Benjamin concluded, stop torturing yourself; know your place and give up any hope that it will ever change.

Snapping back to the present as they neared the Akins family stud farm and home, familiar scents of hay, horse flesh, and excrement wafted toward them, accompanied by the rhythmic sound of a hammer ringing across the quiet countryside.
The Fairfield Farm stretched out, comprising five neatly fenced paddocks of about two acres each, a sheltered barn area for the mares and foals and separate individual wooden stable blocks on the other side of the house for the stallions.

The farmhouse itself boasted a sturdy Tudor design, complete with a tall, thatched roof. Benjamin followed Thomas's gaze to the unmistakable figure of his father, Stephen Akins. Despite being only forty-five he moved with the weight of a man older than his years. His wide-

brimmed hat shaded his weathered features from the sun.
Even from a distance, Benjamin sensed his father's intense
focus, his mind consumed with decisions about breeding,
sales, and the endless demands of running a stud farm.
Years of pain and sorrow etched themselves into his face,
where an unkempt beard streaked with grey framed features that were rough, yet not unhandsome.

Benjamin sighed inwardly; he knew that the moment his
father laid eyes on him, his carefree escapades would
quickly become a distant memory, replaced by a flurry of
tasks and admonishments. As they turned onto the lane
leading to the farmhouse, the boys reined in their horses.

"You must wash both of these lads down thoroughly, dry
them with straw then bush them off, and check their feet
first," Benjamin instructed briskly. "Remove any stones,
then take them to their stables—each has his name carved
into the wooden planks on the doors." Thomas nodded in
understanding, mentally ticking off the tasks.

"Benjamin!" Stephen called out as he strode toward them.
"What hour do you call this?" He approached with purpose
just as the boys dismounted, neatly adjusting their stirrups
and loosening the girth straps.

"Make haste, Thomas. I shall manage my father. Your
uncle is shoeing Micky; he appears nearly finished, so he
can show you where we store the tack and how to put it
away properly clean off any sweat." He gave his instructions in a brisk but discreet manner before responding to
his father.

"Good afternoon, Father. I beg your pardon for my tardi-
ness, both horses were quite spirited this morning and in
need of vigorous exercise," Benjamin replied quickly as
Thomas led the horses away as instructed.

"Indeed, look at them! They both appear blown. I daresay you've been racing them," Stephen remarked, in a disproving tone.

Benjamin shrugged, a hint of mischief in his eyes. "Well, we exercised them well, if that's what you mean."

"I hope it was worth it; you'll be mucking out stalls and fields until sunset at this rate. I need to get going, we have a mare being brought here and I was going to use Ralph as a teaser before Miller goes about his business but the client has little time, so we'll let him get straight to it."

Stephen paused, then continued, "But first, you must go up to the manor and fetch your sister. She's been schooling with Mistress Mary Stephens, reading scripture with young Jane, but she needs to get back here to attend to her duties."

At the mention of Jane, Benjamin felt a flush creep across his cheeks.

"Are you well, son? You look rather flushed," Stephen observed, a knowing glint in his eye. "Be off then and don't dawdle. Mind your manners before Mistress Stephens too and present yourself properly especially regarding that hat, which I might say has seen better days. When she gets back your sister must see to the vegetable garden and prepare supper, and we have much to discuss this evening," he added, a hint of anticipation in his tone.

"Very well, Father. I shall attend to it immediately," Benjamin replied, his thoughts now consumed by the prospect of seeing—and perhaps even speaking with—Jane Stephens, if he were lucky. He dashed towards the house, intent on changing into his finer clothes, the ones normally reserved for Sunday services.

Chapter 2
Little Sodbury Gardens

Benjamin's heart betrayed him, quickening at the mere thought of Jane as he walked the short distance to Little Sodbury Manor. He had considered saddling one of the horses to appear more dashing but then thought better of it; such a display would seem ludicrous for so brief a journey, and his father would surely chide him.

The manor rose majestically before him, its grey stone subtly glistening in the sunlight and framed by ancient yew trees. A young housekeeper, a slender and bright-eyed girl perhaps a little older than he, met him at the gate with a shy smile. "Master Akins, your sister is in the garden with Mistress Stephens. The master is away on business with the steward of the estate. Please forgive me—I'll inform Mistress Stephens of your arrival," she said coyly.

Benjamin, somewhat naïve to the effect his good looks had on the fairer sex, had eyes only for Jane. Following the young girl through the grand front entrance felt like stepping into a world to which he did not quite belong.

The gardens were in full summer bloom, neat and orderly, with the sweet scent of lavender and roses carrying on the gentle breeze. Beneath the shade of a great yew tree sat Mistress Stephens, her daughter Jane beside her, and Benjamin's sister Sarah, all listening intently as Mistress Mary Stephens read from a large, leather-bound Bible with gilded edges and a brass clasp.

Benjamin hesitated at the sight; they had not yet noticed his arrival, however, the housekeeper curtseyed gracefully, and before she spoke, Sarah caught sight of her brother and called out, "Ben!"

At once, Jane turned, and their eyes met. In that moment,

Benjamin felt as though the earth had tilted beneath him. She was stunning—her clear, unblemished skin and striking hazel eyes complemented the pale blue of her exquisite gown. Her delicate features were framed by silky dark brown hair that cascaded in lovely waves from her silk coif.

"Master Akins," Mistress Stephens greeted warmly despite her formality. Benjamin bowed slightly. "Mistress, my father sent me to bring Sarah home."

"Of course," she replied, placing her open Bible on her lap. "But there is no rush, surely! Stay a while; we were just finishing our lesson. A little scripture nourishes the soul. I understand your uncle taught you both to read?"

Benjamin swallowed hard, stealing a glance at Jane, who watched him with curiosity. "Aye, Mistress," he replied quietly, taking a seat beneath the great yew tree in an attempt to calm his racing heart.

"We were looking **at 1 John 4, verse 8**. Would you like to read it aloud for us?" Benjamin reddened at the request, feeling embarrassed. "Yes, if you wish," he replied coyly.

Paul Akins, a deacon, had taught him to read. Although he had made progress, he knew he fell short compared to his younger sister, who excelled at nearly everything, including reading. He silently prayed that today's passage would not be too difficult. Leaning forward, he gazed at the open Bible before him, admiring its elegant craftsmanship.

Mistress Stephens placed her finger beside the passage she wanted him to read:

"He that loveth not knoweth not God; for God is love." Benjamin read nervously
"I will continue the passage it reads, **In this was manifes-**

ted the love of God toward us, because that God sent his only begotten Son into the world, that we might live through him…' What do you think this tells us?" Mistress Stephens asked the group.

Sarah, never shy with her opinions, raised her hand eagerly. "Sarah, go ahead," Mistress Stephens encouraged with a nod.

"God's primary virtue is love and he gave his only begotten son as a ransom for us all."

"Yes, that is correct," Mistress Stephens replied.

"But, what I don't understand is, if God is Jesus and they are the same, then He sacrificed a part of himself for us— the Father and the Holy Spirit as well. It doesn't seem to make sense. Surely Scripture indicates they are separate rather than one. We learned recently that God's name is Jehovah, but he is also Jesus."

"An interesting thought, Sarah," Mistress Stephens acknowledged. "There are many scriptures that add mystery to this fine question, but the answer would be the Trinity. We can explore it another day."

"Where can we find mention of the Trinity in Scripture?" Sarah asked eagerly.

"Well Sarah, you are keen this morning, another good question. While the term 'Trinity' isn't directly mentioned, there are scriptures that priests might refer to, though some debate their translation," Mistress Stephens replied, pausing. "I must remind you Sarah, that while it's safe to discuss such things with me, be cautious about raising these questions elsewhere with those you don't trust—it can be dangerous, especially for us ladies. Some priests don't take kindly to being pressed on such matters. Rest assured, the

Bible holds all the answers, and we must pray to God for insight."

Sarah nodded. "Our Uncle Paul says the same about things he gathers from his study of Scripture."

"Does he? He seems like an interesting man." Mistress Stephens snapped the book closed, causing the distracted Benjamin to jump as his attention was drawn back to her.

With a subtle smile betraying amusement at Benjamin and Jane, Mistress Stephens regained her composure and stood, signalling the end of the lesson. Sarah, beaming, reflected her genuine enjoyment of the learning session.

Benjamin was preparing to depart when Jane approached him. "Master Akins," she began, her voice gentle, "I would be very interested in visiting your father's stables. My father has often praised the quality of your horses and I find them to be the most beautiful of creatures," she concluded with a sincere smile.

Benjamin, caught off guard, stammered, "Indeed, Mistress, I share your admiration." A broad, almost foolish grin spread across his face.

"Jane, you must ask your father, who will then speak with Mr. Akins. It is time for your embroidery lesson; wish Sarah and Benjamin farewell," Mistress Mary declared, cutting short the exchange.

Mistress Stephens' sharp tone had abruptly snapped him out of a trance.

Benjamin bowed and Sarah curtsied respectfully. "Thank you, Mistress Stephens, for the time you spend helping my sister with her reading," he managed, his wits returning.
"It is a gift that all should have, and I pray to God that one

day it will be so. Your sister is a pleasure to teach—a bright pupil. Please send my warm regards to your father. Ruth will see you out. Good day to you both." With a wave of her hand, Mistress Stephens glided away gracefully, followed by Jane, who looked back and offered Benjamin a small, knowing smile before waving to Sarah.

"Bye, Jane! See you next week!" Sarah called out. Benjamin stood with his heart pounding, as if he had just ridden a hard gallop for miles.

"Ben, I think she likes you," Sarah teased, smirking up at him. "You like her!"
"Shh, sister," Benjamin exhaled sharply. "Don't be foolish," he muttered.

As Ruth, the same girl who had led him into the garden, escorted them along the long path toward the road home, she gave him a longing smile, which Benjamin didn't notice. His mind was not on the road ahead or the short Bible lesson he had just attended. It was on Jane Stephens' smile and the tantalising possibility—however improbable—that she might see him as more than just the son of a lowly horse breeder.

Chapter 3
Opportunities

The sun had begun its descent, casting a warm amber glow over the rolling fields of Fairfield Farm. The aroma of a hearty meal hung invitingly in the air of the oak-panelled dining room at the Akins household.

Benjamin sat upright, his back straight and hands neatly folded, quietly observing the gentle rituals of suppertime. His back ached from the day's labour and the hearth remained unlit due to the summer warmth, yet the room still felt cosy and inviting.

Sarah moved around the table, placing bowls of thick broth, seasoned with sage and pepper, and generous chunks of pigeon. In the centre, she laid a large plate bearing a thick slice of crusty bread and a wedge of soft cheese, accompanied by a big jug of frothy ale.

Her father, Stephen, took his customary place at the head of the table, with Benjamin to his right and Sarah to his left after receiving her bowl from the kitchen.

"I shall say grace," Stephen announced, bowing his head and closing his eyes. His children followed suit.

"Our Father, which art in heaven, hallowed be Thy name. Thy kingdom come, Thy will be done in earth, as it is in heaven. Give us this day our daily bread. And forgive us our debts as we forgive our debtors. And lead us not into temptation but deliver us from evil; for Thine is the kingdom, and the power, and the glory, forever. Amen."

Both Brother and sister responded with 'Amen', opening their eyes and eagerly began tucking into their pottage, Benjamin reached for a chunk of bread, still warm. Being freshly baked it cracked with a satisfying crunch as Benjamin broke off a piece.

Stephen cleared his throat, his deep voice breaking the quiet: "How did the new Stable lad go today, Son?"

"He did well father, decent rider and hard-working, quick to learner too."

"Will he earn his keep? because he will need to"

Benjamin nodded "I think he will Father, still early days." They continued eating. "Is there something on your mind, father, you seemed distracted." Asked Benjamin

"Aye well, it seems the Smyths have reached out again" he said, his tone steady though there was a glint of curiosity in his eye as he produced a small letter with a broken seal

"A letter from Thomas at Ashton court father?" his interest piqued. Stephen gave a small nod of his head whilst taking a small sip of Ale from the cup he had just filled.

"What do they want father?" Benjamin asked eagerly

"It seems he has a fresh shipment of Spanish horses in via Portugal to Bristol. Master Smyth is using that riding master of his, Tiago, acting as an agent. You remember him, don't you Benjamin?

"Oh yes, I do!" A bright smile flashed across Benjamin's face in memory of his visits to Ashton Court, where he had met Tiago.

The flamboyant Tiago had shown him how to make a horse dance, introduced him to the impressive stables at Ashton court, and shared insights about the Smyths many horses—some bred for racing, others for hunting. It was the first time Benjamin had seen the Spanish horse.

Benjamin thought of them as some of the most graceful

and agile creatures he had ever encountered. It was said they were bred for war, which struck him as a waste.

"Well, the letter came by courier this morning. It seems Master Thomas Smyth wants me to look over the horses. He claims they are the finest stock, but he wants my opinion on the best ones to sell and ones he should keep and breed. He thinks I may be interested in buying one from him.

Benjamin shifted in his seat "They are very fine horses, they move like nothing I've ever seen, but they are very expensive, aren't they father?"

"Aye". Stephen said, "they are hugely popular with the Nobles. Master Thomas Smyth believes they could be the answer to our problems. With the ten acres we have we will always be limited to the numbers we can have here; you know what my father Walter always said."

"…One acre per horse, nothing more, nothing less," Sarah interjected.

Stephen gave a slight smile at the echo of his father's voice, a bittersweet reminder of his absence.

Keen to move on, Sarah added, "So it will be worth the investment, Father? Some of ours will need to go to make way." Sharp and to the point as always.

A look of horror crossed Benjamin's face as realisation set in.

Stephen exhaled through his nose, noticing his son's pained expression. "Aye, as I've said many times, we are a stud farm and horse traders. We can't get too attached to our horses; they are our livelihood. Trading is the only way we keep a roof over our heads and food in our bellies." He paused to take a bite of cheese, washed down with a swig of ale, emphasising his point. "Look, we are overstocked with too many stallions. The breeding side is slowing down; the gentry want the finished product. They lack patience and knowledge, unlike their fathers."

"However," he continued, "this is pushing prices up. Whispers of troubles in Ireland and the threat of war have the gentry buying horses. So, one or more of the boys might have to go while prices are high. We need the capital, and we don't have the land for more. Nobody around here is selling land, and if they do, we can't compete with the Fosters, who pay way over the odds for anything. Heaven knows why." Stephen stroked his bread, the habit he had when thinking hard on a matter.

"Father, I understand your reasoning, but who do you plan to sell?" Benjamin asked, his voice strained with emotion.

"I'm thinking of Mickey. Master Thomas might be interested in a trade. He rode him during the Seymour's Cotswold hunt this winter and was quite impressed with his quirky and forward nature. He's the kind of horseman Mickey needs to bring out the best in him."

Benjamin was perplexed by his father's ease with the wealthy, a stark contrast to the image he had of his grandfather, Walter, a rough-around-the-edges and straight-talking man who somehow came to hold a prominent position as the Smyth Master of horse at the lavish Ashton Court, before the family's move to Fairfield Farm when Benjamin was just a baby.

"And then I think it's between Samson and Miller," Stephen continued, interrupting Benjamin's train of thought. He felt a wave of relief that his father hadn't suggested Ralph, knowing he would need every penny to purchase a stallion and some pure Spanish brood mares to meet the demands of the high-born clientele. Ralph, being gelded, due to his conformation not meeting his father's standards. However, he was valuable for leading the brood mares and acting as a teaser to check mares where in season, before introducing the stallions. Ralph also participated in hunts, where Benjamin or Stephen made sure that the stallions loaned for trials were used responsibly.

"Miller is a finer mix, with perfect conformation for a medium hunter. I'll keep him as the main stud here to continue our hunter breeding, especially since old Duke is getting on and isn't as impressive for clients when compared to Miller. It must be Samson," Stephen said with resignation. "I'll let you choose the two brood mares to accompany him."

Benjamin nodded, fighting to keep his emotions in check as his heart sank under the weight of the of the decision, but knowing better than to argue with his father once his mind was made up.

After a long pause, Stephen turned to Benjamin, understanding how much he cared for the horses and the bonds he shared with them. "You see, son, the Smyths aren't just offering horses; they're presenting a business opportunity that might change everything for us. The Smyths have always looked after us. Thomas's father, Hugh, loved my father, Walter, and treated us more like family than servants. We owe them everything, and we must trust that Master Thomas has our best interests at heart, even though both our fathers have passed. Thomas is his father's son. I helped raise him and taught him the basics of riding before his fine schoolmasters came along. He spent so much time in the stables, and fortunately for us, he shares his father's passion for horses." He paused to study the letter once more.
"He has invited us to Bristol next Saturday and will begin just after the bells ring for Matins at 8am, this is an invita-

tion only horse auction, near St. James Church, where Thomas will be hosting the worthies of the county and beyond. We have much to prepare." Stephen Akins said excitement, lacing his voice, "This could just be the break we need right now," again stroking his bread,

Once they had finished eating, Sarah cleared the table, and the family settled down for the night.

Benjamin felt a mixture of feelings. but mainly heartbreak at the prospect of saying goodbye to horses he had helped raise from birth. He tried to focus on the upcoming auction and the prospect of visiting Bristol, a welcome break from the monotony of everyday life.

Chapter 4
The Morning Routine.

Looking out of his open window, Benjamin took in the scene. The first golden threads of morning light stretched over the rolling hills of Little Sodbury, casting long shadows across the fields of Fairfield Farm. A thin mist still clung to the pastures, softening the outlines of the wooden fence posts and the grazing horses, their breath rising in the cool air like faint smoke. The air was crisp, laced with the scent of damp earth and freshly cut hay, while the distant call of a lark marked the beginning of another day.

Benjamin exhaled softly, recalling last night's decisions and realising it wasn't just a bad dream.

Samson and Ralph, paddock buddies, both looked up as Benjamin closed his window, their ears pricked and alert. They quickly returned to their rhythmic chewing, bringing their heads back down to graze in unison.

Within the farmhouse, the day had begun; father and sister were already moving about, their footsteps resonating through the timber frame. The usual morning sounds were amplified by the anticipation of their trip to Bristol in five days, a journey for which preparations were now underway.

There was no time to mope. Rubbing sleep from his eyes, Benjamin reached for his linen shirt and wool breeches. He could hear his father, Stephen, moving around downstairs, the sound of the iron poker scraping against the hearth as he stoked the morning fire.
Across the hall, Sarah's door creaked as she started her day.

Benjamin hurried downstairs to the kitchen, where the aroma of oats and honey already filled the air. Sarah had taken over the porridge, a task their father had begun before drifting to the window, his gaze fixed on the stables outside.

"Morning, lad," Stephen greeted him. "You're up just in time. The horses will be wanting their oats soon." Benjamin nodded and ate quickly, knowing his father would soon be pushing him to begin the day's work.

"I want the mares picked out, and Mickey and Samson need a good wash and groom. Take your grooming kit with you; we'll have to do it again after travelling to Bristol. We need them gleaming if we want to fetch the best price they deserve."

"Yes, Father, Thomas and I will get right to it" Benjamin replied

Sarah sat quietly, listening. "I could clean their tack today," she offered.
Stephen nodded approvingly. "Good thinking, lass. We'll need everything in order."

"Will I be coming, Father?" Sarah asked hopefully.

"No, not this time, my girl. I need to devise a plan for that," Stephen replied

"Could I ask Mistress Stephens if she might have me?" she suggested.

"Hmm, best not. I wouldn't want to impose on her; she already does so much for us with your reading. It wouldn't be proper to ask," Stephen said.

Sarah looked downcast by the double blow from her father but she respectfully nodded in agreement.
"A solution will come our way, God willing. I'll need

Benjamin and Thomas, along with his uncle to ride and lead the horses. I should check if my fowling piece is in good working order, and I'll get the boys some clubs just in case. Our stock would be prime targets for highwaymen. Let's pray we don't run into any trouble."

Sarah asked, "Father, if you do, be sure to make a dash for it! I'm sure the average highwayman's horse wouldn't keep up with Samson, Mickey, or Ralph."

Stephen laughed. "True, but we'd still lose the mares and old man Ward will be riding Duke—I'm not sure the old boy would be interested in galloping for long, especially with Ward wobbling around on his back like a sack of spuds."

They all burst into laughter at the thought, lightening the mood for a moment.

Suddenly, there was a knock at the door. Stephen moved to open it and found old man Ward standing there. "I beg your pardon, Master Akins, sorry to disturb you," he said, cap in hand.

"Your ears must be burning," Stephen remarked with a wide smile, turning to his children.

"Master Akins," Ward announced, "a Mr. Cropper has arrived asking to speak with you."

"Indeed, we know Mr. Cropper," Stephen replied, turning to Sarah. "Tell him I'll be there directly. Quickly now, fetch my best hat and doublet."

Mr. Cropper stood tapping his foot, impatience etched on his face as Benjamin and his father quickly emerged from the house, giving themselves a final brush-off.
As the tall, slender man—his severe features framed by a

blend of dark and grey hair—spotted them, a practised smile bloomed across his face, momentarily concealing a hint of irritation.

"Mr. Akins," he began, his voice smooth and measured, "I bring greetings from my master, John Stephens Esquire of Little Sodbury Manor. He seeks a favour of you gentlemen" he paused, allowing the weight of his words to settle before continuing "He would like to visit at your establishment later this morning, with young Mistress Jane, who wishes to see your horses before going on a ride with her father this day."

Mr. Cropper surveyed the farmhouse and paddocks, searching for something that might interest the young Mistress. His nose wrinkled at the pungent aroma of fresh horse manure.

Meanwhile, Thomas tipped a barrow of manure from the field, shovelling it onto the steaming muck heap downwind of the increasingly displeased Mr. Cropper, who drew himself up stiffly as the scent thickened in the air.

"If that is his wish, how could I refuse? The family has been good neighbours to us. Yes, of course—if they don't mind the smell, we will have the place tidied up by then," Stephen anticipated the steward's thoughts.

"Yes, that might be wise," Mr. Cropper replied. "I shall pass on the message. Good day, Mr. Akins. God's blessings upon your day." He turned on his heel and marched away.

"Well, he's a delight," Benjamin laughed as Sarah joined them.

"What did Mr. Cropper want, Father?" Sarah asked.

"It seems Master Stephens and your friend Jane are coming to pay us a visit," Stephen replied.

In an instant, Benjamin's focus shifted from the haughty steward to the exhilarating realisation that Jane was coming; a thrill coursed through him like a bolt of lightning. "We must get the place ready, Father! Let's snap to it!".

Stephen turned to Sarah, raising his eyebrows with a smirk as Benjamin dashed off in a flurry of urgency. "Perhaps we shall have your friend Jane visit us every morning, that foolish boy," he chuckled, shaking his head.

Sarah smiled, tucking her arm under her father's as they strolled back toward the farmhouse.

"Do you know what this is all about, Sarah?" Stephen asked.

Looking up at him with a smile, she replied, "I believe Jane wishes to see the Akins stock."

Stephen appeared puzzled for a moment, then realisation dawned at his daughter's cleverness.

"You, my girl, are too smart for your own good," he said, ruffling her hair with his knuckle.

She let out a cheeky giggle "Oi get off" she said playfully.

"It's going to be a long day I reckon," Stephen said, deep in thought. "But perhaps it's an opportunity..." He stroked his beard in contemplation.

A few hours later, Mr. Cropper returned, accompanied by two riders not far behind him. The Akins family formed a line to welcome their visitors, while Thomas and his uncle stood nearby looking a little awkward at the unaccustomed formality.

"Master Stephens and young Mistress Jane!" Mr. Cropper announced.

"Thank you, Mr. Cropper, but such ceremony is unnecessary," John Stephens responded with a warm smile, nodding toward the family with humility. "The Akins family are both friends and neighbours, and we appreciate your hospitality on such short notice. I hope you can forgive me."

"It is always a pleasure. Thank you for coming," replied Stephen Akins, bowing his head in a gesture of respect to his social superior.

Mistress Jane, dressed in a dark green riding dress, sat elegantly side-saddle atop a perfectly groomed light grey pony.

"Welcome, Mistress Jane, it is an honour that you wish to explore our humble establishment. I fear it may disappoint," Stephen added with an apologetic smile.

"Thank you, Mr. Akins. Though we are neighbours, I have never ventured beyond the private pathway. Your horses are quite splendid, and I would be delighted to see them up close. I am a rather avid equestrian myself; my mother often worries, but I simply adore riding," Mistress Jane said smoothly.

"Yes, she has been rather insistent," John admitted. "I

have been away on business these past few days, but I felt it was time to indulge her. Once again, you have my gratitude."

As he spoke, he dismounted from his black-and-white cob, wincing slightly upon landing—a subtle sign of his advancing age. Once on the ground, he adjusted his belt and the scabbard of his ornate rapier, standing tall and composed.

Of middling height and stature, John wore knee-high riding boots crafted from supple brown leather, which complemented his elegantly tailored green doublet, matching his daughter's dress in colour. The doublet was rich in texture and adorned with intricate stitching. A buff-coloured cloak draped gracefully over his shoulders, adding warmth and refinement to his appearance. His neatly trimmed moustache framed his face, and greying hair cascaded loosely from beneath a broad felt hat, jauntily adorned with a striking feather that added a flair of distinction.

John made his way toward his daughter to assist her in dismounting while Mr. Cropper took the reins of his horse. Jane descended from her side saddle with a grace that contrasted with her father's slight struggle. "I don't need your help, Papa, but thank you," she replied, exchanging warm smiles with him. Her piercing hazel eyes darted toward Benjamin, whose delight at seeing her was clear.

Meanwhile, Thomas and his uncle quickly took the reins of their mounts, while Jane comforted her pony with a gentle pat. "Good boy, Minnie," she cooed fondly before the pony was led away.

"Please," Stephen offered with a warm smile, "join me inside for a bit of ale and some bread and cheese. It must be near lunchtime."

"Now, Stephen, please call me John. Haven't I told you that before? It would be my pleasure," he replied, gesturing broadly. "You have a tidy and well organised establishment here, and I wouldn't expect anything less. I trust my daughter will be entertained in my absence?"

"Certainly," Sarah replied immediately, linking her arm with Jane's. "Benjamin and I will show her around the horses." Benjamin stepped forward with an easy smile.

"If Mistress Jane is interested in our stud farm, she will find no finer specimens than the horses we keep here," he said proudly.

"That remains to be seen," Jane responded playfully, her brown eyes sparkling as she allowed herself to be led away at a brisk pace.

John gave a slight nod in Mr. Cropper's direction. The watchful chaperone picked up on his cue and followed, while John accompanied his host to the farmhouse.

Mr. Cropper maintained a respectable distance, hands clasped behind his back, as he kept a close eye on the trio moving toward the stables. Sarah and Jane fell into comfortable conversation, reminiscing about their lessons at the manor and the time spent playing in the gardens.

Benjamin led the way, heading toward the first stable—Millbank, as it was formally known. However, with an affectionate tone, he spoke of the horse inside, calling him by his stable name: Miller.

"This is my father's favourite," Benjamin announced, gesturing to the tall bay horse. With a long, handsome face and a dark, glossy mane trimmed short amplifying his thick muscular neck, he stood unusually tall at 17 hands, pricked ears alert as the trio approached, as if posing for a painting.

"He's a very good-looking horse," Jane said, stepping forward to pat Miller's nose. The horse stood like a statue, exuding majesty.

"He's the golden boy—tall and well put together, with what we call nice conformation," Benjamin explained. "He's a fine hunter with perfect manners; he rarely puts a hoof wrong."

"And boring!" Sarah chimed in with a cheeky giggle.

They moved on to the next stable, where they stopped.

"This one is Ralph, he's the only gelding in the yard, and he's my personal horse," Benjamin said proudly.

"What's that white patch under his eye? It looks like a tear." Jane reached out to touch it.

Ralph shot his head away with a snort. "It's a birthmark. It's unusual, but it makes him easy to pick out," Benjamin replied, amused by Ralph's reaction.

"He doesn't seem very friendly," Jane noted, as Ralph now stood back in his stable, ears pinned back.

"Alas, he can be a little grumpy at times," Benjamin explained. "He would normally be out in the field at this time, so he's expressing his displeasure at the change in routine. He's quite clever at communicating his feelings." He reached out his hand, and Ralph approached eagerly, his ears relaxing as he nudged Benjamin over the stable door.

"Oh, I'm sorry, Ralph," Jane said playfully, as if addressing a child.

"Give him this." Benjamin whispered, producing a carrot seemingly from nowhere and slipping it into Jane's hand. Jane waved it in front of her, capturing Ralph's full attention. The horse began making excited grunting sounds with his ears pricked, before taking the carrot from her outstretched hand and quickly chomping it down. Once he swallowed it, Ralph lowered his head between his forelegs and emitted further sounds. Jane laughed, "What in heaven's name is he doing?"

"He's used to receiving carrots only after being exercised, when I encourage him with treats to do his stretches," Benjamin explained.

"His stretches?" Jane asked, astonished.

"Aye, I stretch him for carrots as encouragement; it helps keep him supple. If I had more carrots, I would gladly demonstrate," he replied.

He's such a clever boy," Sarah interjected, patting Ralph's nose. "But alas, Ralph, no more carrots for you. We should move on, or Benjamin will sing your praises all day. And this here is Micky, he's, my favourite."

"Indeed," Benjamin chuckled, "mostly because of his cheeky and mischievous nature. But he is quite talented, provided he's in skilled hands."

"I have a fondness for greys," Jane remarked, affectionately rubbing Micky's head. The horse playfully tilted his head to one side, pulling a whimsical face. "What a proper character he is, with such beautiful eyes—light brown, rare for a grey. You're like a giant version of my pony, Minnie," Jane said fondly.
"Yet we must sell him," Sarah replied, a note of sorrow creeping into her voice.

"That is a lamentable truth. What brings about this necessity, dear Sarah?" Jane inquired.

"It's the nature of our business; we can't afford to grow

too attached," Benjamin replied solemnly.

"Ha! You sound just like Father! Pray, dear brother, you had tears shimmering in your eyes when Father spoke to us last eve," Sarah teased.

"No, I did not!" Benjamin protested.

"I admire a man who isn't afraid to show his emotions," Jane remarked, a smile illuminating her face, causing Benjamin to blush with embarrassment.

At that moment, Micky, with Benjamin's back turned to him, took advantage of the revelry and seized Benjamin's finest hat in his mouth. He waved it triumphantly for a moment before casting it upon the ground at his feet. Both ladies erupted in laughter as Benjamin feigned a reprimand directed at Micky whilst retrieving his hat to dust it off.

"See, that is why he is my favourite," Sarah giggled amid her amusement.

Mr. Cropper coughed, reminding them of his presence, prompting a giggle from Jane.

"It is time to proceed; we shan't linger all day, Mistress," Mr. Cropper stated, his disapproval evident.

Benjamin regained his composure and adopted a mock-serious demeanour. "Yes, the last two are Duke and Samson. Duke, my grandfather's steed and now my father's mount, is a venerable twenty-two year old and has sired all the fine males here. They recently turning eight, all sired with different mares of course. Samson resembles Duke most; robust and solidly built, both possessing three white socks—a rare trait among his descendants. Dependable Samson is probably the most laid-back of them all."

"It's a fine selection," Jane admitted. "I must confess, I am rather envious. If I could, I would establish a stable like this. We have some quite large stables at the manor; my ancestors were fond of horses and hunting. My mother tells me they had a fine selection, but alas, it's not the same any more. We each have our own horses, and while we did have some to pull our coach, we never use it, so father sold them."

"You are welcome to visit as often as you like," Benjamin replied lightly. "Perhaps even take one for a ride—under proper chaperonage, of course."

Mr. Cropper cleared his throat. "Mistress, these are not horses suitable for ladies to ride, even one as capable as thyself; they are steeds fit for gentlemen, and I doubt your gracious mother would approve," he interjected, clearly vexed by the exchanges he had overheard. "It is now time for thee to join thy father," he instructed, gesturing toward the farmhouse to reinforce his statement.

Jane went to retort, then appeared to think better of it. She might be Mistress of the house, but her father's Steward was the most respected member of the small household the Stephens' kept these days, and her Father would be displeased if she disrespected him, especially in public and in company. Besides, Jane knew she was pushing the limits of what was appropriate, and was being rather forward for a Mistress of her station. So, she gracefully lowered her head and made her way toward the house, whereupon Sarah quickly linked her arm and began to skip along. "I shall show you my room," Sarah announced.

As Benjamin trailed behind Mr. Cropper, an unexpected wave of nervousness washed over him. Mr. Cropper came to a halt, turning to place a hand on Benjamin's shoulder.

"Pray, take this counsel as it is intended, young Mr. Akins. Your family is held in high regard among ours, and should you desire to maintain that bond, I implore you to consider your position—along with that of Mistress Jane—and the manner in which you conduct yourself in her presence."

After giving Benjamin's shoulder a light pat, Mr Cropper strode toward the house, leaving Benjamin to bear the weight of his admonition. The rebuke struck him like a hammer, stirring a tumult of emotions: embarrassment, a little anger and regret for his own thoughtless behaviour. In frustration, he shook his head and kicked a stone along the path.

As he raised his gaze, he noticed the young housemaid from the previous day hurrying down the private path, a letter waving in her hand. "Mr. Cropper! Mr. Cropper!" she called out.

Turning sharply at the threshold of the farmhouse, Mr. Cropper inquired, "Ruth, compose yourself, girl; what troubles you?"

"It is a letter from Master William Stephens, from the Low Countries!" she exclaimed.

Mr. Cropper's eyes widened. "Hand it over, girl! Has Mistress Mary read it?" He noted the broken seal.

"Yes, she instructed me to deliver it to her husband immediately," Ruth said, still breathless, her gaze fixed on Benjamin with open admiration.

"Is it ill news?" Mr. Cropper inquired.

"Alas, I couldn't say. Mistress seldom reveals her feelings, and I cannot read, nor would I presume to," Ruth replied.

Mr. Cropper swiftly scanned the letter, Benjamin watching with curiosity as a kaleidoscope of emotions played across Mr. Croppers face. He raised a hand to his mouth in thought, then met Benjamin's gaze. With a decisive snap, he folded the letter.

"Go home now, Ruth," he commanded, then retreated into the house, leaving Benjamin to grapple with the unfolding mystery.

Following him inside, Benjamin found his father and John Stephens seated at the table, laughing over a jest. They both turned as Mr. Cropper passed the letter to John.

"It's a letter from Will—I mean, Master William," John declared, rising to seize the letter and reading it, his face a myriad of expression.

Upon finishing, he lifted his gaze, newfound cheerfulness evident. "It is my son; he is returning home by God's grace!" he announced displaying a broad smile. "I must make my way home. Thank you kindly for your hospitality, Mr. Akins. It would be prudent for us to journey together to Bristol in five days; there is safety in numbers." John Paused, evidently distracted by his thoughts "I hope you don't deem me rude, but we haven't heard from my son in several months, and I must speak with my wife. Mr. Cropper, might you fetch Jane for me, and If someone could bring our horses, I would be much obliged.".

"Certainly" Stephen replied

"Good day to you, we shall meet again on Friday and we would be delighted to have Sarah as our guest at the Manor whilst we are away."

Stephen smiled warmly. "You are exceedingly kind, John, as you say we shall meet on Friday."

Chapter 6:
A Letter from Afar, June 1641

Mistress Mary Stephens sat in the drawing room of the manor, soft summer light filtering through the mullioned windows and casting gentle shadows on the worn wooden floor. In her hand was a letter penned by her beloved son, William, dated January—five months ago. The second son born to her, and the only one to survive infancy, William would soon turn thirty in October. She recalled her eighteen-year-old self-cradling baby William, a time when motherhood seemed effortless, and life was free of sorrow.

His words, bold yet tempered by the care of a devoted son turned soldier, detailed a recent ambush and the harrowing loss of his dear horse, Bruce. Though William emerged unscathed, thanks to God's providence. More heartening was his account of gaining favour with young Prince Maurice—a detail that suggested both honour and hope from what Mary saw as a foolish and perilous venture.

A shadow fell across Mary's face, a familiar ache echoing in her heart. Her husband, John, had given his blessing to William's adventure – an adventure William deemed noble, but one that had chipped away at the bedrock of their peaceful marriage. Despite the shared heartaches – the tragic fire that stole her mother, father, brother, and sister, leaving a gaping void in her past – this new tension felt different, a raw and unsettling undercurrent.

She had already endured the agony of losing so many children, their tiny lives extinguished before they truly began. William's words washed over her, and she offered a silent, fervent prayer for his safe return by year's end, a promise he'd made with a confidence she desperately hoped was justified. William and Jane were her world, precious survivors wrestled from the jaws of fate. As if summoned by her anxiety, John entered the room, and Mary rose instinctively, a gesture born of respect.

"Husband, I am penning a response to William's letter. I must confess, the thought of him amid the din of battle, exposed to dangers beyond imagination, fills me with a sorrow that is not easily soothed, John. I wish I could adopt the pragmatic view you possess."

"Dear wife, it's natural to feel the way you do" John replied as he stepped toward Mary-intending to embrace her, however, he hesitated upon seeing Mr. Cropper emerge from the side door. "Mr. Cropper, please, would you leave us?" The steward dutifully turned and exited the room, closing the door behind him to grant the couple their privacy.

John's eyes, steady and contemplative, met Mary's. "I understand your worries dear; however, consider the matter from another perspective. Our William has earned the favour of a royal Prince, a man of notable lineage—indeed, a beloved nephew of our King. If he can cultivate this connection, it may secure William's future and provide us with much-needed allies in royal circles. This could represent the dawn of a rising star for us."

"While that may be true, to what extent can this favour be utilised when the royal nephew and his companions are exiles from their own kingdom, relying on handouts for their survival and to further the war waging in the ruins of Christendom —into which you so eagerly sent our only son?"

As soon as the words left her lips, Mary regretted them. Her husband always viewed their circumstances with optimism—a trait she had once found endearing. However, after the profound disappointments they had endured, she struggled to share his hopeful perspective, often feeling irritated by what she saw as naivety.
With a sigh, John responded, "We have traversed this ground before, Mary. Had I intervened with William, he

would have resisted, seeking other avenues for his ener-
gies, placing himself in jeopardy – physically, financially,
and, indeed, spiritually. You are aware of his proclivities,
and it would not have been long before he crossed swords
with one of the Foster brothers, if not all three, given their
past encounters and the enmity between the families. William must carve his own destiny; he is a man grown, not
your little boy any longer."

Mary held her tongue, opting to change the subject.
"Speaking of the Fosters, is it true that Ruth's parents and
perhaps others, have fallen victim to the cruel machina-
tions of our friends, the Fosters, who have imposed unfair
loans upon them? Are they now pressing our indebted tenants with their band of thugs?"

John's brow furrowed at the injustice of it all. "It appears
to be true, and poor Ruth's father's face bears witness to
their cruel devices."

"John, these are our tenants; many of them have been so
for generations in my family. It is our duty to assist them,"
she paused, realising that rebuking her husband once more
was not fair.

"I intend to seek legal counsel in Bristol on Friday. Surely,
the tenants' illiteracy regarding those agreements signifies
something, and the interest levied defies all moral and
Christian decency. I cannot stand idly by, my dear. Unlike
many landowners, I have foregone rent increases out of
loyalty and to our own detriment. Yet still they resort to
these usurious lenders?"

"My dear husband, I know you are a good and just man,
and I don't mean to be ungrateful for your allowances at
my bequest. However, I worry about confronting the
Fosters directly. This land is becoming restless, and such
unruly creatures like the Fosters may escalate things fur-

ther. I also fear for your safety on the road; they always seem to know our business and comings and goings."

"Fear not, I've arranged for the Akins and their servants to accompany me, along with Mr. Cropper and our stable lad Tim. We'll be armed, with seven mounted men to deter any foolish ideas" John explained reassuringly. "Assaulting a poor tenant farmer over unpaid debts is one thing. I very much doubt they would dare try and harm a gentleman. Besides, I do not fear them, Mary," he professed

"I pray that's the case, but it's wise to be wary. This feud with my family has lasted generations. Whilst the Fosters continue to amass influence and wealth through shipping and money lending, the Welches of Little Sodbury Manor endure solely through the blood of our children and mine."

"But they are Stephens as are you, not Welches, Mary. This foolish feud should have ended long ago. I hoped your sister's betrothal to Richard Foster, your fathers attempt to bring peace, following their tragic loss—would have softened the Fosters hearts." John replied, shaking his head in disappointment.

They won't be satisfied until they have it all. The manor, the lands, everything. Nothing less will do. This thought hardened Mary's resolve. Richard Foster cared nothing for her sister, and the feeling was mutual. Had fate not intervened with that devastating fire, her sister would have been condemned to a joyless, desolate marriage. Mary knew her Christian faith called her to rise above such earthly concerns, to focus on the spiritual, to perhaps even find some measure of forgiveness for the Fosters. But the venom was too deeply ingrained. She couldn't let them win. She wouldn't forgive their countless transgressions, their insidious attempts to undermine the Welches at every turn. The slights, the veiled insults, the land grabs… they were an unending litany of grievances she carried like a stone in her heart.

She desperately wished for William's return; he would know how to resolve this dilemma. Yet, she steeled herself against further complaint and simply nodded. "Yes, my husband, I trust your judgment."

A smile brightened John's face as he took Mary's hand. "I have much to arrange before Friday, my dear. Hopefully, more letters will arrive. Once you've finished your reply, please give it to Jane; she's eager to read it."

"I'd prefer to wait before sharing the letter's contents, my dear. Perhaps we can read it to Jane together upon your return. And if you wouldn't mind, let's keep it from the servants for the moment," Mary suggested.

"I don't see why we should keep such good news a secret, Mr. Cropper already knows all" John said, a hint of confusion crossing his features.

"That is fine. I have a reason which I'll explain when you return. Please, trust me in this," Mary pleaded, her hands covering his, her eyes imploring.

"Very well, my dear." John sighed, then his expression lifted. "Alas, amid these burdens, I find a small joy—securing a worthy steed to replace dear Bruce. Such a gift would symbolise our pride in William's service and ensure a safe and honourable return. I shall seek a worthy one at the Bristol horse fair."

His cheerful demeanour fully restored, he exclaimed, "Yes, all will be well, my dear, you will see!" He turned and exited, closing the door behind him.
Mistress Mary shook her head, determined to focus on her husband's virtues. He was a kind, loving father and a dutiful husband, even if ill-equipped to manage their estate at times. As the second son of a minor gentry family from Gloucester—a family he'd long been estranged from due to

unspoken issues— He lacked the education granted to Mary's brother, the training required to manage their family home, its eight hundred acres of farmland, and two hundred more of woodland. A privilege denied to Mary as well. Only through tragedy had they inherited these roles, constantly battling the feeling of being inadequate. She reminded herself that her husband always tried, even if his best often fell short.

Just then, Mr. Cropper reappeared at the side door, bowing with deference. "Mistress," he greeted her.

Once she was certain her husband had gone, Mary faced Mr. Cropper. "Our plan is afoot," she stated, her tone remaining dry.

Chapter 7
Road to Bristol

Friday arrived with the summer sun warming the Gloucestershire lanes. John Stephens Esquire sat tall on his steady cob, his quiet resolve mirrored in its gait. Beside him, Mr. Cropper rode Mistress Stephens' prized hobby horse with refined nonchalance. Behind them, the stable boy Tim, just younger than Benjamin, proudly clung to Jane's elegant white pony, his youthful eyes full of the promise of adventure on the long ride ahead.

Their company grew as they encountered the waiting party from the Akins household. Benjamin rode at the rear, guiding Ralph while leading two carefully selected broodmares destined for sale in Bristol. He greeted their travelling companions: Thomas sat astride Samson, Benjamin's father was mounted on Micky, and the downtrodden-looking old man, Ward, rode the old Duke. Benjamin felt a twinge of sympathy for both horse and rider as he gazed upon the pair.

Glancing up at the sky, he noted the morning sun's rays were already strong; the flies would soon be out in force, swarming the group like bees to honey, causing irritation to both man and beast.

Together, they formed a moving cavalcade bound for Bristol, each man and horse contributing to the rhythm of the journey. Their plan was simple: ride three miles to Chipping Sodbury for food and drink before continuing to Bristol, aiming to arrive before dusk. Stephen Akins had written to his brother Paul, who reserved rooms for them at an Inn in Bristol—a welcome haven after a long day's ride.

As they traversed the winding lanes, the group revelled in the brief camaraderie born of shared purpose. John Stephens, a man tempered by duty and social rank, led with quiet authority, engaging in conversation with Stephen Akins, with the silent Mr. Cropper following closely behind.

Benjamin noticed the two fine flintlock pistols protruding from John Stephens' saddle holsters, while Mr. Cropper had a carbine secured in his own. With stable boy Tim, who shared his passion for all things equine, Benjamin thought it best to keep the broodmares behind the three Akins stallions, just in case. He regretted not having asked Thomas to ride Ralph, the only gelding among them, as they now trailed behind with two mares in tow. He resolved to swap mounts once they stopped.

The gentle clopping of hooves, the swishing of tails against flies, and the soft murmur of conversation passed the time quickly. Before they knew it, they were turning toward the Market High street of Chipping Sodbury.

Chapter 8
Warnings

The small market town with its cobblestone streets, worn smooth by centuries of trade, lined with timber-framed buildings, their thatched and tiled roofs casting uneven shadows. The main high streets open-fronted shops, displaying wares from local crafts and imported goods, spilled onto the street. The air is thick with the mingled scents of woodsmoke, livestock, spices, and freshly baked bread from Mr. Hobbs bakery. Market stalls set up haphazardly, overflowing with produce, textiles, and hardware. It was bustling with the everyday commerce of life.

Benjamin's stomach rumbled with the promise of a hearty late breakfast—or perhaps an early lunch—making his mouth water. As they stopped outside the Crown Inn, the group dismounted, taking in the substantial stone building adorned with a weathered sign featuring a golden crown. A youth speaking with John received a tossed coin as he led the horses around to the side, aided by Tim and Thomas, who had been instructed to remain with the horses and keep watch over their saddlebags while the rest of the party entered the Inn.

Inside, a low hum of conversation mingled with the clinking of tankards. Upon seeing the party arrive, several patrons nodded and offered warm greetings to John and his father. The landlord quickly wiped down a table near the back of the Inn, accommodating the gathering as they took their seats.

"What would you like to drink and eat gentlemen? Has my lad seen to your horses?" he inquired.

"Yes," John answered on behalf of the group. "He is with a couple of our servants tending to them—thank you."
The landlord proceeded to take their orders in turn, and

Stephen requested some buttered bread with cheese to be brought to the two lads looking after the horses.

The first bite of food had barely registered on John's tongue when the atmosphere in the tavern soured. He hadn't noticed them at first, too focused on the hearty meal before him, but a sudden hush and the nervous glances of his companions snapped him to attention. Looming over the table were two intrusive figures: the Foster brothers. Their presence was a discernible weight, a dark cloud descending on the jovial scene. John's gaze flicked around the room, spotting the hulking forms strategically placed in the shadows – hired muscle, their faces impassive, radiating a silent threat. One of the Foster brothers, a man in his early thirties, leaned forward, his expensive clothes a jarring contrast to his rough, weathered features. A twisted nose, and scars -perhaps souvenirs of a past brawl, dominated his face. He invaded John's personal space, his breath thick with the stale tang of ale.

"John Stephens! Fancy seeing you here," his voice rasped, a gravelly growl that cut through the air. "You'd best keep clear of those indebted tenants of yours. Their troubles are not yours to shoulder, but meddling in their affairs, I fear, may bring you some unwelcome grief." The air crackled with unspoken malice, a clear and unmistakable threat hanging heavily in the silence.

As John started to rise, a calloused hand clamped down on his shoulder, halting him mid-motion. Samuel, the Foster brother, leaned in, his grip surprisingly strong. "No need to stand; we don't intend to linger. We merely thought we'd pop in to say hello. But do ensure that those good-for-nothing tenants of yours settle *our* debts before they pay you *your* rents." The words hung in the air, each syllable a deliberate act of aggression.

John's response caught in his throat. A flutter of fear, quickly suppressed, crossed his face. Mr. Cropper, John's loyal Steward, bristled at the hand on his master's shoulder, but his hand remained firmly at his side. The hulking figures surrounding them, with their predatory stillness, were a clear deterrent. The Akins, their faces etched with bewilderment, looked at John then to the Fosters, waiting for a cue.

Every eye in the tavern seemed to be on them. Conversation died down, and the air thrummed with an overt tension. Finally, John forced the words out, "Very well, I shall ensure they do." But the retort lacked conviction, his usual confidence crumbling under the weight of Samuel's intimidation. The Foster brothers, in contrast, seemed to feed off the unease.

"Matthew 5:42," Samuel drawled, a mocking smile twisting his lips. "'Give to him that asketh thee, and from him that would borrow of thee turn not thou away.'" He paused, letting the silence stretch. "And do not think about whispering to your friends in Bristol; remember we have many more acquaintances in higher places than you, and we tend to take care of our own business." The veiled threat was unmistakable.

With a curt nod to Saul, the youngest Foster brother - slighter of frame, with a deceptively handsome face compared to his brutish brother - Samuel clapped his hands. They turned and strode towards the door, their silent retinue of thugs melting back into the shadows, following close behind. The landlord, who had been watching with a mixture of fear and morbid fascination, visibly sagged with relief. The spell broken, the other patrons slowly resumed their meals, their conversations returning to a hushed murmur.

John exhaled sharply, the tension visibly draining from his shoulders. He sank back onto the bench, his face pale.

"What was all that about, John?" Stephen asked, his brow furrowed with concern. "Are you at odds with the Fosters?"

"I will explain later," John replied, a steely edge creeping back into his voice as he struggled to regain his composure. "But for now, let us continue with our meal. We need to get back on the road."

Chapter 9
The Road Ahead

As the group prepared to saddle their horses, Benjamin ensured that he swapped positions with Thomas, eager to eavesdrop on the conversation between his father and John Stephens.

Now riding at the front on Samson, they navigated the bustling High Street before veering onto the ancient Roman road. The atmosphere was subdued, the group anticipating that John Stephens would initiate the conversation. For the moment, however, they remained content, maintaining a steady pace and hoping that the midday sun's heat would dissipate, as both riders and horses were beginning to feel the effects of the rising temperature.

After a short while on the road, the sound of pounding hooves disrupted their journey. A gang of horsemen emerged, led by Samuel and his brother Saul, with their hired thugs close behind. They charged forward at full gallop, forcing John Stephens' group to veer hastily to the roadside. As they passed, laughter and jeers filled the air, with Saul Foster firing a shot into the sky from a pistol.

The shot rang out sharply, startling the broodmares. They reared in panic, their hooves thrashing dangerously as Thomas and young Tim struggled to maintain control.

Reacting swiftly, Benjamin dismounted gracefully and approached the frenzied mares. Tim's pony was pulled off balance by one of the panicked broodmares, but Benjamin arrived just in time. For a tense moment, it seemed the mare might bolt. However, Benjamin kept his composure, raising his hands and murmuring reassuring sounds. Slowly, the mare calmed at his approach, and he placed his hand on its head, stroking its forehead. Though still tense, it began to settle, letting out soft snorts as Benjamin worked to soothe them.

Dust swirled in the wake of the Fosters' retreating figures, their mocking laughter hanging in the air. John Stephens bore an expression of palpable indignation as he reached for the handle of one of his pistols. However, Stephen swiftly extended his hand, suggesting restraint while trying to soothe Micky, who was also rattled by the shot. The horse's body was tense, making snorting sounds as it jogged in place, attempting to disperse its nervous energy while fidgeting with its hooves.

The momentary impulse to retaliate flickered and faded from John almost as swiftly as it had arisen.

"I apologise for that, Stephen," he said, redirecting his focus. "I will explain everything shortly." He shifted his gaze to Benjamin, a note of appreciation in his voice. "But I must commend your son for his quick reactions. The way he calmed those mares so swiftly was nothing short of remarkable!"

"Aye, the boy certainly has a gift, but if you don't mind, I would like to know what's going on," Stephen remarked.

Once the commotion had subsided, they regrouped and pressed onward toward Bristol, knowing they had some distance to cover. As they rode, John began to explain the details of the ongoing family feud.

Benjamin, still beaming from the earlier praise and excitement, strained to listen in on the hushed exchange between his father and John, both speaking in lowered tones.

"It's a conflict that has spanned generations. The Fosters were once proud owners of Little Sodbury Manor, a symbol of their ascent from the merchant class—far less common back then. However, it was confiscated by the newly crowned Tudor King, Henry VII, which gives you an idea of how far back this goes—some one hundred fifty-six years! The manor then passed to Sir John Welch and his wife, a Foster. Her elder brother was attained for fighting on Richard's side and was required to start again. Since then, the manor has remained in the Welch line."

"Both families have been at odds ever since. My son William is the same age as Samuel, and they grew up in the same area, which led to their fair share of run-ins. Samuel's bent nose is testament to that," John continued, a wry smile crossing his lips.

Unable to contain himself, Benjamin chuckled at the quip, recalling Samuel's distorted features. Realising he had been caught eavesdropping when John and Stephen turned toward him, Benjamin's face to reddened with embarrassment. The stern look he knew well laced across his father's face.

"I'll check on the mares," Benjamin announced, eager to escape the awkward moment. As he passed, Mr. Cropper shook his head disapprovingly, though Benjamin noticed a faint smirk that brought a flash of amusement to his expression.

The road ahead, well-worn, was uneven and rutted by years of wagon traffic. The gentle landscape rolled around them, fields of wheat and barley stretching out on either side, dotted with scattered farmsteads and wooded thickets, creating a tableau of peaceful prosperity that felt increasingly distant. As they passed through Pucklechurch, the road widened, flanked by grazing sheep and occasional travellers – a peddler with a laden mule, a solitary priest with his staff, and a farmer guiding a creaking cart toward the market.

The group paused by a stream to water the horses, pulling up just upstream of three young men who were wrestling their sheep into the water, laboriously washing their long, woolly coats in preparation for the next day's shearing. Thomas and Tim gave the mounts a quick check; despite showing some weariness, they were still sound for the final leg of the journey. The Akins' horses, particularly fresh, were a testament to their excellent condition. Benjamin watched them eagerly devour a patch of cow parsley, its delicate white flowers a common and favoured summer treat for horses found along the hedgerows.

As the sun dipped lower in the sky, they finally caught sight of Bristol in the distance, the towers of St. Mary Redcliffe rising majestically like sentinels. The road grew busier, with wagons creaking under heavy loads, merchants engaged in animated discussions, and common folk trudging along with their belongings slung over their backs.

Benjamin inhaled deeply, soaking in the vibrant atmosphere as he listened to snippets of gossip regarding events and names he had never encountered. Relishing the change of scenery—a delightful break from the usual routine—he turned to Thomas with a smile, glancing ahead at Bristol, now within reach.

Chapter 10
Bristol, June 1641

The city throbbed with commerce, its streets, a vibrant tapestry of trade and lively chatter, underscored by the distant, sonorous toll of church bells signalling evening prayer.

As John Stephens and his party approached, the air thickened with the mingled scents of the river, wood smoke, and the tang of tanneries working along the water's edge of the port city—a testament to Bristol's role as a major centre for leather production.

They entered through lesser-used Frome Gate, where vigilant watchmen eyed each traveller with suspicion. Beyond them, in the distance, the imposing form of Bristol Castle loomed, a reminder of royal authority, though its defences were somewhat outdated, its sturdy walls bore the scars of age, their stones weathered and worn. Beyond the gate, the streets unfolded like a labyrinth of timber-framed buildings, leaning precariously over narrow alleys. Upper stories protruded so far that neighbours could nearly shake hands across the gap.

As they navigated the bustling streets, Stephen cautioned Benjamin for the third time, "Mind the saddlebags for pickpockets this busy street is prime hunting ground for them". They passed the High Cross; the tall stone statue adorned with a cross, a central point where notices were tacked up and criers loudly announced the latest tidings. Shouts about tensions in Ireland filled the air, but the dominant news, causing much gossip, was the trial and execution of the King's favourite, the Earl of Strafford, at the Tower of London for treason by Parliament. This news fuelled the already tense atmosphere in a city divided in its loyalties.

As they proceeded into the merchant quarter down Corn street, the calls of merchants hawking their wares filled the air—fresh fish pulled from the Avon, spices from distant shores, fine woollens, and barrels of ale and beer. Beyond the busy streets, the docks were alive with activity, ships moored closely together as sailors busily unloaded cargo from far-off lands: tobacco from the New World, sugar from the West Indies, and fine wines from France.

John guided them toward the Red Lion Inn; a well-known establishment nestled near the market quarters. This stout two-story building boasted a wide courtyard and stables for horses and a warm glow spilling invitingly from its windows. The savoury scent of roasting meat wafted through the open door, and stable hands hurried to tend to the party's mounts.

"Tim, you are in charge of the horses for the evening," John instructed. "Keep a watchful eye on them for us; ensure they are all brushed down, including the Akins' steeds." He tossed the lad a coin as he spoke.

Inside, the Inn was crowded but inviting, with low wooden beams and a floor sticky from years of spilled drink. A fire crackled in the hearth the strong aroma of ale and pipe smoke. John conferred with the innkeeper while the group settled at a long wooden table. Tankards were set before them, and the tension of travel began to dissipate. Still, the shadow of the Fosters loomed over John Stephens as he sipped his ale, the bitter tang of humiliation, anger and resentment mingling with apprehension about how to proceed.

Stephen Akins pondered the weight of tomorrow's decisions and his family's future, while Benjamin, Thomas, revelled in the carefree joys of youth. Mr. Cropper and old man Ward, weary and drained, struggled to stay awake in the inviting warmth of the fire.
Food was served—hearty pie and peas—which they eagerly devoured. "It has been an eventful day. I shall retire to my chamber for rest; tomorrow promises to be busy," John declared, stifling a yawn.

"I believe I shall do the same," Mr. Cropper affirmed, joined by Stephen in agreement.

"Pray, the night is yet young!" Benjamin exclaimed, brimming with youthful energy.

"You and Thomas can stay down here for an hour longer, if old man Ward agrees to keep an eye on you," Stephen suggested, a slight smile forming despite the day's earlier tensions.

"Aye," came the rare word from the old man, who looked half asleep.

"Very well, but not too much more of that ale. Here, take the keys to your room." Stephen tossed a key to the shared accommodation they would be using.

Benjamin smiled, nodding at Thomas as a camaraderie formed between them. Some time passed, and both young men finished the ale that had been brought for them. They looked over at old man Ward, whose head had slumped on his chest, snoring contentedly.

"Thomas, may I ask you a question? What is your uncle's first name? I don't actually know it," Benjamin inquired.

Thomas chuckled heartily. "Really? That doesn't surprise me; he is a man of few words. His first name is Dick," he replied, amusement twinkling in his eyes.

"I see. Well, it's time we procure some more drinks. I don't think Dick here needs another," Benjamin remarked with a grin.

"I'll get these. Your father gave me my first wages today, so I insist," Thomas declared.

They made their way to the bar, quickly being served by a robust-looking woman who clearly could handle herself.

"Some of your best value-for-money ale, please, good-wife."

"Here you go, lad. This is the best value," she responded, handing them their drinks.

Thomas took a long, hopeful gulp of the ale, but the expression that contorted his face a moment later spoke volumes. This brew was a far cry from the "first water" quality of the two previous rounds John had generously provided. His face reddening, Thomas slammed his tankard onto the table, the force of the impact rattling the nearby cutlery. He erupted in a fit of coughing, sputtering, "This ale is an insult! It's weaker than a newborn babe and tastes as if it were strained through old Ward's boot!"

The tavern wench, unamused, wiped her hands on her grubby apron. "Funny, that's the same ale that put Bill over there under the table."

"Bill must have the constitution of a wet sponge," Thomas grumbled. Yet, taking another long swig, Benjamin lingered over his own drink, taking a slow sip.

"If it's so dreadful, why do you keep drinking it?" Benjamin asked.

"I believe in being thorough in my criticisms," Thomas sniffed, taking another reluctant sip.

At that moment, a large, broad-shouldered man at a nearby table turned toward them. His face was red, his beard patchy, and, worst of all, his knuckles appeared to have personally ended several men.

"You got a problem with the ale here, lad? This is my local, and we work at the brewhouse on the quay that makes it and supplies this place," the man growled, his voice laced with menace.

Thomas, seemingly oblivious to the brewing storm, gestured grandly. "Sir, I do have a problem with this ale! It's so weak, if it were a horse, it would be put out to pasture or shot!"

Benjamin nudged Thomas firmly with his elbow, a silent plea for him to stop while he was ahead.

Finally taking in the hulking figure and his posturing, Thomas amended, "I meant to say it's adequate for its price point." He took a sip, adding, "It's actually growing on me."

The man turned away with a loud laugh, addressing his companions. "Pups!"

Benjamin turned to the barmaid. "Perhaps some mead? What would you recommend?"

"I wouldn't suggest the mead, but this cider will put hairs on your friend's chest," she replied with a teasing smile.

The two young men began drinking their fresh ciders, taking in the lively and raucous atmosphere of the Inn's bustling bar. As Thomas scanned the room, he noticed a young serving girl stealing glances at Benjamin from across the way.

She was a fair thing- rosy cheeks, dark curls escaping from her cap, having a mischievous glint in her eye, she cut a fine figure. Every time she passed by, she seemed to find an excuse to linger.

They both went back to the table with Thomas's uncle still sound asleep. Taking their seats "Well, well, Benjamin," he murmured nudging his friend in the ribs, "It seems you have an admirer."

Benjamin sighed. "Leave it be, leave it be Thomas"

"Leave it be? Leave it be? Thomas clutched his chest dramatically. "You wound me, sir. Here I am your new best friend, ready to help you woo this lovely creature, and you tell me to leave it be? Slurring his words the alcohol taking its toll on the slender youth.

Benjamin narrowed his eyes, "Whatever your thinking don't do it"

It was already too late Thomas jumped up, rising from his seat unsteadily with exaggerated confidence, he strode over to the bar where the young serving girl was waiting for a round-faced bar woman to put together her order of drinks.

Thomas pulled up next to her, believing he looked quite dashing. "Good evening, my fine lass," he declared, flashing the serving girl a roguish smile. "Might I trouble you for another round? My friend Benjamin over there is feeling quite parched, and I daresay he could use the company of a charming young Mistress like yourself to lift his spirits."

The girl had barely drawn breath to reply before fate intervened. In his attempt to appear effortlessly suave, Thomas leaned exactly where the bar's serving hatch stood open. At that instant, the stout, no-nonsense tavern wench—wholly unmoved by flirtation—swung the hatch down with a decisive crack.

The support vanished beneath his elbow, and Thomas pitched sideways with the grace of a dropped sack of meal. For a heartbeat he hung there, grasping at empty air, before crashing flat on his back with a thud that made the floorboards shudder.

Silence…Then, the Red Lion erupted into laughter even the drunk Bill lifted his head to mock.

Benjamin, struggling to breathe through his wheezing laughter, wiped a tear from his eye "Oh, Thomas" he managed between gasps, "your charm is truly unmatched my friend"

The young serving girl covered her mouth, stifling her giggles as she peered over the bar at Thomas, who lay there blinking up at the ceiling. The older wench, arms folded, merely shook her head "Wet Sponge" she said smirking.

"Serves you right" the young girl added.

Thomas groaned, rubbing the back of his head "Well," he mumbled "that went exactly as I planned."

Benjamin now looking over at his friend, still laughing offered him a hand up "Oh, undoubtedly" he agreed.

With that old man Ward appeared, "Bedtime" he said simply

"You two go up, I'll be with you soon, just going to check on Tim and the horses" Benjamin said. The young serving girl was still giving him suggestive looks but Benjamin was completely unaware.

Thomas shook his head "Some people get all the luck," he said as he staggered up the stairs to the rooms with his uncle.

Chapter 11
Rising Sun

Sunlight streamed through the Red Lion Inn's windows, waking the weary. As the group gathered for breakfast, the day's weighty purpose loomed. Benjamin Akins and Thomas Ward, heavy-headed from the previous night, exchanged weary glances.

"I've never felt so wretched," Thomas groaned, rubbing his temples.

"Did I not warn you about excess you foolish boys" Stephen gently chided, a hint of amusement in his eyes.

Thomas, clutching a tankard of water, grimaced. "To be fair, the ale was awful... or perhaps my memory is failing me."

Despite his own discomfort, Benjamin chuckled. "We must shake this off. Today we meet Thomas Smyth; important matters are at hand."

"Indeed," Stephen replied, his countenance transforming into one of resolve. "We must maintain our wits for the auction, and we cannot get carried away. Thomas Smyth possesses a private collection of Spanish horses for sale—an opportunity that could prove transformative for Fairfield Farm."

"Spanish horses," Benjamin echoed, a spark of excitement igniting within him despite his headache. "They're in high demand. Securing even a few could significantly boost our profits."

"Exactly," Stephen said, leaning forward. "If the chance arises, we'll need to sell some stock for funds. How do they look this morning, Benjamin?"

"They're all prepared, Father," Benjamin replied, picturing Micky and Samson, his prized hunter studs, and two broodmares contently eating hay in the stable. He'd groomed them meticulously that morning. Yet, a tension gripped him as he considered the risks of potential profit. The horse trade was uncertain, full of complexities. Perhaps, he thought, he was starting to think like a true horse trader. Still, the thought of parting with the two stallions especially, hadn't truly settled within him.

As they prepared to leave the Inn, the atmosphere in Bristol was charged. City folk paraded through the streets wearing bright ribbons. They quizzed the Innkeeper, who explained over a breakfast of cheese and bread, "Red for the King, Blue for Parliament—each colour a bold statement of where they stand in this growing rift. Especially after that execution, or so I hear."

The city was still alive with talk of the Earl of Strafford's execution, and the rising tensions between the Monarchy and Parliament were nearing a boiling point, sparking diverse opinions.

After breakfast, the group split into two: Benjamin, Stephen, Thomas Ward, and old man Ward headed for the Smyth auction at the horse market, while John Stephens and Mr. Cropper set off for the solicitor's office. Tim remained at the Inn to tend to the horses.

They agreed to meet again that evening and to forgo church on Sunday, setting off early to have clearer roads for the ride home.

As they walked toward the auction area, nausea rippled through Benjamin, prompting him to wipe his brow. "I thought breakfast would sort me out, but I fear the ale has other plans for my stomach," he said with a look of discomfort on his fine features.

"You aren't the only one," Thomas admitted with a frown. "I may start regretting the choices I made after the third mug and mixing it with that cider. Boy, was that strong!"

The groups light-hearted banter mingled with commotion of the market as they arrived. A large area had been sectioned off in the square; a man dressed in the Smyth livery stood with a list at the entrance. As the group approached, he looked up, "Stephen" he said, a wide smile on his face.

"Mark. good to see you boy, well should I say, man" Stephen gave Mark a friendly slap on the back.

"Mark was a stable boy, when we lived at the estate" Stephen explained turning to the group"

"Please go in and get a seat" Mark said warmly.

"Didn't you want to see our invite?" Stephen teased

"No, Master Thomas advised you are to see him around the back of the ring after the auction is over. Good to see you Stephen". He urged them through. Two very finely dressed gentlemen stood in line behind them. They cleared their throats displaying their impatience with the hold up.

The circle of chairs around the ring crackled with anticipation, a stark contrast to Benjamin's growing unease as he took in the obvious wealth of the prospective bidders. Sunlight glinted off the glossy coats of the Spanish horses, magnificent animals that represented both the promise of fortune and the spectre of devastating loss. The horses lined up and fidgeting, were held by handlers in the Smyths' Ashton Court livery, who struggled to maintain their composure.
Standing slightly apart on the raised platform, Thomas Smyth listened as a man beside him announced in a loud

voice, "Gentlemen, take your seats; the bidding is about to begin." The crowd quietened, settling onto the wooden stalls with a palpable sense of anticipation.

Thomas then addressed the attendees, his charismatic presence commanding the attention of the gathered crowd. The Spanish horses stood proudly, their muscles rippling under the sunlight. "Thank you all for attending, and I hope you can appreciate the rare opportunity to buy some of the finest horses on Gods good earth."

Benjamin's heart raced at the sight. "They're magnificent," he murmured, his previous worries momentarily forgotten.

As the auction commenced, he revelled in the atmosphere —enthusiastic chatter and eager bidders surrounded them. Yet, he was all too aware of the stakes involved. They needed to garner enough from their own sales to make the trip worthwhile.

The sound of horses stamping and people murmuring faded into the background as Benjamin scanned the crowd. The pressure was mounting as the first horse was pulled out of the line into the ringed area.

Chapter 12
An Uncertain Path

A sense of foreboding clung to John Stephens as he and Mr. Cropper entered the solicitor's office. The air within the small, book-lined room felt heavy, thick with the scent of aged parchment, black ink, and a pervasive layer of undisturbed dust. Sunlight struggled to penetrate the grimy windowpanes, casting long, oppressive shadows across the worn furnishings. The solicitor had a studious look, with a receding hairline and perpetually anxious eyes, he sat hunched behind his cluttered oak desk, nervously adjusting his spectacles as he shuffled through a stack of legal documents. John and Mr. Cropper took their seats in the two worn, leather-upholstered chairs, positioned opposite him. The silence in the room was growing increasingly strained.

"Mr. Stephens," the solicitor named Mr. Pritchard began, his voice betraying a distinct tremor that did little to ease John's apprehension, "regarding your letter of the 14th...I regret to inform you that I can no longer offer your family legal counsel on this matter."

Incredulity washed over John's features, momentarily displacing the worry that had been etched there for weeks. "What are you saying, Prichard?" he demanded, his voice rising in disbelief. "We are in the thick of it! The Foster's encroachments grow bolder by the day, and with the political climate as volatile as it is, your expertise is more crucial now than ever before!"

The solicitor's demeanour stiffened noticeably, his gaze dropping to the surface of his desk as he avoided John's direct stare. "The Foster family has retained my services, effective immediately," he explained, his voice barely a whisper. "To continue representing your interests would present an irreconcilable conflict of interest. I must withdraw from the case. I am truly sorry, Mr. Stephens, but my hands are tied."

A wave of frustration and a searing sense of betrayal surged through John, making the small room feel as though it were spinning around him. The solicitor's words were a hammer blow, shattering the last vestiges of hope he had been clinging to.

"What!" he exclaimed, his voice edged with barely suppressed anger. "You've served our family for years, man! Have you forgotten the years of loyalty and patronage we've shown you?"

As if on cue, the office door creaked open, hinges groaning in protest, and Richard Foster entered—a tall, well-built, finely dressed figure whose imposing presence filled the cramped room. Ruthlessly ambitious head of the rival Foster family, he was followed closely by his eldest son, Barnabas: a sombre, austere priest whose eyes held a dark, unnerving glint, a zealotry that verged on fanaticism.

"Thank you for your discretion," Richard Foster said with a curt nod to Pritchard, deliberately ignoring John's surprise and indignation. "I would appreciate a moment to speak with John directly, Gentleman to Gentleman. We have much to discuss." A menacing look hardened Richard's face.

John's silence spoke volumes. He nodded curtly in acceptance, his eyes shifting anxiously toward Mr. Cropper, who sat silently by his side. The Solicitors shuffled awkwardly and then exited the room, eager to escape the unfolding confrontation.

The gleaming oak table formed a stark dividing line. Richard regarded John with an unsettling calm. "I understand your older brother, Henry, was a Member of Parliament the last time I heard of him. As you may know, I made his acquaintance some years ago." He cracked his knuckles sharply in the silence. "But you and he are… estranged. Years without speaking. Quite regrettable. Families should stay close, don't you think?"

Without waiting for a response, Richard settled into a seat, his son a silent, cold-eyed sentinel at his right.

"And you, the second son of a gentry family from Gloucester. The Welches probably never imagined their youngest daughter's marriage would carry such significance. Strange how things unfold," he added, a flicker of wistfulness crossing his face. But his eyes soon hardened, fixing on John with predatory intensity. "I understand you plan to challenge me legally over your tenants' debts. A misguided display of loyalty. You may come to regret it."

"I haven't come here to endure threats and insults, Mr Foster," John replied, his voice low and steely, inwardly seething.

"I am simply advising you against it, one gentleman to another. It will only escalate matters. You see, you simply don't have the connections or money to take me on. Your older brother won't help, and you and your family seem to have shied away from decent society—perhaps it's too costly?" Richard's smug smile was like salt in an open wound.

John clenched his fists, struggling to control his emotions. Richard's knowledge of his estranged older brother and family showed he had done some digging. Perhaps he was even aware of his strained finances of the last couple of years.

"What's left of this feud must end, Richard. It only brings suffering to our families and the community," John asserted.

"That's rich coming from you," Richard Foster replied, a smirk playing across his lips. "And yet, here you are, still scheming. I hear many things. I know you run your household on a shoestring, no wonder Little Sodbury Manor has seen better days. Once one of the great houses of the county, now a shadow of itself, fading into obscurity; such a pity."

"How I run my household is no business of yours, Richard. Little Sodbury Manor is a fine house, and always will be under my line," John said with feeling.

"Really? Well, I understand your dear son lies wounded in the Low Countries, his life uncertain. That is truly sad to hear; he was a spirited boy and your only living son. You have none to spare to secure that line," he smirked.

John's mind reeled, struggling to process the information being hurled at him. While the detail about William was clearly inaccurate, the fact remained: the Fosters had sources, informants close enough to know something about their affairs. He risked a glance at Mr. Cropper, who sat ramrod straight in his chair, arms folded, listening with unnerving intensity. Was that a hint of amusement he detected in the old man's eyes at the mention of William?

Richard Foster's booming voice snapped John back to the present, demanding his full attention. "My son Barnabas has had his ear to the ground," Richard thundered, "and he has heard enough whispers about Mistress Mary Stephens. Whispers about her teaching common folk the Bible, questioning established doctrines. Preaching, when it is most certainly not her place in society. And as a woman? It's blasphemy, pure and simple. Especially putting forward ideas that are dangerously radical." The words dripped with venomous disdain; each syllable laced with a potent mix of contempt and outrage.

"Her intentions are noble. She merely teaches some to read, and if that book happens to be a Bible, so be it. She is very charitable," John interjected, feeling the urge to defend his wife.
 "Knowledge is not an enemy." He added

"Oh, but it can be," this time it was Barnabas who spoke, "Some knowledge can breed dissent, and dissent brings disorder and then we will see the whole world turn upside down, it's not only the evil of the papist we need to guide against. Some of the implications of your wife's teachings could be dangerous for her and the community. You would do well to reconsider your next move."

Barnabas, the priest, remained a step behind his father, his face an unsettling mask of serenity. But the subtle tightening of his lips, the cold glint in his eyes, betrayed a simmering menace. Here was a man moulded by the church yet seemingly consumed by an unholy zeal – a dangerous and unpredictable combination, John knew from experience. Raised in a strictly religious family, he had seen first-hand how piety could morph into fanaticism, and how scripture could be twisted to legitimise the most ruthless of agendas.

"Let me cut to the chase," Richard Foster interjected, his voice dropping to a conspiratorial whisper. "Consider this an... olive branch. I can offer you a solution. An end to this petty feud, once and for all."

"I'm listening," John replied, his voice carefully neutral, though a knot of suspicion tightened in his gut.

"I'm prepared to make you an offer for Little Sodbury Manor, at the top end of the market rate, no less," Richard stated, his tone laced with an almost insulting patronisation. "Consider it a generosity born of... well, let's just say I tire of this bickering. I'll extend this offer only once, and you have one month to decide. Refuse, and the consequences... well, let's just say they won't be pleasant."

John sat back, struggling to process the enormity of what was being proposed. The thought of selling Little Sodbury Manor – the ancestral home, the stone and timber infused with generations of his wife's family history – was a prospect he dared not to consider. "You're serious," he murmured, his voice tight with a mixture of disbelief and curiosity.

"Very much so," Richard Foster asserted. "Think of it—a clean break. No more squabbles and feuds, no more needy tenants. You can start anew, perhaps further afield, I hear many radicals like your wife may be at home in the new world, many puritans and the multitude of secs that grow by the day are flocking there. The tendrils of our feud could be removed entirely. All this unpleasantness can become a mere footnote in the histories of our families."

John visibly grappled with the enormity of the proposal, ignoring the snipes about Mary's faith.
The idea had some merits, while Mr. Cropper seated silently at his side, revealing nothing of his thoughts; his face was like a blank parchment. The idea of relinquishing a family's legacy clashed violently with his secret desires to be freed from it all, to live more simply.

"Why now?" John questioned, unyielding. "What's changed Richard?"

Richard leaned back in his chair, confidence radiating from him. "As it turns out, power dynamics are shifting in Bristol, and I'd rather settle old scores privately than let this drag on, I have new ventures and ambitions I wish to focus on. Besides our trading, shipping and money-lending business are thriving—I have more money than I can spend—and I want to clear this burden once and for all.

That manor is rightfully ours, taken from us on the whim of a long dead king. I'm offering you a once-in-a-lifetime chance to put this behind us. Here is my offer."

He waved his son forward with a piece of paper. John glanced at the figure and his eyes widened —it was indeed generous. It wasn't far from what the Tracys supposedly paid for Stanton Court, a larger and grander house with more land, though it sold a few years ago.

"One month is all you have; the expiration date is on there. You won't get another chance like this. If I don't hear back, I'll know my next steps. Rest assured, John, I will be in that hall with the Foster coat of arms over the fireplace one way or another, that I promise you," Richard said with a wide smile. "Good day to you. Call my Solicitor back in on your way out."

John bristled at the man's dismissive tone, the humiliation of the past few days compounding. In shock, he focused on the official-looking purchase offer and the familiar signature of his Solicitors as a witness. Could he convince his wife that this was the prudent course? Was the offer too good to be true, almost reasonable given their history? And who was supplying information to the Fosters?

Chapter 13
A Deal in the Making

The auction was frantic, with bids soaring well beyond Stephen Akins' budget. Wealthy merchants, gentlemen, and nobles—many adorned with red feathers or ribbons—dominated the bidding. Benjamin remembered the Innkeeper's words about the colours symbolising loyalty. Among the crowd, Thomas Smyth stood out in fine attire, a large red feather protruding from his hat. His charismatic presence commanded attention, clearly in his element as he led the proceedings.

As the auction reached a fever pitch, disappointment hung in the air. Mark approached, sensing their deflation. "Stephen would you please follow me," he urged, leading them through the crowd.

Mark guided them to a quieter area, where Tiago, Master Thomas's former riding instructor and now horse agent, awaited. Tiago greeted them warmly, embodying his flamboyant Portuguese mannerisms. "Ah, Benjamin! You've grown into a fine man! How was your last visit to Ashton Court? Have you been practising with Ralph?"

Benjamin smiled. "Yes, Tiago. I've been working hard. He can execute flying changes, Pesade, and capriole with me on the ground and in the saddle."

"Really, that is truly extraordinary! It takes years at some of the finest riding schools... Remarkable, young Benjamin! You have a rare gift, much like your grandfather. I must come and see you and Ralph," Tiago said, grinning as he glanced at Stephen. "And Stephen, your eye for breeding is a genuine talent, sem dúvida." He punctuated his compliment with a playful smile, then added with a chuckle and a wink at Benjamin, "And your riding was above average, vá lá!

Tiago gestured toward a striking Gray Spanish horse nearby. The restless beast pulled at its lead, clearly unnerved by the auction. This horse was larger than the others, around 16.1 hands high, imposing, yet elegant, though smaller and more muscular than the Akins' hunters. Benjamin noticed a scar down its left shoulder. "This is Castillo," Tiago announced proudly, his chest puffed out in a mixture of pride and sadness.

"A magnificent horse," Stephen said, stepping closer to appraise the creature, who snorted in response. "Questionable temperament," Stephen jested.

Tiago's expression grew sombre as he began Castilio's story. "His master, a count of noble bearing and a master horseman, cherished this horse above all others. They fought bravely side-by-side, sustaining wounds together amidst the chaos of the battlefield. Castilio survived the final clash, but sadly his master did not. On his deathbed, the count pleaded with his son to ensure Castilio's life was one of peace—a worthy life, but jealousy and bitter envy clouded the son's heart. He believed his father cared more for the horse than for him. Blinded by this bitterness, he betrayed his father's final wish and sold Castilio to the first passing trader… who, by a twist of fate, was me.

Tiago continued softly, "Learning of this tale through a servant, I feel it's my responsibility to find this beloved horse the best possible home."

As Tiago spoke, Master Thomas appeared, a knowing look on his face. "Ah, I see you've met Castilio. He's a fine animal, though he needs a bit of care. He's had quite a history. I'm sure Tiago's ever-embellished story has already been told," he smiled at Tiago, who feigned hurt.

Thomas continued, "At thirteen, with that scar, I'd hate to see him go underpriced. He's a proven sire, bred for war! He may be too much horse for some, but not for you!" he expressed, "but there is a catch, of course," Thomas continued, his voice now weighted with a newfound gravity. "I would also like you to consider working for me, assisting Tiago in my new breeding venture. I'll pay you a good wage, enough to offset your absence from the farm. Young Benjamin could take the reins in your stead, and you could hire additional staff as you see fit to ease the burden. It won't be full-time at first, but as success is all but assured with your guiding hand, it will likely grow into something substantial."

"There's a whole fraternity of nobles invested in this – the Earl of Newcastle's chef among them – all with the same goal: to improve the quality of horses in this country. It's even said the King himself is keen on the idea and has some fine animals in the royal stud. Sadly, he's rather preoccupied with his troublesome Parliament at present, but that will blow over."

He paused, leaning closer to Stephen, a speculative glint dancing in his eyes. "You can see the potential here, Stephen, can't you? What an opportunity for someone of your talents. The chance to shape the future of equine breeding in England!"

He clapped Stephen on the shoulder, who appeared to be caught in a whirlwind of possibility, his eyes wide with a mixture of excitement and disbelief.

"Now, let's talk about a deal on the horses," Thomas continued, lowering his voice. "How about your fine grey, Mickey, In exchange for my Castilio? Plus, I'll include two of these superb broodmares in exchange for two of your best hunter mares. I'll even throw in a third mare if you agree to gift me the first colt produced or you can buy her outright from me at a fair price," he added with a playful nudge. Stephen's head was reeling, the enormity of the offer threatening to overwhelm him. "That's... that's quite an offer, Thomas," he stammered, struggling to maintain his composure.

As Thomas spoke, a small throng of clerks approached, each vying for his attention with urgent whispers and outstretched documents. "I must go, Stephen," Thomas said, his tone suddenly brisk and businesslike. "Please, take some time to consider my proposal. It could be a turning point, not just for you, but for horse breeding in this county." He clapped Stephen on the shoulder once more, his expression conveying genuine gratitude. "Thank you for joining me today. I'll do my best to catch up with you later this evening. Which Inn are you staying at? I'll send word."

"The Red Lion," Stephen replied, deep in contemplation, as they parted ways.

As they lingered, the magnitude of the decision settled heavily – a monumental opportunity to shape the future of horse breeding, backed by patrons of considerable wealth and ambition. Moreover, the arrangement concerning Castilio, a decidedly advantageous bargain, held immense potential. Despite the inherent risks of any horse purchase, the breed's high demand at auction made the potential for profit undeniably clear.

Benjamin stood beside his father, his face alight. He envisioned selling to the high-born, running Fairfield Farm, and perhaps even becoming a worthy match for Jane Stephens! His heart raced, and he couldn't help but hop in place, bubbling with exhilaration.

Thomas Ward, his new friend and stable hand, smiled warmly at Benjamin's enthusiasm, his hangover forgotten.

"Some people do seem to have all the luck," he said, chuckling at Benjamin's innocent ambition and infectious excitement. The atmosphere buzzed with opportunity as they stood on the brink of a new chapter.

Chapter 14
Uneasy Nights at Little Sodbury Manor

The evening had draped its shadowy veil over Little Sodbury Manor, the last vestiges of sunlight fading beyond the horizon, leaving behind a band of twilight that painted the sky in hues of purple and deep indigo. Inside, Mary Stephens sat at her writing desk, the quivering candlelight casting shadows that dance across the parchment before her. Her nimble fingers moved with intent as she penned a letter to her son William, sending him news from home and words of encouragement from a mother's heart.

Pausing her writing, she gazed out at the estate. Dusk veiled the fields, rolling toward a horizon where the last daylight flickered. The old oak stood sentinel, its branches swaying gently. The tranquil landscape contrasted sharply with the turmoil in her heart: a deep longing for William and a gnawing worry that unsettled her even in the estate's calming embrace.

Just as she refocused on her letters, a light knock broke the silence

"Mistress Mary?" It was Ruth, the young servant girl, her voice soft but urgent. "Mistress Jane is waiting for you. She wishes to pray with you before bed."

Mary smiled gently, setting aside her pen. "Of course, Ruth. Thank you."

With that, she moved through the corridors adorned with portraits of her ancestors, the faces of the past watching over her as she made her way to her daughter's chamber. The house was quiet, save for the soft creaks of the floorboards beneath her feet.

As she entered Jane's room, a warm light shimmered from the bedside candle, illuminating her daughter's fair complexion. Jane was nestled beneath a cover of soft linens, her large hazel eyes sparkling with innocence and curiosity.

"Mother!" Jane exclaimed, a smile breaking across her face. "Will you read to me?"

"Of course, my sweet," Mary replied, settling beside her on the edge of the bed. Taking up Janes small, well-worn Bible, she began to read of Jesus walking on the water, her calming voice filling the room. As she spoke of the waves and Peter's tentative steps on the surface, she watched Jane's eyes grow wide with wonder, enraptured by the tale.

"Do you think he was scared?" Jane asked, her voice a whisper. "I would be frightened to walk on water!"

Mary chuckled softly, closing the book as she tucked Jane beneath the covers. "Perhaps a little frightened, but he had faith, just as we must have faith in those we love, even when they are far away."

"I miss William, I miss riding out on horses with him and the way he always made me feel safe," Jane confessed.

Mary nodded, her heart aching at the mention of her son, now far from home. "I have some news to share, but not now, just have faith all will be well" Mary replied as she stroked Janes face with affection.

With a contented sigh, Jane's eyelids fluttered as sleep began to take hold. Mary kissed her forehead, whispering gentle reassurances that lingered in the twilight air, then rose quietly to leave the room.

As she exited, she exchanged a knowing glance with Ruth, who had just appeared by the door, awaiting further instructions. "Is Sarah Akins settled for the night in the guest room?" Mary asked.

"Yes, Mistress. I had Anna tend to her needs and she had retired for the night" Ruth replied.

Mary ensured that the house was locked up tight for the night, her heart easing as she checked each window and door—an instinct honed by years of managing the estate and its safety.

With the last of her duties done, she gave the keys to Ruth to put away and bade her goodnight. Mary climbed the staircase to her own chamber, grateful to rest after a long day. But sleep would elude her for a little while longer as it always did, her mind ever active and restless.

An hour passed before a scream shattered the manor's fragile peace. Mary jolted awake. With her heart pounding deep inside her chest, she snatched a tall candlestick from beside her bed and lit the tallow candle it held. Her instincts on high alert, Mary rushed out of her room and down the hallway with the dancing flame illuminating her every step.

As she descended the staircase, the previously quiet manor now echoed with chaos. Running into the main hall, she found Ruth in a state of near hysteria, her hands clasped tightly to her chest as if trying to contain her panic.

"Mistress Mary!" Ruth exclaimed, her voice a choked gasp. She pointed a trembling finger towards the whitewashed stone wall. Mary's eyes followed, landing on a chilling inscription scrawled there in what appeared to be blood: "HERETIC."

Mary's pulse quickened at the sight, but instead of succumbing to fear, she acted. "Ruth, pull yourself together," she commanded firmly, her voice cutting through the girl's panic. "Clean this up at once! We cannot leave such a vile thing on the wall."

Ruth, still visibly shaken, nodded, ran to fetch a rag and water then promptly began to frantically scrub the ominous message, her hands trembling. Just then, Anna Baker rushed into the hall, her face etched with worry. "Anna, send for Glen immediately," Mary commanded, her voice firm despite the unease she felt. "We need all available men here; any tenants we can muster to safeguard the manor and guard against intruders."

As Anna scurried off, Mary's resolve hardened; she could not allow this act of intimidation to unsettle them. The Fosters were undoubtedly behind this foul display, and she knew they would stop at nothing to undermine her family's position.

With a surge of determination, Mary strode purposefully toward the manor's back door, her grip tightening on the candlestick. If an intruder was indeed present, she would face them. Reaching the door, she found it slightly ajar. The inky blackness of the outside world seeped into the house, sending a shiver down her spine and raising goosebumps on her arms. Too afraid to look outside she quickly closed the heavy door, bolting it firmly behind her.

With her back against the solid timber, Mary turned to see her daughter's face, stricken with panic, her eyes wide and glistening in the dim candlelight. She held hands with her equally frightened friend, Sarah Akins. Instantly, Mary adopted a practised calm, her voice steady and reassuring. "There is nothing to fear, my dears. Stay close to me. Let us return to your bedrooms."

Inside, however, Mary's mind raced, her thoughts spiralling down a path that tightened her stomach with dread. She suspected a traitor within the very walls of her home – treachery lurking where she ought to feel most secure. The mere notion unsettled her deeply, the implications sending waves of icy anxiety through her veins.

She forced herself to breathe evenly, reminding herself of the hardships they had already weathered. "I will not let fear rule us," she murmured, her gaze sweeping the hall, her senses sharpened, alert to the slightest unusual sound. "We will protect our family, and our home, come what may."

Chapter 15
Tensions at the Red Lion Inn

John Stephens sat heavily at a corner table within the bustling Red Lion Inn, candlelight painting shadows across his furrowed brow. An untouched tankard of dark ale sat waiting to be consumed. The recent meeting with the Fosters pressed heavily upon him, Richard Foster's proposition echoing in his ears, stirring a wave of different emotions and possibilities.

Across the table, Mr. Cropper, the family steward, maintained his vigilant composure. He raised his tankard in a formal salute, his voice steady, though laced with concern. "To resilience, Master Stephens, and to finding our way through these troubled times."

Tim Jones, the young stable hand, looked up with bright eyes. "This ale is lovely, so it is!"

John forced a smile, trying to shake off the day's weight. "You think so, Tim?"

The Inn buzzed, but John was lost in thought, the noise fading as he replayed the Fosters offer over and over in his head. They were a direct threat to his family's legacy. Could the feud end with their offer? Many troubles would vanish and he did long for a simpler, more agreeable life.

Sensing his master's mood, Mr. Cropper cleared his throat. "If the Fosters attempt anything, we will fight at your side. You have the local tenants' support, and together we can defend what is ours."

John took a long drink, the ale refreshing his nerves. "Thank you, Cropper. We will need every ally we can muster. Alas I don't really know what they are truly capable of, what lengths they will go to, if I don't give them what they want."

Just then, the door swung open, bringing a gust of chilly air. The Akins group entered, spirits buoyed from the horse auction. Benjamin, excited, rushed to John.

"Master Stephens, you won't believe what we've accomplished!"

John smiled, warmed by the sight of Benjamin and a welcomed lift in the atmosphere. "What is it, Benjamin?"

The Akins settled at the table to explain the day's events and the barmaid began taking their orders as joy and laughter filled the air, offering John a reprieve.

Meanwhile, Benjamin and Thomas Ward noticed a group of rowdy men at a nearby table, including the burly figure from the previous night, now sporting blue ribbons. Their loud discussions about Parliament and the King's supposed weakness stirred unease in John.

A quick glance at Mr. Cropper confirmed they both felt the tension as the group grew increasingly boisterous.

As the Akins family celebrated their auction success, John's thoughts appeared to drift back to the troubling path ahead. He ordered a bottle of wine, determined to set his concerns aside and let the alcohol wash away his worries.

In high spirits, Benjamin animatedly recounted securing a deal involving Micky and two broodmares for Castilio, their magnificent Spanish stallion. "We'll have the finest horses in the county, Father!" Benjamin exclaimed, his youthful confidence brightening the room

Stephen ruffled his son's hair, a rare sign of affection and look of pride on his face only heightened Benjamin's spirits.

"That is splendid news!" John declared. His usual positive demeanour was rekindled by the Akins' jubilant mood and the potent wine beginning to weave its enchantment.

Turning his thoughts to his aspirations for his son William, John speculated, "I might be inclined to make an offer on that splendid horse, Samson. It would help you secure that third mare from Thomas Smyth." He said recalling the details of the potential deal.

Stephen hesitated, visibly contemplating. "Indeed, we could sell you the horse, but I would prefer not to finalise a deal just yet. At present, I find myself rather thinly stretched and can only entertain a strong offer, John. Nonetheless, I appreciate your proposition."

"Nonsense! I seek no special rates; I shall pay the market price for such a fine animal. I merely ask that you hold on to him until the end of the year, or alternatively, you could work him to maintain his condition until William returns this winter, we can work that as part of any deal."

Stephen nodded, a smile breaking across his face. "I am certain we will be able to arrange something."

With all the uplifting talk, the group was soon revelling in their newfound prospects and the mercurial day didn't end there. The dashing figure of Thomas Smyth, flanked by his entourage now entered the Inn. Among them was Matthew, now dressed in civilian attire rather than livery, followed by a familiar face—Paul Akins, Benjamin's uncle and a deacon. Benjamin sprang up to greet them.

"Uncle Paul!" he exclaimed, rushing forward with open arms.

Stephen extended his hand to Thomas Smyth and Matthew in greeting. "Good to see you, Thomas. Brother it's been too long!" he said giving his brother a manly hug.

Stephen made the introductions, "This is John Stephens of Little Sodbury Manor."

"I know your son, William," Thomas replied, shaking John's hand. "He's a couple of years my senior. My friends and I always looked up to him on the hunting field; he tackled the largest hedges and ditches without a second thought. A fine, fearless horseman."

John beamed at the praise for his son. "He is away fighting for the Protestant cause in the Low Countries," he explained.

"Yes, I heard he joined the volunteers. A brave man indeed," Thomas said solemnly.

As they settled in, more wine was poured, and tables were pushed together to accommodate the growing crowd. Laughter mingled with the rustic sounds of the Inn and for a moment, John allowed himself to relish in the camaraderie surrounding him.

However, the joy at the table was being stifled by the unruly group of men who continue to denounce the King's court as papist and tyrannical devils. The voice of the hulking man with a blue ribbon growing louder with each drink and the slurring cheers of his comrades beginning to overpower the Inn.

"Look at these King's toffs, thinking themselves above us!" his voice booming. "They're just pampered dogs at the king's beck and call—privilege of Parliament, down with the Bishops and that Catholic wench pulling Charles's strings!" He waved a pamphlet in his hand.

A murmur of agreement rippled through his companions,

emboldened by his rhetoric but getting weary glances from others in the Inn. Tensions in the tavern thickened, and John felt his light-heartedness begin to dissipate once more, as yet more trouble seemed to have found them.

Glancing at Thomas Smyth, Benjamin noticed his shift in demeanour. Despite his attempts to ignore the provocative rhetoric against the King, Thomas shot a sidelong glance at the large man and his rowdy companions, who seemed to be gesturing toward their smaller group. The man had clearly identified them as Royalists, likely by the red ribbon Thomas Smyth wore.

Thomas seemed to be weighing up his options before speaking, his voice firm yet measured. "Could you ask your patrons to temper their speeches? Such words are better whispered in shadows than spoken aloud in good company," he said to the Innkeeper.

The innkeeper, having overheard the conversation, stepped closer, sensing the rising discontent. "Gentlemen, might you kindly keep the noise down?" he requested, his tone diplomatic.

The large, brawny figure leading the unruly group, stood up abruptly, the movement drawing attention as he cracked his neck and rolled his shoulders, a menacing look in his eyes. "What's that to you? We'll speak as we please. This isn't an Inn for your kind!" he be bellowed towards them, knowing full well the request for tempered speech came from Thomas.

"I think the drink has clouded your judgment," Thomas Smyth retorted, his back to the man, his expression composed but firm. He turned, adding, "We may disagree on political matters, but that doesn't grant you the right to incite trouble."

The air grew further taut as the brute man stepped closer "And who do you think you are, telling me what I can or cannot say?" he sneered, puffing out his chest.

Instantly, Matthew rose from his chair, revealing a concealed pistol and dagger beneath his cloak, creating a barrier between Thomas and the thug. "You will address my Master with respect, or you'll find yourself in grave trouble."

A deadly silence fell. The innkeeper paled. "Enough!" he called, stepping forward, his burly barmaid flanking him as backup. "This is a public house; any further trouble will not be tolerated."

"Tell him to retract his statements, or you can join him in the stocks!" Matthew stated, his voice low and threatening. Gasps could be heard rippling through the crowd.

The Innkeeper hesitated, then addressed the large man. "Edward, please, you'd best leave if you want to avoid trouble. This doesn't need to escalate. Last warning."

Seeing their precarious position, Thomas Smyth stood, commanding attention. "I suggest you heed the Innkeeper's advice and leave in peace. I have no wish for violence. Your incendiary words might cause repercussions, especially if my friend Robert Yeamans, Bristol's Sheriff, hears of these treasonous statements."

Edward's face flushed with anger. He glared at Thomas, sneered, then gestured for his companions to follow him. "The King's lapdogs have had their time," he spat, as they headed for the exit, leaving behind a tense silence.

"But I haven't finished my drink," one of his companions protested.

"We're going!" Edward snarled, grabbing the cup and throwing it across the room in a childish act of defiance.

As the large man's voice faded, Thomas Smyth turned to the group, a mix of concern and relief on his face. "It seems the political climate in Bristol is becoming ever more heated. You should pick your accommodation more wisely next time."

"Indeed," John replied, his heart still racing.

With the threat averted, the group breathed a collective sigh of relief and poured more wine, settling back into easier conversation. The earlier anxiety began to dissipate, although the dark shadow of division loomed larger than ever. John silently appreciated the camaraderie of his friends as they rallied around one another in these precarious times.

"Now, Stephen, we have a deal to conclude," Thomas Smyth said.

As they resumed their discussions, Benjamin exchanged a knowing smirk with Thomas Ward, both young men relishing the excitement of the past couple of days, far removed to their normal, mundane routines. As the hangovers from the previous night subsided they sipped on the finest wine the Red Lion could muster. "Hair of the dog," Old Man Ward said as he raised his glass to the air, seemingly piping up for nowhere.

Chapter 16
The Journey Home

It was a muggy Sunday morning, the summer warmth lingering as the group prepared to leave Bristol, skipping church for an early start. The Akins and Stephens group gathered outside Red Lion Inn.

The night before, Thomas Smyth finalised a generous deal with the Akins family, securing a splendid stallion, Castilio, and three pure-bred Spanish mares. Stephen used the promised funds from Samson's sale to facilitate the transaction.

While Benjamin was excited about their new prospects, a deep sense of loss and pangs of regret lingered as the reality of selling Samson—second only to Ralph in his affections, began to sink in. He comforted himself with the knowledge that the horse would only be down the road at the Manor. An additional benefit of the deal his father had arranged was that Benjamin could continue training and keeping Samson fit until William Stephens returned from the Low Countries at the year's end. Meanwhile, Old Man Ward would remain in Bristol to assist Tiago and Matthew in transporting the new horses to Little Sodbury. Afterward, they planned to advance their breeding endeavours at Fairfield Farm.

"In six months, you'll be knee-deep in breeding these Spanish beauties with me and your very own. We could even look to mixing their blood with Arabians or native breeds—the sky's the limit. We will put England back on the map for breeding fine horses!" Thomas Smyth had said, with ambitious and genuine enthusiasm. Stephen had accepted Thomas Smyth's proposition to work part-time alongside him, eager to embrace this new chapter in horse breeding. Without the financial restraints and limitations, he faced at their own stud farm, he could focus his talents and passion. The handsome financial reward and the security that brought his family was the cherry on the cake.

Stephen had remarked to Benjamin that evening, how fortunate they were to have the patronage of the Smyths, their generosity to the Akins family was truly remarkable.

As they prepared to leave, Benjamin felt sad saying goodbye to Micky. Benjamin approached Micky and stroked the horse's velvety muzzle. "You're going to the best home, my friend," he whispered, knowing Micky was going to a skilled horseman.

With the horses tacked up and their hooves checked, the group set off down the winding path into the countryside. The humid summer day clung to their skin, causing them to sweat beneath their woollens. As Benjamin glanced upward, he noticed dark clouds ominously gathering on the horizon, hinting at an approaching rainstorm.

They made good progress, leaving Bristol behind. Benjamin pulled his horse alongside his Uncle Paul, who had joined them after arriving with Thomas Smyth the night before, riding an old looking but study cob. "So, what brings you to Little Sodbury, dear Uncle?" he asked, genuinely curious.

Paul smiled broadly, his face lighting up. "To see my dear family, of course!" he replied warmly. Benjamin couldn't resist teasing him. "And what else?"

"Well," Paul continued, his tone shifting to one of elation, "Anthony Rogers, the priest I'm studying under, is taking over parish church in Little Sodbury temporarily, so I will be hanging around for at least six months, maybe longer."

"Six months?" Benjamin exclaimed with wide eyes. The thought of spending more time with his uncle filled him with anticipation. Paul was a fountain of knowledge, a wellspring of stories and insights. "So, what will be your duties as deacon under Anthony Rogers? What kind of priest is he? The last one wasn't very nice and wouldn't answer my questions. He just said I must have more faith."

"Under Father Rogers, I'll be assisting with the services and learning more about managing parish's affairs. It's a worthy challenge, even if it's a relatively small parish," Paul replied, his expression serious. "He's quite engaging, if a bit unorthodox—though, in my view, that's a good thing." Paul waved away a pesky fly that was weaving around his face.

Benjamin grinned, feeling relief. "That sounds promising! I'd love to learn more about what's going on further afield. Bristol seems awash with news and intrigue compared to Little Sodbury, where the complaints are usually about the weather and annoying neighbours."

As they rode on, the conversation flowed freely, filled with plans. Paul mentioned that his mentor, Anthony Rogers, was considering a move to the New World with a religious community, a notion that captured Benjamin's imagination. "They seek to preach in a place where they can explore new truths and have open discussions about scripture. It's compelling," Paul said, his enthusiasm evident.

"I heard stories of people with red skin and painted faces out there. Are the stories true, Uncle?" Benjamin asked, wide-eyed.

"There are natives, yes, with different complexions to us and clothes and customs, and little to no knowledge of the Bible. Can you imagine teaching someone Bible truths for the first time?" Paul looked wistfully at the thought, his excitement clear.

Benjamin enjoyed learning stories from the Bible, taking the lessons from them, but wasn't practically studious and didn't remember much of what he was taught, unlike his Sister and Uncle. On the contrary if it was learning about horses his mind was a sponge, absorbing everything. In that way he was like his father.

The camaraderie kept spirits high despite the thickening clouds, hinting at a brewing storm. Suddenly, the first drops of rain began to fall, pattering softly on the leaves and dry mud.

"We'd best pick up the pace," Stephen called out, urging the group to ride harder. The darkening clouds and cooling air temperature made it clear they needed to return home before the weather turned treacherous.

With bursts of laughter and urgent shouts, they spurred their horses into a frantic canter whenever the road permitted, the landscape dissolving into a blur as they stormed along the twisting, hazardous roads back to Little Sodbury. Above them, the heavy clouds unleashed their fury and a relentless downpour drenched the earth and pounded against the trembling leaves, as if nature itself was unleashed in wild, roaring protest.

Chapter 17
Homecoming

Rain plastered John Stephen's mud-streaked face as he leaned forward to give his exhausted cob a reassuring pat while they trudged up the long path to the Manor. Behind him, Mr. Cropper and Tim Jones pressed on, their sodden wool cloaks clinging heavily to their rain-soaked, weary bodies. Even Jane's usually spirited pony—borrowed by Tim—seemed out of sorts, its head bobbing in protest. Before their parting, Benjamin had noticed the pony's uneven gait and seeing Tim's concern, had promised to examine the animal's left hind leg—the likely source of the trouble —when collecting his sister from the Manor the next morning.

They had parted ways with the Akins family less than a mile back, while distant rumbles of thunder echoed ominously in the background, the rain pounded down relentlessly, a true summer monsoon.

Approaching the main house, a hooded figure detached itself from the shadows. Despite the concealing cloak, John instantly recognised Glen Jones, who nodded respectfully as he revealed his face.

"Good to see you, Glen. What brings you to the house at this hour? Is everything all right?" John asked, concern etching lines across his tired face.

"Nothing to worry about, Master. Just a bit of extra security, I assure you. Mistress Mary will explain." Glen ushered them forward. "Come on, let's get you all inside and dried off. I'll get the fires going." He turned his attention to Tim. "You okay, lad?"

"Yes, Father!" Tim replied, brightening, barely able to contain his eagerness to tell him everything. Unlike his older companions, he seemed to draw from an inexhaustible well of youthful energy.

"Sounds like you've had quite the adventure. Get these horses into the stables and rubbed down dry before you join us. Cooks got some of her special stew simmering." Glen's words were brisk but delivered with his usual warm reassurance.

Dismounting stiffly, the men hurried indoors just as a massive clap of thunder reverberated overhead, rumbling the very foundation of the manor. Inside, Ruth and Anna, both maids, hurried around fetching warm blankets for John, informing him that fresh clothes had been laid out on his bed.

Though Mr. Cropper offered to assist his master in dressing, John, feeling a sense of autonomy despite his weariness, waved him off. "You see to yourself, Cropper. You deserve a warm meal too."

As John climbed the staircase, each step felt heavy after the long ride, but he was greeted at the landing by the presence of his wife, Mary. "Husband!" she exclaimed, her eyes shining with relief. "I have missed you dearly! My heart feels lighter to see you safe." She rushed forward, helping him shed his damp cloak and layered garments.

A sudden spark ignited between them as Mary leaned in and kissed John, her lips pressing hard against his in an unexpected display of affection. Taken aback, he smiled broadly. "Perhaps I should go away more often," he teased lightly, though the weariness lingered in his voice.

Mary met his gaze earnestly, a shadow crossing her face. "Husband, I have much to tell you."

The tone in her voice made John's heart sink. "And I you,

my love," he replied, the fatigue now a tangible presence, making his limbs feel like lead. "Let's discuss it after I've changed into something dry."

Together, they stepped into the adjoining chamber, where the pulsing hearth cast a warm glow that seeped into John's tired bones. As he changed into fresh garments—laid out by Mary atop a dresser, for the sodden wool would take days to dry—the comforting scent of woodsmoke mingled with the aroma of stew drifting through the house, offered a measure of solace. It was Mary's troubled expression that held his gaze; he could feel the weight of whatever news she bore pressing between them like a gathering storm.

"Have you heard anything from William?" John asked, breaking the silence as he adjusted his collar, his heart filled with apprehension.

"No more letters have come," Mary answered, her voice tinged with worry "it's not that."

John looked at her, his eyes already heavy with the warmth of the room and promise of rest, but he steeled himself to listen. Outside, the storm raged on – thunder rattled the windows of the bedchamber and the fire cast wild, dancing shadows on the walls.

Mary glanced at the closed door before turning back, her voice low. "I think we have a traitor in this house."

John met her gaze, a grim understanding dawning. "I was about to tell you the same thing."

Chapter 18
Ratcatcher

After the household sat in silence during the evening meal, the warm, Savory smell of stew clung to the air, punctuated only by the soft crackling of the fireplace. Mistress Mary and John Stephens Esquire exchanged knowing glances across the table, their unspoken communication revealing the weight of their shared concerns.

Once the meal was concluded, John rose from his seat with a slight clearing of his throat. "Mr. Cropper," he said, his tone formal yet earnest, "I would like you to gather all the servants in the main hall once the table is cleared. I have matters of importance to discuss with them."

Mary interjected, "Mr. Cropper, if you would accompany me for a moment before attending to that?" She turned her gaze to her husband, nodding respectfully.

"Of course, Mistress," Cropper replied, bowing his head slightly as a sign of compliance before stepping aside with Mary.

Moments later, the two maids, the cook, Tim Jones, and Glen Jones entered the hall. Glen, his bald head glistening under the candlelight, stood tall among them, while the cook—a round-faced woman with fiery red hair—looked weary after rising from her post in the kitchen. She fidgeted with her hands, clearly uneasy about the summons.

Mr. Cropper took his position at the head of the line, addressing the assembly. "You may wonder why I have called you here on this tempestuous evening." John said whilst he circled the makeshift assembly, scrutinising each face before continuing.

"I will ask you all in turn; are you content with Mistress Stephens and myself as your masters?"

The group looked taken aback by the unexpected question, but soon their expressions shifted to compliance, nodding and murmuring, "Yes, Master" or "Aye."

"Do we not treat you with the respect and consideration that your diligent service deserves?" John continued, his tone steady yet firm. Another round of agreement echoed through the hall, though the murmurs were tinged with uncertainty and confusion.

"Excellent," he replied, unable to fully mask his relief. "Mary, please share our concerns."

As Mistress Mary stepped forward, she met the anxious eyes of the household staff with a steady gaze. "Most of you have served this family since you were very young. Many of your parents have been tenants sworn to this house for generations, like Mr. Cropper, who has dedicated his life to our service."

She paused, letting her words hang in the air. "Therefore, I am distressed to inform you that there is a disloyal traitor among us." Her eyes flicked to Mr. Cropper, who offered a subtle, almost deferential, nod.

A wave of shocked gasps rippled through the room. John noted Jane standing silently in the corner, her wide eyes reflecting surprise and a hint of unease. Sarah Akins had been asked to wait in her room, this being deemed a family matter.

Then, Mary's sharp voice sliced through the stunned silence. "Just over a week ago, we received a letter from William. I confided in each of you privately, sharing its contents and urging absolute secrecy. Now, I must ask: Anna Baker, did you share that information with anyone?" The weight of her question hung heavy in the air, all eyes turning to Anna.

No, Mistress! Of course not!" Anna's voice rose in indignant protest.

"How about you, Glen?" Mary continued, her gaze unwavering, seeming to bore into him. She searched his face, looking for any hint of deceit.

"Absolutely not, Mistress," Glen asserted, his response firm, but a flicker of something unreadable crossed his features. Perplexity? Defiance?

"Lacy, our esteemed cook," Mary's voice dropped, tinged with a subtle threat, "did you tell anyone?"

"No, Mistress," Lacy whispered, her eyes wide with fear.

Mary turned to the young maid, Ruth, her voice chillingly calm. "And you, Ruth? What about you?" The silence stretched, thick with unspoken accusations.

Trapped in Mary's unwavering gaze, Ruth began to tremble uncontrollably. "I—" she stammered, her voice cracking before she burst into tears and collapsed at Mary's feet. "I am sorry, Mistress! They were blackmailing me... threatening my family!"

A glimpse of something akin to pity crossed Mary's face, quickly replaced by steel. Her voice, though, remained sharp. "You Judas! We shared slightly different versions of that letter's details with each of you, precisely to expose the one feeding information to the Fosters. How could you betray us, Ruth, after all we have done for you and your family?" Mary said, reflecting genuine hurt which turned to anger, her scrutiny, a crushing weight on the young maid.

Mary pulled the girl roughly to her feet, but Ruth only sobbed uncontrollably, consumed by shame. In a surge of fury, Mary struck her across the face, sending Ruth reeling back to the floor in stunned silence.

"And you let them into our house as well, didn't you?" Mary's voice was dangerously low, a barely suppressed fury trembling beneath the surface, like a volcano before eruption. She silently battled to regain control, willing herself to remain composed.

John surged to his feet, his voice sharp and commanding. "Mr. Cropper, take Ruth to her quarters. Bolt the door. We will discuss her punishment in the morning. She has jeopardised the safety of this house, and her punishment will be proportionate to the severity of her betrayal." Ruth flinched, her sobs stifled, as Mr. Cropper moved to obey. The room fell silent, heavy with the consequences of her actions.

Turning back to the remaining staff, John's voice firm and loud, echoed around the hall, using the remaining reserve of his strength. "I must ask you all: Have any of you had contact with the Foster family regarding loans or information? Speak freely; now is the time for full disclosure!"

Anna stepped forward hesitantly, her voice trembling slightly. "Master John, the Fosters have extended offers of loans at favourable rates to my father, but he has not accepted them. Other than that, we have had no further contact."

"Thank you Anna, is there anyone else among you?" John inquired, his gaze scanning the assembly, each servant's head bowed in shared shame at Ruth's betrayal.

Mr. Cropper cleared his throat, stepping forward with the posture of a diligent steward. "If it pleases you, my Master, I shall dismiss the staff now. In the morning, I would like to summon all our tenants to this hall to address the matter at hand."

"Yes, Mr. Cropper, that would be prudent. I trust you will make all the arrangements first thing," John replied, his tone stern, compelling deference from the man before him.

With a respectful bow, Mr. Cropper exited the room, joined by the others, as they left the hall an uncertainty lingered in the air.

John turned his attention to his daughter, his expression softening. "My dearest Jane, come hither," he called gently. As she approached, he enveloped her in a warm embrace.

"Now, you must return to your chamber, my dear. I will be up shortly to bid you goodnight and say a prayer with you."

Jane replied, a look of shock and concern for Ruth, readable on her face. "Okay, Poppa. Can I just pop into Sarah's room to say goodnight?"

"Yes, of course, my darling. And I apologise for making you witness that. One day, you will run your own household, and sometimes they aren't always loyal or obedient," John replied.

She nodded dutifully. "What will happen to Ruth, Poppa?"

"Of that, I am still undecided, but do not concern yourself, my dear. Off to bed now; I'll be up shortly."
Jane nodded respectfully, obeying her father, her heart lightened by his affection as she left the hall.

Once she had departed, John faced Mary, an earnest glint in his eyes. "Well handled, my dear," he acknowledged, appreciating her strength in the tense situation.

"I should not have lost my temper like that," Mary admitted, a shadow of regret crossing her delicate features.

John stepped closer, drawing her into a gentle embrace. He could feel the tension in her body, stiff against him as if bearers of the world's sorrows lay heavy on her shoulders. "It is only natural to feel such turmoil after the betrayal of one you trust, my love," he reassured softly. "But I shall say one thing…"

Mary turned her head to meet his gaze; curiosity lit within her expressive eyes. "What is that, my husband?"

"I am grateful that I am not counted among your enemies," he smiled, his tone lightening the weight that had clouded the room. The warmth of his words coaxed a slight upward turn of her lips, gradually easing the rigid tension that had enveloped her. With a gentle sigh, she relaxed into his embrace, drawing solace from his steadfast presence.

As John contemplated their next steps, anxiety threaded through his thoughts regarding Ruth's fate and the unpleasant task of handing out a fitting punishment. "But what shall we do with the girl?" he mused aloud, the formality of their situation stark against the backdrop of familial warmth.

The sound of thunder continued to rumble in the distance, fitting to the storm of uncertainty brewing in their secluded haven.

Chapter 19
The Morning After

The morning broke fair, the sun casting its golden light abroad, while the air bore a briskness most welcome—a blessed reprieve from the tempest that had raged the day before. The ground, once cracked and thirsting, now lay dark and rich, as though the hand of God had poured forth and it had drunk its fill. Benjamin Akins, the chill of night still clinging to his limbs, paused for a moment to collect himself after the hard and hasty ride out of Bristol the day before.

Leading his impressive bay hunter, Samson, up the private path to the stables of Little Sodbury Manor—large, though sparingly filled—Benjamin could not help but admire the majestic beast, as he so often did. He recalled the many times over the past years he had watched Samson and Ralph prance side by side in their paddock—the only two males they dared turn out together, for the others were too quick to quarrel and vie for dominance. Ralph and Samson shared a rare bond, one made all the more evident that morning as they called out to each other as Benjamin led Samson from his stall, as if each sensed this parting was different, more final.

Samson's fine breeding was plain in every measured step —powerful and proud, showing no sign of weariness from the hard ride the day before, a true testament to his fitness and condition.

At eight years of age, Samson was in the prime of his physical prowess—a steadfast companion who held a treasured place in Benjamin's heart. As he gently caressed Samson's forehead and the spot just under his forelock that always seemed to calm him, a wave of melancholy washed over Benjamin at the thought of parting with the noble creature, now destined for the Stephens family. He reassured himself however, knowing that Samson would remain nearby and that he was still expected to work the horse for the Stephens for some time yet, this cushioned the blow.

Though Benjamin had yet to meet William, murmurs about him, coupled with comments from the astute Thomas Smyth at the Inn, painted a portrait of a soldier—brave, skilled, and a competent horseman. He reflected on the nature of such men; while some boasted of their prowess, many proved to be little more than users of the bonds they shared with their steeds, treating them as mere objects or tools rather than noble partners. The knowledge that William sought a replacement for his previous mount, unfortunate victim of battle, kindled a flicker of unease regarding Samson's fate. With a gentle pat, Benjamin sought to comfort the stallion, bolstered by their enduring bond.

As he approached the house, he noted the frantic activity inside, Mr. Cropper ushering people in and out with an authority befitting a steward managing a great estate. Suddenly, he spotted Tim Jones signalling him from the stable block. "What's all this commotion, Tim? Why are so many souls gathered?" Benjamin asked as he led Samson, the bay hunter's ears pricked forward, his head turning to take in the unfamiliar sights and scents stirred by the unusual bustle about the manor grounds.

Tim looked momentarily uncertain, casting a glance toward the gathering before replying, "I cannot say for certain, Master Benjamin. It seems to be a family matter—all the tenants have been summoned for a meeting with Master John. But please, bring Samson to the stable block. His stall is all prepared."

Benjamin gave a slow nod, a faint unease settling in his chest. "How fares the pony you rode yesterday? He seemed a touch lame toward the end of our journey. Mr. Stephens, I noted, was disinclined to slow the pace—what with the rain coming down like the Flood itself."

Tim's expression turned serious. "He's not quite himself this morning, sir. Would you take a look at him?"

"Of course I will, Tim," Benjamin replied, the concern in his voice unmistakable.

He turned toward the stable block—a solid, well-built structure, its stone-flagged floor cool underfoot and timber-framed walls weathered but sturdy. The scent of horses, hay, and damp earth hung in the air. Inside, ten generous stalls lined either side of the central aisle, all clean but only three currently occupied, a large hayloft at the far end brimming with the sweet, golden cut of the season.

As he stepped inside, the familiar sounds welcomed him—the soft clatter of hooves on stone, the rustle of straw, and the low, contented murmurs of horses. Tim led Benjamin to the third stall on the left, where Samson would be stabled. Removing his head collar, Benjamin watched as the bay moved off to investigate the generous heap of hay piled high in the far corner beside a large wooden crate filled with fresh water.

In the adjacent stall stood Jane's grey gelding, shifting uneasily from one hind leg to the other. His gait was uneven as he moved about the ample space, his discomfort plain to see.

"Easy now, lad," Benjamin soothed, kneeling to examine the pony's left hind leg. The creature nickered softly, its large eyes reflecting a trusting innocence.

As he examined the leg running his hands over each limb, Tim stood close by, worry written across his features. "What do you suspect? Is it a grave matter?"

"I'm not certain yet," Benjamin replied, feeling around the

joint of the left hind once more with care. "It may be a mere strain from yesterday's exertions. A spot of rest and some gentle exercise afterward may do him well. I notice only a slight warmth in the pastern of the left hind leg the others seem to be fine."

Just then, Mr. Cropper's authoritative voice echoed from the main house, summoning everyone to gather. "I must attend this meeting," Tim declared. "Keep an eye on the place whilst I am gone—would you?"

"Of course, but I have matters at the farm that require my attention, and I need to fetch my sister. Do not tarry too long," Benjamin replied, his sense of duty evident.

Benjamin gave Samson some attention before, making a quick inspection of the other horses to ensure their well-being. He noted John Stephens' white-and-black cob appeared stiff yet sound.

"How is my boy Minnie doing?" A voice suddenly startled Benjamin, raising the hairs on his neck.

"Good morning, Mistress, Jane!" he exclaimed, bowing deeply. "I apologise for not noticing your approach."

"I am merely escaping the household drama. Sarah is gathering her belongings to return home. We spied you coming down the drive. It has been lovely having her stay, she is like a sister to me," she said shyly, her gaze lingering intently on Benjamin before continuing.

And how fares my pony, Benjamin? What's your expert opinion?" Mistress Jane smiled, a playful gleam in her eye that lent levity to the morning air.
Benjamin felt an unexpected flutter of nervousness, unaccustomed as he was to being alone with the young Mistress of the manor. There was something in her gaze—bright, teasing—that unsettled his usual composure. He

cleared his throat quietly, steadying himself with the thought of duty.

"Your pony, Minnie, shows a touch of warmth in his left hind leg, Mistress," he said, his voice even, though his heart beat a little too fast for his liking. "There is no swelling as yet, but the limb is warmer than the rest. I'd advise a few days of box rest. I shall return to trot him up and see how she fares."

For a moment, their eyes met—hers curious, perhaps amused, his; a touch too earnest. The silence between them held just enough weight to feel like more than courtesy.

"I am no true expert, of course" he added with quiet humility.

"Thank you, Benjamin. I shall heed your counsel nonetheless," Jane replied earnestly, stepping a little closer. Her gaze lingered on his, warm and unguarded. "In truth, I would be most grateful if you might look in on him each day. Would you be so kind as to do that for me?"

In that moment, Benjamin found himself wholly disarmed by her nearness. The delicate fragrance that clung to her— lavender, perhaps, or something sweeter still—seemed to wrap around his senses, deepening the quiet spell she cast. His heart quickened, stirred by a yearning not solely born of duty but of something far more dangerous: the desire to please her simply because it was, she who asked it.

"I am your humble servant, Mistress," he replied almost without thinking, gently taking her hand and pressing a soft kiss upon it—a gesture both respectful and daring in its intimacy.
Jane giggled, a light, delightful sound that lingered in his ears. To his astonishment, she leaned forward and placed a gentle kiss upon his cheek, her warmth sending a chilling thrill coursing through him. Awestruck, Benjamin felt a

broad smile spread across his face as she turned to leave.

"I will send Sarah down shortly," she said, casting a playful glance back over her shoulder, a mischievous sparkle dancing in her eyes before she disappeared around the corner and onto the main house.

The moment lingered in his mind, filling the space between heart and reason with a heady mix of joy and trepidation. He returned to his task, though a distracted vacancy had taken hold—his thoughts adrift, his spirit soaring far above the heaviness that had settled over him since Micky and Samson's sale. In that fleeting instant, it was gone. The mere memory of Mistress Jane's smile cast everything in a brighter light. He felt lighter than he had in years—happier, even—as though, at last, things were beginning to fall into place for him and his family, and as he had secretly hope he realised Jane Stephens did indeed feel the way he did about her.

Tim's sudden return tore Benjamin from his reverie, the jolt sharp and unwelcome. One look at the boy's face—pale, eyes wide with disbelief—and the lightness Benjamin had felt vanished like mist under the sun.

"I can scarcely believe it, Benjamin—Master John has ordered a flogging for Ruth!" Tim blurted, his voice thick with outrage.

"A flogging?" Benjamin repeated, stunned. "What in God's name could she have done to deserve such a punishment?"

Tim glanced around nervously, lowering his voice. "My father always warned me not to speak out of turn about family matters," he said, hesitating. "But you ought to know. Ruth let intruders into the house while we were away. And... she told them things—family secrets. It was those Fosters we passed on the road."

Benjamin's brow furrowed, the shock on his face giving way to anger and disbelief. "That is serious indeed... what a foolish girl," he said, though his tone carried more worry than scorn. A protective instinct stirred within him—not only for the family of the girl who had so thoroughly captured his admiration, but also for his own sister, who had been staying in the same household.

"She wasn't trying to be foolish," Tim insisted, his voice rising. "The Fosters have been blackmailing her. Her father's already taken a beating from those brutes. Ruth thought she had no choice."

He swallowed hard, eyes pleading. "It's not right, Benjamin. Ruth is a good lass. She doesn't deserve this."

"Ah, I detect the scent of a crush!" Benjamin teased, a playful smirk dancing on his lips.

"Perhaps you do, I won't lie," Tim admitted, though his tone quickly shifted to seriousness. "But that doesn't change the fact that the Fosters' actions are utterly deplorable. If anyone deserves punishment, it should be them," he declared passionately. "I understand the Master cannot allow such a breach of trust to go unaddressed and Ruth is fortunate they haven't escalated the situation to the higher authorities; however it still feels unfair she is to receive a flogging."

"How many lashes is she to endure?" Benjamin asked, his stomach tightening at the thought. Such punishments were hard enough to stomach, but when the recipient was a girl —a Mistress —it always struck him as doubly cruel.

"Twenty, I believe," Tim replied grimly. "And Mr. Cropper is to deliver them. He won't hold back. That poor girl..." He shook his head; sorrow etched across his face.

Benjamin swallowed hard, a surge of sadness rising in

him. Desperate to shift the mood, he said, "I must be getting back to Fairfield Farm. I've settled Samson in—he's happily at his hay in the stall"

"Thank you for your help, Benjamin," Tim said with a grateful nod.

Just then, Sarah appeared, carrying the small bag packed for her long weekend at the manor. Her presence offered a momentary reprieve.

"Hello, dear brother," she said. "I had a lovely time. How is Father?" she asked.

"We are all very well, and we have much good news to share." Benjamin paused. "Oh, and before I go, Mistress Jane has requested that I return each day to check on Minnie" Benjamin added casually.

"She came here?" Tim asked, his brow furrowing with concern.

"What troubles you, Tim? It was merely a brief encounter," Benjamin said, feeling a twinge of unease himself, at the thought of being alone with Mistress Jane, an undeniably unseemly situation.

"It's not the meeting that worries me—I fear Mistress Jane will lay the blame for Minnie's condition at my feet," Tim confessed.

"She said nothing of the sort; she understands that such mishaps can occur," Benjamin reassured him.

"Thank goodness for that. Mistress Jane has a special fondness for that pony."

"Well, I must ensure Minnie gets back to fitness. I'll be exercising Samson three times a week to keep him in shape, but you may need to lunge him once weekly until your master's son, William, returns. We'll be seeing more of each other," Benjamin replied.

"That sounds good, Benjamin. I must admit, managing three horses and this pony, along with Mr. Cropper's additional duties of which are many, was becoming a daunting task," Tim confessed.

"Don't worry, Tim. I'm just down the road if you need any help or advice," Benjamin assured him.

"I cannot wait for my brother Owen to return with Master William. I miss him—and in these troubled times, the house sorely needs a man like him. Once they are back, these rogues will not dare be so bold." Tim paused, then added with quiet sincerity, "Thank you again."

Mary flinched at the sharp crack of the whip striking flesh from behind the closed door. Mr. Cropper was delivering Ruth's twenty lashes with grim efficiency. Whatever resentment Mary had once harboured toward the girl had long since melted away, replaced by a deep and aching pity.

Ruth—only seventeen—was left to endure the full weight of this punishment alone. After word of the family's dealings with the Fosters had reached her parents, they had vanished from their small holding in the village, fleeing to who knew where. And now, abandoned and disgraced, Ruth was left to face the consequences alone.

Mary had come to understand, the full story of the Fosters' treacherous plot to ensnare the family in such a predicament. Now, it was Ruth who must absorb the repercussions. Mary had offered the girl two choices: leave the family service without references to find work elsewhere, or accept this punishment.

Initially, John considered dismissing the poor girl, but she pleaded for another chance, willing to accept her punishment in hopes of redemption. To minimise Ruth's humiliation, it was decided to reduce from a public flogging before the household and tenants, to a private yet still agonising punishment. However, Mr. Cropper insisted that the twenty lashes must be carried out as planned, arguing that leniency might encourage betrayal among the staff and tenants, who could easily succumb to the Fosters' bribes and threats. He believed a firm hand was necessary to maintain order and loyalty.

Mary felt weary, her spirits heavy after the toils of the day. That morning's assembly of tenants—some twenty families who tilled the eight hundred acres let by the Stephens, the remainder of two hundred, being for the most part woodland, kept under the family's own care—had proved most draining. The meeting swarmed with petty grievances, which swiftly gave place to tiresome bickering, aggravated, doubtless, by the vexation that the previous day's violent rain had thwarted their designs for the midsummer revels. It was an ancient custom: to light bundles of wood upon the fields, that the fire might banish ill fortune, and thereafter to feast and dance in mirth. Mary found the practice both distasteful and touched with pagan folly; yet she knew its value well, for it kept the tenants' content, and thus obedient.

Somehow, Irene Jones, the wife of Glen and stepmother to Owen and Tim, had become the subject of unjust suspicion. The spirited and attractive woman, in her mid-thirties and much younger than her husband, had fiery red hair that matched her fervent responses. She was unjustly blamed for the unreasonable downpour, likely simply for being Irish and Catholic.

John had struggled to maintain order during the tenants' assembly; his voice often lost in the clamour until Mary intervened. "Silence!" she commanded, her authority silencing the crowd, respecting her family lineage.

She reminded them firmly of her husband's fairness. "He is the only landlord who has not raised rents sharply, despite inflation. He's shown patience with mismanaged pastures, knowing full well the toll the labour shortage has taken. Do not mistake his generosity for weakness." Her gaze swept the room. "And as for this nonsense regarding Goodwife Jones—we will hear no more of it. The Jones family has served this estate loyally for generations." It was a warning, unmistakable and final.

Having captured their attention, she deferred back to John, who laid out the threat posed by the Fosters, detailing Ruth's betrayal and the ensuing consequences. He emphasised that while Ruth was forgiven for being disloyal, any future act of betrayal would be met with a far harsher penalty.

Mary and John had yet to discuss the Fosters' offer at length, their initial conversation having devolved into a heated argument. Mary remained shocked that John would even entertain the notion, finding it impossible to trust what she perceived as a potential snare.

As the tenants dispersed, a priest's arrival proved a boon. Father Anthony Rogers presented himself as polite and understanding, unlike many clergymen Mary had encountered lately.

John, feeling at ease with the older man's gentle demeanour, sought counsel regarding Irene Jones. He anticipated the villagers would raise the issue with their new priest, especially given the rise in anti-Catholic and anti-Irish sentiment fuelled by newly distributed leaflets in nearby Chipping Sodbury, which seemed to be embracing Puritanism.

Mary held. Goodwife Jones in high regard; she was a kind and amiable woman, despite what Mary considered to be her misguided beliefs. Her family—devout Protestants—remained steadfastly loyal, not only as tenants but also as cherished friends. In this spirit, Mary interjected, praising Irene and suggesting that she might even contemplate conversion, though her journey was still in its early stages. She felt compelled to add, "Glen's son Owen fights alongside my son in the Low Countries for the cause of Protestantism." Mary was unsure why she felt the need to make such statements; perhaps the violent messages left by the Fosters and the threats issued by Richard and his priestly son regarding John's recent trip to Bristol had affected her more deeply than she realised.

"Pray, good Mistress Mary, there's no need to reassure me," the priest said with a warm smile. "My deacon is an

Akins, and they speak very highly of the Stephens as pillars of strength in our parish. The divisions and unrest in our land contradict the guidance of Scripture and our Heavenly Father's grace. I strive to remain detached from worldly politics and focus on guiding souls to know our Father and His Kingdom."

These words were a soothing balm to her worries; could it be that a priest shared her convictions? Eager to learn more about him, she listened intently.

"Paul would surely love to visit your household if you would graciously host him. He has a keen interest in William Tyndale, who once served your family generations ago I understand. Paul has thoroughly studied Tyndale's work and seeks to uncover all he can about him," Father Roger said, pausing to meet Mary's eyes, as if reading her thoughts before continuing, confident and trusting.

"In truth, we have much to be grateful for, as Tyndale's translation work enables us to partake in God's Word in English. Yet, I must entreat you to keep my sentiments on this matter to yourself," he had added with a playful wink, delighting her with his candidness.

"Indeed, I happen to know a little of him myself; my great-grandparents were taught by him! You and Paul will be most welcome at our table," she had responded, feeling a renewed sense of hope.

"Well, I look forward to that," Father Rogers had smiled. "I pray you forgive me; it may be a few weeks before I can join you, for I have much upon my shoulders. However, Paul is not so burdened as I and will be keen to make your acquaintance."

"Pray, let us know when it is convenient, and we shall accommodate you," she had assured him.
Back in the present, Mary stood outside the room, acutely

aware of the grim reality Ruth was enduring within. John remained focused on practical matters, seemingly oblivious to the pitiful cries echoing from the chamber.

"I propose we take Glen into our household on a more permanent footing, alongside Irene," he said thoughtfully. "It would keep her safe from any further hostility, and in turn help restore the strength of our household. We could make the small dairy-house cottage free for their use."

Mr. Cropper, still red-faced from his recent grim duty, looked up with renewed interest as John spoke, clearly heartened by the prospect of such a practical and kindly solution.

"How is Ruth?" Mary asked softly.

"I would give her a moment, Mistress," Mr. Cropper replied. "She endured her punishment with commendable fortitude." A sickening churn gripped Mary's stomach, and her motherly instinct to comfort Ruth surged within her.

Sensing her turmoil, John raised a hand. "Mary, we must not make it too easy for her. She has wronged this family, and an example must be set," he said seriously.

Mary hesitated, then replied, "Yes, as you wish, my husband."

William Stephens and Owen Jones were busy packing their belongings in the dim light of their inn chamber, preparing to depart at first light. A fortnight had passed since their arrival with Prince Maurice. Though they had been graciously received into the King's court at Whitehall, William soon found himself adrift amid its splendour.

Despite the easy friendship he had forged with the Prince during their campaigns—and the brief weeks spent in his company at The Hague and upon their return journey to England—the rigid ceremony of court life had now placed a gulf between them. Maurice, once so familiar, was surrounded by lords and flatterers, bound by rank and etiquette, and William found himself a stranger amid the glittering pageantry he could neither share in nor wholly comprehend.

With his funds now depleted, it was time for William to return home. Owen, however, was particularly eager to reunite with his family in Little Sodbury.

"We are all set for tomorrow, Will," Owen remarked, shaking out a tunic and tossing it into his satchel. The formalities of Master and Servant had long since dissolved; their bond had been forged in the fires of nearly two years of gruelling campaigning with various armies, marked by both triumph and peril, and considerable hardship. The experiences they had shared had fostered a brotherhood that transcended the boundaries of rank.

William leaned back against the Inn's crude bed, the rough fabric over a straw mattress felt like a luxury, a stark reminder of some of their trials. "Aye, I suppose it is time," he replied, his voice tinged with a mix of relief and melancholy. Returning home promised familiar comforts, yet the thought of leaving behind the camaraderie of the campaign felt bittersweet, he had found something he was good at;

despite not relishing war he enjoyed leading men, Strangely, he did feel at home there.

"I can't wait to return to the fields and the sounds of home," Owen said, his eagerness shining through. "Nothing quite compares to a clear sky over Little Sodbury sat at the old Roman fort looking up at the night sky."

William couldn't help but smile in response. "I miss the family—and all the servants," he added with a hint of nostalgia.

"Even Mr. Cropper?" Owen teased, a cheeky glint in his eye.

"Yes, even that old fish!" William laughed, the sound echoing warmly in the small room.

As they continued their packing, William's expression shifted to one of practicality. "We must swing by the smithy to pick up my armour; he opens at seven so if we rise when the church bells ring for Prime at six that will give us plenty of time to get there for when he opens. I hope having my back and breastplate blued will help protect it from rust when it hangs at home in its retirement."

"And it will match that fine Flemish Zischagge helmet the Prince gifted you," Owen quipped, giving William a playful nudge. "Shame you cannot afford to have it gilt to match as well. It certainly makes you stand out on the battlefield!"

William drew the helmet from his bag, turning it over in his hands and admiring its fine craftsmanship. It was, without doubt, a worthy piece—but a poor consolation for two years of hardship. All he had to show for his efforts were a handful of scars, an empty purse, and, most bitterly of all, the loss of his beloved horse, Bruce.

Bruce had been a gift from his father on his twentieth birthday—a spirited youngster he'd backed to the saddle himself. In many ways, they had trained each other. The memory brought a wistful smile, followed swiftly by a pang of grief. The sorry nag he'd acquired for the journey home was no comparison.

The war had taken much, and the lingering shortage of quality horses across the continent was only one of its many cruel legacies.

He regretted not securing an audience with Prince Maurice to bid him farewell, but he had left a letter with a royal servant, conveying his departure and warm respects, along with his Little Sodbury address, should the Prince wish to contact him but he suspected he wouldn't remain in England for long.

As the two men finished packing, the room filled with echoes of shared laughter and stories of the unwavering camaraderie that had sustained them through the darkest of times. They spoke of close calls on the battlefield, nights spent huddled around meagre fires, sharing what little food they had and the unwavering support they had offered each other through personal losses.

Tomorrow would mark the beginning of a new chapter, one that would lead them back to their roots—a comforting thought as they prepared to leave behind the trappings of court life. William decided he wouldn't mind a bit of quiet, albeit often boring, country life; it might suit him for a while. He looked forward to some peace and quiet to reflect on what he wanted to do with his life. Perhaps it was time to settle down, maybe even find a wife and start a family, as was expected of most gentlemen of his age and standing.

Chapter 22
The Irish

Both men trudged through the bustling thoroughfares of London—England's vast and restless capital, teeming with near four hundred thousand souls. The streets were already thronged: apprentices sweeping doorways, merchants laying out their wares, and hawkers crying their goods beneath breath that misted in the cold air. The noise rolled and echoed through the narrow lanes, a constant hum of wheels, hooves, and human voices.

The air was thick with odours—smoke, dung, fish, and the sour reek of refuse—a sharp contrast to the clean winds of the countryside. After weeks in the city, William wondered if he had grown half insensible to the stench, or merely resigned to it.

Their weary horses plodded behind a modest pack mule they had lately purchased—an unfortunate necessity that now pricked William's pride. He still owed Owen money for the creature, a humbling thought, and what little remained of his purse would soon be swallowed by the blacksmith's bill.
He was astonished at how quickly the journey home, coupled with the indulgences of court life, had drained his funds. True though, he had acquired some fine clothes during his stay, garments fit for the elite, yet likely to see little use back in Little Sodbury. He pushed the thought aside; his father would sort him out upon his return, and he would receive his allowance once more. All would be well, he assured himself. Yet a wave of guilt washed over him as the memories of the debts he had burdened his father with came flooding back – debts accrued from his excesses and the considerable expense of kitting him out for service.

Despite countless opportunities to indulge alongside the

officers of his regiment, William had abstained from both excessive drinking and games of chance during his time away. Taverns were frequented, dice rattled on oak tables, and wine flowed freely among his comrades, yet he held fast to his restraint. His promotion to lieutenant, and with it the honour of being selected to serve in Prince Maurice's lifeguard, was a distinction he bore with quiet pride. He would not risk tarnishing such a privilege through recklessness or vice. Every decision he made was weighed with the gravity of duty and the promise he made to his father.

However, since arriving in London, the pressure to drink among the noble elite at court had become relentless—an unspoken expectation woven into every gathering, toast, and whispered aside. It was a culture alien to him, and the disquiet he often felt in their polished company only deepened his temptation. In time, he succumbed. One night of drinking became several, and with them came the inevitable card games—high-stakes affairs played with casual arrogance by men who could afford to lose fortunes. William could not. Yet the hard-earned wages he had amassed over two years of disciplined service as a mercenary ebbed away, lost to the turn of a card and the clink of coin upon velvet.

The financial loss stung, but the deeper wound was far more grievous: the quiet oath he had once sworn to his father—a solemn vow of temperance and self-mastery— lay in ruins. In the aftermath, shame settled over him like a shroud. He saw with painful clarity that half-measures would never suffice. Henceforth, he must abstain entirely from drink in any company where cards or dice were present, for the moment his judgement slipped, he ceased to be the man he strove to become. Instead, he became a shadow of himself—drawn helplessly toward the thrill of risk, the sharp jolt of chance. It was never about the winnings. It was the rush he craved, the reckless surge of adrenaline, the only time he ever truly felt alive—and it was leading him to ruin.

As they arrived at the blacksmith's workshop, both men dismounted and tied their horses outside. The blacksmith, a man nearly as robust as Owen, greeted William with a hearty clap on the back. "Master William! Good to see you! I have your armour, breastplate, and rein hand gauntlet ready. They turned out well! I hope you will speak well of my work to your friends at court; not many around here know the craft as well as I do."

William examined the pieces with a discerning eye, noting the fine work he done of blueing the armour that made them appear as good as new. He traced a small ding on the breastplate where a musket ball had grazed him, he told that to be left, a reminder of a harrowing day. "A close call that," he remarked aloud as his finger traced the indentation on his breastplate, shaking off the memory of the event.

Suddenly, a great cry erupted from the street. A throng of people pressed forward, waving pamphlets and shouting, "The Irish! The Irish in full revolt! Slaughter in Ireland!" The words sent a chill down William's spine.

"What in the world is happening?" Owen exclaimed, seizing a young urchin who was waving a leaflet in the air. "Let's have one of those, boy!" He tossed a coin at the lad and snatched a pamphlet from his hand. "Master William, what does it say, if you wouldn't mind?"

William took the leaflet, knowing that Owen's reading skills were quite basic. He scanned the contents, his heart sinking as he read aloud, "It's happened as they have feared: in Dublin and Ulster, there has been mass killing of Protestants."

Owen's eyes went wide with shock. He knew this news would incite further turmoil back home, especially with his stepmother being Irish. "I hope Mistress Mary has converted her faith at least," he murmured, a sense of helplessness settling over him. He had been fighting against Catholic influence but held no strong convictions himself; he simply tolerated, and even liked, his stepmother, who brought his father much joy.

An angry mob had quickly gathered outside, led by a man clad in austere black, his short-cropped hair marking him unmistakably as a Puritan. Clerks and apprentices trailed behind him, brandishing pamphlets and waving them with righteous fury. The air crackled with tension, voices rising in a discordant chorus of outrage.

William instinctively collected his armour from the blacksmith's bench. "I think—"

"I know," Owen interrupted, as if finishing the thought they shared. He cast a wary glance at the swelling crowd. "If this unrest carries on, we may find ourselves swept up in something far beyond a longing for hearth and home. And I've no wish to be sent to Ireland—I hear it rains more than here," he added with a dry smile.

"They call it a soldier's graveyard," William said grimly. "It's time we left."

With a resolute nod, paying the blacksmith with what little coin he had left, stepped away from the forge. The clamour of the mob rang through the streets like a war drum.

He and Owen mounted their weary horses, the familiar weight of their gear settling heavily, matched only by the weight of the news they had just received.

As they rode away, William cast a final glance over his

shoulder at the crowd. The Londoners faces twisted with a dangerous mix of rage and fear, their anger rising like smoke before a fire. He had seen unrest before—seen what it could become. He had no wish to be caught in the first sparks of another conflict.

"Let us make haste for Little Sodbury," he said, spurring his horse into a steady trot.

Benjamin approached the appointed meeting place dressed in his finest. He wore his red doublet and best shirt, trimmed with bone lace at the collar and sleeves, with matching baggy breeches. His high riding boots, though dulled by frost, still caught the light with the sheen of careful polishing. Upon his head sat his broad-brimmed hat, newly adorned with a white feather.

The outfit had been purchased for him by his father at no small expense—garments reserved for those occasions when he presented the stallions to their wealthiest clients. Together with the show tack and finely trimmed red saddle cloth, it lent both horse and rider a certain pageantry that never failed to impress. Benjamin smiled faintly to himself. Dressed thus, he felt almost the equal of those gentlemen in this moment. His hand brushed the plain sword at his side—another of his father's insistences, given the troubling rise in horse thefts across the county. He thought it lent the perfect finish to his appearance.

He guided Ralph, who had been groomed to a standard far beyond the usual field-ready preparations, the horse's iron-shod hooves striking a steady rhythm against the frost-hardened earth. Each step gave a muted crunch, while plumes of mist billowed from Ralph's nostrils like great white blooms, curling into the crisp morning air before vanishing in the pale light of dawn.

As they crested the rise atop one of the ancient Roman fort's mounds, they paused to survey the view. A broad, open field stretched before them, bordered by ragged hedgerows, while the unnatural ring of earthworks—softened by centuries—stood as a silent monument to the passage of time. Beyond, in the pale winter light, the faint silhouette of the manor's old family chapel nestled among the tree line. Wisps of wood smoke curled from the manor's many chimneys in the distance, half-obscured by the bare branches of a small woodland and the sloping hillside upon which the house stood. The trees—primarily oak and beech, their limbs stark against the sky—formed a skeletal fringe around the manor rear, as if nature itself kept watch in quiet vigilance.

Ahead, Benjamin caught sight of Tim and Ruth stood in the middle of the field, arms folded tightly across their chests in a vain effort to hold off the cold. Their breath hung in the air in short, silvery clouds, rising like smoke into the stillness of the morning. Jane Stephens rode her pony, Minnie, her laughter ringing out like a merry tune carrying on the breeze. "Oh, what a delightful surprise to find you here!" she exclaimed, cheeks flushed with exhilaration as Benjamin approached. "Would you care to join us? I'm exercising Minnie—he's wonderfully fresh and sprightly this morning!"

With Minnie's injured leg long healed and strengthened under Benjamin's careful guidance, Jane added with a gleam in her eye, "I believe we should race!"

Tim and Ruth exchanged knowing glances. Though the prospect of joining in the merriment clearly tempted them, a sense of duty tugged them back to propriety. "Your mother would not approve of such folly," Tim said, attempting to uphold the decorum expected of them, though a faint smile betrayed his own amusement.

Yet, before Benjamin could voice a response, Jane was off, her little grey pony darting forward with remarkable speed. "Mind the ground—it's a bit hard for racing!" Benjamin called after her, a little too late. He spurred Ralph into a canter, eagerly following Jane who took a path that would lead them both behind the peculiar crenulated rings of the fort remains.

As soon as they were out of sight of the hapless servants, Jane reined in and dismounted with practised ease and Benjamin, catching up, did likewise. They embraced passionately, sharing a long, intense kiss that made the world around them fade to nothing, leaving only the soft whispers of the wind and the gentle rustling of frozen leaves.

"We have received word from Will," Jane said breathlessly, her voice tinged with concern. "He has returned to the country and shall be home any day now."

"Well, that is splendid news! You have missed your brother dearly, as has your family," Benjamin responded, a hint of confusion clouding his features.

"Yes, but this also means you may not come to exercise Samson any more," Jane lamented, her brow furrowing. "My excuses to see you shall be limited, my love."

Benjamin's heart sank at the realisation—she was right. It had been challenging to steal moments for themselves as it was. Their friendship with Tim felt strained, and he sensed that Tim was becoming aware of the affection blossoming between him and Jane. Meanwhile, he knew Tim's own feelings for Ruth, though genuine, remained unreciprocated and Tim was becoming less compliant when asking for favours and moments alone.

They kissed once more, the flutter of butterflies igniting in Benjamin's stomach at each meeting of their lips. Jane giggled, her laughter like a gentle chime. "I think I hear them approaching; you must show me those tricks you keep promising!"

With a flourish, Benjamin made a mock bow. "Your wish is my command!" he declared — a convenient excuse for why they were both dismounted, though in truth he wished only to impress Jane. It was enough to make him set aside his usual caution, despite the ground being less than ideal for such a display.

He took his place beside Ralph, the horse standing proud and alert. With a soft word and the lightest touch upon the rein, Benjamin drew the animal's attention. His voice fell to a gentler tone, part command, part fondness. "Do not shame me now, my boy."

At the faintest movement of his wrist, Ralph responded. The horse gathered his strength beneath him, drawing his hindquarters under, his forehand lifting. Then, with a poised spring, he raised his forelegs from the ground—not wildly, but in perfect balance, his knees bent and neatly tucked. For a heartbeat he seemed suspended, a living statue of strength and grace, before settling softly back upon all fours.

It was no reckless show, but the mark of true schooling—discipline and elegance in harmony.

"This is the best one—the capriole!" Benjamin announced, a spark of pride in his voice.

At his signal, Ralph gathered himself once more, drawing his hind legs well beneath him, every muscle coiled like tempered steel. Then, with a sudden bound, he sprang into the air and, at the height of the leap, struck out powerfully with his hind legs—precise, measured, and true—before landing lightly again upon all fours.

The movement was brief, yet full of controlled strength: a leap of defiance and splendour, born of trust between man and horse.

Tim and Ruth, who had just arrived, gasped aloud at the sight.

"That was simply marvellous!" Jane exclaimed, her face alight with wonder. "Perhaps I can persuade *Poppa* to let you teach Minnie those splendid tricks!" She laughed, eyes bright with excitement at the thought.

Benjamin grinned, his chest swelling with pride at Jane's admiration. Beneath the light grey winter clouds and the watchful gaze of the ancient fort, the burdens of the world seemed to slip away, leaving only the joy of youth and the endless possibilities that that offered.

Meanwhile, Ruth watched from a short distance, her gaze wistful, the affection she held for Benjamin Akins unmistakable in the softness of her expression. Tim, noticing the look and frowning slightly, spoke with quiet tact.

"It is time we returned," he called out to Mistress Jane. "Your mother will begin to worry. Come along, Ruth— we've much to attend to back at the manor."

"Goodbye, Benjamin," Ruth said, her voice gentle as she offered a shy smile. But as her eyes lingered on the playful warmth exchanged between Benjamin and Jane, a stir of jealousy crept into her features. She turned away, her smile fading, and joined Tim as they began the walk back toward the manor.

After a moment, she leaned closer. "Did you see what I saw, Tim?" she whispered, a coy note in her voice.

"I think it's best we keep such observations to ourselves," he replied cautiously, "for our sake—as well as Benjamin's and Mistress Jane's."

Still, as they walked, Tim cast a glance back at Benjamin. There was a look in his eyes—a quiet envy. Benjamin seemed to lead a charmed existence, his easy manner with both horses and young ladies a sharp contrast to Tim's own daily struggles.

At Ruth's side, resentment simmered just beneath the surface. Her feelings toward Mistress Jane were shifting, sharpened by the growing awareness of the unspoken affections beginning to blossom between her and the man Ruth had long admired in silence.

"I shall help you onto your pony now," Benjamin said, his broad smile directed solely at Jane.

She giggled—a light, melodic sound that danced on the crisp morning air. "Honestly, when those two are together, they do seem rather useless," she said with a playful nod toward Tim and Ruth as they made their way back toward the manor. Her eyes sparkled with amusement.

With an easy grace, Benjamin offered his hand to help her mount her Side Saddle. Each time she was near, he felt it —that sudden spark, a current of energy that hummed just beneath the surface. Something unspoken, but unmistakably real.

Once they were out of earshot, Benjamin leaned in slightly, his voice lowered and sincere. "When can we meet again?"

"Shall we not convene at the stables tomorrow? It is your day to tend to Samson, and I shall be there around noon to groom Minnie," she replied, with a wink, brightness in her eyes.

"Until then, my love," he whispered, taking her hand and planting a quick kiss upon it—a tender farewell that made her blush deepen.

As she rode away, Benjamin watched her retreating figure and felt an overwhelming sense of longing and anticipation. His heart ached for more moments like this, where the world outside faded away, and it was simply the two of them under the vast sky.

Turning away from the path Jane had taken, Benjamin cast a glance toward Tim and Ruth, now some distance ahead, making their way back toward the manor. An uneasy sense of finality hung in the air—an unspoken awareness that something between them all had shifted. It unsettled him, though he couldn't yet name the change, only feel its weight pressing at the edges of his thoughts. As he returned home the uneasy feeling began to dissipate, transversing the frost-kissed countryside, the serene beauty enveloped Benjamin in unexpected calm. The gentle wind whispering through the grass created a soothing melody, a silent promise that time would reveal the path ahead.

Arriving back at Fairfield Farm, Benjamin was filled with resolve. His connection with Jane flourished but teetered on a knifes edge, exhilarating yet fraught with uncertainty, as they both knew the truth could not remain hidden forever. Thoughts of proposing swirled within him, despite knowing the uproar it would cause both families.

Mistress Mary regarded him favourably, yet financial and social disparities loomed large. John Stephens aimed to bolster his family's standing through Jane's marriage. Recalling her mention of several suitors' weeks ago, a wave of jealousy surged in him, though she'd since avoided the topic, valuing their shared moments.

After walking Ralph back to the stable, brushing him down with meticulous care, and offering him a juicy carrot, Benjamin laid his cheek against the horse's velvety muzzle and whispered warmly, "I love you, boy. You did me proud, as always." Ralph snorted softly, nuzzling his head into Benjamin's chest, a silent acknowledgment of their deep and unwavering bond. The scent of hay, sweat, and horseflesh hung in the air, a comforting aroma that spoke of shared labour and mutual connection and trust. As the sun dipped below the horizon, the temperature dropping with its departure, Benjamin stood silhouetted against the vibrant sky. He watched as the shadows lengthened, stretching across the fields like grasping fingers, and resolved to navigate the emotional and societal maze before him with courage and conviction.

Paul Akins sat at the sturdy table that served both for the family's mealtime and the administration of their modest affairs. His brow furrowed in concentration as he perused a ledger filled with numbers and notes, the soft clinking of pots and pans resonating from the kitchen where Sarah was busy preparing the evening meal. The warm aroma of stew wafted in the air, mingling with the earthy scent of the farm.

Just then, the door creaked open, and Benjamin entered, hanging his hat on the hook by the door. He stretched his back with a satisfying crack, shaking off the chill of the late Autumn afternoon.

"While your father is away at Ashton Court attending to matters of business, he has asked me to keep a vigilant eye on the farm," Paul announced, glancing up from his work. "Moreover, I am tasked with making heads or tails of his accounts and ensuring he remains current with his debts. I may need your assistance in sorting through it all."

Benjamin nodded, his expression shifting from weariness to curiosity. "I noticed a receipt for the sale of Samson; however, the accounts still show time booked for exercising him. According to the agreement, that was to conclude in October. Yet you still seem to be working him three times a week. Why are we not billing the Stephens' for this?" Paul questioned, incredulity lacing his tone.

"Ah, I recall my father mentioning that such arrangements were to remain until young William returned, but that was meant to be in October. Perhaps he has been waylaid on his journeys," Benjamin replied, a note of concern threading through his voice.

"Then we should consider billing them for your labour, shouldn't we? Heaven forbids but what if William never returns?" Paul pressed, a frown deepening on his forehead.

"My father would call them gentlemen's agreements, Uncle," Benjamin replied, a mischievous glint in his eyes. "His records are certainly full of such arrangements."

"Indeed, and he moans he doesn't make any decent money; anyway, how have you been, Benjamin? It's been a while since we've had the pleasure of your company," Paul asked, attempting to lighten the mood.

"All is well, Uncle. Just the regular routine. Castello is progressing wonderfully; he's an extraordinary horse. I believe he's starting to trust me, which is a real achievement!" Benjamin exclaimed, his spirits clearly lifting. "Although, he did throw young Thomas Ward off the other day during his first attempt to ride him—poor lad ended up face-first in the muck! You should have seen it!" He chuckled, the thought bringing a light-hearted tone to the conversation.

"Oh dear, that indeed sounds unfortunate," Paul responded, a small smile breaking through his otherwise serious demeanour.

"I thought our boys were swift on the riding aids and well-schooled, but this horse is like comparing a rapier to a cook's meat cleaver! I often wondered why I struggled with him at first. It seems we were both speaking different languages, yet slowly we are learning to understand one another." Benjamin's tone turned more reflective as he continued, "He is remarkable to ride—so flexible, powerful, and compact. He can canter and weave around that line of beer barrels that Thomas and I set up. We keep pushing them closer together. His agility is truly astonishing; no wonder they are sought after as fine war horses."

"But how does he perform in his main duties?" Paul inquired, a hint of awkwardness in his tone.

"Again, we believe all three mares may be in foal; he is indeed a worthy stud," Benjamin replied. "I hope he proves worth the sacrifice it took to acquire him and those mares. I think word is starting to spread about them. It might be worth riding him out at some point to visit some of the estates nearby."

"That's a great idea—and good news about the mares being in foal," Paul said, relief flickering in his eyes. "We could certainly use a cash injection. Without your father's wages from Thomas Smyth, we'd struggle to cover the costs of hay and bedding this winter. We need to secure some stud fees or bookings for next season, but opportunities seem scarce." He sighed; concern etched on his face as he studied the books.

As they pondered the future of Fairfield Farm, Benjamin asked, "Does Father Rogers not need your help, Uncle?"

"Do you want me gone already, young Ben?" Paul teased, amusement sparkling in his eyes.

"No, it's been splendid having you around," Benjamin replied earnestly, grateful for his uncle's company.

"I'm only jesting, lad. Father Rogers prefers to handle things himself and isn't much for delegating—he likes his own company most of the time. I don't think he'd volunteer to take on a deacon to teach, if I'm honest. But when he gets going on scripture, he truly becomes alight with the Spirit you then struggle to get away from him, but he does have a way of opening up the Bible," Paul said with a chuckle.

"Well, that means less work for you then! I wish my father delegated half as well," Benjamin grinned, drawing a hearty laugh from Paul.

"Oh, he's always been good at that—but the paperwork..." Paul sighed, waving a hand in frustration. "I've got a long night ahead sorting it all out."

"I'm off to bed—I'm exhausted!" Benjamin declared. "Sarah, is dinner ready? I'll eat quickly and then retire."

Sarah appeared with a steaming bowl of stew and fresh bread. "Thanks, sister!" Benjamin said, settling at the table cluttered with papers.

"Remember to pray before you eat," Paul reminded mock-seriously.

Silence fell as Benjamin enjoyed his meal, warmed against the evening chill.

Breaking the silence, Paul said, "We're invited to dine with the Stephens tomorrow. Can you come?"

Benjamin, almost spitting out his food in excitement, nodded. "I'd love to!" he replied

"Brush up on your table manners then," Paul joked with a grin.

"Can I come?" Sarah asked eagerly.

"Yes, we're all invited, and your father should be home to join us," Paul assured her with a nod.
They continued discussing tomorrow's plans. The warmth of the hearth along with hearty laughter and shared family stories wrapped around them like a warm blanket, creating a blissful atmosphere as the burdens of the day began to lift. The evening wore on, and soon Benjamin excused himself, bidding his uncle and sister goodnight as he made way to his chamber.

As he settled into bed, staring at the ceiling with his arms behind his head, thoughts of Jane flooded his mind. Spikes of anticipation filled him as he imagined the two opportunities he might have to see her the following day. Excitement bubbled within him, tempered by a tinge of anxiety about the possibility of being discovered.

He sighed deeply, wishing that their affection need not be shrouded in secrecy. Deceit was not in his nature, and the very thought of having to lie made his stomach churn. He feared that if ever questioned directly about his feelings or intentions, he would surely buckle under the pressure; his ability to spin a tale was woefully inadequate.

Yet, as the moonlight filtered softly through the window, casting a silvery glow across the room, Benjamin felt a glint of hope. Perhaps, in time, this secret could be embraced rather than hidden. He longed for the day when he could openly express his affection for Jane without fear of repercussions.

As sleep began to wash over him, he resolved to cherish what moments he could steal with her, to enjoy the thrill of their secret rendezvous while remaining mindful of the delicate balance they were navigating. Even amid the uncertainty, the thought of Jane brought warmth to his heart, offering solace against the chill of the night.

With one last fleeting image of her bright smile, Benjamin succumbed to slumber, his dreams filled with visions of promise of tomorrow.

Chapter 25
The Weight of a Woman's Decisions

Mistress Mary Stephens sat by the window of her bed-chamber, her gaze fixed on the gardens and the private path leading to the manor—a silent, unwavering plea that her son might soon ride through the gates and return home. The afternoon sunlight streamed through the tall panes on an unseasonably warm autumn day, the frost of recent weeks retreating beneath the gentle warmth that now illuminated her refined features, still untouched by the full ravages of age or grief. Yet the weight of her thoughts etched a subtle shadow across her expression.

With a sigh, she lifted a quill and began absently tracing the edge of the parchment before her. The list of potential suitors for her daughter, Jane, lay open—each name a delicate negotiation between status and sentiment, hope and apprehension, as she weighed the future with a mother's quiet determination.

"Mary," her Husbands's voice broke through her reverie as he entered the room, his expression grave. "Have you given further thought to Jane's prospects? We must begin getting arrangements underway, exercising prudence, especially with the Fosters lurking nearby. We want of connections and the protection those afford."

Setting down the quill, Mistress Mary's brow furrowed with quiet resolve. "I have considered it carefully, John. Each candidate on this list holds some promise, but we must weigh their alliances as closely as their virtues. I will not sacrifice Jane on the altar of mere familial ambition."

John nodded, his tone measured yet firm he replied. "I agree. We must find a match that not only brings influence and protection but one that pleases Jane —both vital to our security and her future, especially now."

A heavy sigh slipped from Mary's lips. She understood his meaning clearly—their decision to refuse the sale of Little Sodbury Manor had only served to deepen Richard Foster's resentment.

"Declining their offer has done little but stoke their anger. But I will not entertain the slightest notion of yielding to their schemes. We must remain steadfast in defending our legacy—and in securing the future of our children."

As John moved to sit across from her, a shadow passed over his face. "And yet, my dear, I worry for William when he returns and discovers all they have been doing; he will likely take a direct, perhaps rash, course of action, as he always does." John breathed out heavily, anticipating conflict.

"I am more concerned as to why he has yet to return home; are you not?" Mary replied, her heart twisting at the thought of her son's prolonged absence.

"Yes, his safety weighs heavily on my mind as well. In his last letter, he stated he was in the company of Prince Maurice, I am keen for him to return home, even if he is making fine connections." John, stung by Mary's implication, replied with a hint of annoyance.

They fell silent, the room thick with unsaid worries. The sunlight shifted through the window, casting moving patterns upon the floor, but Mary's thoughts remained anchored firmly on Jane's future. "Perhaps we should wait until William returns. He may have elevated prospects to consider for Jane."

"You mean my consideration," John interjected, his tone taking on an unfamiliar note of authority.

"While we must prioritise our family's position, I would not have our daughter robbed of a say in her own future," Mary replied, her voice steady, striving for an assertiveness that masked her inner anxiety.

"In this matter, I must insist," John said, leaning forward, his tone measured but edged with strain. "Jane is indeed a beauty, and I would see her well and happily married. Yet we must accept that our choices are no longer what they were. Those most fitting to our needs may not, perhaps, prove pleasing to her. Were we not entangled in this wretched business, we might afford her more freedom in the matter—but necessity, alas, must now prevail." His voice carried the weary weight of frustration.

Mary heard the undertone—the lingering resentment that still smouldered over her refusal to entertain the Fosters' offer for the manor. She drew a slow breath, choosing her ground with care. Though every instinct urged her to answer him, she forced herself to yield for the moment, hoping to forestall another quarrel that would only deepen the rift between them.

"Very well, husband, but consider this: William's return may open doors that are currently shut to us. Saving a Prince—even a foreign one—must surely grant us some favour with King Charles this Princes uncle."

John paused, contemplating her words. The air lightened with uplifting possibilities. "You make a compelling point," he conceded, a hint of admiration dancing across his expression.

Mary's heart swelled with gratitude for this momentary alignment in their viewpoints. "Let us pray he returns soon with both good news and prospects for our dear Jane and then onto a match for William".

Just then, a knock at the door interrupted their musings. "Come in," John commanded.

Mr. Cropper entered, bowing his head in respect. "How goes the preparation for this evening's meal, Mr Cropper?" Mary asked.

"Very well, Mistress. Cook has everything in hand, and the great hall is laid for our evening guests," he reported efficiently.

"Excellent, Mr. Cropper," Mary replied warmly, her gratitude evident in her tone. "Is there anything further you require?"

"I have managed to locate the manuscripts and letters you requested from the library, Mistress," Mr. Cropper responded, a hint of pride shining through his formal demeanour.

"Oh yes! I knew they must be in there!" Mary glided across the room to take the manuscripts from him, her fingers brushing against the aged parchment. She thanked him sincerely and waved him away.

Mr. Cropper, once again bowing his head, exited the chamber.

"What are those, my dear?" John inquired, his curiosity piqued.

"They are the early works of Bible translation and sermons from William Tyndale, taken from my great-grandmother's diary. I promised I would find them to show Paul Akins," she replied, her excitement bubbling beneath the surface.

John's brow creased at the thought. Mary had expressed a keen interest in spending time with Paul—an educated, relatively handsome man, well-versed in Scripture among other things. When the pair engaged in conversation, John found himself a mere observer, watching the excitement and joy their debates brought to Mary. It left him feeling slightly envious of their intellectual camaraderie.

"Do you think that is wise?" John asked, concern threading through his voice. "I recall you telling me how William Tyndale was burned for heresy!" He emphasised the poignant word, the gravity of history weighing heavily in the air. "Didn't the Church send people to search and destroy any information that could be found on the man? Such connections are what led to much of your family's decline in influence did it not? Now you plan to reveal to a Deacon of the church what your family has long concealed?"

John shook his head in bewilderment.

"My dear John, so much has changed since those dark days. For one, the Church is no longer Catholic, and translations of the Holy Scriptures are no longer persecuted in the same way," Mary countered, her conviction clear.

"Still, not everything has changed," John persisted, "The political and religious divisions plaguing this country are more dangerous than ever. What if this information draws unwanted scrutiny upon our family? Besides, the Tyndale translation is still banned, is it not, despite it being used to create the King James translation?"

"That is true. However, I have not seen it actively enforced, and despite the churches' efforts, many copies still abound," Mary replied calmly.

"Mary, we must be cautious. The Fosters will seize any opportunity to undermine us, twisting our words to their advantage. Such matters could lure them out of the shadows once again when they make their next move." John said forcibly, his voice rising slightly with growing concern.

Mary met his gaze with unwavering determination. "I truly believe we can trust Paul and Father Rogers. They share a more enlightened understanding of God's word, much like what I have gleaned from the teachings of William Tyndale. I cannot express how blessed I feel to converse openly with them about my thoughts on our faith. Each time we explore the Scriptures together, we enrich one another's understanding and unravel the depths of meaning hidden within," she explained, her passion evident in her tone.

"While I will admit that Sunday church has become far more engaging under Father Rogers, and the notion of unity and holiness has provided comfort amidst the unrest, even amongst our tenants and the village folk, we are still in perilous times," John countered, a note of caution lacing his voice. "The Fosters already have your progressive ideas in their sights; Richard's eldest son is gaining influence as a priest. We cannot forget this, Mary. Please, for once, heed my counsel." John said in a more pleading tone.

Once more, Mary struggled to maintain her composure in the face of her husband's concerns. She understood the merit in his words, recalling the Scripture from **Ephesians 5:22: 'Wives, submit yourselves unto your own husbands, as unto the Lord.'** This was a principle she often grappled with. John had granted her considerable freedom, which fostered harmony within their marriage, yet there were moments she needed to be reined in, knowing her forthright manner sometimes caused him embarrassment.

"Husband, I shall keep your concerns in mind this evening, and I will endeavour to focus on more secular topics when we converse if that pleases you," Mary said, offering him a placating smile that disarmed him, transforming his tension into his usual positive demeanour.

"Thank you, my love," John replied, his expression softening. "I simply want to ensure our family's safety as we navigate these trying times, it is out of care I council you." He said softly

With the weight of their responsibilities still hanging in the air, Mary glanced at the manuscripts she had gathered. She understood the delicate balance she must try and maintain and the neglect she sometimes gave her husband. She put the papers down to one side, and walked to her husband, giving him a forceful kiss.

John's face lit up with a huge smile as she pulled away, "What was that for?"

She kissed him again, longer and with a long forgotten passion, then pushed him gently onto their bed.

Chapter 26
Dinner at the Manor

The Akins family—Benjamin, Sarah, Paul, and Stephen—embarked on a short journey to Little Sodbury Manor, while Father Rogers would join them separately. The day began with crisp, refreshing sunlight, but dark, ominous clouds loomed overhead now.

Benjamin felt a mix of excitement and anxiety as he was granted a rare day off from his duties to visit Chipping Sodbury. There, he collected new clothes for the family from the tailor on High Street, commissioned by their father before leaving for his latest assignment for the Smyths. His sister, Sarah, was equally delighted, eagerly anticipating wearing her new dress for the manor dinner—a rare treat.

The siblings carefully navigated the muddy road, avoiding wet patches that could mar their appearance. While Benjamin had visited the manor many times, this was his first time as a dinner guest, a prospect that both thrilled and intimidated him. He also felt a twinge of envy towards Paul, who frequently visited and seemed to be in Mistress Mary's favour.

Sarah, too, had reasons to feel attached to the manor; she had spent time studying with Mary Stephens, enjoying their reading lessons and keeping Jane company.

Benjamin admired the intricately slashed sleeves of his new doublet, which fit him perfectly, unblemished and tailored; he hoped to present a dashing figure before Jane this evening and hoped to impress Mistress Mary and John Stephens in turn.

"You must put those clothes to good use—at church and on special occasions," Stephen reminded them, his voice a blend of firmness and affection. After receiving a small bonus from their patron Thomas Smyth, he felt moved to pass the generosity on. Always careful with money, this rare gift reflected his quiet desire to provide for his children when circumstances allowed.

As they approached the front of the Manor, Benjamin glanced up at the gathering clouds. "We should quicken our pace; those skies look ready to burst, and that would surely spoil any impression we hope to make."

Stepping through the grand front doors of the manor, Benjamin was greeted by the familiar figure of Mr. Cropper, the steward, who offered a formal bow. A wave of apprehension washed over him, making him feel like an intruder in this elegant world he had yet to fully embrace. Just inside the threshold, he spotted Ruth, Irene Jones, and Anna Baker lined up near the hallway that led to the great hall on their left. Ruth's warm smile brought him comfort, easing some of his tension, she respectfully inclined her head to Paul and Stephen and they passed.

As they entered the great hall, Benjamin's gaze was immediately drawn upward to the impressive, exposed timber beams soaring high overhead, a testament to the skilled craftsmanship of a bygone era. The weight of history settled upon him, palpable in the very stones of Little Sodbury Manor. The room was adorned with portraits of the Welch family, their stern, aristocratic faces seeming to follow his every step with silent judgment. Dominating the space was an immaculate, long oak table, its varnished surface reflecting the pulsing candlelight like a still pond. It was lavishly set with fine pewter plates, their surfaces gleaming softly in the dim light, and glistening silverware that hinted at countless formal dinners and hushed conversations. A warm hearth crackled cheerfully, casting an amber glow across the room and softening the otherwise austere atmosphere, contributing to an ambiance that was both inviting and undeniably intimidating.

Father Rogers seated at the right side of the head of the table, a place of honour due to his clergy status, welcomed the Akins family with a nod of acknowledgment. His presence exuded warmth and authority, embodying the spirit of fellowship that would soon envelop the evening.

"Good evening, may God's blessings be upon you all! It is wonderful to see you looking so well," he greeted, his voice smooth and melodic. "I trust your short journey was pleasant, despite the threatening weather?" Father Roger said smoothly. As he said the words the heavy hammering of a rainstorm was unleashed hitting the windows as if in reply.

"Quite so, thank you, Father," Stephen replied with a smile, as he approached the table. The excitement bubbled within Benjamin, even as the watchful eyes of their guests danced around the room.

As the family settled in their seats, Mr. Cropper moved to one of the doorways, ready to announce the evening's hosts. "Ladies and gentlemen, I present Mr. and Mrs. Stephens," he declared as John and Mary walked in, both wearing welcoming smiles for their guests.

"And not forgetting Mistress Jane!" Mr. Cropper added as she entered behind them, a flurry of youthful grace.

The guests rose in unison, displaying their respect, as Mistress Mary took her seat to the left at the head of the table, with John settling at the head.

As Benjamin took his seat, he could not help but admire Jane. Her dark hair fell in soft ringlets, framing the brightness of her face, while the deep red silk of her gown caught the candlelight and set off the grace of her figure. His heart quickened as their eyes met. She managed it with poise, never letting him feel exposed, yet a fleeting, knowing glance passed between them—a moment's understanding hidden amid the company.

As the guests resumed their seats, conversation flowed once more—gentle pleasantries, quiet laughter, and the occasional stolen look across the table. Each glance seemed to weave a thread of pride and fondness about the young Mistress whose heart Benjamin, in silence, so dearly cherished.

Glen Jones and Tim appeared, both father and son wearing aprons over their Sunday best clothes, they brought around large napkins which the guests placed over their left shoulder as was custom. This was quickly followed by bowls of water for all to wash their hands before food could be served.

The evening promised both companionship and an underlying air of unease. With trouble brewing beyond the familiar walls of the manor, the gathering felt like a brief, cherished reprieve. Mr. Cropper, the steward, held out a bottle of wine for John Stephens' approval before expertly uncorking it and offering it to the guests in turn. As the maids brought the first course up from the kitchen – a delectable spread of roast beef accompanied by a rich, spiced sauce, and fine manchet bread – Father Rogers offered a prayer of thanks to God and soon the cheerful sounds of conversation began to fill the great hall, the clinking of silverware harmonising with laughter.

Benjamin's stomach was soon protesting at the richness of the food laid before him. He silently battled with himself, determined not to let the inevitable wind escape—he could not imagine the embarrassment of such a faux pass in front of their esteemed hosts.
As conversation flowed around the table like the wine in their cups, Benjamin found himself struggling to keep pace with the many overlapping discussions. His thoughts, dulled by the strong, expensive wine he had sipped too eagerly in hopes of calming his nerves, drifted from one voice to the next. Jane spoke animatedly with Sarah, their

laughter rising like melodic chimes above the din, but he caught only fragments of their words. Shaking off the haze, he turned his attention toward John, who had just begun addressing his father.

"So, I understand you have just returned from Bristol, Stephen. What is the latest news? It can sometimes take a while to make out to these parts".

"Well, word is the Irish Catholics have carried out great slaughter among the protestants. Some stories are too grim to grace this fine table." Stephen replied respectfully.

Benjamin caught a glimpse of Irene Jones in the corner of his eye, taking sudden interest in what was being discussed, standing at the edge of the hall awaiting her next instructions from Mr. Cropper.

"Such a great shame, the things man does in the name of our Father Jehovah. We are all his children, misguided sheep without a Shepard," Father Rogers replied with genuine feeling.

Mary, eager to keep the conversation from straying too far into theology, yet feeling the silence too constrained for comfort, drew breath to speak.

But John forestalled her. "Tell me, Father," he said, leaning forward, "what is your view in all this? Do you hold that retaliation is unjust?"

Father Rogers paused a moment before replying, a faint smile touching his lips. "As I am oft heard to say—and it has grown something of a jest among my congregation, I fear—"

"What does the Bible say?" Paul interjected lightheartedly, echoing the reply he knew his mentor often used when speaking on any weighty matter.

"Yes, you got it. You are listening to some of what I say after all," Father Rogers jested, smiling at his understudy.

"My mind goes straight to **Matthew 5:44: "But I say unto you, love your enemies. Bless them that curse you. Do good to them that hate you. Pray for them which do you wrong and persecute you."**

"It goes on, of course—but I didn't come to dine with you just to deliver sermons," the old priest added with a grin.

"Interesting viewpoint—it differs somewhat from your colleagues in Bristol," Stephen added. "The clergy there are in uproar, stirring the mob and speaking of righteous vengeance. From what I'm hearing, the reported atrocities sound like unthinkable conduct for any civilised person— let alone those who claim to follow Christ."

"I can believe that. Truly, I say to you—what a world it would be if we actually followed the guidance God has given us in His Word the Bible," Father Rogers said, frowning. "But unless we meditate on scripture and apply it in our lives, how can we call ourselves followers of Christ? We can't be hearers only—we must live by it. After all, the prime marker of one true faith can be found in **John 13:35 "By this shall all men know that ye are my disciples, if ye have love one to another."**

"Let us toast to that fine sentiment," Paul Akins said, raising his glass. The others in the room followed suit.

Benjamin marvelled at the priest's effortless recall of scripture; however, his attention soon drifted from the conversation as he noticed Tim, the young stable hand, looking decidedly out of place and unusually nervous while serving wine and attending to the guests at the head of the table.

When John Stephens drained his glass in a series of generous gulps—his expression betraying a hint of disinterest in the direction of the conversation—Tim hurried over to refill the silver goblet. In his haste, he caught his foot on the edge of his apron and sloshed wine onto the floor.

"By Jove!" Tim exclaimed, wide-eyed with a mix of surprise and horror as the room fell momentarily silent. All eyes turned to him, his cheeks flushing the same shade as the spilled wine.

In a bold attempt to recover, he raised the wine jug in a mock toast, still smiling despite his embarrassment. "A toast—to the floor, for always being there to catch me when I trip!"

For a heartbeat, silence held—but then laughter broke out around the table. Even Benjamin chuckled as Tim, grinning, leaned into his own misstep with charm.

"Tim, I believe that serves as a reminder to us all," Benjamin chimed in, seizing the opportunity to lighten the mood. "Much like our horses, one must always watch one's footing to avoid a slippery situation!"

"Or a slippery floor!" Tim added, laughing along as he started to clean up the spill.

John smirked, shaking his head wryly as he replied, "Well, at least the floor will be well-marinated for the stew!"
With the tension dissolved, Tim resumed his duties with renewed enthusiasm. "Don't worry, Master Stephens, I'll be sure to check my footing next time—wouldn't want to send the entire meal flying, would we?"

The atmosphere lightened further, filled with laughter and friendly banter. In the midst of the joviality, Benjamin stood to excuse himself, catching Tim's eye. "Where might I find the privies?" he asked quietly.

"There's a garderobe at the far end of the house, or the privy outside, Mr. Akins—but it's coming down in sheets out there now," Tim said, offering quick directions, all formality of his temporary role for the evening briefly forgotten.

As Benjamin navigated the corridors, he made his way to the garderobe, a small room built into the manor's outer stone wall, featuring a seated hole that led to a ditch outside. Once inside, he quickly relieved his discomfort and felt much better. However, he was startled by the sound of two sets of footsteps approaching. He darted out of the door, closing it behind him, only to find Jane standing there with a cheeky grin on her beautiful face. "Jane!" Before he could say anything more, she stepped forward, kissed him, and wrapped her arms around him.

"This is too risky, Jane," he said, panic lacing his voice, though he hesitated to push her away.

"I know, but I've been wanting to do that all evening, it's also very exciting is it not? you look so handsome tonight," she replied, her expression radiant.

"And you are more beautiful than I can find word to describe, my love," he whispered back, his heart racing.

At that moment, he spotted his sister's head peeking around the corner with a giggle. "You told my sister?" he asked, mildly indignant.

"Sorry, but she is my best friend. She will keep our secret," Jane smiled, her eyes sparkling with mischief. "Now you best get back to the table, before we are all missed" Jane gave Benjamin another long kiss, smiling widely.

"Will you two stop that?" Sarah said with a giggle, clearly delighted that her brother and her best friend seemed to be in love.

Chapter 27
Unexpected Guests

As the evening drew to a close, the final course was served: a delightful assortment of nuts, dried fruits, raisins, figs, and lightly spiced cakes, accompanied by tankards of rich spiced ale and creamy posset. Laughter and conversation filled the great hall, creating a merry atmosphere that contrasted sharply with the tumultuous weather outside. Flickering candlelight danced across the room, illuminating the faces of friends and family gathered around the table.

Mary stood and gently tapped her spoon against her glass to capture the attention of her guests. "If I may have your ears, dear friends," she called warmly. "My darling daughter, Jane, has prepared a piece to play on the harp for us tonight."

Just then, Mr. Cropper wheeled in a large harp, its graceful curves catching the candlelight, along with a small chair that he positioned in the corner with practised efficiency.

With a hint of nervous excitement, Jane approached the harp, her skirts swishing softly against the polished floor as she settled onto the chair. Pausing to look around the room at the eager faces, she smiled and began to play. Her fingers glided over the strings, filling the hall with soothing melodies that wove a tapestry of sound, drowning out the relentless rain and wind battering the manor's stone walls. The room's acoustics amplified the harmonious notes.

Benjamin watched in awe, captivated not only by the enchanting music but also by Jane's undeniable talent. Each pluck of the string seemed to magnify her beauty, highlighting her grace and poise and for a moment, all thoughts of the storm and their predicament faded away.

As Jane played, the guests listened intently, their faces reflecting a mixture of admiration and tranquillity. The delightful sounds enveloped them like a warm blanket, and even Mary's heart lit at the sight of her daughters' talents truly shining.

Their reverie was shattered by a sudden, thunderous bang at the front door. The sound cracked through the house like a musket shot, jolting several guests upright in their seats. Laughter died mid-breath. The warm, jovial atmosphere collapsed into a hush of unease. Without a word, Mr. Cropper rose and strode swiftly from the hall, his footsteps echoing as he disappeared into the corridor, his brow knotted in a deep, foreboding frown.

"Who could that be at this hour?" Mary wondered aloud, exchanging worried glances at John.

Mr. Cropper wrestled with the latch, the wind howling through the gaps like a warning.

"Who disturbs us at this hour, Mr. Cropper?" John called out, a note of apprehension in his voice as he stepped quickly into the main hallway.

"Let us find out, Master Stephens," Cropper replied, his face drawn with tension as he braced against the storm raging beyond the door.

Mr. Cropper heaved the door open, muscles straining against its stubborn weight and the howling wind that battered it like a living thing. Before the doorway stood two tall, cloaked figures—rain-soaked and motionless, their faces swallowed deep within the shadows of their hoods. Water streamed from their garments, pooling silently at their feet like a moment frozen in time.

John raised a hand to the others gathered in the hall, signalling for silence. He made his way to the hallway, where Mr. Cropper stood to one side of the cloaked figures as they stepped across the threshold. John's eyes narrowed as he peered into the rain-lashed gloom, his other hand moving instinctively to the dagger at his belt.

"Who goes there?" he demanded, his voice sharp and commanding as he stepped further into the corridor, ready to confront the unexpected visitors.

Emerging from the shadows, the first figure pulled back his hood to reveal the familiar face of William Stephens—drenched and mud-splattered, yet grinning broadly. Close behind him came Owen Jones, equally soaked but glowing with his usual excitement.

"Father, I am home!" William proclaimed, bowing his head respectfully. The gesture, though informal between families, reflected the decorum that still held sway.

Hearing her son's voice, Mary rose swiftly from the dining table, her heart leaping with relief and joy. "William!" she cried, her tone rich with warmth as she hastened toward him. All formality was forgotten as she met him in the entrance to the hall and gathered him into her arms.

Around them, the guests rose from their seats, some leaning forward with smiles of delight, eager to witness and share in the joyful reunion between mother and son.

Father Rogers offered a courteous nod, embodying the spirit of fellowship that filled the room. As William and Owen shook raindrops from their cloaks, candlelight danced over their mud-streaked faces and drenched, dishevelled beards. Despite the tempest raging outside, a warm atmosphere of camaraderie and relief settled over the hall, the shared joy of reunion resonating quietly among all present.
"Welcome home, my son!" John proclaimed, his earlier sternness giving way to a dignified and heartfelt embrace.

"Mr. Cropper, I pray thee, gather what fresh linens you may find; bid these worthy gentlemen warm themselves beside the fire and attend to their needs."

Mr. Cropper nodded to the maids, prompting them into swift action.

As William shed his damp cloak, he turned to the assembled company, bowing slightly in respectful acknowledgment of each guest. "I apologise for disturbing your fine dinner and for the foul weather that attended my return," he said, his voice steady despite the weariness that clung to him.

Owen, brimming with enthusiasm, stepped forward. "And fear not! I come bearing tales of our adventures, and I assure you at least half of them are true!" His exuberance sparked warm laughter from those present.

Mary chuckled, a comforting sound that echoed in the chamber. "We have missed you dearly, Owen," she replied, her eyes twinkling with fondness.

Tim and Glen Jones approached, exchanging glances with John, who offered them a nod of approval, their duties done for the evening. They both rushed forward to the hug Owen, relief evident in their expressions as they welcomed a son and brother back into the fold, Irene, his stepmother though close in age, looked on, her pretty face alight with joy of seeing the reunion.

Observing the scene, Benjamin felt a wave of happiness wash over him. Just then, Jane rushed over, her face radiant, to greet her older brother. Benjamin felt a surge of emotion, barely contained, at the jubilant sight.

"Dear sister, I hardly recognised you! When I left, you were but a girl, and now I behold a beautiful Lady." Said William

Jane giggled with delight, her eyes sparkling with affection. "And you, brother, left as a fine young man and have returned looking like a grizzled old soldier! The war has certainly taken their toll on you, dear brother," she said with a wink.

"Still as cheeky as ever, I'm pleased to see. I must say, I am not at my best, I will admit," he smiled widely, the weariness in his eyes betraying his words.

William Stephens, though nearly six feet tall, appeared smaller next to the taller, broader Owen. Both wore time-worn buff coats - thick, protective leather garments essential for both travel and war. William's was finer but equally weather-beaten, bearing the marks of their journey. They presented the image of seasoned soldiers, swords sheathed at their sides on baldrics, high riding boots and spurs glinting from the glow of the fireplace.

William, his light brown hair now long in locks and his once boyish features matured and shadowed by newly grown facial hair, cut a rugged figure. He had inherited his mother's broad, blue eyes, which remained the most striking feature of his otherwise unassuming face. Despite his slightly dishevelled moustache and beard, he exuded an endearing familiarity. The dirt and weariness etched into his face did little to dim the warmth of his homecoming.

"Cook is warming a stew for you both even now; we would gladly hear of your travels once you have eaten," John said, ushering them closer to the welcoming warmth of the hearth.

In a firm, commanding voice, William instructed Mr. Cropper to see that their horses were properly tended—one had lost a shoe a mile back, and the pack horse, carrying their belongings, was to be securely stowed. Catching young Tim's eager eye, he acknowledged the boy's readiness to return to the stables—a task Tim undertook with enthusiasm, undeterred by the driving rain and eagerness to hear news of their adventures, his admiration of both men clear to see.

As they gathered around the great table, Mary felt a quiet surge of gratitude swell within her chest. The room, alive with laughter, warmth, and the clink of glasses, was a fitting homecoming for her son—a rare moment of peace in uncertain times. In the heart of Little Sodbury Manor, bathed in flickering candlelight, she allowed herself—for the first time in many years—to feel contentment and a fragile sense of security. Long may it last, she thought, watching her family and guests with a soft smile as the evening wore on into the hush of midnight.

Chapter 28
Morning After

Benjamin awoke, bleary-eyed, in a modest yet comfortable guest chamber at Little Sodbury Manor. The room—furnished with carved oak furniture and hung with heavy damask drapes—carried a warm, musty scent that mingled with the faint aroma of linen and beeswax. An exquisite feather mattress, topped with a woven coverlet embroidered in floral thread, had cradled him through the night, the rope-strung frame beneath it firm yet forgiving.

The dreadful weather from the previous evening had compelled Mistress Mary to extend hospitality to all guests. The storm had howled through the night, rain thrumming against leaded glass and wind rattling the casements, a reminder of the raw power of the elements intruding upon the estate.

 Now, Benjamin drew aside the heavy drapes and gazed out through the leaded mullioned window. The grand front façade of Little Sodbury Manor loomed below, its weathered stone glistening where the storm's rain had carved dark rivulets down its surface. The once-manicured front gardens, proud in summer, now slumped in quiet disarray—shrubbery bowed and leaf-littered, flower beds churned with fallen debris, their edges blurred beneath the bruised weight of late autumn. The ancient hedgerows that framed the forecourt stirred gently in the cold breeze, their branches stripped of colour, thinned to wiry silhouettes.

Down the slope upon which the manor stood, a series of stone steps descended the terraced hillside—three wide tiers, cut centuries earlier into the natural fall of the land. The steps, their edges worn by age and slick with lingering damp, glistened with moss and pale lichen, glimmering like tarnished silver in the overcast light. Pools of water had gathered in the lower grounds, reflecting the heavy grey sky in broken, trembling fragments.

Beyond the gardens, the fields lay sodden and silent, the last of the harvest long since gathered. The bare trees that lined the distant hedgerows stood stark and watchful, their limbs blackened and skeletal against the pale wash of morning. Wisps of chimney smoke curled upward in the still air, the only motion on a land hushed in the aftermath of the storm.

After dressing, Benjamin made his way cautiously along the corridor and descended the grand staircase, the worn treads creaking softly beneath his boots. As he stepped into the main hall, a chorus of cheerful voices met his ear.

At the long table of the great hall sat his father, Father Rogers, and Uncle Paul, gathered amid the remnants of what had plainly been a hearty breakfast. Scattered crumbs, half-eaten loaves, and emptied cups bore witness to the good humour and lively talk that had lately filled the room.

"Lad, you're up late, you missed breakfast," Stephen remarked, a hint of disapproval in his tone.

"I never slept in such a comfortable bed," Benjamin said, a grin breaking through his lingering drowsiness.

"Aye, I'll not deny it was a fine rest," Stephen replied. "But there's no time for dawdling, lad. You're needed back with the Wards—the horses would have been in last night, and all the stalls will want mucking out."

"Come now, Stephen, give the boy a little peace," Paul interjected, smiling warmly at Benjamin. "He works his stockings off all week."

"That's life for most of us, brother," Stephen said with a chuckle. "Don't fret—I'll be joining him soon enough. What of you?"

Before Paul could answer, Father Rogers gently stepped in, his tone mild but firm. "Paul, I'd have your help at the parish this morning. There's much to prepare before tomorrow's service."

"We best take our leave before we overstay our welcome. The family has much to discuss with their newly returned son and would no doubt wish for some privacy," Paul Akins added, stepping further into the main hallway leading to the front door.

Just then, Sarah and Jane entered, their youthful energy lightening the atmosphere. The guests offered Jane a respectful nod, and Father Rogers stepped forward. "Please convey our warm regards to your parents for a splendid evening, Mistress Jane. Your harp playing was enchanting."

"You're ever so kind to say so, Father Rogers. It was a true pleasure to have your company. I will be sure to pass on your message," she replied courteously, her tone gracious as she prepared to bid farewell to their guests. Her gaze lingered briefly on Benjamin—a fleeting look of longing, passing just for a moment, as her carefully composed mask slipped, revealing her true feelings before she swiftly regained her composure.

As the group prepared to leave the hall, they were kindly escorted out of the estate by Mr. Cropper, who ensured they departed with proper decorum. Outside, the air had turned brisk.

Descending the private pathway, the rhythmic thunder of hooves echoed across the grounds as a column of about thirty horsemen approached. Their guidon fluttered gently in the breeze, emblazoned with a golden stag on a deep crimson banner—an unmistakable mark of the county militia horse. Leading the procession was a heavily built man of medium stature, riding with a commanding presence.

His ruddy complexion and round face, framed by a well-groomed, long moustache and a small, pointed beard. He wore an elaborate buff coat over a polished back and breastplate, the metal gleaming subtly in the morning light. Atop his head rested a wide-brimmed hat, decorated with a flowing white plume. The hilt of his sword shimmered elegantly as he adjusted his reins.

"I desire an audience with John Stephens," the man declared loudly.

"Good day, Sir Humphrey Redmain," Mr. Cropper said politely, bowing his head slightly as the gentleman drew nearer.

"I am just seeing our guests out. How can I be of service?" Mr. Cropper added, taking in the troop of horsemen behind him.

"Summon your master at once; this is a matter of utmost urgency," Sir Humphrey demanded abruptly. He then turned, catching sight of Father Rogers for the first time. "You must be the new parish priest here?"

"I am, indeed, Father Rogers. How may I be of assistance, Sir Humphrey, I believe?" the priest replied calmly and respectfully.

Sir Humphrey Redmain doffed his hat as a small token of respect toward Father Rogers.

At that moment, John and William emerged from the manor, drawing Sir Redmain's attention.

John's expression shifted from surprise to concern as he noticed the troop of horses and the urgent visitor. "Sir Humphrey, it's a pleasure to see you. But what brings you here with such an escort?" he inquired.

"There is trouble brewing in Chipping Sodbury," Sir Humphrey Redmain began, his face marked with excitement. "We've received reports of a mob gathering, targeting those suspected of being Irish or Catholic. They're committing acts of violence and creating disturbance; there is talk of whippings and ear-clippings and the like. We happened to being doing our quarterly muster, when a constable brought the alert."

Benjamin's mind conjured unsettling stories of individuals subjected to such degrading punishments. The mental image of those acts lingered, troubling him deeply.

"In Chipping Sodbury, you say?" John's brow creased – with concern. "While I cannot condone their faith, this is England. The people have rights and certain liberties that must be upheld!"

"Yes, if you say so, John—but my chief concern remains the maintenance of the King's peace," Sir Humphrey Redmain declared firmly. "We intend to quell this unrest swiftly and decisively. We will not allow this county to fall into the same disorder that consumes London, where insolent apprentices and grasping merchants run riot. They must be reminded of their place." He tapped the hilt of his sword with a devilish grin.

John paused in thought before replying, "I shall accompany you. Our family is well regarded in these parts—the Welches, my wife's kin, have held considerable influence among the common folk for generations."

"I am glad to offer my assistance, should it be needed," Father Rogers added, his tone sincere.

"A familiar face may help to calm tempers, and Father Rogers here has quickly gained the peoples respect," said John, welcoming his help with a nod.

"I'll come too, Father!" William said eagerly.

"No, William," John replied firmly. "You'll remain here and see to the manor's security—should the unrest reach our doorstep; someone must be prepared. I must insist."

William's expression evidently displaying frustration. "But, Father, I wish to help! I can't simply stand by while there's danger lurking in our community."

"You've no cause for worry, William," Sir Redmain declared with a confident air. "Our men will soon put the fear of God into those ruffians."

He turned to John with a crooked smile. "You're welcome to ride with us, as are you, Father—but best keep to the side when we set about our business," he added with a low chuckle.

Then, almost as an afterthought, he continued, "As I was passing, I thought you might wish to join the hunt—and perhaps we might speak further on your recent letter... regarding my Henry and your Jane." His tone was light, but a certain glint in his eye belied the weight of his words.

Benjamin felt a bolt of dread and a sick feeling of jealousy at the last statement, so Jane was right; they were making plans for her future.

"Very well, then," John said, a trace of resignation in his voice. "Have my horse saddled. Father Rogers can ride him. I shall take Samson." He turned to Benjamin with a knowing wink, then looked at William.

"Yes, son, that fine-looking horse you've likely seen in the stables, is indeed meant for you. Consider him a gift. But for now, I'll have to borrow him."

The sting of being left behind softened instantly. Though William tried to mask his disappointment, a smile crept across his face at the unexpected news, William had spied the horse in admiration.

As the party readied themselves for the ride, a quiet unease settled over Benjamin. A rising fear stirred in him—not only for John, whom he had grown to respect, but also for the unrest now encroaching so perilously close to home. And beneath that, a more private anxiety gnawed at him: what would all this mean for his future with Jane?

Once mounted, John took his place at the head of the group beside Sir Humphrey, the steady rhythm of hooves mingling the clatter of sword hilts and tack. They trotted briskly down the manor's private path, splashing through puddles left by the storm, and turned toward Chipping Sodbury.

Benjamin's gaze lingered on William, who stood watching them go, his expression taut with restrained worry. Though his posture remained composed, shaped by years of discipline and duty, Benjamin saw a glimpse of conflict in his eyes.

William turned abruptly, waving a hand in a gesture that seemed more dismissal than farewell. "Good day to you all," he said curtly, before striding back toward the manor with purposeful steps, his shoulders stiff with silent frustration.

Chapter 29
Preachers

Benjamin was busy shovelling manure onto the muck heap alongside Thomas Ward, the familiar scents of horses, hay, and earth filling the air. Days had passed since the excitement at Little Sodbury Manor, and the Akins family had resumed their routines, each member silently grappling with thoughts about recent events. That morning, Old Man Ward had sent Thomas to Chipping Sodbury to purchase some horseshoes. He returned in the late afternoon, eager to share his story with the family and reveal the unsettling happenings in the market square.

"There were people gathered, some I didn't recognise, being preached to by a priest I've never seen before," Thomas recounted, shaking his head thoughtfully. "But I did recognise the men flanking him—Samuel and Saul Foster. Samuel, with that unforgettable bent nose, was hard to miss," he added with a snicker.

"The formidable priest passionately recounted the supposed atrocities inflicted upon Protestants by the Irish Catholics, he was speaking of unimaginable slaughter with fervent conviction, there was anger in his voice and the crowd was angry too" Thomas recalled feeling a surge of emotion himself, as everyone had been horrified by the stories printed in pamphlets about the supposed wrongs occurring there. He had attempted to inch closer to the makeshift pulpit, but found himself swept along by the throng, as even the local traders paused to absorb the incendiary rhetoric.

Thomas continued describing how a cart was brought forth, and tied to it was a man—red-haired and seemingly a thief—left only in his breeches, clearly having endured a beating. As the crowd pressed in, they hurled insults, some even spitting in his direction. The sight churned Thomas's stomach: he remembered having witnessed such brutal treatment before—a horrifying display of shame and cruelty.

"Samuel seized a whip and began to lash the unfortunate wretch, all while the priest proclaimed hellfire and damnation for all Catholics. I could hardly fathom what I was witnessing!" Thomas recalled

Then it escalated quickly," he continued, his voice dropping to a whisper as if recalling a terrible dream. "They brought forth two women and a man, known to be Catholics. They didn't deny it, and the mob dragged them through the high street, pelting them with insults and, I dare say, even some horse dung. They put the man in stocks and lashed him, clipping his ears, as the mob jeered. It was a gruesome sight."

The horror of it all made Benjamin shudder at the thought. "That is barbaric!" he exclaimed, the injustice stirring his spirit.

"It was," Thomas said solemnly. "Then I saw—" he hesitated again, his fists clenching. "I recognised one of the women and I realised it was Ruth's parents; they had chosen to flee once their betrayal to the Fosters became known."

"The poor souls," Benjamin murmured, his voice heavy with a mix of sympathy and simmering anger. Ruth's family had already endured so much, only to flee into the cruel grasp of the Fosters, and now this act of mob justice.

"They aren't even Catholic, are they?" Benjamin had asked, his tone edged with disbelief.

"Not as far as I'm aware," Thomas replied, continuing his grim tale.

"There was so much noise and lots of shouting, the mob's fury was reaching its peak and Ruth's parents lay battered and broken in heaps on the floor, I sensed the tide turning, the crowd was roaring for more, it was terrifying,". Thomas' voice trembling as he recounted the memory to Benjamin. "I decided it was best to make myself scarce, but just as I was about to make my leave a voice boomed from behind me, it halted me in my tracks. 'Stop right there,' this familiar raspy voice hollered at me. It was Samuel Foster, I tell you Benjamin, my heart was racing" Thomas explained. "He confirmed he recognised I worked for the Stephens' household, and asked me if they harbouring a Catholic. He demanded I speak. I thought briefly about running but decided against it, I figured to flee would imply guilt, so instead, I replied, "You're mistaken, friend. I work for the Akins' stud farm down the road from the Manor, I could feel the crowds eyes shifting toward me, they felt hostile".

Benjamin could sense the unease in Thomas's voice as he continued to recount the days affairs in great detail.

"Do you know what he said? He asked me if the Stephens had Catholics working in their household. I just replied, 'I wouldn't know; I'm just a simple stable boy who doesn't venture much beyond fetching supplies,' but my words did little to ease their scrutiny. He carried on pressing me, saying 'I think you do know and you're protecting them.' He was right up in my face and he had his hand resting purposefully on the hilt of his sword. I just wanted to get out of there." Thomas expressed.

"My heart was racing as the mob began to close in around me, their faces all twisted with suspicion and rage. I feared I would be seized, but as if a gift from God, there was a sharp crack of gunshot and a bunch of horsemen appeared, armed with carbines, pistols, and swords. They hadn't yet drawn their weapons, but their presence was enough to distract Samuel from me and I spotted John Stephens on Samson and Father Rogers riding John's cob. I can't tell you how relieved I was to see them."

Thomas described how among the riders there was a particularly imposing figure that caught his eye. He held a wheel-lock pistol in his hand, smoke still curling from the barrel of the recently discharged shot. "I will have order here!" He bellowed, his commanding voice echoing down the now-silent street. "In the name of the King, disband and return to your homes at once!" His face was flushed with indignant anger, and his words carried the weight of authority.

"It was great, the mob just stood frozen, their fury turned to silence, you could hear a pin drop and now they were the ones that looked uneasily, they didn't know what had hit them." Thomas' unease shifted to almost smugness as he recalled the sudden twist of fate. "I edged in amongst the crowd to get a good ear on the unfolding exchange of words between the head horseman and the Priest."

"Sir Redmain, how do you fare this day?" the priest said smoothly, an insincere smile curling at the corners of his lips.

"Barnabas Foster," Sir Redmain then replied curtly, his tone sharp and unyielding. "What is the meaning of this assembly, and what—" barbarity is this?" He gestured dismissively; the weight of his authority palpable as he put his pistol away into one of the saddle holsters.

"It's Father Foster," Barnabas corrected him, straightening slightly. "Do you mean these thieves and Catholics?" His voice carried an edge as he spoke loudly, then softened conspiratorially, "I know it's got quite out of hand; I am glad you are here to restore order, but their horrific crimes have caused much anger."

"Puritan fanatics, it seems to me, they always go too far," Sir Redmain declared, his voice ringing across the gathering crowd.

The remark spurred grumbles from the mob, caught the echoes of dissent among them—shouts of "the King's tyranny!" and "Pompous toad, Cavaliers" as well as other inflammatory insults came in quick succession filtering into the simmering atmosphere.

"Who said that?" Sir Humphrey Redmain demanded, as he draw his sword, the movement mirrored by the thirty or so troopers who stood at attention behind him.

The priest and his retinue began to withdraw, stepping back cautiously, while the rest of the mob surged forward, emboldened by their numbers—at least two hundred strong, their voices rising in a cacophony of grievances and insults. "Get back, you swine!" Sir Redmain bellowed, slashing his sword dangerously close to the man at the front of the crowd. Yet the mob pressed on, undeterred, their resolve unshaken.

"Stop this madness!" a commanding voice boomed, cutting through the chaos. It was Father Rogers, pushing through the back lines of soldiers with John Stephens at his side, both resolute and determined to restore order.

"You are all good Protestants, are you not?" Father Rogers called out, his voice firm, capturing the crowd's attention holding out a bible in his hand like a shield to the evil.

The mob hesitated, their bravado faltering as shock rippled through them at the sight of the old priest advancing. A few recognised John Stephens, and their shouts of defiance wavered. "Aye, yes we are!" they chorused, their voices united but revealing cracks in their earlier conviction.

"The true path, as revealed in the Holy Scriptures," Father Rogers declared, his steady voice belying his frail appearance. He continued, his words measured and deliberate, **"Colossians 3:12-13: 'Put on therefore, as the elect of God, holy and beloved, bowels of mercies, kindness, and humbleness of mind, meekness and long-suffering, forbearing one another, and forgiving one another...'"**

As he closed the Bible, a profound calm descended over the assembly. The crowd, once a seething mass of anger, now stood in uneasy silence contemplating the fathers' words.

He then said, "If you are indeed God's elect, delivered from Babylon the great," addressing the Puritans among them—marked by their simple dress and cropped hair—who now appeared thoughtful and subdued, "then let us heed the Scriptures. Let us extend forgiveness to those who stray from the right path. In love and unity with the Lord, we pave the way for enlightenment." He raised his arms skyward in a prayerful gesture, his eyes closed, as if summoning divine grace to settle over the gathering.

The crowd, stirred by his words, began to murmur among themselves, their earlier fury giving way to a reluctant sense of reflection. The air, once thick with hostility, now carried a fragile hope, as if the old priest's invocation had momentarily bridged the chasm of their division.

"It was amazing, Benjamin," Thomas said, his voice still tinged with awe as he recounted the moment. "The crowd was entranced, as if their anger had completely dissolved. And then, as if the heavens themselves were moved, a ray of sunlight broke through the clouds, illuminating Father Rogers as he told them all to go home, study and mediate on their bibles and the Prayer to the Father" The amazement in his tone was palpable, as though the memory still held him in its grip.

Thomas finished the recount by explaining how even John and Sir Redmain exchanged glances of amazement as the crowd slowly began to diminish, the fire in their hearts quenched by the priest's wise words. Some townsfolk, filled with regret, began untying and aiding the beaten victims, lifting them from the dirt as if under a spell that had finally been broken.

"It was a miracle," Thomas said, "that is the only way to describe it."

Chapter 30
Castilio Unleashed

Thomas had recounted the events from that day numerous times, Benjamin always listening eagerly, his curiosity piqued. "What about the Fosters? What did they do?" he asked, captivated by the unfolding tale.

"They scarpered pretty quickly," Thomas replied, a hint of amusement in his voice. "I reckon they were worried about getting the blame for it, I told John Stephens all about it that day."

"How did he react?" Benjamin inquired, leaning forward with interest.

Thomas paused, before considering his words. "He spoke quite seriously with Sir Redmain afterward. Other than that, he seemed mostly concerned about what had taken place."

Benjamin's thoughts briefly drifted to the letter concerning Jane, but he quickly rebuked himself for such selfishness. "What became of Ruth's parents?" he asked, recalling their grim ordeal.

"John Stephens took them back to the manor," Thomas explained, his expression sombre. "Father Rogers did his best to attend to their wounds and handed them over to your uncle, who has some medical training. But they were in a right state," he added, shaking his head at the memory.

Minds back in the present, Benjamin suggested, "We should swing by there. It's been days now, and we haven't had any word. Even Sarah couldn't get an invitation, it seems." Concern was evident in his voice.

Sensing the heaviness of the moment, Thomas quickly changed the subject, a glimmer of mischief in his eyes. "I know we have tack cleaning to do, but do you think today's the day?"

Benjamin looked knowingly at Thomas; they had been planning to take Castilio for a proper test. The firmer ground after a couple of days of sun and wind created ideal conditions for galloping and some hedge hopping.

"Today feels perfect; the air is crisp, and there's not a breath of wind," Benjamin observed, his eyes scanning the horizon. "Castilio was worked yesterday and is fairly settled. Let's do it!" he added, a broad smile spreading across his face.

"Can I take Miller? He could use a good blowout," Thomas asked, his excitement palpable.

"Of course," Benjamin replied. He watched as Thomas stepped down from the muck heap, only to miscalculate his footing. Thomas slipped, landing heavily in a mountain of horse manure.

"That's a fine start!" Benjamin chuckled, shaking his head at his friend's clumsiness. "Best get changed, Thomas."

Once dressed in their riding attire and with the horses tacked up, they mounted and made their way through Little Sodbury Woods. Benjamin soon sensed that Castilio was on edge. The stallion's body tensed beneath him, spooking at every twig that snapped in the underbrush. In stark contrast, the ever-composed Miller ambled along calmly, highlighting Castilio's pent-up energy.

"You seem to have quite the coiled spring beneath you," Thomas commented with a knowing smile, observing the tension in Benjamin's posture. "It doesn't matter if he's in front or behind; his demeanour is the same—a powder keg waiting to explode."

"This is going to be interesting," Benjamin muttered under his breath, striving to maintain a steady hand on the reins. Castilio began to dance and jog on the spot, unable to contain his enthusiasm for the open fields ahead.

As they entered the fort fields, wide expanses lay before them, inviting and open. Benjamin felt a jolt of excitement course through him. "Let's keep a steady canter, shall we?" he smiled at Thomas, who nodded in eager agreement.

And then they were off. Castilio responded to a subtle command as always, and the horses thundered across the field in a powerful canter. Benjamin struggled to contain Castilio's explosive energy, feeling the raw power beneath him as they raced across the open ground.

"As soon as we go into a light seat, he's going to take off," Benjamin exclaimed with nerves and excitement in his voice.

"Race you to the fort!" Thomas shouted, pressing Miller into a gallop with a smooth change of pace, but Castilio, no stranger to speed, rocketed forward. The acceleration felt thrilling, a surge of raw power underneath Benjamin as the stallion bolted ahead, leaving clumps of mud in his wake.

"Wow!" Thomas exclaimed, watching as Miller, though no slouch, suddenly faced fierce competition.

"I have no control!" Benjamin laughed, his heart racing at the sheer exhilaration. "And no stop either!" The distance between them grew, but soon Miller's longer stride began to close the gap again.

"Should we try some hedges?" Thomas asked joyfully, his eyes sparkling in anticipation

"If I can bring Castilio back to me first!" Benjamin urged,

focusing intently as the tense energy began to dissipate from the stallion after covering two fields. Regaining control, he spotted their favourite hedge approaching.

With adrenaline coursing through him, Benjamin felt a burgeoning confidence. Riding alongside his friend amidst the stunning beauty of the open countryside, he savoured the freedom of the moment as the wind rushed past him.

"Let's do it!" he encouraged Castilio. As they approached the hedge, Benjamin steadied the horse into a more balanced canter. However, Castilio, filled with exuberance, leaped a stride sooner than Benjamin had predicted, launching them both high over the hedge. They soared above the height of the obstacle, landing smoothly on the other side. Though Benjamin felt slightly unsettled in the saddle, he quickly regained his seat, grinning widely. "You jumped like a baby Castilio, but that's some scope you've got boy," he said whilst patting Castilio on the neck.

Thomas, riding Miller, executed the jump perfectly, clearing the hedge at just the right height and maintaining his speed on the other side. He surged ahead of Benjamin, but Castilio quickly caught up, showcasing his superior acceleration.

"Let's bring them back to a walk and let them catch their breath," Benjamin suggested playfully, clearly enjoying the friendly competition.

"Do you mean your breath, Benjamin?" Thomas chuckled.

As they slowed to a leisurely pace, Benjamin's attention was drawn to a familiar sight across the field. He spotted Tim, standing nearby erecting a wooden pole with arms adorned with shields, an interesting training exercise for the horses. Mounted on Samson was William Stephens. A pang of jealousy surged through him seeing Samson with his new owner, but he looked very well.

Alongside him rode Owen Jones riding Johns robust cob, looking slightly comical, being such a large man on a 15 hand horse, each man wielding wooden sword. They took turns charging at the pole, slashing at the shields as they cantered past, their laughter mingling with the rustle of the wind.

"Look at them go!" Benjamin exclaimed, "It seems William and Owen are getting quite the workout!"

"Indeed," Thomas remarked, grinning as they took in the playful display of horsemanship. "That pole won't know what hit it!"

Benjamin watched the two young men ride with fervour, their lively spirits resonating in the air. "Let's go over and say hello" Thomas said, already spurring Miller to a canter without waiting for a reply.

"Thomas wait."

As they cantered over, William turned his horse to face them. "Have you leave to use this land as a racecourse?" he called, his tone cool and formal.

Benjamin inclined his head respectfully. "Yes, sir. We've your father's permission to exercise our horses here. We've been coming these two years now," he answered with easy good humour.

"And do you pay for this privilege?" William asked, his expression still grave.
"We offered, at the first," Benjamin replied carefully, "but your father would not hear of it."

William gave a short laugh. "Ha! That sounds like him."

"Stop teasing the boy, Will," Owen said lightly.

Benjamin observed the easy familiarity between William and Owen—more the manner of comrades than of master and servant—and could not help but reflect on how swiftly such bonds might form. His thoughts turned to Thomas and himself, and how quickly their own friendship had grown beyond mere formality.

"Tim and my dear sister have been singing your praises as a horseman," William went on, resting a hand on his hip, a playful glint in his eyes. "Tell me, have you heard of the Old Sodbury Frog Hops?"

"You mean the run of hedges and ditches yonder, once used for the Roman Hill Chase?" Benjamin asked, glancing toward the overgrown ground.

"'Once used,' you say? Why did they stop it?"

"A lad was killed there just over a year ago," Benjamin said quietly. "His horse broke its leg and had to be put down as well."

"By George!" William exclaimed. "Accidents happen! Whose bright notion was it to end the sport for that?"
"That would be your father," Benjamin said quietly. "He felt responsible, as it was on his land."

"Well, let's go and prove to him it's perfectly safe. I need to properly test Samson, and there's no better way to do it." He paused for effect, then added with a playful smirk, "Care to join me, or are the tales of your horsemanship somewhat... exaggerated?"

He urged Samson towards the overgrown course, where a challenging array of obstacles awaited. The circuit stretched for about eight furlongs, just under a mile in length, encompassing jumps, ditches, and open fields. It even featured a rustic bridge spanning a small stream, adding an extra element of excitement to the ride. The varied terrain would put both horse and rider to the test, winding through patches of countryside that had clearly seen better days but still retained a wild charm.

Benjamin felt torn between competitive spirit and apprehension. Castilio's apparent lack of experience over hedges or greenness as they would call it, weighed his mind; a fall on this neglected course could be catastrophic. The horse represented a crucial investment for his family's precarious finances; one they couldn't afford to lose recklessly.

The overgrown course itself posed hidden dangers. Uninspected for years.

Benjamin struggled between proving himself and shouldering responsibility. This wasn't just about pride—it was a gamble that could significantly impact his family's future.

"Looks like the boy's scared," William drawled, a mocking edge to his voice. "No worry, I've been doing this course since I was eleven. It's not for the faint of heart, I suppose."

Benjamin's pride stung. "Let's swap horses," he said, a touch of forced nonchalance in his tone. "Miller's done the course before when he was younger. It's less risky."

"Do you think this is wise, Ben?" Thomas asked, his voice laced with genuine concern.

Hearing a voice of reason from Thomas of all people only amplified Benjamin's unease. He ignored it, focusing on the task at hand.

Benjamin shortened the stirrups, instinctively adjusting for jumping. He swung onto Miller's back, the familiar feel of the saddle a small comfort. "Let's show him what we can do," Benjamin murmured into Miller's ear, a whisper of encouragement to his father's favourite, the golden boy of the stable.

Chapter 31
Silly Games

Both riders instinctively shifted their posture, muscles tensing as they prepared for the demanding course ahead. Their focus narrowed, the world beyond the immediate path fading away as horse and rider became one unit of purpose and movement. The first obstacle loomed before them: a narrow ditch followed immediately by a thick hedge – a formidable combination designed to test precision and timing. The tight squeeze would force them to navigate single file, adding an extra layer of challenge to their approach.

William's voice cut through the tension, a mixture of excitement and bravado. "I'll lead the way; try to keep up," he declared, his confidence bordering on arrogance. His eyes gleamed with a competitive fire, reflecting both the thrill of the challenge and his unwavering belief in his own abilities.

"Just be careful with Samson," Benjamin cautioned, a flicker of genuine concern beneath his own rising excitement. He couldn't shake the worry for Samson's well-being.

"He's safe with me; fear not, boy!" William retorted, then spurred Samson into a canter. The stallion responded instantly, leaping bravely over the ditch, then gathering himself for the hedge. With a powerful surge, Samson cleared it, William a seamless extension of the horse.

Benjamin followed closely on Miller, feeling the familiar thrill of their partnership. They cleared the ditch and the hedge effortlessly, but the overgrown hedgerow pressed in on them. Branches snagged at Benjamin's face and shoulders as they rode single file, the constricted path amplifying the urgency of their pace. The course narrowed further, leading them along a series of three hedgerows, each taller and wider than the last – evidence of the course's long neglect. The hedge jumps were overgrown, the track increasingly narrow, and the wooden planks of the makeshift fences appeared rotten and broken.

As Benjamin carefully adjusted Miller's pace to maintain balance, he watched Samson launch himself over the next hedge. William remained perfectly balanced in the saddle, a testament to his skill. A surge of both pride and trepidation washed over Benjamin for Samson.

Miller followed, clearing the imposing hedge with a powerful leap. However, the landing was heavy, and sharp branches raked across his legs. Benjamin fought to maintain his seat, his body instinctively adjusting to absorb the impact. Years of practice allowed him to regain his balance with fluid grace, barely missing a beat.

They pressed on, adrenaline, coursing through their veins. The thrill of the ride mingled with the constant awareness of danger, creating a heavy mixture of endorphins that sharpened their senses. As they approached a low wooden fence marking the entrance to an open field, Benjamin could feel Miller's excitement building.

The horse's powerful strides betrayed his eagerness to run, and Benjamin found himself walking the fine line between control and release. "Let's keep a steady rhythm, golden boy," he murmured, a blend of affection and caution in his tone. His hands held the reins with practised ease—firm yet forgiving—subtly guiding Miller's exuberance into collected movement. It was the delicate balance every good horseman learned by feel, restraining just enough to maintain composure, while still allowing the horse his momentum and spirit.
They cleared the fence and onto open space for about two furlongs, Miller gaining ground tucking in just behind,

keeping pace with Samson at full gallop. "Care to lead, then? Be my guest!" William taunted, goading Samson into a faster pace.

"Are you bottling it?" Benjamin blurted out, the challenge escaping his lips before he could censor himself.

"Ha! Come on then, lad, keep up! Let's see what you're made of!" William retorted, urging Samson forward with renewed vigour.

Approaching the gate, William effortlessly collected Samson, transitioning into a balanced canter before launching him into a smooth jump. Benjamin followed suit, but as they soared over a shallow, water-filled embankment, their horses' hooves sent up a spray of droplets that glittered in the air.

"Just a bit further!" Benjamin shouted encouragingly to Miller as they cleared two more tall hedges. The rough brush scraped against Miller's legs, eliciting a grunt from the horse, but he powered on undeterred.

Their momentum carried them towards the small wooden bridge spanning the stream. Suddenly, Benjamin's heart leapt into his throat. A fallen tree lay sprawled across the structure, its branches tangled with the railings, completely blocking their path. The obstacle loomed larger with each stride, leaving precious little time to react.

Benjamin's mind raced. The stream's banks were too steep for a safe descent, and the bridge's remaining narrow width left no room to manoeuvre around the fallen trunk. As the thundering of hooves filled his ears, he grappled with a split-second decision that could mean the difference between triumph and disaster.

Panic flared. Before he could think, Benjamin hauled back on Miller's reins, bringing him to an abrupt halt. "Wait, don't jump it!" he yelled, but his warning came too late. With a determined flush on his cheeks, William had already committed. "Here goes!" he shouted, recklessly urging Samson forward.

"Stop pull him up!" Benjamin screamed, his voice cracking with panic as he watched William and Samson leap over the treacherous debris, landing hard on the far bank. Samson scrambled for purchase, his hooves scrabbling against the muddy ground. Benjamin's heart pounded with terror for both horse and rider. But Samson strength and heart pulled through, as he pulled them both up the bank and to safety.

"Victory!" William whooped, his chest swelling with pride. "What a horse!"

Something snapped in Benjamin. "That was madness! How dare you risk Samson like that, you dam fool!" The words burst from him before he could stop them, sharp and unfiltered.

William froze, stunned by the outburst. Then his expression twisted with rage. "Who do you think you're speaking to, stable boy?" he spat, his voice laced with venom.

Benjamin's anger faltered. "I—I'm sorry. I just... I care for that horse," he said, his voice dropping, the fire giving way to remorse.

"Care for him all you like," William sneered, "but remember your place. Lucky for you, your cowardice kept you from trying to cross with us. Otherwise, you'd be flat on your back right now!" He pointed sharply toward the manor. "Off with you! Get off my land—this instant!"

Blinded by wounded pride, William couldn't see reason, and Benjamin—burning with shame and disbelief—turned without another word.

Cursing himself inwardly, Benjamin turned Miller away, patting the horse reassuringly. He glanced down, noticing a few superficial cuts on Miller's legs. He'd have to bathe and treat them when he got home. "Sorry, boy. That was stupid." After what felt like an eternity, he reached the fort fields.

He saw Thomas hand-walking Castilio, a mixture of annoyance and relief on his face. "What happened?" Thomas asked.

"What happened to you?" Benjamin countered, noticing the mud smeared up Thomas's backside and boots.

"Castilio bucked me off as soon as you two took off, I think he wanted to follow. Lucky Owen grabbed his reins before he got far," Thomas replied, still clearly irritated. Benjamin managed only a weak smile, the sting of his argument with William still fresh.

"What happened, then?"

"I called William a fool, and now we need to leave his land," Benjamin said, his face deadpan, his voice serious.

Owen, who had overheard the exchange, burst into laughter. "Well done, lad! Someone needed to remind him of his folly from time to time!" He clapped Benjamin on the back, his mirth infectious. "But for now, until he cools down, best head home."

As they guided their horses back toward Little Sodbury, the tension gradually eased, but the damage lingered. He had squandered his opportunity to impress Jane's brother. Would William ever see him as more than a stable boy? The thought gnawed at him, twisting together genuine concern for Samson and a growing resentment toward William's recklessness. It seemed unlikely he'd receive an invitation to the manor anytime soon. The realisation struck sharp and cold, fuelling his longing to see Jane once more.

Chapter 32
Best Laid Plans

William pulled his horse up alongside Owen as they watched Benjamin and Thomas disappear into the distant woods.

"I heard the boy upset you. You weren't too harsh, were you, Will?" Owen asked, amusement flickering in his eyes.

William grinned and shook his head. "Sometimes, these ambitious upstarts need a reminder of their place."

Owen chuckled, a warm, knowing smile. "Or perhaps he just brought you down a peg or two?"

William laughed. "I'll give him this: the lad has spirit," he said, a smile spreading across his face as he recalled their exchange. "And he certainly knows how to produce a fine horse." He patted Samson's neck with genuine affection, grateful for the powerful animal beneath him. "He reminds me a little of dear Bruce, may he rest in peace," he added softly, a hint of wistfulness in his voice.

"You miss that horse, don't you, Will?" Owen observed, sensing the deeper grief beneath William's words.

"Aye, I can't deny it," William admitted, his expression darkening. "It's foolish, I know, but when I think of all the friends we've made, the hardships we've endured and the losses we've suffered out there… Oddly enough, the hardest thing for me is losing a horse; strange, isn't it?" He shook his head, carrying the weight of the memory. "Maybe it's because they don't ask to be there—their loyalty, obedient spirit, and willingness to lend us their strength are truly remarkable."

Owen gave his friend a reassuring pat on the shoulder.

"Don't start getting soppy on me, Will," Owen said with a tense smile.

"We better get back. My dear mother has a 'significant announcement' for the household—she's been plotting away in the study for days," William added, his tone sharp with anticipation but tinged with apprehension. "I'll probably find out I'm betrothed to some fat, ugly heiress."

"Oh, you should count yourself lucky that anyone would put up with you!" Owen snorted, playfully shoving William's arm.

William glanced towards the roof of the manor, just visible through the bare winter branches. "Perhaps it is time to settle down," he mused, the words escaping him with a strange mix of amusement and genuine contemplation.

"Tim, put their training equipment out of sight in the hedgerow. We'll be back to practice tomorrow!" Owen called to his younger brother.

As they began their ride back toward Little Sodbury, the conversation was filled with their usual playful banter. Suddenly, Irene Jones, now Mary's personal maid, appeared, scolding William for being absent when everyone was needed at home.

"What's going on?" William asked with curiosity in his eyes.

"We've all been summoned to the main hall, Master. Would you like me to inform Mistress Mary that you need some time to change?" she replied, her gaze lingering on the mud-splattered horse and rider.

"Yes, that would be prudent," William replied, nodding earnestly. "Tim, see to our horses. Give Samson a thorough brush down and a couple of carrots for his troubles."

William swung down from the saddle, adjusting the stirrups and loosening Samson's girth before giving the horse an appreciative pat. "I best make myself presentable," he said with a chuckle.

Mistress Mary and John approached the great hall, standing at the head of the household, which had regained nearly its full strength in recent months—"back to fighting weight," as Mr. Cropper would say. With Mr. Cropper as steward, Glen serving as butler, and Irene acting as head maid, the household operated like a well-oiled machine. Ruth and Sarah Smith quietly maintained order, while Cook and Tim continued their duties in the kitchen and stables, respectively.

The main hall buzzed with anticipation. As Mistress Mary and John finished a hushed conversation, William arrived, a striking transformation evident. His facial hair was freshly trimmed, his long hair neatly brushed back, and he was dressed in fine attire—clothes that undoubtedly met Mistress Mary's approval. Yet, a wry thought flickered in her mind: "That's where all his money goes—arriving home like a beggar."

John addressed the household. "We have some exciting news," he announced, instantly capturing their attention.

William and Jane exchanged glances, a flicker of concern in Jane's pretty eyes while awkward bemusement settled on William's face.

"We are planning a dinner party in three weeks' time, just before Christmas. We will be hosting some of the local gentry and other notable figures of the county – something we have not done in many years."

"Sir Thomas Berkeley and his wife, Lady Eleanor, will be coming from Horton Hall, bringing their children Henry, and Charlotte with them," John continued, emphasising the importance of such alliances.

Mary's mind was already racing as she considered the prospects. Sir Thomas, a second son, wielded influence equal to their own, and Horton Hall rivalled Little Sudbury

Manor in grandeur. Their estates—less than two miles apart—bordered each other's lands, if united would form a formidable power base in the region. With extensive holdings and noble lineage, the presence of Henry, the heir, along with the intelligent and charming Charlotte, offered promising prospects for Jane and William. A strategic match could greatly elevate the family's standing.

John continued, "We will also be hosting Sir Humphrey Redmain and Mistress Redmain, along with their son, also Henry."

Mary sighed inwardly. Sir Humphrey was a pompous bore, overly proud of his title. He could be tolerable company—so long as he didn't drink too much. His son, however, had a reputation as a mama's boy. Mary regarded him with a mixture of fondness and caution. Still, the family's wealth, derived from his wife inheriting her father's flourishing merchant business, brought benefits that could not be ignored. The new hall they had recently completed was splendid, located four miles west of Chipping Sodbury. Sir Redmain would be eager to forge a connection with Jane, whose Welch lineage still held influence in the area.

"And, we shall welcome Thomas Smyth and his wife, Mistress Frances Smyth, along with their eldest son, you guessed it, another Henry." John's voice carried the weight of optimism, which mingled with Mary's hope for a well-connected match for Jane in the midst of swirling uncertainties.

She pondered the potential benefits of Henry Smyth, although he was only eleven. His wealth eclipsed all the other suitors, and the mercantile family were very well thought of, especially with his family's connections in Bristol. Margaret, Henrys younger sister, would be too young for William, but Mary anticipated getting to know this family and what alliances they might bring.

"And finally, Father Rogers and Deacon Paul Akins, who will regrettably be moving on from our parish in the new year. This will be a farewell of sorts, sadly."

The news landed like a hammer blow. Mary had deeply valued both men and their positive impact on the Little Sodbury community. She was determined to learn the circumstances of their departure; she hadn't had a chance to speak with them beyond the brief announcement at church that morning.

As John continued to outline the details of the dinner party, Mary felt a renewed sense of purpose ignite within her. "We must ensure this gathering reflects our utmost hospitality. I will secure additional help for the kitchen, obtain the finest provisions to delight our guests, and perhaps even investigate engaging some musicians, depending on the cost."

John nodded, a faint smile playing on his lips. "Indeed. I want you to enjoy this event as much as our guests. I shall have Mr. Cropper coordinate with the kitchen and the rest of the staff. Ensure that no detail is overlooked; the guest rooms will be needed, along with space for their servants."

"Rest assured, I will make it a splendid occasion. It is of the utmost importance to this house that we impress our guests!" Mary declared, her voice firm.

William and Jane turned towards their mother, sensing the weight of her expectations. "The guest list is confirmed, and you two have the most to prove," she said, her smile both encouraging and calculating. "Your father will discuss your duties to this house and our family privately after this meeting." She paused, turning to Jane.

"Yes, Mother," Jane replied, sounding strangely subdued, much to Mary's surprise.

"We must get you down to the tailor in Chipping Sodbury. A new dress might be in order," Mary said.

Jane's face immediately lit up. "That's more like it", Mary thought, satisfied.

"Can I bring Sarah Akins with us?" Jane asked, her eyes wide and pleading.

"I suppose so," Mary conceded, her mind already racing with plans.

"Now, to the preparations," John announced, dismissing the assembled servants and handing Mr. Cropper a list of supplies. He then turned to his son and daughter. "You two come with me to my study. We have much to discuss."

Chapter 33
Secret Meeting Places, December 1641

Benjamin blew into his cupped hands, his breath puffing out in a fleeting cloud against the winter chill. He sat nestled beneath the gnarled branches of the ancient oak tree. Nearby, the neglected Welch family chapel stood in silent decay, situated just east of the manor and accessible through the old hill fort fields. Once a sanctuary of quiet solace, it had fallen into disrepair in recent years, Mistress Mary favouring the more vibrant congregation of the church in the village.

Over the past few weeks, this secluded spot had become their secret haven – a meeting place for him and Jane. To avoid suspicion, they'd been exchanging carefully worded messages through Benjamin's sister, Sarah. Each clandestine encounter sent a jolt of excitement and a prickle of anxiety through him.

With his father away in Bristol again and the workload on the farm mounting, the weight of responsibility pressed more heavily on Benjamin than usual. Recently, they had managed to acquire—and swiftly resell—a pair of unbroken hunting horses, turning a respectable profit. It was a much-needed boost, enough to carry them through until the busy stud season in March.

Thomas Ward had quickly proven himself an invaluable hand—keen to learn and remarkably tenacious. Even when the lessons were hard-won, such as breaking in a young horse to saddle and rider, he met each challenge head-on. Benjamin chuckled, recalling how Thomas had steadily improved his score on the so-called "fallers board" they kept in the yard. The wiry lad had a knack for surviving spectacular tumbles, always managing to bounce back to his feet, grinning through the mud.

Suddenly, a rustle in the nearby undergrowth snapped Benjamin from his reverie. He stilled, straining to listen. It was probably just a bird or a rabbit, he reasoned, but then he made out a familiar shape moving towards him through the gathering twilight. "Ben!" Jane's voice whispered urgently as she approached.

"Yes, over here!" he called, relief washing over him as she hurried towards him. She wrapped her arms around him in a comforting embrace, a brief defiance against the cold winter air.

"That was a close call," she said, her heart still racing against his chest as he shrugged his coat around her shoulders.

"Where have you been?" Benjamin asked, concern lacing his voice.

"No one spotted me, but when I passed servant quarters, Tim came out, and I had to duck out of sight. Everyone's so busy with preparations for the dinner that I think they've forgotten I exist... except for Ruth, who seems more attentive than ever," she replied, forcing a nervous laugh.

"Perhaps Ruth is just grateful that her parents got their tenancy on their smallholding back. That was very generous of your parents, considering what happened."

"To be truthful, I think my parents are struggling to find good tenants, and before the nonsense with the Fosters, Ruth's family were some of the better ones!"

"Oh, I see," Benjamin said, slightly taken aback by her frankness.

"I didn't mean to change the subject, but..." Jane paused, her eyes sparkling with mischief. "I didn't come here to talk about tenants – kiss me!"

"Yes, Mistress," Benjamin replied, leaning closer. Their lips met, the thrill of stolen moments amplifying the excitement between them.

"Oh Ben we just don't get any time together. They are such precious moments for me, but so fleeting" Jane said before pressing a long intense kiss on Benjamin's lips.

Suddenly, a twig snapped nearby, shattering the intimacy. Both of them jumped apart like startled deer.

"Shh!" Benjamin whispered urgently, his heart pounding. He darted towards the bushes. "Stay close!"

He crept cautiously towards the sound, fists clenched, glancing back to ensure Jane remained behind. Each rustle of leaves, each snap of a twig, ratcheted up the tension. He reached the bushes, the air heavy with the scent of damp earth. Venturing into the thicket, he pushed aside branches, his heart hammering against his ribs at the thought of an intruder, or something worse, lurking nearby.

"What was it?" Jane's voice trembled behind him, fear etched on her delicate features.

"I don't know. I thought I saw a figure move, but it was too dark. Whatever it was, it's gone now," he replied, trying to mask the unease that was settling in his gut.

"Hold me, Ben. It's scary out here in the dark." She burrowed into his chest, shuddering. He couldn't tell if it was fear or cold that gripped her. "What if someone saw us, oh Ben?"

"Don't worry my dear. In a way, would that be so bad?" he asked. "I am tired of this sneaking around. I love you and I don't want to hide away like that is wrong in some way". Benjamin said with meaning.

"Oh, Ben I wish it was that easy" she stroked his face with her hands which were as cold as ice.

"Can you walk me closer to the house? I'm a bit unnerved, and I want to get back. I'm sorry," she said, her teeth chattering.

"Of course, my love you are freezing, do you want my coat?"

"No that's ok, thank you," Jane replied.

A biting wind sliced through the bare trees as they crept down the overgrown path, the scent of frost and decay heavy in the air. Each footfall was measured, the snap of twigs a potential betrayal. Winter-stripped woods pressed close as they skirted the manor grounds, reaching the looming, dilapidated servant's quarters. Hugging the tree line, they moved carefully, cold seeping in.

The last yew tree offered a meagre cover, casting distorted shadows on the frosting ground. They paused, breath held, peering across the exposed ground – a silent, vulnerable stretch under the winter sky. Every rustle and creak amplified the tension, each moment drawn out by the heavy threat of discovery.

"When can we see each other next?" Benjamin asked quietly, searching her eyes.

"I truly cannot say, Ben. I won't be able to come tomorrow. There's this grand dinner," Jane lamented, her voice laced with disappointment. "Honestly, one might think we're hosting the King himself! My mother's been spending money as if it were growing on trees and my father has all but given up trying to rein her in." She forced a giggle, desperately searching for humour amidst the turmoil.

An uncomfortable question surfaced in Benjamin's mind, but he hesitated to voice it. "What will happen if your father arranges a betrothal? This dinner is about that, isn't it?"

"Oh, Ben, please don't spoil the moment," Jane replied earnestly, her expression turning serious. "I really didn't want to discuss it."

"But we must confront the reality sooner or later," he insisted gently.

"Poppa won't force me into marriage; he'll allow me to choose, I'm certain of it. All I must do is refuse any suitors they put in front of me. Besides, if they manage to find a match for William first, that will keep them occupied for a while," she reassured him, her gaze warm and comforting, melting his resolve to continue the uncomfortable conversation.

"I love you, Jane," he said, his voice filled with sincerity.

"And I love you too, Ben." She leaned in and pressed a soft kiss on his cheek. "Will you watch me to the house before you leave?"

"Of course."

As Benjamin watched Jane lift her skirt and dart across the open lawn, slipping through one of the back entrances to the grand manor house, his heart swelled. He stood frozen for a moment, contemplating the vast chasm between them. How could he ever be a suitable match for someone of her station? What could he possibly do to be deemed worthy in the eyes of her father, her mother, not to mention her brother? The weight of his feelings and insecurities washed over him. It seemed hopeless, but he must find a way.

Chapter 34
Evenings of Hopes

Mistress Mary Stephens watched as Father Rogers and Paul Akins approached, a bittersweet ache settling in her chest. Their visits had brought comfort and familiarity—things she knew she would soon miss. The serenity of the morning stood in stark contrast to the troubling news that had reached her: Bishop Godfrey Goodman, under increasing pressure from Puritan factions who accused him of harbouring Catholic sympathies, was being urged to recall Father Rogers. The priest, now unjustly blamed for the recent unrest in Chipping Sodbury, had become a scapegoat.

The weight of this injustice pressed heavily on Mary, and she could see in Father Rogers' eyes that he, too, was fully aware of the storm gathering around him.

The priest had sought to ease her concerns, explaining that the bishop—beset by mounting troubles—found it expedient to recall him, especially given that his assignment had always been temporary. Still, Father Rogers believed that statements from both Sir Redmain and John would go a long way toward clearing his name of the accusations. Yet, despite his reassuring tone, Mary's resentment toward the Foster family only deepened.

She and John had agreed not to burden William with the full weight of their recent struggles, though it was clear he had matured—and perhaps softened—since his departure two years ago. Neither of them doubted, however, that William would adopt a far more direct approach should he need to confront the Fosters.

Thankfully, it had been easier than expected to keep him uninvolved. Since his return, William had remained somewhat aloof, preferring the company of Owen. Still, having them both back from the war had brought Mary a profound, if fragile, sense of security—one she had not felt in years.

She mused that a wife might be the perfect remedy to settle her son's restless spirit, and this thought fortified her resolve to ensure the evening's dinner was an unequivocal success. Her thoughts drifted back to Father Rogers, who had become an unexpectedly reassuring figure in the community—one she was loath to lose.

The familiar clatter of horses' hooves and the rattle of carriage wheels abruptly interrupted her reverie. Two splendid carriages entered the courtyard: one bearing the distinguished Berkeley coat of arms, the other adorned with the emblem of the Redmains.

As a swell of panic rose within her, Mary rushed to rally the servants. Despite weeks of meticulous preparation, an unyielding sense of urgency enveloped her. Every moment felt precious, and she could not afford any missteps this evening. The weight of the occasion
loomed large; this was not merely a gathering but a pivotal convocation that could determine the fortunes of their family.

Upon reaching the main entrance, Mistress Mary took her place by her husband's side, flanked by their children, Master William and Mistress Jane, both presenting a most comely visage. Jane's new gown enhanced her natural loveliness, while William was adorned in the very latest fashion from the London court. His garment blazed like fire against the grey stone of the manor; scarlet silk, resplendent, clung to his figure in the rich folds of his doublet, its surface threaded with gold brocade that shimmered in the light emitted from the open entrance. At his throat fell a collar—wide and flat—a falling band of linen in Flemish lace, ivory against his blood-red coat. Mary thought how dashing he looked and prayed it would have a similar effect on their visitors this evening. The servants arranged themselves in an orderly line, with Master Cropper leading the way to bid welcome to their esteemed guests.

"Have Father Rogers and Deacon Paul already been admitted, pray tell?" Mistress Mary enquired.

"They wanted to avoid a fuss and know their way around here," John said, smiling to reassure Mary.

The first carriage arrived, and Sir Thomas Berkeley, still youthful and dignified, helped Lady Eleanor alight. Her grace and beauty sparked a pang of envy in Mary. Their children, Henry and Charlotte, aged nineteen and eighteen, followed, resembling their parents closely. Charlotte was the spitting image of her mother but retained the unspoiled freshness of her youth: a pale complexion with a delicate flush upon her cheeks, her light brown hair curled under a silk hood, her face sweet and self-assured. This reminded Mary of her own hopes for her children, strengthening her desire for a match for her son, despite the age gap.

The Berkeley's greeted the family with the appropriate formalities, as Glen Jones ushered them towards the great hall and their appointed seats, while Tim attended to the carriage.

A second carriage clattered up, and Sir Humphrey Redmain, all impatient, flung the door open. His servant leapt down to assist, but Sir Humphrey strode forward with an air of consequence, leaving Lady Beatrice to descend with her son's help.

"Good day to you, Sir Redmain," John greeted politely.

Sir Humphrey puffed himself up, as if expecting cheers. "These roads abouts are most plaguey ill-suited for carriages, wouldn't ye say, John?" he drawled, affecting concern.

"Truth be told, I scarce used mine; we're a family of riders, and prefer to travel on horseback," John replied with a goodly measure of cordiality.

"Ah, a man after mine own heart! I'm a cavalry man, much like your son, Master William, here," Sir Redmain chuckled, his voice thick with self-importance.

William offered a wry smile. Sir Redmain attempts at camaraderie were slightly comical, given William's two years of brutal warfare as a lieutenant in a Royal Prince's Lifeguard, surrounded by veterans. It was a stark contrast to these part-time, "pretend" soldiers, who likely had more experience in local taverns than on any real battlefield. Nonetheless, he nodded respectfully, indulging the robust knight.

Sir Humphrey, now approaching Mary, seized her hand and kissed it in what he likely considered a gallant gesture. A shiver ran through Mary, masked by a carefully composed smile. Beside him stood Lady Beatrice, plump and unremarkable, showing the wear of time. She offered a warm smile, her dutiful son by her side—stout and well-built like his father, but without his excess. His kindly demeanour contrasted sharply with Sir Humphrey's, especially as he cast an admiring glance at Jane, who responded with cool indifference compared to her warmer greeting to the Berkeley lad.

Mary mused on the need for Jane to maintain a delicate balance, showing equal courtesy to both young men, lest she prematurely limit her options.

As Mr. Cropper ushered the families toward their places, the carefully planned seating arrangements, a topic of much debate, came to fruition. The Berkeleys and the Redmains, younger brothers of nobility and knights in their own right, presented Mary with the thorny question of who would sit at John's right hand. Finally, they decided Father Rogers would occupy the esteemed position, avoiding any potential slight. Once again, the old priest's steady presence served as an unwitting peacekeeper.

Finally, the grandest carriage yet appeared, bearing the Smyths of Ashton Court. Thomas Smyth and his wife, Mistress Frances Smyth arrived with their son, young Henry, who bowed low to Jane with a winning smile; and with him came his sister, little Florence, peeping shyly from behind her mother's skirts.

Thomas greeted John warmly, "Pray, no pomp or ceremony for me; I'm but a humble merchant." He winked mischievously at Mary, though his opulent attire belied his words. Nevertheless, she felt an immediate warmth toward him. "My friend Stephen Akins sends his regards; we just returned him home. I hear my good friend Paul Akins is in attendance this evening."

"Indeed, he is in the hall. I understand you're once again a Member of Parliament for Bridgwater?" John replied, steering the conversation away from the Akins.

"Please, make little of it; it's a long tale—more a curse than a blessing, I might add. But I eagerly await this evening and a respite from the towns and cities." He turned to William, adding, "It's been many years since our days on the hunting field. I've always admired your courage," clasping William's arm.

"We must take up such pursuits once more now that I'm home. I acquired a fine horse from your friends, the Akins." William replied

"Ah, Samson! A fine horse indeed. Stephen and Paul may not have told you, but the story of how our fathers met and how his line of hunters came to be is quite amusing. As I recall, it began as a fortunate accident between Walter Akins, their father's prized draft mare, and one of my father's Arab stallions that managed to escape at the Ashton Tide Horse Fair." Thomas Smyth smiled widely at the fond story.

"No, I can't say they have, but it sounds like a good story," William replied.

"It is a long story, so perhaps over dinner. But indeed, a splendid return gift from your father," Thomas Smyth remarked, patting John's shoulder.

"A most generous gift; indeed, my father always looks after me," William replied, nodding in appreciation.

Meanwhile, Matthew, his faithful man, inquired of Glen Jones regarding the stowing of their considerable luggage and was promptly directed to the guest chambers.

As the guests settled into their places, the atmosphere in the grand hall shifted—soft murmurs of genteel conversation mingling with the fragrant aroma of a sumptuous feast. The long oak table, draped in fine linens and polished silver, commanded respect; a setting truly befitting the ambitions of all in attendance.

Father Rogers, seated gracefully at John's right, beside Paul Akins, engaged in a light-hearted discourse with Sir Thomas Berkeley about the New World and his own aspirations to venture there. Mary's gaze wandered around the table, observing the unfolding dynamics. Each family was eager to leave a mark on the evening; every shared laugh and exchanged glance carried the weight of future alliances.

"Pray, do tell us more of your exploits in service, William," Sir Humphrey Redmain interjected into a conversation William and Thomas Smyth were having regarding horses, his voice booming across the table, eyes a-glint with a mix of ambition and bravado. "Surely there are tales of great merit that would inspire us all!"

"Ah, 'tis the camaraderie I hold most dear from those days," William began, his voice imbued with a blend of humility and quiet pride. "In truth, few battles were fought, and we spent more time mounting sieges and relentless patrols and skirmishes, coupled with the ravages of illness, that claimed more lives than sword, pike or shot ever could. I sincerely pray to God we are spared such devastation in this fair land as I witnessed on the Continent. Yet, I must confess, it appears we move ever closer to the madness that brews in the air."

Mary felt a pang of unease; Sir Redmain's heavy-handedness often stifled conversation, straining the delicate cordiality she endeavoured to maintain. Nevertheless, she remained steadfast in her purpose, resolute in fostering connections and seizing opportunities for her family.

"Indeed, wisdom and understanding must be the keys to unwinding these troubled times," Thomas Smyth gently interjected, seeking to steer the conversation toward a calmer course.

Sir Humphrey waved a dismissive hand as if to brush aside reason. "Nay, my good sir, one must acknowledge that strength is what shapes the future! Our King has shown far too much leniency; he has compromised far too readily. The time has come for our sovereign to defend his legacy vigorously, for there are those in this country, his own subjects, who wish to strip him of his rightful kingship!"

Lady Beatrice, sitting rigidly beside her husband, nodded in agreement. Her gaze softened as she cast a subtle glance at her son, Henry, who was maintaining a steady, unwavering regard toward Jane. Mary offered Henry a small, approving smile; his composed demeanour stood in stark contrast to his father's impetuosity, revealing potential for alliances more rooted in thoughtfulness than in hubris.

As the conversations resumed with vehemence, the servants began to serve the first course, filling the air with the rich aromas of the feast. A prayer was given by Father Rogers followed by lively chatter that rippled through the table, punctuated by laughter and the harmonious clinking of goblets. Yet, amidst the merriment, Mary remained acutely aware of the evening's stakes, her thoughts restless. She sought to guide the dialogue toward topics that could forge a lasting connection with the Redmain boy, seeming smitten to Jane. Every other glance he made was toward her, with a look of enchantment in his eye. It was a pity about the father, Mary thought.

"Lady Eleanor, might I beseech you to enlighten us?" Mary requested, shifting her focus to the matron of the Berkeley family. "What say you regarding the mounting tensions in our fair region? The Puritan faction seems increasingly emboldened in their pursuits."

Lady Eleanor, poised and graceful, seized the moment with admirable ease. "Indeed, dear Mary, it is a matter of grave concern. The very peace of our beloved communities hangs in a delicate balance, and it is imperative that we act with prudence to maintain it."

Paul Akins, intrigued by the unfolding exchange, interjected thoughtfully, "I must posit that the term 'Puritan' is indeed a broad and sweeping generalisation."

Lady Eleanor arched a brow, her interest piqued by his assertion. "Pray, do share your thoughts, Mr. Akins. What do you mean by that?"

"While I cherish the virtues of order and uniformity in worship—for God is a God of order—I find myself am sympathetic to certain elements among those labelled Puritan. Their desire to purify our worship in accordance with the practices of the first-century Christians, before the encroachments of papal corruption and tradition, has merit— so too does a close adherence to the Bible," Paul Akins said smoothly.

Mary interjected, her tone warm yet firm, "I believe we can all acquiesce to that last statement. But, Mr. Akins, I wonder—what say you regarding their stance on abstaining from recreation on the Sabbath, save worship. Their aversion to sports following church services, for example, does strike me as rather extreme, as do measures they'd implement if they had their way."

Paul nodded thoughtfully. "Indeed—a case in point. They take offence at the Book of Sports chiefly because pastimes such as maypole dancing are said to spring from pagan rites of old—fertility customs, and the like. Such things, I grant you, are unseemly. Yet wholesome recreations—archery, or honest exercise—can hardly be condemned. We are not bound by the old Messianic law; still, the Lord's Day ought to be kept for worship and rest. Some, however, in their zeal, seem bent on drawing the line so narrow that it tends more toward Pharisaical severity than true devotion."

"A refreshing and balanced perspective you possess, Mr. Akins," Mary remarked, striving to capitalise on the moment of discourse. "And if I may inquire, to what camp would you assign your own religious inclinations?"

"Ultimately, my loyalty lies in the camp of God and His Kingdom," he responded earnestly. "Yet alas, the Scriptures enjoin us, as articulated in **Peter 2:17: 'Honour all men. Love the brotherhood. Fear God. Honour the King.'** We must respect the authorities ordained by God, so long as doing so does not conflict with our obedience to Him," Paul answered elegantly.

Mary continued smoothly, "It seems, regrettably, that our world has little room for moderate discourse. Extremes reign; one is either with us or against us—such appears to be the mantra of our times."

Lady Eleanor nodded, a sombre expression gracing her features. "Indeed, I fully concur. The art of moderation has regrettably fallen out of fashion."

The conversation weaved through the table, reflecting the tensions and complexities of their surroundings. Each speaker, with their own convictions and interpretations, displayed the layers of thought and belief that distinguished them while simultaneously drawing them close in their shared experiences and concerns.

As their conversation unfolded, Mary noticed Jane glancing at Henry Berkeley, a hint of innocent curiosity in her eyes that she seemed to be suppressing. The handsome young man was now engaged in a spirited discussion with William, who appeared to be deliberately avoiding topics of religion, politics, and war. Amidst the pleasantries, Mary hoped something more profound might emerge from the evening – an alliance based not just on convenience, but on genuine respect and admiration.

As each course was served and conversations ebbed and flowed, the threads of fate wove a grand tapestry of evening hopes, intertwining the destinies of all present.

Just then, Sir Thomas Berkeley began discussing Thomas Smyth's recent appointment as Member of Parliament for Bridgewater. "The House of Commons is now ruled by a boisterous few. The Grand Remonstrance—a mere list of complaints, some valid, but mostly exaggerations and misinformation—is a step too far, I say. I may even relinquish my seat, as I have no desire to spend more time in that snake pit. John Pym is the worst of them, London is riotous, and closer to home, Bristol is deeply divided, though leaning towards Parliament, in my estimation. Troubling times indeed, my friend."

John listened carefully, absorbing the words of these influential men, but refrained from joining in. It was clear that everyone present, sympathised with the King, though with varying degrees of fervour.

"The King must treat with these curs—but only with an army at his back," declared Sir Humphrey Redmain, his tone firm and unyielding.

"Bringing armies to bear upon the field shall only usher in the spectre of civil war," Paul Akins retorted, caution colouring his words.

"Or perhaps we should simply round up the upstarts and hang them then!" Sir Humphrey thumped the table, a flash of ire crossing his visage.

"Then one would render our King a tyrant," Thomas Smyth interjected, his tone laced with distaste.

Mary's heart raced with concern as the discourse around the table grew increasingly heated. Desperately, she racked her brain for a topic that might divert the conversation from its perilous trajectory. She longed for an atmosphere of peace to envelop the gathering once more, her thoughts weaving frantically for a way to restore harmony.
"William, why don't you share with our guests the tale of your friend Prince Maurice the king's nephew?" she urged, her tone light yet earnest. "Come now, son, your humility does you considerable credit, but saving a prince of the blood royal is a story most deserving of recounting."

All eyes turned eagerly toward William, anticipation shimmering in the air.

Mary, with a subtle gesture, summoned Mr. Cropper. "Have the musicians ready to perform," she whispered, urgency in her voice.

William, his cheeks flushed crimson, demurred. "There's little to tell, Mother. I merely put my horse before some ambushing dragoons, taking three balls, one of which

felled my noble steed. I found myself on the ground, un-
conscious. Thankfully, the musket balls landed providen-
tially, my Armour absorbing their force. Alas, there's little
more to say.

"Dear son, there is indeed more – you are far too modest!"
Mary interjected, her eyes gleaming with pride. "And if
you will not share, then I shall! The Prince placed you in
his personal lifeguard and bestowed gifts upon you, expressing his deep gratitude, and you have not long returned
from the King's court in London!"

Her proclamation drew raised eyebrows and cheers from
the guests, laughter rippling through the air. Mary noted
the genuine admiration and intrigue on their faces, especially Charlotte Berkeley's. The young ladies enchanting
gaze flickered toward William, and in that instant, Mary
reflected on the innocent thrills of youth—flirtations that
blossom like fresh blooms in the summer sun. A fond
smile touched her lips as she recalled the sweetness of first
loves and tender infatuations.

As the third course was elegantly served, with artfully arranged dishes gracing the table, Mary turned to Mr. Cropper, her excitement bubbling forth in a soft gasp. "It is
time to unveil Jane's harp! It shall be the crowning delight
of this splendid evening!"

An air of anticipation enveloped the room as the servants
set about preparing the cherished instrument, envisioning
the music that would weave into the hearts of all present.
Mary felt the atmosphere shift subtly, a gentle current of
joy and expectation flowing through the gathering. She
could already picture Jane, luminous in her talent, captivating the admiration of the young gentlemen in attendance,
exactly as her mother had hoped.

Just then, Mr. Cropper approached Mary, his expression
polite yet urgent. "I beg your pardon, Mistress, but may I
be excused for just a moment? I have a matter requiring
my attention."

"Of course, Mr. Cropper," she said, dismissing his request with a wave of her hand, her focus shifting resolutely to the impending performance. Her mind was alight with thoughts of Jane's poised entrance and the enchantment that would surely follow. With a respectful bow, Mr. Cropper retreated to the study, the door closing softly behind him. The sound faded, leaving Mary to savour the anticipation building in the hall, eager to witness the harmonious blend of her daughter's artistry and the evening's carefully laid aspirations.

First, Jane presented a delicate performance on the harp, its melodies weaving through the room, captivating the assembled guests. As the final notes faded, three musicians entered, bearing an array of instruments – a lute, a viol, and a recorder. The servants, with practised efficiency, cleared the tables and chairs, transforming the dining hall into a spacious dance floor.
The guests, eager to participate, formed two lines, ladies and girls on one side, gentlemen partners on the other, facing each other with polite anticipation. The musicians struck a lively tune, a popular country dance.

Sir Thomas Berkeley, with surprising agility and eagerness, led out Lady Eleanor. Their movements were graceful and practised, a testament to years of dancing together. Across from them, Sir Humphrey Redmain, with a touch more bluster than grace, partnered Lady Beatrice, who looked eager but somewhat uncoordinated.

Young Henry Berkeley eagerly took Jane's hand, a shy smile gracing his lips. Mary watched them, her heart filled with a mother's hopes. William, however, remained by the edge of the dance floor, a contemplative expression on his face. Thomas Smyth, noticing his reticence, clapped him on the shoulder. "Come now, William," he said with a wink, "a handsome fellow like you cannot let the ladies have all the fun!"

With a reluctant smile, William bowed to Charlotte Berkeley, who looked delighted to be asked, and they joined the dance. As the music swelled, the dancers moved with increasing enthusiasm, their laughter and conversation filling the hall. The rhythmic steps, the swirling skirts, and the playful glances created a scene of vibrant gaiety. As the dances required partners, they took turns, each interaction revealing subtle dynamics. Charlotte seemed enchanted with William, while Henry Berkeley gave Jane polite attention, though he was less readable than the other Henry, who couldn't wait for his turn dancing with Jane, despite being a far less accomplished dancer than young Berkeley.

Mary danced with her husband, but then Paul Akins requested a dance, which Mary coyly obliged, not noticing John's clear disquiet as he watched from the corner, sipping a glass of wine. The scene, a microcosm of their society, played out under the warm glow of candlelight, masking the anxieties that lingered beneath the surface, a temporary illusion of peace in an increasingly troubled world.

Chapter 35
News from London, January 12th 1642

Benjamin nestled closely against Ralph, who lay dozing in the stable, his eyes flickering open and closed, content in the warmth of the hay. A dark mood hung heavily over Benjamin. It had been over three weeks since he'd received any word from Jane.

Even Sarah, who had made several trips to the manor, reported back that Jane was "busy" and that it wasn't an opportune time to visit, a message relayed by the ever-present, and obstructive Mr. Cropper. The twelve days of festivities and feasting for Christmas had come and gone, the Yule log reduced to ashes in the Akins' fireplace. It struck him as odd that, the absence of an invitation to visit over the festive period and even their father was concerned perhaps they had caused some offence.

Knowing this, Paul had teased his older brother about how splendid the evening had been, regaling them all with tales of the enchanted young suitors Mistress Mary had lined up for Jane and William the lively conversation, the music and dancing. Instead of receiving swift assurances Benjamin had expected from Jane regarding her affections, he had found himself with the cold shoulder, not knowing the reason why, which deepened his sense of melancholy.

Only Sarah seemed to understand the heaviness in his heart. Alarmed by Jane's aloofness, she had quizzed Benjamin in private about whether he had offended her in some way. Her concern turned into a gentle rebuke, suggesting that he might be ruining things with her only friend, not believing for a moment that he was not to blame.

His foul mood did not go unnoticed. Thomas often bore the brunt of Benjamin's irritability and uncharacteristic indifference, while their father had grown increasingly weary of his son's brooding and lack of enthusiasm around the stud farm. Only Ralph—his steadfast steed and closest companion—offered any true solace. The horse's calm presence brought Benjamin fleeting moments of peace, allowing him to lose himself, if only briefly, in the quiet rhythm of grooming or the steady sound of hooves on soil. With Ralph, the ache in his heart dulled, and the weight of his thoughts lightened—if just for a little while. In these moments, Ralph seemed to sense his master's unrest, responding with unusual gentleness, as if he understood that Benjamin needed it.

He had regrettably neglected Ralph of late, as he had become preoccupied with a string of young horses they had backed and sold. Meanwhile, he struggled to manage Castilio, the stallion who had grown increasingly unruly without the benefit of regular exercise. The horses had been brought into the stables for the wettest months to prevent the fields from being churned into muddy ruin and giving the horses mud fever. They had limited the turnout to a small, fenced-off area, allowing the horses just enough space to stretch their legs and indulge in the joyful ritual of rolling—a simple pleasure that always seemed to bring them a sense of happiness.

Thomas had grown fearful of the spirited horse, particularly after his last attempt to exercise the beast had ended in a rather unfortunate tumble into a thorn bush. The incident had left Thomas sore and his pride bruised, yet even the humour of it failed to bring a smile to Benjamin's face.

"What in heaven's name are you doing?" Thomas Ward's head popped over the stable door, amusement evident in his voice at the sight of Benjamin nestling against the hefty horse.

"I'm glad you have time to linger about, Master Benjamin. I know you're the master's son, but we have horses to exercise! Your father has asked me to go to Chipping Sodbury to fetch his riding boots from the cobbler, and to pick up some news pamphlets while I'm at it. He insisted I'm not go alone and to take his turnip of a son with me—his words, not mine!" Thomas chuckled, tossing an apple toward Benjamin. "That should wake Ralph up."

Catching the apple, Benjamin smiled as Ralph's ears perked up, his eyes widening at the sight of the treat. The horse began to grunt in anticipation as he always did at mealtimes, he made to get up.

Benjamin sprang to his feet, giving Ralph ample room as he stretched out his front legs in that peculiar manner horses do before propelling themselves upright. Shaking off the remnants of hay like a dog, he turned his attention to the apple in Benjamin's hand, nudging him softly with his nose, eager to hasten the offering.

Thomas placed Ralph's saddle over the stable door "come on Master let's get going"

It was a brisk winter day. The short ride from Fairfield Farm to Chipping Sodbury was both invigorating and serene. The air was crisp with frost as Benjamin mounted Ralph, feeling the horse's familiar warmth.

Their well-worn route led them through dormant fields, a landscape of muted greens and browns beneath the wintry sky. The frosty countryside invigorated both horse and rider.

Approaching Chipping Sodbury, the market town emerged: quaint stone cottages lining winding streets, smoke promising warmth. The bustling market town was a lively contrast to the peaceful fields they had left behind them.

They both entered the high street which was alive with motion and sound; market-goers wrapped tightly in their thickest woollens, cloaks drawn close and caps pulled low against the wind. Steam rose from their breath as they haggled and chatted, their voices mingling in a cheerful din that echoed off the stone buildings.

Merchants called out over their stalls, their hands red with cold as they rearranged wares—spiced apples, smoked fish, bolts of rough cloth, and tin candlesticks. The scent of roasting chestnuts and woodsmoke drifted through the frosty air, mingling with the earthy tang of wet straw underfoot. Children, their cheeks flushed pink, darted between carts and barrels, laughing as they chased one another along the ice-slicked cobbles.

Farmers stamped their boots and shared news beside the inn's door, their breath misting as they spoke in low tones. A sheepdog lay curled near a brazier, while a peddler nearby warmed his hands over the coals. Despite the cold, the market thrummed with warmth—of community, of trade, of the small comforts that stitched a harsh winter day into something bearable.

Thomas, who had taken the old Duke as his mount for the trip—at the behest of Master Stephen—smirked as the aged stallion gave a disgruntled snort. The horse's stiff joints clearly resented the confinement of the stable and the chill of the day. As they made their way down the bustling high street, Benjamin recognised many familiar faces among the crowd, nodding absently as they passed.

Suddenly, the sharp voice of a village crier rang out above the clamour. "News from London! The King has entered Parliament—sword in hand—to make arrests!"

The announcement cut through the market's noise like a bell. Passers-by turned, curiosity piqued, and began to gather around the crier, straining to hear the latest word from the capital.

"Members of Parliament John Pym, John Hampden, Denzil Holles, Arthur Haselrig, and William Strode—accused of treason!" the crier continued, repeating the message with a practised cadence. "But they have escaped the King's grasp!"

A murmur rose among the growing crowd. Some muttered approval, voicing support for the King's show of strength. But most stood in stunned silence, expressions dark with unease. Whispers passed quickly—traitors to some, heroes to others. The market's cheerful buzz had shifted; a shadow had crept into the heart of the day's dealings, and Benjamin could feel the weight of it pressing in like the cold.

Chants of "Privilege of Parliament" were taken up by a few men, the ones they had been heard talking in favour of the move made themselves scarce, fearing trouble whilst more people took up the cry. The sense of community from moments before was shattered by the political divisions.

"Let's go grab those boots and get out of here Ben, back to the sanity of Little Sodbury and home"

Heading swiftly back, taking Portway Lane for the ride home, the tranquil scenery was momentarily disturbed by the distant sound of cantering hooves approaching from behind.

As they turned to glance back, a figure on horseback emerged—a royal messenger, judging by the coat of arms on his saddlebags, clad in a dark green cloak that billowed around him as he rode swiftly. His expression was earnest, and his mount appeared lathered from exertion, snorting puffs of mist against the crisp air.
Benjamin slowed Ralph's pace, sensing the urgency of the approaching man. The messenger drew closer, his breath visible in the cold, and without preamble, he called out,

"Good sirs! I seek Little Sodbury Manor, the residence of one William Stephens. I have a message that must reach him promptly."

With a slight nod, Benjamin replied, "Aye, you've found the right path. Little Sodbury Manor lies just beyond this village, a short ride down the road." He gestured onward, his tone serious. "But may I inquire as to the nature of your message?

The messenger looked both relieved and eager to be off again. "I was tasked with delivering private news that requires his immediate attention. There are matters afoot that call for his involvement."

Benjamin was captured by interest– an opportunity and an excuse to visit the manor, perhaps even see Jane. Sensing the weight of the message, he offered, "Pray you, good sir, do not tarry. I can provide swift guidance to ensure you reach him without delay. You may follow us, if you wish."

"Thank you, kind sir," the messenger replied appreciatively, gathering the reins of his horse. "Time is of the essence." He glanced back down the road, preparing to resume his journey.

"Thomas, let's take this chap to the Manor. We'll cut across the fields; it will be quicker." Putting the horses into a canter, they dashed off.

Chapter 36
The Messengers

As the company trotted toward the manor, the silhouettes of four men came into view—dismounted, horses in hand, standing at the front of the house.

Benjamin, recognising John and William Stephens, surveyed the other two men—whose features seemed only vaguely familiar. He cast a longing glance at the manor's windows, hoping to catch a glimpse of Jane, but to no avail.

Upon halting their mounts, the Royal messenger proclaimed, "I bear a private message for Lieutenant William Stephens of Prince Maurice's lifeguard."

"That would be I," replied William, a look of surprise crossing his features.

"I possess letters, along with a verbal message that I must deliver in solitude," the messenger added, lowering his voice slightly for discretion.

"Very well, then. Pray, accompany me to the stables; I shall see to the welfare of your steed."

The messenger's striking black mare stood lathered in sweat, her flanks heaving despite the frosty air. With a brisk nod, the rider turned and departed, leaving John and the other gentlemen exchanging puzzled glances.

"Allow me to introduce myself," said one of the men, stepping forward with a courteous nod of acknowledgment. "I am Sir Thomas Berkeley, and this is my son, Henry, of Horton Hall."

As John stood watching, William led the messenger and his horses off toward the stables. Still lost in thought, he suddenly realised his lapse in courtesy.

"My apologies," he said, turning back to Sir Thomas. "This is Benjamin Akins, son of the esteemed horse breeder we spoke of—he lives just down the lane."
Thomas Ward instinctively fell back, maintaining a respectable distance, while Benjamin dismounted to greet the newcomers at ground level, bowing respectfully.

"It is an honour to make your acquaintance. I believe we have met previously. I recall purchasing a bay gelding from your father about a year ago. A fine hunter, indeed—one of my most cherished." Sir Berkeley said cheerfully.

"Ah, yes, I remember! That was indeed one of ours. His stable name was Hector, one of Duke's final batches," Benjamin replied, gesturing toward Duke whom Thomas was now dismounting from. "He has since retired, and Miller, one of his progenies has assumed those duties. You must come to visit us sometime. We also have a splendid grey Spanish stallion available for stud—equally impressive and I have some younger horses for sale."

"I may very well take you up on that invitation," Sir Thomas replied, then added with a wry smile, "Though my wife will surely scold me if I bring home another horse." He cast a knowing look of amusement toward his son.

At that moment, Mr. Cropper and Tim walked over briskly to give assistance from the main house, Tim casting a surprised glance at Benjamin, Mr Cropper appearing not to notice him.

"Pray tell, how is it that you find yourself escorting this mysterious messenger, Benjamin?" John enquired.

"We were returning from Chipping Sodbury when he appeared somewhat lost, and thus we offered to guide him here' Benjamin replied. "It is fortunate he did not wander into the market town. Rumours of the King's attempted arrests are igniting quite a stir among some of the folk there once again."

"Is this so? I have not heard such news."

"It seems quite recent. The pamphlet I acquired for my father made no mention of it. Names such as John Pym, John Hampden, and Haselrig were listed, though I can't recall the others. Given the recent unrest in the town, we thought it best not to linger."

John, cocked an eyebrow, turning to Sir Thomas Berkeley. "It appears the matter is escalating further in London. A conflict of some kind is brewing."

"Grows ever more likely," Berkeley observed gravely. "I'll write to my relative, Baron George Berkeley, in the House of Lords. He'll likely have news, as he's probably at his London residence if the Lords are in session."

"Indeed. This royal messenger might have insight, but please keep us informed," John said, turning to Benjamin, before smoothly changing the subject. "I've heard little from your father lately. Is Master Smyth keeping him busy?"

"Nay, Father's at home. He'd welcome an invitation; you're always welcome at Fairfield Farm Master Stephens."

"Indeed, that's most comforting. Please convey our sincere compliments and express our gratitude for your kind assistance to the courier. Good day to you," John stated affably, signalling their dismissal.

With a flash of inspiration, Benjamin inquired, "I wonder if I might prevail upon you for the loan of a hoof pick from the stables? I rather suspect Ralph has picked up a stone."

Thomas, though briefly exhibiting a flicker of bewilderment, maintained his silence, likely carrying such an instrument in his saddlebag for precisely this eventuality.

"Very well," John conceded, proceeding purposefully toward the house to rejoin the Berkeley gentlemen in their conversation.

Guiding Ralph toward the stable block, Benjamin glanced up at the manor windows and caught a fleeting glimpse of Jane before she vanished from sight. A sudden, fierce desire to rush inside and seek her out seized him—but he mastered himself at once, rebuking such ill-mannered and imprudent impulses.

Within the stables, he found William deep in conversation with a messenger, the man gesturing toward the house as they spoke. After a moment, William nodded, offering him lodging for the night. The messenger bowed his thanks, and the two departed together, William clutching a small packet of letters, seemingly unaware of Benjamin's presence.

Tim was diligently attending to the horses, draping rugs upon them and meticulously grooming their coats. As Benjamin drew near, the boy appeared visibly discomposed. "What brings you here?" he queried abruptly, his customary cheerful disposition replaced by an air of surprise.

"Good day to you, Tim. I trust you are well? Might you be so obliging as to lend me a hoof pick?" Benjamin inquired with polished courtesy.
"Aye, there is one over there, by the wall. Why do you not carry your own, sir?" Tim retorted, his tone noticeably more curt than usual.
"Indeed, I generally do. Forgive my lapse in memory. Tim; have I inadvertently given offence?" Benjamin responded, experiencing a disquieting pang at Tim's uncharacteristic reserve.

Before Tim could offer a reply, the figure of Mr. Cropper filled the doorway, casting a long shadow across the stable entrance. "Ah, Mr. Akins," he remarked, with a distinct note of censure in his tone. "I see you have once again honoured us with your uninvited presence."

His gaze was as cold as winter's breath, and Tim seemed to wither beneath the weight of Mr. Cropper's scrutiny, leaving Thomas in a state of bewildered silence.

"I merely aided a Royal messenger in locating William and am in need of a hoof pick. We shall soon take our leave," Benjamin stated, unease creeping in as he felt the sharp edge of Cropper's watchful gaze bearing down upon him.

"See that you do," Cropper retorted curtly. "We are engaged with important guests and desire no distractions." With that, he pivoted sharply on his heel and strode purposefully back toward the house, his demeanour brooking no further conversation.

"What was that all about?" Thomas inquired, brows knit in confusion as he absorbed the palpable tension that hung in the air.

"Tim, what have I done to invoke such disdain?" Benjamin pressed, searching the younger boy's face for answers.
"We have been told by Mr. Cropper to maintain our distance from you, lest we risk our positions," Tim replied, his voice dropping to a near whisper, a flicker of empathy mingling with genuine fear in his eyes.

"Is that so? You possess no knowledge of the reasoning behind this?" Benjamin's expression hardened, hurt and indignation igniting within him.

"Well, I—" Tim stammered, but the words stuck in his throat.

Struggling to contain his hurt feelings, Benjamin turned to Thomas with a weary sigh shaking his head.

Just then, Ralph lifted his head, ears pricking as he caught sight of Samson in the gloom of the large stable barn. The stallion had pushed his nose over the stable door, his silhouette just visible in the dim light.

The two horses nickered to each other—soft, familiar sounds that drifted across the yard like echoes of a bond untouched by time or distance. For a moment, the tension eased, and the world fell quiet.

"Sorry, boy," Benjamin murmured, placing a steadying hand on Ralph's neck. "We're not welcome here... not any more, it seems. I know you miss him—I do too." He cast a longing glance toward Samson, taking in the stallion's proud, handsome features. Samson's ears pricked forward, as if he too felt their absence.

Ralph called out again, and this time Samson answered—a high, powerful whinny that rang with unmistakable longing. The sound tightened Benjamin's throat. With a quiet sigh, he gave the reins a gentle tug and led Ralph toward the mounting block at the edge of the private drive. He mounted up, the ache in his chest deepening as the bond between the two horses echoed his own sense of loss.

As the two young men took their leave, a heavy silence settled over them, thick with unspoken grievances, dashed hopes, and the sting of humiliation that clung like the coldness of the air. Halfway down the long path, Benjamin reined in. Turning in his saddle, he cast one last glance back toward the manor. Its tall windows glinted coldly in the grey morning light, reflecting nothing but distance. He searched them, almost pleading, for some sign—some flicker of understanding.

The house remained silent. Impassive. Unforgiving.

But then, movement. In the upper window, he caught sight of Mistress Mary—still as a statue, framed in glass like a figure cut from marble. Her face was unreadable; eyes fixed upon him with a piercing stillness that sent a shiver down his spine. Benjamin bowed his head out of habit, out of respect. She did not respond.

Something twisted in his gut. A touch of dread. Had they been discovered? The memory of that shadow moving in the brush that night returned to him with sudden clarity. Was it possible she knew?

As they rode on, the manor fading into the distance behind them, a knot of unease tightened in Benjamin's stomach. John seemed untroubled—if anything, merely puzzled by the long absence of the Akins family.

"You didn't use that hoof pick, then, Benjamin?" Thomas asked at length, breaking the uneasy silence.

"There was no stone," Benjamin replied shortly. "Let us make haste for home." He gave Ralph a light touch of the heel, and the horse broke into a brisk trot.

Chapter 37
Storm Clouds of War, March 1642

Several weeks had passed since the arrival of the messenger from London had cast a pall over the household. Mary, deeply troubled by the unfolding events yet powerless to influence them, observed the comings and goings of local gentry and knights with keen interest. She recognised old Sir Robert Poyntz, who, to her dismay, did not seem to recall her, despite having been a frequent and affable visitor during her youth when he called upon her father.

William, with a newfound intensity, seemed busier than ever. Perhaps, Mary mused, it was the soldierly qualities Prince Maurice had observed in him during the campaigns in the Low Countries—qualities that had clearly earned the prince's esteem—that now led to this new and weighty responsibility. Even so, she fervently hoped these preparations were not the harbingers of open conflict between their sovereign king and his discontented, restless, and power-hungry Parliament.

William had confided in her regarding the charge entrusted to him under the patronage of the Prince, though carried in the King's name. As a trusted man, he was to identify and confirm a list of local gentry and nobles judged loyal and steadfast. His task was to deliver the King's private instructions, bidding them to make quiet preparations for what might soon become open conflict with Parliament— or, as His Majesty now termed them, the rebels.

Several of these notable gentlemen had since come to the manor, holding private counsel with William—meetings from which Mary and John were, to their frustration, politely but firmly excluded.

"These are military matters, dear mother," William had reiterated on numerous occasions, "and it is for your and Father's protection that you must remain unaligned in such affairs." Yet, she and John reminded him of their long-standing hospitality and the advantageous marriage alliances they had cultivated, all of which bound them firmly to the King's cause.

As she wandered through the garden, inhaling the fresh scent of spring, her thoughts turned to Jane. She recalled the betrothal to Henry Redmain—an arrangement that John regarded as a significant triumph, given the remarkably modest dowry that the Redmains had happily accepted, their son being the sole heir to a decent fortune. This, of course, was despite the necessity of enduring the company of Sir Humphrey Redmain. John considered this a trifling cost for the benefits to be gained, a detail he had revealed to Mary weeks prior.

Furthermore, and best news of all, the connections and prestige of the Berkeley family, secured through William's betrothal to Charlotte Berkeley, further enhanced their status, forging a strong power base with their neighbours at Horton Hall. Charlotte's dowry would provide essential financial support for William. Mistress Mary was very satisfied with this match from every aspect.

Mary had been overjoyed by the outcome, albeit somewhat frustrated that the wedding plans had been postponed until the current troubles were resolved. Nevertheless, her meticulous preparations for that December evening had indeed borne fruit. She had not, however, anticipated the heartbreak and distress now enveloping her cherished daughter, Jane.

Mr. Cropper had discreetly informed her of a clandestine romance said to be blossoming between Jane and the Akins lad—an affair reportedly witnessed by one of the servants. With measured delicacy, Mary had broached the subject with her daughter, and under gentle yet firm questioning, Jane had admitted to the attachment. To Mary's relief, the confession revealed the affair to be innocent— her daughter's virtue still intact.

Yet relief warred with dread. Should word of this liaison reach society's ears, innocence would offer no protection. Jane's reputation would be irrevocably tarnished; her prospects ruined in a single breath. Worse still, her betrothal to Henry Redmain would be in jeopardy—his father, a proud and exacting man, would surely call it off.

Mary endeavoured to comprehend Jane's feelings and chided herself for not picking up on the signs before Mr. Cropper' revelation. The Akins boy was undeniably handsome and charming, and had he possessed wealth or station, she would have harboured no reservations. She held a respectable view of his family despite their humble origins. Nevertheless, Jane had a duty to her family and her own future happiness, and Mary was resolute that Jane's infatuation was no true love. Yet Jane remained steadfast in her belief that she was truly in love.

Mary had granted her daughter time to reflect, yet Jane continued to reject the prospect of marriage to Henry, professing her love for Benjamin. This compelled Mary to resort to gentle persuasion, emphasising that should Jane reveal the secret affair to her father, he would never forgive her, and she would never see Benjamin or Sarah Akins again—that would be a certainty.

Mary painted a stark picture of the consequences of their liaison, warning of a life spent mucking out stables on a Provençal farm, along with the danger of placing their family in a precarious position. She impressed upon Jane her duty and prospects, allowing her a little more time to contemplate her recent actions.

At length, Jane relented, agreeing—albeit with quiet sorrow—to sever ties with Benjamin. It was tacitly understood that word of her engagement to Redmain would soon reach him, a truth that needed no formal declaration. In her solitude, she clung to the hope that one day she might rekindle her friendship with Sarah, whose absence she also felt keenly.

Mary, meanwhile, had quietly asked Mr. Cropper to explain the circumstances to Benjamin, trusting that the boy's better judgment would prevail when the time was right. Until then, she made certain that all contact with the Akins family was firmly curtailed.

John, for his part, had become increasingly preoccupied with visiting tenants. The sting of being excluded from William's dealings left him uneasy in his own home, especially as prominent men came and went with little regard for his presence. Instead, he threw himself into a personal mission: attempting to justify the need for higher rents to increase the estate's income. It was a task met with resistance and no small measure of discontent from those who leased the land—despite it being the first increase in many years.

Mary found it quietly amusing that she had once fretted over the trouble William might stir, only to now see him utterly captivated by the young Mistress Berkeley. At just eighteen, the girl possessed a grace and intelligence far beyond her years, and William, for his part, seemed eager to step into the next chapter of his life—if she was on the next page. In the little free time he could spare, he had joined the Berkeleys on a hunt at Horton Hall and was quickly becoming a trusted friend to both Sir Thomas and his son, Henry.

Jane, too, seemed taken with Charlotte—a connection Mary was keen to nurture. Encouraging such a friendship with a Mistress of similar station, she hoped, would both strengthen their social ties and help Jane grow more comfortably into her own role in society.

And yet, beneath her quiet satisfaction, Mary could not help but lament how cruelly the shadow of unrest had pursued them home. The world, it seemed, was not yet ready to grant her son the peace or promise that he had been so

near to embracing. His sense of loyalty to Prince Maurice
—and to the Kings cause—had grown all-consuming,
leaving little room for the life she had once hoped he
might reclaim.

The familiar sound of hooves thundering up the private
path roused Mary from her reverie, for it appeared the
Royal messenger bore yet more letters for William. This
had become customary. He took his horse to the stables
without ceremony, while William, flanked by Owen breaking from his meeting, accepted the message as if it were
common routine, then strode into the Great Hall, which increasingly resembled a command centre.

Mary chose to approach one of the open windows. It was a
warm spring day, and she found a small stool upon which
to rest and listen intently to the discussions within, while
fiddling with the ivy that clung to the walls in some parts
of the manor.

William had gathered with him Sir Humphrey Redmain,
Sir Thomas Berkeley, and Francis Seymour, 1st Baron
Seymour of Trowbridge—a magnate of the county and the
most senior visitor thus far. In this moment, pride swelled
within her heart for her son. The last Seymour to visit
Little Sodbury Manor had done so over a century ago, accompanied by the King of England. Since then, the manor
had not hosted such distinguished guests, and the influence
of the Seymour's had dimmed, akin to their own, albeit on
far differing scales.
"This," he began, holding the paper aloft, "is a letter from
the Royal Court, now at Windsor, though soon to move
north. Prince Maurice writes that he and his elder brother,
Prince Rupert—newly arrived in England to offer his service to His Majesty—had accompanied the Queen to Hol-
land for her safety, following threats of attainder like those
that brought down the Earl of Strafford.

"The King yet makes one final attempt at peace," William continued, his tone grave. "But Prince Maurice reports that Parliament now runs amok, seeking to seize command of the militia. Such an act draws a clear and perilous line between the two sides, even as they press on with bills that strip the King of his lawful authority."

"We must prepare for war. We must amass arms, horses, and men, for only from a position of strength can peace be achieved," declared Sir Thomas Berkeley.

William gave a light, amused grin as he continued reading the correspondence.

"What brings you mirth, Mr. Stephens?" The Baron's voice rang out with authority, cutting through the room.

"My apologies, Baron. The Prince Maurice has enclosed funds for a horse for me—one His Grace felt he owed me from our time in Low Countries together," William replied, his expression earnest.

"When you saved his life, you mean, William?" interjected Sir Thomas, eager to enhance his future son-in-law's credentials with the Baron and his family – a notion Mary reflected upon favourably, eavesdropping with keen interest.

William, scanning through the letters, added, "I also have a brief message here from the King, addressing his loyal servants in the southwestern part of his realm, beseeching prayers for England and aid for defence of the realm."
"He might as well say prepare for war, without overtly declaring it," remarked Sir Humphrey Redmain, his brash voice unmistakable.

"Very well. It would seem we have weighty matters before us," declared Baron Seymour, his tone measured and austere. "I shall send word to my brother, the Marquess of

Hertford, with all due haste. We shall act as His Majesty implies. See that my carriage is made ready—and take care that discretion be our watchword. These affairs must proceed with the utmost circumspection.”

He paused, his gaze settling on the gathered men with sombre intensity. “A dark hour indeed, should this kingdom fall upon the sword of civil strife. Yet let us pray that reason and loyalty may still prevail—by God’s mercy, if not by man’s.”

Turning then to William, the Baron inclined his head—graciously, though but a little. “Master Stephens, I am in your debt. Your welcome has been generous, and your counsel not without worth.”

William bowed respectfully. “I am merely pleased that our King can count upon such loyal support from some of his most important subjects such as you.”

“Indeed,” nodded the Baron, before striding out of the hall.

Mary swiftly rose to her feet, feigning interest in a patch of daffodils just beginning to stir from their winter slumber, as the Baron approached. His stride, though deliberate, bore the unmistakable stiffness of a man in the ripening of his years—no longer young, but not yet bowed by old age, somewhere in his early fifties. He did not see her, his attention fixed on the carriage where his attendants moved with haste, securing trunks and adjusting harnesses in preparation for his departure.

Once the carriage was down the private path, she returned to her seat, her thoughts abuzz with the implications of the meeting.

“Well, the Baron seemed rather lukewarm, didn’t he?” ventured Sir Redmain, his tone quizzical.

Sir Thomas Berkeley replied, "He has not been on good terms with the King until recently; he had been vocally against Ship Money in the past. However, with his brother now a Marquess and himself a Baron, coupled with the rising influence of radical views in Parliament, I am certain he will align himself more closely with the King when lines are drawn."

"Let us hope so. Many seem to be sitting on the fence," Sir Redmain observed.

"What I did not mention is that the Queen has taken the crown jewels abroad to raise arms and recruit soldiers in the Low Countries. The King knows full well that war approaches; else he would not resort to such desperate measures. If it must come to pass, we shall need to deliver the Rebels a swift and crushing victory to put an end to this foul business. There is much to be done—we are but halfway through the list" William spoke with quiet authority, drawing them into his confidence.

Mary listened intently, the weight of their words pressing heavily upon her. The spectre of war loomed ever closer, and the urgency of the moment seeped into her thoughts, impossible to ignore. With the fate of their family—and their future—hanging precariously in the balance, she could only hope and pray that reason would prevail before it was too late.

She could not bear the thought of William going off to fight another wasteful war, but the idea of him fighting against his own countrymen was still unthinkable—yet it seemed increasingly likely as the world around them descended into madness.

The troop of horse had arrived in Little Sodbury, yet Sir Redmain was notably absent. He had ridden to Wells to confer with Sir Ralph Hopton, recently released from the Tower of London, where Parliament had held him as a delinquent. Now free, Hopton busied himself rallying the local gentry to the king's cause.

Meanwhile, Parliament was growing increasingly uneasy, issuing the Militia Ordinance to seize control of county bands, city militias, and the supply of weapons and ammunition across the realm.

The King turned to a rather antiquated document concerning the rights of the commission of Array, written in Latin, which did cause some confusion among the ranks. Regardless, preparations were firmly underway; the land was fraught with divisions of loyalty, with many still hesitating, choosing to bide their time and observe which way the tide might ultimately turn.

William found some hope in the fact that Sir Redmain's militia cavalry mostly stayed loyal to the King, even as Gloucester's support seemed to shift towards Parliament. The thirty-one men, making up a mere half-troop compared to typical formations and including Owen, were assembled as if for battle. Their mismatched helmets and equipment, sourced by gentlemen with means, starkly highlighted the country's lack of preparation for war.

Some donned simple but effective pot helmets with neck guards resembling the tails of lobsters, fitted with triple-bar face guards at the peak to shield against sword slashes while maintaining necessary visibility for the modern cavalryman. Others sported burgonets, popular in the Elizabethan era, likely handed down from fathers or even grandfathers. Among them, William's gaze was drawn to an ancient Medieval sallet, a peak fitted for additional protection, conjuring tales of long-past battles. Most had stout buff coats of differing degrees of quality. The thick, versatile coats gave good protection against swords but not so much against musket balls. Less than half had back and breastplates, most proofed against pistol shots, and they were armed with swords of varying types, as well as pistols and carbines held in saddle holsters.

The more fashionable younger gentlemen—a couple William recognised from his misspent youth—eschewed helmets, favouring instead finely crafted felt broad hats lavishly adorned and designed to conceal "secrets": metal skull caps that offered some protection without compromising their stylish appearance.

William, however, wore his blued and gilded Flemish Zischagge helmet, a prized gift from Prince Maurice. It featured a single horizontal bar and a more articulated tail, crafted from thinner, numerous plates. He found it far more comfortable and less restrictive than his old three-bar pot helmet.

Owen had mocked him as a show-off when William emerged proudly clad in his blued armour to match, a small scrape marking its surface alongside the original proofing mark from the armourer on his breastplate and back and his rein hand gauntlet simple but effective protection.

They departed from the manor that morning, taking the route to the Roman fort field, where training exercises for the horse troop had been arranged.

Owen, favouring a single-handed cavalry pole-axe, rested it casually on his shoulder atop his new, large draft horse —the best he could afford.

William retorted, "You look like a brute with that thing, Owen," gesturing to the pole-axe.

"Precisely the effect I desire. It's simple, but far deadlier than you think," Owen grinned, his confidence unwavering.

"Much like yourself, my old friend," William laughed heartily.

"You won't be laughing when you need me to get you out of trouble with it," Owen teased, a mischievous glint in his eyes.

"Now, Corporal Jones, we must inspect these soldiers whom Sir Redmain believes will be the very pride of the King's army," William declared with a smirk.

"But he also believes he shall be the finest captain!" Owen interjected, sharing in the light-hearted jest.

William chuckled again, "I must endure him as his lieutenant—God grant me strength! At least we shall have ample opportunity to discern the metal of these men and endeavour to prepare them for the trials that await."

Upon reaching the thirty men milling about, William noted their excitement as they chatted animatedly, displaying their weapons and horses to one another like children on their first proper hunt. Owen called them to attention, finally getting them into an untidy formation.

"Good start," William muttered under his breath to Owen, a hint of amusement in his eyes.

William walked down the line, inquiring after their names; each gentleman presented with differing degrees of lineage —the Cornet, a second son of a knight. In fact, most appeared to be second sons, as William observed them proudly offering their credentials, though no one boasted about any meaningful experience beyond the obligatory gatherings of the militia, where they often spent more time indulging in drink and merry making than in any real soldiering or drilling, frequently bragging without compunction.

William listened to their carefree chatter, his expression a mix of bemusement and concern. What else could he expect? England had enjoyed an unusual peace for years.

Save for a few aborted expeditions and scattered skirmishes with the Scots in recent years, the only significant battle—an English defeat at Newburn—defined the clashes now known as the Bishops' Wars. Yet these conflicts had exposed the military fragilities of both the English and the King of the three kingdoms.

As he joined in their light-hearted banter and the easy jesting that flowed among them, William noted most of the men were in their early twenties, with only a handful older than his own thirty years. All were second sons. His expression hardened at the thought of the challenges ahead shaping this ragtag group into a semblance of soldiers. He reflected on his own early days as a volunteer: bright-eyed and bushy-tailed, blissfully unaware of the horrors that awaited him and the steep learning curve he would need to survive them.

"Gentlemen! That's enough of your prattling; it is time to attend to the task at hand," he shouted, his voice imbued with authority.

"Corporal Owen and I have seen two years of fighting alongside Swedes, Dutch, Germans, and even a few Englishmen. These soldiers have been engaged in warfare for over twenty years. We have learned from them, and now we shall instruct you, with the hope of improving your chances of surviving your first battle—and, God willing, your last—when we vanquish these Rebels!"

This proclamation earned a rather unwelcome cheer from the assembled troopers, and Owen quickly countered, "Shut your mouths!" he barked, employing his best parade ground voice.

"I beg your pardon," one of the troopers retorted, casting a look of disdain towards Owen not accustomed to being addressed in such a manner especially from a commoner.

"Corporal Owen's role in the upcoming weeks is clear. He answers only to me whilst we are in training". William ordered.

"I must object," the Cornet interjected, his tone laced with the authority of a knight's second son and the troop's guidon bearer – a rank surpassing Owen's within the troop.

William responded resolutely, leaving no room for debate: "I beseech you, sir, do not object. This is my order. Owen possesses more experience than all of you combined, and I assure you, in the Army, social status and wealth do not automatically make for a good soldier. The ability to learn, take orders, and cultivate discipline – these are what truly matter as much a bravely and honour." His unwavering gaze silenced any further dissent.

"Form up—get into line!" Owen bellowed, his voice cutting through the thud of hooves and the men's chatter.

"We are in line!" a few protested, tugging at their reins.

"That is not a line!" Owen shot back, spurring forward and tapping a rider's boot with the hammer-end of his pole-axe for emphasis. "Dress your ranks—knee to knee, shoulder to shoulder! Close up, gentlemen, close up!"

"That's it!" William called out from the flank, his voice

ringing over the field. "We want you knee to knee! Hold steady now!"

Achieving some semblance of order, he then commanded them to walk forward, insisting they maintain their formations, "While keeping yourselves knee to knee!" he repeated.

"Sort out that line!" Owen commanded, taking the left flank while William anchored the right.
"Now, trot!" His sharp, commanding voice cut through the air. The trumpeter, uncertain of the notes, struggled to sound a clear call, trying to stay focused and maintain formation. But as the troop lurched forward, the line immediately faltered, prompting a shouted litany of corrections that mingled with the strained, faltering notes of the trumpeter struggling to relay the commands.

"We are not cantering, gentlemen!" William barked, his voice barely audible above the sudden eruption of equine enthusiasm. Some horses surged forward into a gallop, while others merely shuffled, heads held high, as their riders fought for control amidst the ensuing chaos.

"What a mess!" William exclaimed, exasperated. "What a damned disgrace! You call yourselves horsemen?" Owen echoed, directing his rebuke at the overly refined gentlemen struggling in the ranks.

Frustration edged William's voice as he turned upon the flustered trumpeter. "Sound the reform!" he ordered sharply, raising his arm in signal. The response was ragged, the movement sluggish.

"By George, gentlemen, this is elementary work!" he cried. "We are not wheeling or filing ranks—only forming a straight line and passing cleanly through the gates on command. Now, come on, lads! Keep your order!"

He rode down the line, his stern gaze sweeping over each man in turn. Then, the sight of one trooper—his ancient, ill-fitting sallet slipped clean over his eyes, the chin strap long since lost—broke the tension at once.

Trying to keep a straight face, Owen pointed and shouted, "Look at this!" He tapped the back of the helmet with his pole-axe, sending it tumbling off the trooper's head and into his lap. The trooper's face flushed with embarrassment. "I suggest you get yourself a decent pot and give that back to whatever museum you stole it from," William said, his tone deadpan, eliciting a chuckle from most of the troop.

Realising the stakes were far greater than mere pride, William and Owen exchanged a look of shared resolve. They both understood that this motley band of second sons would require serious training if they were to become soldier's worthy of the King's favour.

"Rise to the challenge!" Owen called out, his voice now imbued with a newfound authority that cut cleanly through the din of uncertainty.

"We shall make soldiers of you yet," William added, his voice rising with conviction. "No longer merely gentlemen, but true cavalrymen for our King—Cavaliers, as they've taken to calling us!"

His appeal to their pride seemed to take hold. With renewed focus, the troop hastened to comply, gradually finding their rhythm. Most were good horsemen as individuals, but they needed to learn to work as one, they began to trot in unison, hooves striking the earth with the first signs of cohesion taking form.

William observed them with cautious optimism. Perhaps, with time, patience, and unwavering discipline, these second sons could indeed rise to meet the demands of the hour. In the uncertain days ahead, it would not be blood or title that defined them, but courage and resolve in the face of adversity.

The troop spent the better part of the day drilling basic manoeuvres, tirelessly repeating the exercises in a bid to forge discipline and coordination into a group of men and horses more accustomed to comfort than combat. By day's end, both riders and steeds were thoroughly exhausted, their bodies aching from the unaccustomed exertion.

"We return on the morrow to repeat these same drills," William declared, striving to foster a sense of camaraderie amongst the tired wearily men. "Once you demonstrate competence in these foundational skills, we advance to weaponry training. We must ensure both you and your mounts grow accustomed to the roar of gunfire, and learn the tactics we've gleaned from the Swedish cavalry: charging cold steel in hand, discharging pistols and carbines at near point-blank range, enveloping our foes in a swift and lethal embrace."

All would come in due course, William mused — one step at a time. The name Second Sons had a fine sound to it, and he resolved that Sir Humphrey Redmain should be brought to believe it had been his own conceit. It should be their name; it would grant them an identity, one that in time might grow into a soldier's pride, stiffening backs and steadying hearts when resolve was most required.

As the sun dipped, painting the field in amber, the men dispersed, their chatter and murmurs revealing spirits lifted by his own call to arms, William watched the men as they set about tending their horses, and felt a fresh surge of determination rise within him. He would labour without cease to ready these men — these second sons — for the trials that lay ahead, and he and Owen took a quiet delight in the challenge. Though he had once yearned for peace, Prince Maurice's confidence in him — which he suspected sprang partly from personal regard and trust, and partly from the manor's obscurity and his family's relatively low station, rendering him a convenient and inconspicuous bearer of messages to his betters — now urged him on, both thoughts sharpening his resolve to prove his worth. Bound to this was his loyalty to the Prince and to his uncle, the King.

Thus, he stepped willingly into what was fast proving an inevitable Civil War, yielding himself to whatever fate it might yet decree.

As Benjamin and Thomas made their way back to Fairfield Farm, their recently purchased wagon laden with hay for the horses, they took the time to pass through the charming village of Old Sodbury. This small parish, home to fewer than one hundred families, was a sight to behold with its well-kept but modest sized houses and gardens blooming with vibrant wildflowers.

As they travelled, Benjamin made sure to greet the people he knew along the way. "Good morning, Mrs. Carver!" he called out to an elderly woman tending to her garden, receiving a warm smile and wave in return. "Afternoon, Mr. Hales!" he nodded to a local craftsman working diligently on his latest project by the roadside.

Approaching the old village pub, Thomas exchanged friendly words with its owner, Mr. Griffith, promising to return later for a pint if he could. Nearby, St. John's Church stood prominently, where they worshipped every Sunday, and one of the bustling bakeries owned by the Hobbs family, famed for its delectable small cakes infused with aromatic herbs and dried fruits—a truly irresistible treat.

Determined to make a brief stop, Benjamin climbed down from the driver's seat and handed the reins to Thomas, instructing him to keep an eye on the sturdy cob hitched to the cart—a good-natured beast that had come as part of a recent trade, and whom they'd unceremoniously named Bob.

He stepped into the bakery to the cheerful ring of the small bell above the door, announcing his arrival to the flour-dusted baker bustling behind the counter. Benjamin had come with a purpose: to procure a few sweet cakes and a fine loaf of manchet bread, a modest indulgence to mark their recent triumph.

In just four weeks, they had bought, backed, and sold no fewer than three promising young horses—each yielding a tidy profit. Benjamin hoped the achievement might at last elicit his father's approval—perhaps even, dare he dream it, a word of praise. By any measure, it was a modest but meaningful success.

Yet the mood at home had soured since his father's return from an extended stay at Ashton Court in Bristol. To Benjamin's growing frustration, the elder Akins had done little but find fault with the state of the farm. He grumbled about the number of horses cluttering the paddocks, scolding Benjamin for exceeding the "one-per-acre" rule—an old maxim handed down from his grandfather. He also scolded Benjamin for going out and buying a new cart and horse to pull it, without consulting him first despite the very good deal he had managed to negotiate for both.

Thus, this excursion to acquire extra hay was essential, for their ten acres of paddock lay bare, and it was only June. Though a small price to pay for the profits they had accrued, Benjamin knew that it would not assuage his father's discontent.

Meanwhile, Paul, his uncle, overseeing the Stud farm during his father's absence and Father Rogers' departure, contemplated his future amidst the church unrest, considering resuming his medical studies, perhaps apprenticing with an apothecary, since university was beyond his means.

Ever the meticulous bookkeeper, he had told Benjamin that the farm's finances had improved markedly under his management—much to Stephen's annoyance. Paul, who delighted in teasing his elder brother, observed the scene with a knowing smile. Stephen, however, seemed troubled and distant, as if he were battling something within his conscience. After a tense pause, he finally confided in them the weight he had been carrying.

He explained how Richard Foster had approached him in Bristol with an exorbitant offer for Fairfield Farm—an offer that he felt was too good to decline. The sale proceeds would enable them to acquire a new farm, three times more land and closer to Ashton Court. Thomas Smyth had already suggested several potential properties, and despite Fairfield Farm being a gift from his late father's will to the Akins, Thomas Smyth had given his blessing for the move. Still, he remained uneasy, especially given the animosity between the Fosters and the Stephens. He suspected the inflated offer was a calculated ploy to further provoke the Stephens family—a scheme Benjamin found both distasteful and deeply concerning.

The Stephens' long neglect of them mattered little now. The news of Jane's betrothal—confided by Ruth, now her personal maid—had struck Benjamin to the heart.

Seeing his distress, Ruth had taken pity and quietly embraced him, whispering that some among the servants— bound by oath to silence—knew of his secret courtship with Jane. She also admitted that Mr. Cropper, somehow, had found it out.

This revelation did not surprise Benjamin. He had long suspected that both Mr. Cropper and Mistress Mary were aware, and that they had quietly conspired to keep the matter contained. At least, he thought with a small measure of comfort, John and William remained ignorant of it—for now.

Awaiting his purchases, Benjamin was consumed by thoughts of the farms sale and the potential disruption to their family legacy, generating a sense of urgency and unease. Life often felt tedious, especially when his father returned, relegating him to a stable boy's role once more. While he loved working with horses, he yearned for more. His romance with Jane had enriched his life and filled him with happiness, but it had been cruelly snatched away, a dream shattered by reality, replaced by anger and resentment at his powerlessness to alter it.

The simplicity of the bakery and the delight of its wares did little to lift the weight on his shoulders as he contemplated the implications of his father's dealings with the Fosters. As Benjamin gathered his purchases—a small collection of spiced cakes nestled in a paper wrap and a fresh loaf of manchet bread, still warm from the oven—he felt the baker's crisp gaze upon him. The man, a stout fellow with flour-dusted hands, offered a knowing smile.

Young Master Benjamin," the baker said, placing the goods into his outstretched hands and quickly swiping the coins Benjamin had laid on the counter without checking them. "You heard we've got a new Rector coming to take charge of St. John's parish, our church, and the chapel in Chipping Sodbury. Apparently, he's a Puritan—one of those killjoys who won't let us enjoy our village sports or anything fun!" he said shaking his head in disapproval.

I had not heard," Benjamin remarked, reflecting upon Paul's disaffection from the Church.

"He bears a good Christian name, yet he is one of those Fosters—the oldest, by all accounts. That does not bode well if he is anything like his loan shark brethren."

Benjamin's eyes widened at this news, recalling the tales of the vicious and vengeful priest who had stirred the unrest against Catholics just months prior, a scandal outrageously attached to Father Rogers!

"Apparently, we might meet him next Sunday," the baker continued, his expression a mixture of concern and curiosity.

"Thank you for this, and may God bless your day." Benjamin remarked wanting to get home and share the news he had gleaned with his father.

"Farewell, young Master Akins. Do send my regards to your family, won't you?" the baker called as Benjamin departed.

"I shall see to it," Benjamin replied with a warm smile, before jogging back over to Thomas to share the news—that 'Devil Priest,' as Thomas sometimes called him, was coming to Little Sodbury.

As they continued back to the farm, enduring the uneven ruts along the Cotswold way, passing the manor to their right, they were met by a group of horsemen—a trio of armed cavalry clad in buff coats of the county horse, whom they had frequently seen practising their drills by the old Roman fort in recent months and were billeted at the manor.

"Begging your pardon, gentlemen, but this is business for the King," one cavalryman asserted, stepping his horse forward to block their path.

"This is the entrance to my farm. Please, move aside," Benjamin replied respectfully, though annoyance crept into his tone.

The trooper appraised him coolly, as if assessing his worth.

"Let the boy pass," came a voice from a fourth horseman descending the pathway from the farm. It was the recognisable figure of Owen Jones.

"Yes, Corporal," replied the trooper, wheeling his horse round while the other two made way for the cart. Owen offered a nod of acknowledgment, though his gaze bore a regretful look.

Upon reaching the main house, Benjamin caught sight of his father engaged in an intense discussion with the unmistakable figure of Sir Humphrey Redmain, who was flanked by William Stephens, mounted upon the familiar sight of Samson.

"I am telling thee, my horses are not for sale," Benjamin's father's voice rang out, now audible to Benjamin.

The flush of anger and irritation upon Sir Redmain's countenance was unmistakable. "I hold a commission of Array from the King, and we must purchase horses forthwith! I shall not ask thee again!"

Hearing the escalating tension, Benjamin quickly leapt off the wagon and strode purposefully toward the confrontation, deeply concerned about what he was hearing.

William interjected, "Mr. Akins, it's true we could take the horses, but given your family's friendship with mine, we'd offer a fair price—more than what the Array provides—considering the quality of your stock. Sir Humphrey and I both need additional mounts. If we don't take them, the Rebels will seize them without hesitation, likely offering far less. We simply cannot allow that!"

"Friends? What manner of friend comes to take away another's livelihood?" Benjamin shouted, his indignation boiling over.

"Benjamin, stay out of this, my boy!" Stephen admonished, holding out his hand to reinforce his authority.

Thomas had approached Benjamin's side, his sinewy frame tensed as if prepared for a fight, clearly matching Benjamin's agitation.

"Shut thy mouth, boy! Such insolence in the face of a King's order—father like son, I see!" bellowed Sir Humphrey. With that, the three cavalrymen from the main path came trotting forward, hands resting fiercely upon the hilts of their swords.

William, sensing the tempest brewing, leaned in close to Sir Humphrey, whispering calming words into the red-faced knight's ear, his hand resting gently on his shoulder.

"I understand this comes as a shock, but rest assured, if it be not us who purchase these horses, the Rebels shall soon take them. Quality horses such as these are rare now; everything is being brought up or taken. We need but two, and I promise we shall pay in hard coin, not promissory notes as the Array wants to offer," William expounded earnestly.

Stephen surveyed the troopers poised for action, their hands itching on their weapons, and noted the formidable countenance of Sir Humphrey, whose demeanour suggested he was prepared to strike at a moment's notice.

"It will have to be Miller and Ralph," Stephen conceded with a heavy heart.

"No! You can't take Ralph!" Benjamin's voice cracked, raw with desperation. Each word was a shield against the inevitable, as he surged toward Sir Humphrey Redmain, fists clenched so tight his knuckles shone white. "He is my horse, and I tell you—no!"

The air hung thick with anticipation, Then, with a sickening crack, the world tilted. Sir Redmain's riding crop, a polished extension of his cruel authority, lashed out, a brutal red streak blossoming across Benjamin's face. He crumpled, the taste of dust and defiance bitter on his tongue.

Steel hissed as the two cavalrymen, now flanking Sir Humphrey unsheathed their swords. The polished blades glinted menacingly under the unforgiving sun, each a promise of swift and brutal violence.

"How dare thee, scum!" Sir Humphrey bellowed, his face a mask of apoplectic rage. A dismissive wave of his hand unleashed his troopers.

Guilt twisting his gut, William hurled the heavy bag of coins, its contents a pathetic offering against the injustice unfolding. It landed with a muffled thud near Stephen, who knelt beside his son, his own face etched with anguish. Benjamin lay still, a crimson tide rising on his cheek, the once-bright blue of his eyes now clouded with pain and disbelief. Rage contorted features that were normally open and kind.

"Get up, Ben!" Thomas's voice trembled, a fragile tremor of fury in the face of overwhelming power. He glared up at Sir Humphrey; his youthful features hardened with a defiance that bordered on madness.

"This is an affront! You will answer for this!" Benjamin shouted, still seated on the ground, pushed himself up with grim determination, fury igniting within him. "I stand my ground against this tyranny! This isn't right; it cannot be lawful!"

"Enough of your insolence! One more word, boy, and I shall have you flogged!" Sir Humphrey spat, his patience evidently at an end. "You—" he gestured dismissively at the troopers, "—bring those horses forth. We do not have time to squander on the whims of a recalcitrant child. I will also have their saddles and bridles."

With an affirmative nod, the troopers dismounted and began to move, their steel glinting ominously in the morning sun. The grim determination in their eyes-only fuelled Benjamin's resolve to resist.

Stephen's hand, rough and calloused from years of toil, clamped onto Benjamin's shoulders, halting his reckless advance. He turned his son, forcing him to meet his gaze. The air crackled with unshed tears and unspoken rage. "Ben," he said, his voice a low rasp, barely audible above the thundering in Benjamin's ears, "that will suffice."

He saw the fire in his son's eyes, the incandescent love for the horses warring with a helpless fury. "I know your love for these horses runs deep, deeper than any well," Stephen murmured, his voice laced with a grief that mirrored Benjamin's own. "But there is naught that can be done... not in this moment." A muscle ticked in Stephen's jaw. "I shall seek redress for this outrage, I swear it. But now... now is not the time." The pained look in Stephen's eyes reflected not just the welts rising on his son's face, but the deeper wound to his spirit.

As the white-hot anger began to ebb, despair surged in to fill the void. The tears, held back by sheer force of will, now erupted, a torrent of grief and helplessness. The harder Benjamin fought to dam the flow, the more violently they broke free, carving tracks through the grime on his cheeks. A sob, ragged and broken, escaped his lips.

Stephen pulled his son close, enfolding him in a fierce embrace, a father's desperate attempt to shield his child from the harsh, unyielding gaze of the world. He felt the tremors racking Benjamin's frame, each one a testament to the storm raging within, the flood of emotion that had finally breached its dam. All he could do was hold him, a silent promise that somehow, someday, justice would be served.

"Take them to the horses, Thomas," Stephen commanded, casting a look toward William that brimmed with accusations, his sense of betrayal unmasked.

"I am truly sorry, Stephen, and Benjamin," William replied, his voice laden with sincerity. "You have been compensated well for your loss," he added, gesturing toward the bag of coins.

"There best be a sight more than thirty pieces of silver in that bag!" Stephen spat, his brow furrowing with discontent. "Tell your father I desire a word with him!"

William seized upon the biblical analogy, sensing the rising tension. "He has no part in this matter; it is purely a military necessity. Once these troubles pass, I will ensure they are returned to you, God willing I give you my word."

"Aye, a noble gesture indeed," Stephen retorted, "but it concerns another matter—one involving your father's friends, the Fosters. They seek to bring your father further trouble I suspect!"

William's brow furrowed in confusion. "The Fosters? What troubles do you speak of?"

A slow smirk spread across Stephen's face, a flicker of amusement in his eyes as he realised the Fosters' troubles had been carefully kept from William. "What do you know, truly?" he asked, a playful challenge in his tone, though the undercurrent was sharp. "I may share my knowledge... once I have spoken with your father!"

William offered no reply, his face a picture of confusion. The carefully constructed facade of composure cracking to reveal a blend of puzzlement and a growing unease. He sensed something was amiss, a thread he couldn't quite grasp.

In that moment, Benjamin turned, his heart seizing in his chest. He watched, paralysed, as Ralph and Miller were led away by Sir Redmain and the troopers. A wave of pure, agonising sorrow washed over him, a pain so profound it echoed the grief he'd felt at the passing of his mother, and loss of gentle kindness and fountain of knowledge that was his dear grandfather. Ralph, in particular, was more than just a horse; he was a confidante, a partner, a brother in spirit and his best friend.

Then, Ralph turned his head, his brown eyes locking onto Benjamin's. A mournful whinny escaped his throat, a sound laden with confusion and a premonition of loss, as if sensing Benjamin's anguish, mirroring it with his own. The sound tore through Benjamin, a fresh wave of pain crashing over him. The trooper, impatient and uncaring, yanked brutally on Ralph's head collar, silencing his protest and forcing him onward.

"Where are you taking them, William?" he choked out, the weight of his feeling thickening his voice until each word came with painful effort.

William, wrenched from his own reverie, met Benjamin's gaze. His eyes were shadowed with a tangled mixture of regret and resolve, the one hardened by necessity. He drew a steadying breath, mastering himself before he spoke.

"Only to the Manor for now," he said, his voice tight with restraint. "But we shall soon make our way north, to join the King." He hesitated, then added, "You are welcome to come to the Manor and take your leave properly. I shall arrange a meeting with my father, Stephen. My sincerest apologies, once more. This has been… poorly handled."

Just then, Sarah Akins and Paul emerged from the house. Sarah rushed to her brother's side, wrapping him in a comforting embrace, while Paul added his own disapproving glare to that already cast by his elder brother.

As William's eyes drifted to the strutting form of Sir Redmain, a chilling realisation settled over him. There was a perverse satisfaction in the man's expression—not only in seizing the horses but in the fear, he sowed among the honest folk who bred them. A cruel glint lit Redmain's eyes, as though he didn't see farmers and tradesmen but enemies of the Crown—Rebels deserving of punishment.

Disgust curled in William's stomach, bitter and corrosive. He shook his head in dismay, the weight of his own complicity pressing down like iron. With a subtle squeeze of his thighs against Samson's flanks, he urged his faithful horse forward, joining the departing troop. Each hoof-beat fell heavy, a reminder of the injustice now tied to his name.

Owen stood nearby, his usual stoicism cracked, a deep unease shadowing his features. It was a silent exchange between the two—a shared recognition of Redmain's cruelty, and the quiet shame of taking part in this act. William held his posture, noble and composed, but beneath it burned a simmering shame.

Chapter 40
Goodbyes

John Stephens stood indignantly before his son. "Why did you think it was acceptable to force our neighbours and friends—damn it—to sell their horses? This is their livelihood, William! How could you allow such a thing?"

"Father, I assure you, there was no ill intent!" William responded, his voice earnest, bordering on pleading. "Sir Redmain required a horse, specifically one capable of bearing him in his new cuirassier armour." He paused, a flicker of frustration crossing his face. "I could hardly point out the folly of wearing such antiquated armour on a modern battlefield, particularly after the considerable sum he'd invested in it!" He rushed on, explaining, "Few horses possess the requisite strength and agility to effectively carry such a load on top of the strains of battle"

"By all accounts, Sir Redmain had already set his eyes upon that very horse," William explained, urgency sharpening his tone. "With time so pressing, we could not afford to overlook a steed of such quality—fit for a king's soldier and near at hand. Swift action was needful. It is but a matter of time before Rebel horsemen ride this way. Many of the Bristol merchants lean toward Parliament, as do those in Gloucester, and the Rebels have already seized much of His Majesty's weapons and stores across the realm."

John's gaze, cool and unyielding, betrayed no softening under his son's justifications.

"They are mobilising father, and we must not for a moment believe..." William trailed off, the unspoken threat lingering in the air— "that the Akins will be spared when they seek recruits and horses."

"That may be true, son, but it doesn't justify how it was carried out. I've heard the son was struck—such conduct is unbecoming of a gentleman! And why did you take a horse that belonged to the boy?"

"I concede, Father; it was poorly handled. Sir Redmain didn't take kindly to the rebuff from the Akins and lacked the patience to understand. He was overly eager to offer them a promissory note, and it took considerable persuasion for him to part with what I believed was a fair price for such exceptional animals. As I need at least two warhorses for my rank, it was necessary."

"I see," John said at length, releasing a weary sigh. "Well, the harm is done. Stephen means to sell his stud to the Fosters—and now those vermin will hold land upon our very doorstep."

Mary sat in silence as the quarrel played out within the great hall. John had only moments before concluded his meeting with Stephen Akins and his son, who had laid out their grievances plainly — how they had been abused by Royalist cavalry and compelled, at sword point, to surrender two of their horses...

John had apologised profusely, promising to mend the situation, having been ill-informed about the whole affair. Stephen lamented the loss of his primary stallion, now left with only one remaining and an elderly retired Duke.

This lament led to revelation of the Fosters' offer to purchase Fairfield Farm—an agreement Stephen now felt compelled to accept. Distressed by the news and gripped by thoughtless panic, John forbade them from selling to the Fosters, a command that only deepened Stephen's indignation, rubbing salt into a fresh wound.

Angered, the Akins stormed out of the hall to say their

goodbyes to the horses, as William had agreed they could. John called after them, hastily promising to match the Fosters' offer, but his words fell on deaf ears. They left in silence, their disappointment heavy in the air.

Mary laid a gentle hand on her husband's arm, her touch a quiet plea for restraint. "Let tempers cool, John," she had murmured, her voice soft yet steady. "It would be best to let things settle before reaching out again."

John sighed, the strain of their circumstances was etched deeply across his face. He then spoke barely above a whisper. "I doubt we could afford such a purchase, Mary... or at least not act swiftly enough to secure it."

The unspoken truth had lingered between them.

Mary had gently pressed the matter, asking why the household funds seemed so short. She had suggested they go over the finances together—perhaps there might be a way to remedy the situation if they worked through it as one.

John had raised a hand, halting her before she could continue. But before he could speak, William had entered the hall—cutting the conversation short and shifting it toward the matter now at hand.

Now, in the present, William's voice turned incredulous at the mention of the Fosters, his tone sharpening into one of rebuke. "When were you planning to tell me about the trouble the Fosters have stirred up in my absence?"

This time, it was John who stood under the weight of his son's displeasure. But before voices could rise, Mary stepped between them, her tone composed but urgent. She recounted the events in full—every decision made, every attempt to secure an alliance—her voice steady even as the truth of their unravelling efforts hung like a storm cloud over the room. The promise they'd once seen had been steadily eroded by the ever-growing threat of war.

William listened in silence, though the pressure behind his eyes betrayed his mounting rage. He kept it in check—just barely. Self-control was a discipline he'd fought hard to master over the years, but now it frayed at the edges.

When Mary had finished, he spoke at last, his voice low and cold. "And you both decided I couldn't be trusted with this?"

Mary answered gently, "We had only just got you back from war. We didn't want to burden you—not when your father and I believed we had things in hand."

She turned to John, but he stepped forward, voice clipped and bristling. "William, I am master of this house. I've handled the matter. And let's not forget—you're about to leave us again, are you not? Best we learn to fend for ourselves in your absence." The sarcasm was unmistakable. So was the bitterness.

William's response came sharp and swift. "It doesn't sound to me like you have the situation in hand at all, Father."

"Enough!" Mary's voice cut through the air, cracking like a whip. "Both of you—stop this madness!" She stood rigid, her composure shaken. "How did it come to this? Have we all gone mad?" Her voice wavered now, heavy with the weight of a mother's fears. "We've sleepwalked into civil war, and now this manor—our home—is a target; a base for Royalist troops. And you, William…" She looked at him with eyes clouded in worry. "Your father is right. You're leaving again. To join the King. You're abandoning us once more."

The words hung in the air, raw and final. The unspoken

truth beneath them—the fear that this parting might be the last—tightened the silence that followed, and made the very walls seem to hold their breath.

"Mother, these Rebels must be crushed swiftly. It's imperative we secure a rapid victory; otherwise, this rebellion will spread like wildfire, igniting the entire country, just like the chaos across the English Channel. The horrors I've witnessed there cannot find their way here. We must put a stop to this Parliament's ambition for power. It's time for us to move on; as you say, we are indeed painting a target on this manor by staying here, you are correct. Our plan is to retreat to Berkeley Castle, gather more men, and push forward once we confirm the King's whereabouts—last I heard, he was in York."

In the main hallway, Jane listened intently, her heart pounding. She made a dash to the doorway and slipped out, running towards the stables, where she had overheard, the Akins were heading, taking this desperate opportunity, she had been longing for to speak to Benjamin.

In the dimly lit stables, Benjamin rushed to Ralph, throwing his arms around the horse's strong neck and burying his face in the thick, familiar mane. The scent—earthy but sweet, warm, and comforting—was like home. Ralph responded with a soft nicker, a low rumble of recognition and reassurance that pierced the gloom like a small, steady beacon.

The stable barn loomed vast around them, sectioned into unfamiliar blocks and filled with the mounts of the assembled troop—utterly foreign to Ralph. He, like Benjamin, had been raised on the quiet rhythms of a small farm, with the same stall, the same routines, day after day. Now, surrounded by strange horses and strange voices, Ralph must feel as lost and unmoored as his master - his former master now, the thought making Benjamin feel sick.

The only solace Benjamin found was the sight of Samson, Ralph's old paddock friend, reunited in the next stable. A flicker of warmth touched his heart as he watched the two horses playfully nipping at each other over the stable doors, their noses rubbing in a silent language of companionship. It was a small reminder of home, a thread of connection in this bewildering new reality.

Nearby, Stephen Akins rested a hand gently on Miller's neck. The horse stood proudly—an impressive specimen, the result of years of careful breeding and tireless dedication. To Stephen, Miller embodied everything a true hunter should be: strength, grace, perfect conformation and dependability.

Now, heartbreakingly, he was to be surrendered—repurposed as a war horse under a man who showed little empathy even for his fellow humans. They all feared for Miller under such brutish hands.

A bitterness rose in Stephen's chest. It was a quiet grief, a lament not only for the animal but for what his fate represented—a loss of beauty and purpose, twisted into the brutal service of war. The cruel irony stung: that a creature bred for harmony with man was now condemned to serve in his darkest work.

"I should have given that fool Castilio, instead," Stephen mused, a hint of regret in his voice.

"Castilio would have had him on the deck before you could say 'eat dust,'" Benjamin replied, managing a wry smile at the thought of the famously sensitive, sometimes unruly horse.

"Aye, you're right, lad, but sadly, Castilio will fetch more

money. Besides, Sir Redmain was asking for the big bay on his grand arrival," Stephen admitted.
"I thought that blotted bladder was eyeing up Miller during the rare times we saw Sir Redmain practising with his troop; I should have known," Benjamin remarked ruefully, shaking his head at his own oversight.

"Don't blame yourself, lad. This war means folks like us will be pushed around for what is rightfully ours. All the more reason we must accept the Fosters' offer. It's a generous one. I cannot afford to ignore now."

"But Father, can we truly trust them? They don't seem very kind or honest," Benjamin replied, trying to plant a seed of doubt in his father's mind, though he knew the futility of such an endeavour. Once Stephen had made up his mind, it was nearly impossible to change it. "What about old man Ward and Thomas? What will happen to them?"

"That's for them to decide. I'll speak to the Symes; they're the sort of men we need around the Estate. Thomas will be taking most of his best men from his estate with him to join the King. He has also sold many of his horses to his Royalist friends leaving mainly younger stock for myself and Tiago to manage.

At that moment, Jane entered the stables, her watery eyes locking onto Benjamin with a mix of desperation and longing. Her delicate features betrayed the ache inside as she took tentative steps toward him. "May I speak with Benjamin in private, Mr. Akin's?" she asked softly, her voice trembling with urgency beneath the veneer of respect.

Flickering with a moment of confusion, Stephen's face shadowed with concern as he studied her, then shifted to a look of dawning realisation upon Benjamin. "Very well, Mistress. I'll give you a moment. I'll wait outside," he said, offering a subtle, knowing glance to Benjamin before stepping outside to engage the trooper guarding the stable in conversation.

Benjamin's heartbeat quickened as he watched her approach, a mixture of worry and curiosity flooding his mind. "What brings you here?" he asked quietly his voice edged with concern.

Jane hesitated, then reached out to gently touch the red mark on his cheek. "I had to see you. I overheard the conversation—about Sir Redmain. Are you… are you hurt?" she almost whispered.

His jaw clenched involuntarily. "You mean your future father-in-law," he snapped, a bitter edge slipping into his tone filled with unbridled jealously.

She looked down, voice trembling. "Ben, do you think I really have a choice? If it were up to me, I'd marry you in a heartbeat. But my family's expectations… they won't allow it."

Her words cut deep, leaving Benjamin momentarily speechless. He felt a surge of frustration, fear, and heartbreak all at once. "I know I'm not worthy of your family's station. We're just peasants—you, so far above me. You even took my horse without permission and—" his voice broke, the anger giving way to anguish "—you hurt me in the process!"

"That's not fair, Ben! That was neither my doing nor my family's!" Jane replied, her eyes earnest. "My family thinks highly of you despite our different backgrounds." Jane's face fell, the weight of her guilt plain to see. Silence stretched between them, thick with unspoken pain and impossible longing.

"Soon, he will be your family. I wish you good fortune

with that. Sir Redmain is nothing but an arrogant fool. If that is what passes for proper breeding, then so be it. I truly hope his son is nothing like him. I have nothing more to say to you, Jane. It appears our courses are set.”

The words stung, heavy with emotion. Benjamin’s anger was palpable, a brittle shield against the raw yearning that threatened to consume him.

He longed to bridge the chasm between them, to confess the depth of his love and the pain of their separation, but the knowledge of their impossible situation held him captive. "Leave me, then, to say goodbye to my loyal friend," he said, his voice colder than he intended. The passionate fire in his eyes dimmed, replaced by a desolate regret. Pride, a cruel master, forced him to turn away, masking his true feelings as he faced Ralph.

Tears blurred Jane's vision as she whirled and fled the stables, a storm of emotion driving her. She raced past the bewildered trooper and Stephen Akins outside talking, leaving them to grapple with the sudden, inexplicable outburst.

Stephen sighed, the weight of all that remained unspoken pressing heavily on his shoulders. He stepped into the stable, his tone urgent but not unkind. “Ben, we must leave. Now.”

“Father, just a moment—please,” Benjamin pleaded, his voice tight.

“There is no time, you have much to answer for it would seem. We must go, it’s not a request,” Stephen said, more firmly this time.

Benjamin stood beside Ralph, gently running his fingers through the horse's forelock—a small gesture the gelding had always favoured. He lingered there, savouring every heartbeat of the moment, hollowed by sorrow: the pain he had caused Jane, the girl he loved yet could never truly claim, and the ache of parting with his faithful companion.

Leaning close, he pressed a soft kiss to Ralph's brow and whispered, his voice thick with emotion, "I'll mend this, somehow. We'll be together again—soon, I promise you, my dearest Ralph."

There were no tears left—only a deep, aching emptiness and a silent vow that this would not be the end. He forced himself to leave turning his back to follow his father, and braced himself for what he knew was to come.

Panic clawed at Benjamin as he crammed a meagre collection of garments and personal items into his satchel. The fragile peace of their home had shattered into shards the evening following their return from the Stephens'. His father had just left for Bristol to finalise the sale of Fairfield Farm, but the preceding night had been a maelstrom of accusations and bitter recriminations. The source? Benjamin's perceived folly in becoming entangled with Jane. Sarah, in her passionate defence of him, had only poured fuel on the fire by inadvertently revealing her knowledge of the clandestine affair.

The argument had been a crescendo of fury, voices rising and falling like waves crashing against a cliff. For a heart-stopping moment, it seemed father and son would come to blows, their anger a tangible force in the small room. But Sarah, always the anchor, had stepped in, her calm voice a fragile thread pulling them back from the brink. The uneasy truce that followed was no less agonising. In the weeks that ensued, a heavy, suffocating silence had descended upon the household. Stephen and Benjamin moved through their days like ghosts, performing their chores without a single word exchanged. The tension stretched, taut and unbreakable, until Stephen finally announced his trip to Bristol to finalise the deal with the Fosters. He promised a swift return, just long enough to sign the papers and collect the funds, after which they would uproot their lives and relocate to lodgings closer to Bristol and Ashton Court.

But even that promise offered little comfort. Today, a fresh wave of anxiety crashed over Benjamin. Tim Jones had arrived with alarming news: the Royalist horse troop was mobilising. They were ruthlessly stockpiling supplies for their campaign, seizing carts and provisions from the locals in the king's name. Tim, having learned the full extent of the family's troubles from his brother Owen, was enraged by their treatment. He urged Benjamin to hide their wagon, to conceal it at all costs should the soldiers return. Benjamin sank into a chair, his mind reeling. The path ahead was shrouded in uncertainty, the future a dark and ominous landscape. The absence of Ralph and Jane was a dull ache in his chest, a constant reminder of his powerlessness as the world he knew crumbled around him. Then, as if struck by inspiration, a daring thought seized him, and a plan formed.

Why not offer his services as a groom to William Stephens? If William truly had compassion, he could not refuse such a sincere plea for inclusion. Who better to tend to Samson and Ralph than he, then at least he wouldn't be parted from Ralph. Such an undertaking would lead to an adventure worth recounting for years to come. More importantly, Benjamin would ensure that Ralph and Samson received the care they deserved and who knew what opportunities might present themselves.

Thus, on this fateful night, he resolved to slip past his uncle Paul and stealthily make his way to the Manor, where he would endeavour to persuade William to take him into his service.

However, he had barely reached the halfway mark up the path to the manor when a voice rang out, sharp and commanding.

"Who goes there?"

The sudden challenge stopped Benjamin in his tracks, his heart leaping to his throat. A figure stepped out of the gloom—a vigilant trooper, carbine resting in the crook of his arm, eyes glinting beneath the shadow of his hat.

"I wish to speak with Lieutenant Stephens," Benjamin said, summoning what confidence he could muster. "About joining the troop."

The trooper gave him a long, appraising look, the corners of his mouth twitching in faint amusement—half sneer, half smirk. Still, duty prevailed over disdain, and with a curt nod, he turned. "This way," he said, gesturing toward the house.

Benjamin followed in silence, his boots crunching against the gravel, every step echoing with uncertainty. The looming manor ahead was lit by only a few flickering lamps, casting long shadows across the lawn. Something about the place felt changed—more guarded, less like home.

The trooper said nothing more, and Benjamin could not tell whether the silence was indifference or quiet warning. As they arrived at the main entrance, they were greeted cordially by Mr. Cropper the last person Benjamin wanted to see. He swiftly informed them that William was unavailable, and that the Stephens family was currently at their evening meal and not to be disturbed.

The trooper was about to comply, but Benjamin quickly inserted his foot in the doorway, his determination unwavering. "I beg your pardon, but I must see him," he insisted.

Mr. Cropper frowned, clearly displeased with Benjamin's forthrightness. "You are not welcome here," he retorted, his tone rigid as the sounds of their exchange carried into the main hall, the stand-off thick with tension, both unyielding.

"Who is it Mr Cropper" John Stephens' voice called out from within."
Mr Cropper hesitated before he replied, "It is Benjamin

Akins. He was just leaving, Master"

"Mr. Cropper, send him in before he does. I would like to speak with him" John replied

With a slight, triumphant smile, Benjamin met Mr. Cropper's glare before stepping through the hallway into the great hall, where he found Mary seated to John's left and William perched on his right. Next to him was Jane, who glanced up, her eyes widening in surprise at the sight of Benjamin.

"I wish to join the Royalist horse as William's groom—if he'll have me," Benjamin blurted, his voice trembling with a mixture of nerves and resolve. He stood as straight as he could, hands clasped behind his back in what he hoped passed for a proper soldier's bearing. At his feet lay his meagre belongings, bundled neatly within a small leather haversack, scuffed from travel and tied fast with cord.

"Really?" replied William, eyebrows raised in intrigue. "I admire your spirit, young Akins. I could certainly use a groom, as Owen is quite burdened with the duties of his rank and the tasks of preparing the troop. However, I must confess that I can scarcely afford a groom. The wage for a lieutenant is a mere five shillings a day, in addition to two shillings per horse for maintenance. Moreover, the timing of our payments remains uncertain, so it may not constitute very steady employment for you, young Benjamin." His tone took on a jovial note, particularly in the latter part, seemingly directed more towards his own father, John Stephens, than to Benjamin himself.

"I don't require much in terms of pay—just enough to get by," Benjamin replied eagerly, his heart racing at the prospect.

"What does your father say about this?" John interjected,

scrutinising him closely, seeming surprised by the revelation.

"I'm sixteen now, and he isn't opposed," Benjamin said—though it was a half-truth, for his father remained blissfully unaware of his intent.

John regarded him steadily. "I value my friendship with your father. To his credit—and despite all that has come to pass these last few weeks—he even offered me the chance to match the Fosters' price for your farm before he departed for Bristol. Regrettably, I could not do so without courting debt, and that I would rather avoid. Still, I would see you have his blessing, lest we strain the friendship further."

"He's still in Bristol and won't return for several weeks," Benjamin lied smoothly, though a note of unease crept into his voice. "I understand the troop is to depart on the morrow."

William raised an eyebrow. "Pray, how came you by such intelligence?"

Benjamin's lips curved in a faint, evasive smile. "I am resourceful," he said simply.
William chuckled. "Resourceful and inexpensive. It seems it's a deal I shouldn't refuse. I know you're an adequate horseman, but do you have any knowledge of arms and armour? Your duties will also include looking after my kit and tack as well as my horses. You will also need to be able to sew and cook our meals."

Benjamin bit his lip at the thought that he could once again get close to Ralph "I'm a quick learner. Anything I don't know now, I'll soon pick up" he said, trying to sound confident.
Jane, who had been silent until now, turned to her father.

"You should check with Stephen, Papa," she pleaded, concern etched on her face.

"Jane, my dear, this is a military matter," William said firmly, then, with a respectful glance toward his father, added, "And with respect, sir, I am not in a position to turn away good recruits."

He let the silence stretch for a moment before turning to Benjamin. "You may serve as my groom—on one condition. You will obey my orders without question. You are my servant, and your conduct will reflect upon me. Yet so long as you follow my command, you shall have my protection. Defy me, and I will have no use for you. Do you understand?"

"Yes, Master William," Benjamin replied, his grin breaking wide with triumph.

"And keep clear of Sir Redmain, if you can," William added wryly. "He remains my captain—at least until we rejoin the Prince, God willing."

Jane once again turned to her father with pleading eyes. Mary noticing, now interjected,
"I think it's a splendid idea," casting an intense stare at Jane that made her shrink back slightly.

"May I be excused, Father?" Jane said, already rising from the table, her food only half-eaten, shoving her chair back under the table harshly, before storming out the main hall.

"What ails dear Jane of late, I wonder?" John muttered, his brow furrowed in perplexity at her melancholy airs and mercurial humours. Turning once more to William, he added with a measure of cold restraint, "You have already done much to imperil my standing with Master Akins, yet you will do as you please, for it is plain your regard for your father's wishes withered long ago."

He rose, dabbing his face with a linen napkin in deliberate silence. "I shall retire to the study. There is no end to the papers that require my attention. It seems the only military matter ever to trouble me is the strain upon my purse and the upkeep of this gallant troop of Royalist horse I now find myself obliged to host."

As John took his leave, the others rose with polite nods, acknowledging his departure.

"Very well, Father, if that is your wish," William said quietly. "Be advised that Sir Redmain is expected in the morning. He has promised to leave payment for the fodder."

"Ha! Then I shall prepare a proper invoice for him. It's quite a hefty one," John muttered, reaching for the door to the library that led to his study. "Good evening to you all."

Turning then to Benjamin, William offered a faint glimmer of camaraderie. "You may sleep in my chamber tonight— the guest rooms are presently spoken for. You'll find my kit there; I'll instruct you on its proper care in due course. For now, let us return to our supper."

He gestured to the steward. "Mr. Cropper, be so good as to show my new groom to my room."

"Very well, Master William," Mr. Cropper replied dutifully. "Come along, Master Akins."

A mix of excitement and unease swirled in Benjamin's chest as he followed him up the stairs.
At the threshold of William's bedchamber, Mr. Cropper halted and turned abruptly. His expression darkened. "You

jumped-up stable hand," he hissed, the venom in his voice catching Benjamin off guard. "Humiliate me like that again, and you'll regret the day you were born. And if you so much as think of seeking out Mistress Jane tonight, I'll see you flogged raw." He stepped closer, voice low and cold. "By God, boy—you've been warned."

With that, he turned on his heel and stalked down the stairs, pausing only to cast a final, scathing glance over his shoulder. "I will be watching you, Mr. Akins."

Mary ascended the stairs some while later, after her conversation with William, her heart weighed down by a discourse that had offered scant comfort. Her earnest entreaties that he remain had fallen upon deaf ears, for William's sense of duty to Prince Maurice pressed upon him with unyielding force. He had received word that the Prince intended to sail back to England with his brother Rupert, bringing arms and men to strengthen their uncle's cause — the message set down in cipher, as was their practice in the Low Countries.

William deemed his presence essential, particularly as his soon-to-be father-in-law and the broader Berkeley family were concentrating Royalist strength at their ancestral seat, preparing to press northward and join the King. Though their numbers remained troublingly thin, recent reports delivered by Sir Redmain lent some reassurance. Recruitment efforts south, led by Sir Ralph Hopton, were yielding fruit, heartening Royalist hopes. It was a balm, however slight, against the fear that the southern counties might yet abandon their sovereign.

William lamented the situation; the Rebels seemed to hold London and many of the arm's stores, effectively stealing a march on the King. Communications had dwindled since the King moved north with his court.
Mary had questioned the prudence of choosing sides so

early, suggesting they might sit back and observe which way the wind would blow. To William, the very notion was unthinkable.

"I am a King's man," he said, his voice firm with conviction. "This family has ever stood loyal to the Crown. Forgive me, Mother, but I had thought you better than that."

Mary, seeing that her son's mind was firmly set, relented with a sigh of resignation. Not wishing to part on bitter terms, she offered a gentle apology. "Forgive me, William, for entertaining such unworthy thoughts. We are for the King, you know that—but we are against this dreadful prospect of civil war."

"On that we can both agree my dear mother" William made his way around the table to embraced Mistress Mary fearing his rebuke too harsh "I will come back to you, and when I do it will be for good" William promised

Before retiring to her own bedchamber, Mary sought out Jane. She found her daughter in bed, her tear-stained face a stark indication of her despair.

"Why, Mother? Why did you encourage William to take Benjamin? Now they're both in danger!" Jane exclaimed, her frustration erupting.

"My dear child, it is for the best that you and Benjamin are apart. Time heals many wounds, and you are betrothed to Henry. You must focus on that now, not on the Akins boy. We agreed that you would sever all ties with him," Mary said, her voice laced with a gentle, almost desperate plea.

"It's not that simple, Mother! I love him!" Jane's words were choked with the raw, fresh pain of tears.

Mary reached to embrace her daughter, settling on the

edge of the bed, but Jane recoiled, flinching away from her touch. "No, Mother! I won't forgive you or William if any harm comes to Benjamin. I don't want to marry Henry. His father is vile, and doesn't the saying go, 'the apple doesn't fall far from the tree'?"

Mary sighed, the weight of her daughter's heartbreak settling heavily on her shoulders. "Jane, I understand your feelings, but you must think of your future. Marriage to Henry Redmain offers security and stability during these turbulent times. Benjamin is a path that is not open to you. and cannot be open to you, can't you see that dear daughter."

Jane twisted her hands in her lap, her knuckles white with frustration. "But what about my heart, Mother? What good is security if it comes at the cost of my happiness? I cannot simply forget him, nor can I accept a life with someone I do not love."

Mary's own heart ached at her daughter's anguished words. She desperately wanted Jane to find happiness, but felt the cold, unyielding grip of reality tightening around their lives, suffocating any chance of true joy. "I do not wish for you to suffer, but sometimes we must make difficult choices for the greater good. Ruth will check on you throughout the night, and Mr. Cropper will be patrolling the hallway."

A flash of anger hardened Jane's tear-streaked face. "You're keeping me prisoner, then?" The question hung in the air, sharp and accusatory.

"If you wish to call it that, my dear," Mary replied, her voice hardening, brooking no argument. "I have been tolerant and understanding, but this ends here. You are confined to your room. Your brother will be in shortly to give you his farewell, so unless you wish your secret to be known to all, keep your noise down and pull yourself together and be the Mistress I know you to be: dutiful and obedient."

Down the long corridor in Williams bed chamber, Benjamin heard a firm knock at the door. "Who is it?" he called out.

"It's Ruth. Master William has sent me up with some bread and meat for you."

"Okay, come in." she entered the room with a plate of food and a jug of ale balanced on a serving tray. She placed them on a small writing desk in the corner of the room.

"Thank you," Benjamin replied, his attention fixated on the array of armour and weapons laid out on a cloth on the floor, he was crouched down examining the Wheel-lock Pistol's wonderful design, in revery of the skill of the maker.

"I hear you're leaving with the soldiers in the morning," said Ruth, stepping closer.

"Aye, that is correct," he answered, his tone practical.

"I will miss you," she said softly, now gaining Benjamin's full attention. Her eyes sparkled with a mix of longing and seduction, as if a veil had been lifted. In that moment, he couldn't help but notice how pretty she looked, not the great beauty that was Jane, but more approachable, perhaps. A quiet prettiness, with intelligent eyes, flecked with hints of mischief that now held him captive. She took off her Linen coifs, letting her long Strawberry Blonde hair spill past her shoulders like a whispered promise. The movement exposed the delicate curve of her neck, a detail he hadn't noticed before, and a fresh wave of awareness washed over him

"We have some time before Master William arrives, he has gone to speak to his father. I would like to be with you. I have always desired…. You, Ben"

The words struck him like a physical blow, Benjamin lurched to his feet as Ruth moved to embrace him, a knot of apprehension tightening in his stomach. His first instinct was to recoil, to put distance between them, but the raw vulnerability in her eyes, the naked yearning he suddenly saw there, held him rooted to the spot.

As her warmth enveloped him, a reluctant sigh escaped his lips, the tension bleeding away as he found a strange comfort in her closeness. The embrace was undeniably pleasant, a primal warmth blooming within him, a sensation far removed from the gentle affection he felt for Jane. But as her hand ventured lower, pressing herself against him, a wave of conflict crashed over him. He allowed the moment to linger, a silent battle raging within as conscience wrestled with desire.

"Please, Ruth, this isn't right." The words escaped him, a softer plea than he intended, as he gently, almost reluctantly, pushed her away, struggling to maintain his composure. "I'm sorry. You're a very attractive girl, and I'm fond of you, please believe me. But my heart belongs to-"

Before he could finish, she surged forward, her lips seeking his. Again, Benjamin didn't react as swiftly as he should have, his hesitation a silent invitation. He managed to pull away, the taste of her kiss a lingering temptation.

Ruth's expression crumpled, disappointment etched on her features, yet she pressed closer, her voice a desperate whisper. " I just want to be with you." With renewed determination fuelled by his hesitation, she kissed his neck, her fingers threading through his hair, pulling him close. "Benjamin, why can't you see? Jane is beyond your reach, a fantasy. I am real, Ben. I care for you. No—I love you," she declared passionately, her breath hot against his skin. "Let us be together tonight. I expect nothing from you, just to have you in the moment." Ruth said pleading

"You're right. Jane is beyond me," Benjamin said, pushing her back once more, this time with a newfound resolve hardening his features, his voice steady. "But it wouldn't be right for me to use you in that way, nor would it be respectful to you, nor honourable and proper. Please, let's pretend this didn't happen. Besides," he grasped for a lifeline, an excuse that might soften the blow, "do you not see that Tim is longing for you? It wouldn't be fair to him."

"Please, Ben," she pleaded, her voice laced with a raw desperation that tugged at his resolve, "I am to Tim as you are to Jane. If that's your choice, so be it. But you're missing out, I assure you." She bit her lip, her eyes gleaming with a suggestive promise that sent a shiver down his spine. "When the reality of life hits you, when you realise Jane is nothing more than a dream, I'll be here waiting. I could be yours; you only need to take me. Think about that tonight when you're alone on the floor of your master's bedchamber." She smiled, a slight chuckle escaping her lips, the mirth barely concealing the sting of rejection.

Putting her coif back in place before leaving, She left a thick silence behind. Benjamin felt a wave of relief wash over him, though it was tinged with a flicker of regret for what might have been—a thought he quickly rebuked himself for. He recalled the stern warnings from Sunday sermons: the perils of temptation, the sin of fornication, and the snares laid for the unwary. A quiet gratitude stirred in him that he had managed to resist.

And yet, unease lingered. He couldn't shake the guilt that he hadn't recoiled more swiftly—that in his hesitation, some part of him had betrayed Jane. He had never been with a girl in that way, nor did he intend to be until marriage. That conviction, shaped by faith and upbringing, was etched deeply into his soul.

He knelt, offering a silent prayer to God, seeking guidance and asking for the Holy Spirit to be with him for the trials that lay ahead. Laying on the hard floor, he closed his eyes, striving to keep his mind focused on his new course and path, batting away the alluring thoughts of Jane and the more primal, unsettling images of Ruth, stirred by her unseemly suggestions.

William, standing in the library, knocked gently on the door of his father's study. "Enter," John called, his voice weary.

William found his father hunched over a mountain of account books in the flickering candlelight, the shadows dancing across his brow as his tired eye strained to look at the figures. A half-empty glass of wine sat beside a clutter of papers, a testament to the late hour.

"Father, I—"

John raised a weary hand to stop him, his gaze lifting from the papers, fixing William with a sharp, knowing look. "You are about to ask me for money, am I correct?"

"Well yes, Father. As I mentioned, I am uncertain when I will receive my wages; at present, all expenses are being drawn from Sir Redmain's purse for the troop, and he is unlikely to forward to me what I am owed anytime soon. I will require some means to get by, though I can always repay you upon my return," William explained earnestly, though a flush crept up his neck under his father's scrutiny.

"Ha! My son, when have you ever repaid me?" John shot

back, exasperation sharpening every word. "Do you even grasp the debt you left in your wake? I was near ruined settling with your creditors and their cursed interest. You return after two years of campaigning with a worn-out nag, a few fine outfits, and a packhorse I was obliged to repay Owen for!"

"Well, yes, Father. Living expenses were quite high, as was the fare to return home," William stammered, his confidence faltering.

"William, I did not just descend from the last shower! Owen returned home with ample coin, and I dare say he would have spent less than you, yet he would have been paid far less to match, yet you are broke. I am merely grateful that was the only debt I was obliged to settle upon your return," John said, his gaze drifting back to his papers, scratching something off a list with unnecessary force.

"I am thankful, Father," William responded, feeling like a scolded boy of ten.

"I am grateful you're home—that is all that mattered to me," John began, his voice low and strained. "But now you're preparing to leave again. Do you even comprehend what it does to your mother when you're gone?"

He paused, the weight of unspoken burdens settling between them. "I've spent the past two years trying to untangle the mess of your debts—quietly, without ever letting her know the full extent of your folly. I did it to spare her the shame... and to protect you."
His expression darkened with the memory. "You know how pious she becomes when the mood takes her. She couldn't understand why I was pleased at your leaving in the first place, not knowing what trouble you'd stirred. She blamed me for every day of your absence—blamed me when I tightened the purse strings, when I sold off my fine

hunter and the carriage team, when I began managing the household on a shoestring."

John's voice cracked slightly, his frustration rising. "She wouldn't hear of raising rents—not even modestly. I even had to scrimp on our church offering... giving as little as I dared. Do you understand? I was left to bear it all, while she looked to me for answers I couldn't give." His words spilled out now, the dam broken—years of resentment and buried exhaustion rising to the surface.

"I am truly sorry, Father; I thought you had forgiven me," William said, abashed, the weight of his past mistakes pressing down on him.

"I do, but I fear you have broken our promise. I am, to be truthful, past caring; you will soon become a husband and, God willing, one day a father, and you will have responsibilities. Hopefully, you will marry the lovely Charlotte Berkeley, who will bring you an element of your own wealth. You will have to be a provider for her and, one day, run this household once I leave this world." John paused, his gaze drifting towards the window, lost in contemplation for a moment.

"William, did you know there was an opportunity to be freed from the burdens of this place? I would have had funds to buy you a place of your own, and myself, your mother and sister could have lived in a place more manageable than this." He said, a look of profound regret etched across his face.

"No, what do you mean, Father?" William asked, perplexed, a knot of unease tightening in his stomach.

"Yes, your mother omitted that detail. The Foster family made an offer to purchase this estate for a very handsome sum. And more importantly, we would be free from this feud!" John slammed his fist onto the table in frustration, making the candle flicker wildly.

"Why did you not accept it, then, Father?" William inquired, his voice barely a whisper.

"Because of them." John gestured wearily toward the imposing portrait dominating the study. The first Sir John Welch stared down from the canvas, a man strikingly like William – strong, resolute, and forever captured in oil. "He fought at Bosworth Field," John continued, his voice a blend of pride and bitter resentment. "He won Tudor favour, secured this manor, and transformed it into the house you see today." The knight's stern gaze seemed to follow them, a silent judgment emanating from the aged canvas.

John's shoulders slumped slightly, his voice softening. "Everything I've done has been for your mother, for the legacy that will be passed down to you and your sister. I strive so desperately to please everyone, and I fail miserably. Even your sister, the usual ray of sunshine, has been clouded over recently; I can't discern the reason why. And you, my son," he continued, turning his gaze fully to William, "you've relegated me to the role of a mere tenant in my own home these past months. Shutting me out of all matters concerning your military pursuits, only deigning to converse when you require funds." The fight seemed to drain out of him, leaving behind a deflated and resigned figure.

"Father, that is unfair. I hold you in the highest esteem. I only aim to protect you, I assure you," William replied with a pained expression, guilt twisting in his gut.

"Yet you are content to have a troop of Royalist horse here, consuming our resources and disrupting our friends' livelihoods and even taking from the tenants and village folk of old Sodbury. William, I must say; if this is how you treat family and friends, I can only imagine how you treat your enemies."

John placed a hand upon his brow, exhaling heavily. "You may have forty shillings to ensure the Akins boy receives a reasonable wage and to keep your own head above water but promise me you will return home safely and as soon as you can for your mother's sake, if not mine. Be sure to look after the Akins lad, and do visit your sister now to bid her a proper farewell; you were once very close. You have kept your distance from us all since your return." He counted the shillings into a worn leather purse and tossed it to William, who skilfully caught it in his hand.

As William reached for the door, John moved quickly to a small drawer and drew forth an intricately carved wooden box. Opening it, he revealed a delicate gold locket that glimmered softly in the candlelight.

"Here—take this," he said quietly. "From me to you. A gift, if you will."

William accepted the locket, his calloused fingers, still bearing the marks of years gripping a sword, carefully tracing the delicate filigree. He flipped it open, revealing two miniature portraits: his mother, and Jane. The resemblance, strikingly accurate and recent, snagged at his heart. "Thank you, Father. It's a thoughtful gift," he managed, the words feeling stiff and strangely foreign on his tongue.

He cleared his throat. "I shall do that." He hesitated, struggling to bridge the chasm of unspoken emotions that yawned between them. "And I apologise; it was not my intention to create such distance." He shifted his weight; his gaze fixed on a point somewhere beyond his father's shoulder. "Father… it's been…hard to adapt back to normal life, as it were." The words tumbled out, clumsy and insufficient to convey the stark, jarring contrast between the brutal realities of war and the suffocating civility of the drawing-room.

The silence lingered, heavy with all that had gone unspoken.

"I promise to return as soon as I am able," William said at last, his tone carefully measured. "And I will write when I can. Once we have crushed these rebels—and with that, perhaps reclaim our place among the higher ranks of society."

His voice hardened slightly with conviction as his eyes flicked toward the grand portrait of his forebear, the stoic face staring down from the canvas like a reminder of duty and legacy. A vow passed silently between them: To restore our honour. "I bid you good night," he added, offering a respectful bow that felt more ceremonial than heartfelt.
Without waiting for a reply, William turned and walked from the room. He closed the study door slowly, deliberately; the soft click of the latch sounding like a final word—a quiet attempt to seal in the tension that still crackled in the air behind him.

"And may God protect you, my dear son," John murmured, scarcely above a whisper, his gaze fixed on the closed door long after William had gone. The candle guttered in its socket, casting long, wavering shadows that danced like spectres upon the walls—a mute reflection of the fears that gnawed at his heart, not for William alone, but for all his household.

Chapter 42
Road to Berkeley Castle

The troop of horses rode down the winding country tracks, their rhythmic clinking of tack, swords, and armour harmonising with the sound of hooves striking the dry earth. The melody of their journey was further complemented by the creaking wheels of three wagons, heavily laden with supplies, weapons, and armour necessary for the days ahead. Dust kicked up in their wake as the morning sun cast a golden light over the vibrant greens of the English countryside, painting a picturesque scene of adventure.

Benjamin felt happier than he had in a long time, as if the weight of his old life was being left behind. He was back astride Ralph, his loyal steed and trusted friend. The familiar warmth of the horse beneath him instilled a sense of comfort and purpose. William, riding Samson, led the way at the front alongside Sir Redmain, while Benjamin was content to be at the rear with the baggage wagons, accompanied by the quartermaster, Farrar, and the groom of Sir Redmain. The camaraderie among the riders infused the air with an exhilarating mix of excitement and anticipation.

As they pressed forward, Benjamin's thoughts spiralled back to their departure. He recalled the image of Jane standing by the window, her expression a complex blend of sadness and resolve as she watched him ride up the long private path and through the gates. He assumed William had offered his farewells in private—it had been some time before he appeared in the bedchamber. When he finally did, he'd given Benjamin a crash course in weapons and gear maintenance, listing his expectations with brisk authority before they settled into a restless sleep in the early hours.

The farewells had varied starkly in tone. Glen Jones, with his wife Irene and their son Tim, had exchanged tearful goodbyes with Owen—their emotions raw, unrestrained, and wholly sincere. The Stephens family, by contrast, displayed a more composed front, their emotions mastered and masked behind a veneer of propriety. They bore the weight of duty as though it were part of their attire.

Amidst it all, Ruth had approached him, her voice a soft murmur of apology for the night before. She had asked if she might hug him goodbye—as a friend—and Benjamin, caught in a tangle of feelings, had seen no harm in it. The embrace was brief, yet charged with something unspoken, a moment that lingered in his thoughts long after they parted. He remembered how she glanced toward the window —toward Jane, who stood watching.

Summoning his courage, he had waved. Jane remained motionless, her expression unreadable.

Just then, Mistress Mary Stephens swept in, neatly placing herself between him and Jane's gaze. A warm smile lit her face, but her eyes hinted at something less benign.

"I'm glad to see you're moving on," she had said, casting a knowing glance after Ruth, who was already halfway to the house, her step light—relieved, perhaps.

"Um, Mistress Stephens—Ruth is just a friend," he had offered, hoping to clarify.

"I see." Her smile faded, her voice taking on a cooler edge. "While I wish you well, do look out for my son. And I urge you—move on with your life."

He had feigned puzzlement, but she leaned in, lowering her voice.

"Please. I know all that has transpired," she whispered. "I understand—you're young, full of feeling—but we live in a world where we cannot always follow our desires."

Then, softer still, she continued "We cannot choose the paths our hearts dictate. Sometimes, we must use our heads. If you truly care for my daughter, the kindest thing you can do—for her and for yourself—is to let her go. You're a handsome young man with some prospects. In time, you'll find someone like dear Ruth, someone who can make you happy."

Her tone was almost maternal, yet beneath the surface, there was a quiet steel—a veiled warning wrapped in warmth.

"Mistress Mary," he had said gently, "I appreciate your honesty. But I fear I will never feel for another what I feel for Jane." He had looked down, the weight of the truth heavy in his voice.
"Still… for her sake, I will try. Perhaps this journey will help us both find hope again."

"That's very wise of you, Benjamin." She had nodded, her manner composed. "May God keep you safe—and watch over my son." With that, she had turned back toward the house, her gestures restrained, her steps measured and deliberate.

As the troop had made its way down the tree-lined private path, Sarah and Thomas had appeared in the distance, waiting with anxious anticipation. In their hands were the notes he had left behind—bittersweet tokens of his departure. He remembered the look on Thomas's face, a blend of sadness and excitement, caught between mourning their parting and the thrill of the unknown. Sarah, in contrast, had worn an expression etched with concern and quiet disappointment.

"What do you think you're doing, Benjamin? How can you leave without telling Father?" she had called out as he momentarily pulled out of the column.

Her words had struck him hard. He had guided his horse closer, lowering his voice so William wouldn't hear. "Please, hush, dear sister," he had said gently. "I need to do this, Sarah. I want to see what lays beyond these fields. And I promise—I'll make sure Ralph, Samson, and Miller return safely."

"But Ben…" she had said, her voice trembling. "You don't understand the dangers ahead for those who ride to war. Think of Thomas Ward's father—he never returned from the king's last campaign."

"I understand," he had replied, trying to keep his voice steady. "But I have to follow this path. It's my chance to stand for something greater... to be my own man. And to protect the horses."

He remembered how she had stepped back, her eyes brimming with unshed tears, torn between pleading and letting go. Thomas had placed a comforting hand on her shoulder as she struggled to stay composed.

"Just promise me you'll take care of yourself," she had whispered.

He never forgot the way she said it—barely above a breath, but heavy with love and fear. "I promise," Benjamin had replied, feeling a swell of determination mixed with an undercurrent of sorrow at the impact of his decision. "Look after my sister, Thomas, and keep an eye on the farm. Father will need you in my absence."

With one last glance at Sarah, he had turned his focus toward the road ahead, his mind sharpening as he prepared for the adventure to come, batting away his reservations and feelings of guilt.

Back in the present, as the troop forged onward, Benjamin felt the rhythm of hooves beneath him blend with the steady heartbeat of the land.

Before long, they entered the familiar bustle of Chipping Sodbury's market square. The sun hung high, casting a golden glow over the vibrant stalls where merchants called out their wares—fresh produce, bolts of cloth, tools, and trinkets. The sights and sounds stirred a quiet excitement in Benjamin, a comforting echo of the world he knew. Yet something felt different now.

As he rode in alongside the King's men, pride swelled in his chest. He was no longer merely an onlooker—he was part of something new, something greater than himself. His eyes lifted to the troop's standard—the Gideon—fluttering in the breeze, carried by the cornet, third in command. Nearby marched Owen Jones, ranked just below as the troop's corporal, his bearing stern and watchful.

Among themselves, the men had begun to call their unit The Second Sons—a wry nod to their shared lineage, and to the fact that few of them were heirs to anything but their own ambition. "Our fathers' spares," they often joked, though behind the laughter lay a quiet resolve to prove themselves something more.

The convoy comprised thirty-eight riders, three wagons each with its own driver, and six spare horses, one of which was Miller. Sir Redmain's groom led Miller, one of the three chargers the knight had brought along, monitoring the horse with a practised hand as Benjamin settled into the rhythm of the ride.

As they made their way through the busy market street, townsfolk parted for the troop. Beneath the curious gazes of the townspeople, Benjamin noticed a mix of hostile looks and envious glances directed at the handsome cavaliers. Some young ladies swooned at the sight of the well-groomed riders; their admiration unmistakable.

"Let's halt here," Sir Redmain ordered as they reached a clear area near a trough. "Let the horses drink and rest for a moment."

"Sir, we have a long journey ahead, and there are too many distractions here that could lead to trouble," William said quietly in response to Sir Redmain's command, casting a sideways glance at the ladies engaging some of the troopers in flirtatious conversation.

Sir Redmain shot back, impatience flaring in his voice, a vein throbbing visibly in his temple. "Lieutenant Stephens, let me make this perfectly clear to you, so you're under no illusions whatsoever: in no uncertain terms, I am the captain of this troop. I will not tolerate second-guessing on every decision I make. I expect a lieutenant who executes orders swiftly and without question. I expect an obedient lieutenant. Is that clear?" He punctuated his words with a sharp, unwavering stare, boring into William as if daring him to even consider a challenge.

William's jaw tightened almost imperceptibly, but he maintained a facade of composure. "Very well, Sir," he replied, his voice carefully neutral, betraying none of the resentment that simmered beneath the surface.

As the horses drank their fill and the sun climbed higher in the sky, Benjamin took a moment to survey the lively market scene. The sound of laughter and chatter from the townsfolk sharply contrasted with the gravity he felt swirling in his gut. They were headed toward uncertainty, and he couldn't shake the feeling that for every joyous moment, unseen perils lurked around the corner, which scared and excited him in equal measures.

After allowing the horses a rest, Sir Redmain signalled for the soldiers to bring out jugs of ale. "Let them indulge; we have a fair journey ahead" he ordered, casting renewed eyes toward the flirtatious ladies who had captivated some of the troopers.

"Corporal Jones, I want you to put out a call for recruits" he commanded. "Surely the allure of soldiering and the splendour of our ranks will attract a few more riders. Get to it at once."

William added "We could do with a Saddler if you can find one Corporal."

A handful of men stepped forward, showing interest, while others lazily lounged about. Benjamin noticed William's growing frustration; he felt powerless to countermand his captain. Resigned, he grabbed a jug of ale, taking a few refreshing sips as the afternoon warmth settled in.

Still tending to the mounts, Benjamin bestowed special attention on Ralph and Samson when his ear caught sounds of shouting coming from the direction of the Portcullis Inn followed by the sound of shattering pottery. Curiosity piqued, William and Owen strode over to investigate the commotion.

As they neared the Inn, the sounds of a scuffle intensified —boots scuffing against cobbles, muffled grunts, and the strained cries of a man in distress. Rounding the corner, they came upon a trooper pinned against the brick wall of the Inn's entrance, his face twisted in pain and alarm. Two burly figures held him fast while three more loomed in the shadows, their features obscured but their intent clear.
"Give us the coin you owe, and we'll let you go," growled a voice—gravelly, unmistakable.

From the knot of men stepped Samuel Foster. He turned at the sound of footsteps, his eyes narrowing at the sight of William. A smug grin curled across his brutish face, the expression made all the more grotesque by his nose— clearly broken, bent at an unnatural angle. The sight confirmed Benjamin's earlier suspicion beyond all doubt.

Seeing red, the simmering anger that had been brewing within since being informed of the goings on, William's anger erupted. Ignoring the usual protocols, he strode forward without hesitation, the countless tales of Samuel's underhanded dealings and ruthless acts flooding his mind. He channelled his rage into a lightning-fast right hook, catching Samuel completely off guard. The force of the blow, amplified by years of training and pent-up frustration, sent him crashing to the ground. Blood splattered like a grotesque fountain across the cobblestones, staining the already filthy street.

As Samuel's two brutish companions, roused to action by their leader's sudden downfall, lunged forward, William met their charge with impressive skill. His trained reflexes kicked in; he skilfully blocked their clumsy strikes, deftly manoeuvring around their wild swings with swift and balanced footwork, a whirlwind of controlled aggression against their brute force.

Owen, a true powerhouse among their ranks entered the fray, sending one attacker sprawling to the ground with a single punch that would knock a mule off its feet. This moment gave William the opening he needed to swiftly handle the other would-be assailant. With all the grace of a gentleman who had tragically skipped etiquette lessons, he delivered a deliberate kick straight to the groin. The unfortunate target's eyes bulged in disbelief as he doubled over, clutching himself in abject agony, eliciting a low groan from the onlooking crowd. It was a sight that— despite the gravity of the situation— might have sparked laughter, had the moment not been so serious.
The two men who had been holding down the trooper turned to confront these fresh threats, but soon a swarm of additional troopers arrived, eager to join the fight and rescue their comrade.

"What is happening here?" Sir Redmain appeared pushing through the gathering spectators, flanked by several troopers with swords drawn, ready to spring into action.

"He did lay hands upon me!" Samuel cried, one hand pressed to his bloodied nose, his voice warped into a high, nasally whine. He thrust a trembling finger toward William, who stood hatless and unkempt, his hair in disarray and a grin tugging at the corners of his mouth. Behind him, the supposed assailants—now shawled and thoroughly battered—looked far the worse for the encounter. "That rogue—and his unruly company—fell upon one of our own like common footpads, Sir.

The trooper, having been rescued, was now bloodied and visibly shaken, confirmed the accusation.

"This… gentleman owes us money, and his father claims he has fled, refusing to pay the debts of his good-for-nothing son. We found him here buying ale for his friends, dressed in an expensive buff coat and carrying a fancy sword with coin to spare. We were merely reminding him of his debts," Samuel spat, blood trickling down his face.

"By God, sir, you have assaulted a King's soldier and officer! I shall have you hanged for this outrage!" Sir Redmain barked, fury contorting his features.

""No, you shall not!" interrupted a crisp, authoritative voice, cutting through the charged atmosphere. Emerging from the gathering crowd, Father Foster, a tall, imposing priest, exuded an aura of quiet resolve, his dark cassock flowing around him. Yet, beneath the facade of piety, a sinister coldness flickered in his gaze.

"Father Foster," Sir Redmain said, recognising him with a curt nod, sliding his sword back into its scabbard. "Is it not curious how you always seem to appear at the scene of civil unrest? One might think you were orchestrating it."

"It's quite curious, Sir Redmain, how trouble seems to find you," the priest countered smoothly, his tone silkily polite, though contempt flickered beneath the surface. "My purpose was simply to welcome you to my new parish. However, I must also inform you that two troops of horse are en-route from Gloucester, dispatched by Parliament's orders. They're investigating a rogue militia from this county —one that has been… ignoring Parliament's directives. That wouldn't be your troop, would it, Sir Redmain?" He arched an eyebrow, the unspoken threat hanging in the air, fully aware of the answer.

"We respond to the King's Commission of Array," Sir Redmain snapped back, his face reddening with anger. "Parliament has no power without the King's approval, and this document, signed by His Majesty himself, is the only lawful authority we recognise, priest." He gestured dismissively towards Father Foster.

"Time shall tell what is lawful and what is not. In that case, I would respectfully ask you to withdraw; your presence here, it is unsettling my flock. It would spare them any misunderstandings when Parliament's forces arrive to carry out their investigations." The priest's words were a thinly veiled threat, a promise of future trouble.

"We were planning to move on shortly. Nonetheless, we do not wish to cause your flock any unnecessary trouble," Sir Redmain replied, his voice laced with sarcasm.

"Apart from depriving them of their goods and livestock, so I have been told," Barnabus Foster shot back, stepping forward, his eyes blazing with righteous indignation. "A 'tax' levied at sword point is hardly a charitable contribution, is it?"

"As I said," Sir Redmain retorted, his patience wearing thin, "as per the King's Commission of Array, they will all receive fair payment once the rebellious factions that plague this Kingdom are eradicated." He offered a sardonic smile, a flash of white teeth in his grim face, before turning away from the scornful priest. "Round up the men, it's time to go" Sir Redmain said to William and Owen.

"Saddle up, men! We're leaving!" Owen bellowed, his voice ringing across the high street, invigorated by the brief scuffle. The order cut through the din like a drumbeat, rallying the troops. A few were slow to rise—still clinging to their jugs of ale and the flirtatious company of local women, their loyalties clearly divided between duty and delight.

But there was iron in Owen's voice—and a glint in his eye sharp enough to slice hesitation from the air.

"I said move...Now!" The men scrambled to their saddles, some with reluctance, others with haste, ale forgotten and farewells to local beauties left half-spoken. Amidst the flurry, William turned to Samuel Foster, a smirk curling at his lips.

"I believe I've mended thy nose, Master Foster," he said with a dry chuckle, then turned smartly on his heel to re-join the ranks.

"This is not finished, Stephens!" Samuel howled, voice thick with fury and pain. Blood sprayed anew from his ruined nose, each word marking his fine coat with fresh crimson.

"Join the rebels," William called back, his tone laced with scorn, "dress yourself like a soldier, and I'll meet thee on the field. Try and fight like a man—rather than skulking behind schemes like the nest of vipers you call family."

Samuel spat a dark glob of blood and spittle onto the earth —a defiant gesture aimed squarely at William. "Perhaps I just might," he growled, his voice low but edged with menace, eyes glinting with cold promise. "Aye, you may count on it, William." The words hung in the air like the shadow of a drawn blade—an oath, plain and bitter, fore-telling a reckoning yet to come.

William laughed—a short, sharp bark laced with contempt. "Good! I shall welcome it," he said. "But be warned—next time, it shall not be fists you feel, but cold steel." He tapped the hilt of his rapier for emphasis, then turned and, in one fluid motion, swung himself into the saddle. As he settled into the seat, the image of Samuel's bloodied, wrathful face lingered in his mind—bringing with it a flicker of grim satisfaction. At last, a measure of redress for the slights dealt to his family.

As the troopers mounted, a boisterous group – friends of the indebted soldier, fuelled by ale and anticipation – raised a mocking toast. "Three cheers for the Lieutenant! The loan shark slayer and the dirtiest fighter in the county!" The raucous cheers echoed through the village square, drawing laughter and back-slaps from the ranks. William cast a final, contemptuous glance at Samuel Foster before leading his troop onward. The receding hoof-beats left Samuel Foster choking on his rage, turning to berate his own men in bitter frustration.

The familiar landscapes of home blurred as they rode onward. Benjamin couldn't shake the image of Jane's brother, so quick and brutal in the fight. He, on the other hand, had never thrown a punch in his life. The prospect of William finding out about him and Jane, and facing that same fury, sent a shiver down his spine. He concluded that flight would be the best option.

As they rode onward, the trees lining the path began to thin, revealing the rolling hills that led toward Berkeley Castle. The sun hung low in the sky, casting the last warm rays upon the troop. William ordered scouts ahead to check for rebels, much to Sir Redmain's amusement. "William, you are very jumpy. We are not even officially at war; these rebels have no lawful authority. Relax a bit; you're unnerving the men."

"We must be vigilant," William said earnestly. "We know not how matters stand—there may already have been a battle, for all we can tell."

"Don't be foolish, William," Sir Redmain replied with a

dismissive shake of the head. "These rebels will scatter the moment they set eyes upon the King. This is but a formality. Who in his right mind would dare raise arms against an anointed sovereign?" His tone carried amusement, as though humoured by William's caution.

But William remained unconvinced. The smirk faded from his face as he thought on the growing unrest across the realm. "You underestimate them, Sir," he said gravely. "They are desperate men. Parliament has pushed too far, and now many see no path of return. They will fight—clinging to the power they have seized, knowing that if they fail, they lose not only their cause but their heads. Desperation breeds dangerous choices. We must keep watch and have the men ready."

Reaching the crest, the vast lands of Berkeley Castle unfolded before them, gilded by the setting sun. The castle, a bastion of power and security, promised welcome respite for the exhausted men and horses. For the first time since departing, William thought of Charlotte Berkeley, a distant relative of the castle's owners. The connection to her family, he realised, might soon be his own. He felt a pang of guilt for not visiting Horton Halls to say goodbye, praying his hurried letter would be enough, to satisfy the Mistress for now.

Chapter 43
Change of Order, August 1642

In the historic parish church of Old Sodbury, Mary, John, and Jane took their places in the gentry pews near the front, beside Lady Beatrice Redmain and her son Henry, who—despite the solemnity of the occasion—cast keen glances at his betrothed, much to Jane's discreet annoyance. Both were recent attendees, seated among other local notables. Many sons and husbands were notably absent, having answered the Royalist call to arms—the Berkeley's having raised their own half-troop of local gentlemen. Behind them, the common folk—tenants and servants alike—filled the rear of the church.

Father Barnabas Foster, a commanding presence, greeted the congregation with a measured gaze, remarking on the return of several "prodigal sons," as he liked to call them, while pointedly noting the continued absence of others. He added, with ominous weight, that the churchwarden's upcoming visits would address such lapses in devotion and "negligence in duty to God."

Mary shifted uncomfortably, aware he referenced Irene Jones, who had boycotted services after Foster's first very anti-Papist sermon. Mary feared heavy fines for the Jones family.

Paul Akins, under mounting pressure, had reluctantly accepted the role of deacon under Father Foster—more to preserve his position and income than out of conviction. As the service wore on, the air in the church grew taut with tension, reflecting the broader unrest gripping the nation.

Father Foster began his sermon and though Mary tried to focus, her thoughts drifted back to the priest's earlier comments, feeling as if another knife had been plunged into her family, now aimed towards Catholic maidservant.

301

Parliament's cavalry had conducted harsh interrogations, reinforced by threats of fines and sequestration, casting a pall of fear over the region. Yet Mary knew they were not alone; she maintained regular correspondence with Mistress Frances Smyth and Lady Eleanor Berkeley—both enduring similar trials as Royalist families in an area increasingly falling under Parliament's grip. With their husbands gone to join the King, Mary took some comfort in having her own husband still by her side.

The Foster family's firm alignment with the Parliamentarian cause—and the considerable influence they wielded through Richard Foster—posed a formidable threat. Though their loyalty seemed born more of convenience than conviction, Mary had no doubt they would seize upon any power that afforded them, especially in their long-standing feud with the Stephens family—now further stoked by a recent altercation between one of their sons and William.

"I declare to the congregation that the Book of Sports and its pagan activities are hereby abolished, as passed by Parliament," Father Foster proclaimed. "Instead, spend the day in Scripture and thank God for your deliverance from the great Harlot of Rome." He launched into a venomous stream of anti-Catholic rhetoric, heavy with condemnation.

Mary drifted into silent prayer, seeking guidance. The once-uplifting sermons of Father Roger had given way to Father Foster's bitter tirades, laced with division and spite. Though few in the parish upheld Catholic doctrine, most—Mary included—believed that difference did not warrant hatred. Did not the second commandment say, **"Thou shalt love thy neighbour as thyself"**? Evidently not, in Father Foster's gospel.

As the service ended, the congregation filed out quickly but respectfully. Mary glanced back to see Father Foster gesturing animatedly to Paul Akins, pointing toward the door. Paul looked as dispirited as the rest.

As Mary stepped onto the church grounds, the sight of a gravestone stirred her usual unease—a stark reminder of mortality. Feeling the weight of neglect, she made her way to her family's stone to pay overdue respects. Nearby, she spotted John speaking with Stephen Akins, recently returned from Bristol to find his son had run away with the Royalist troop. Stephen had come to the Manor seeking answers, accompanied by his brother Paul, whose calm presence had likely steadied the conversation.

The men emerged from the study hours later, seemingly reconciled. Yet the news that the Fosters had withdrawn their offer for Fairfield Farm left Mary both relieved and uneasy. What was their true aim? What would follow?

The familiar path brought no comfort. Each step toward the clearing was heavy with unspoken sorrow. She paused before the weathered stones—her parents' marker standing watch over the faded names of her siblings.

The face of her dead sister, Anne rose in her mind: her laughter in the trees playing as children, sunlight in her hair, the effortless charm and beauty that drew suitors in droves. She missed the quiet nights brushing each other's hair, whispering dreams of the future. Here lay the remnants of their lives, claimed by fire. Time had blurred the inscriptions, but not the memories. As she touched her mother's stone, the chill of the stone met a warmth within —a silent bond, enduring still.

"Forgive me for my absence," she whispered, the weight of her neglect settling in.

"Mary," a voice interjected, causing her to jump. "I sincerely apologise, Mistress Mary; I did not mean to startle you."

Turning to find Paul Akins beside her, she observed the unease etched across his handsome features. "I did not intend to interrupt your moment of remembrance, but I felt it necessary to inform you that Father Foster intends to send the church warden to visit your residence concerning Irene Jones, your maid," he conveyed, his tone heavy with concern.

"Yes, I anticipated this. Irene remains steadfast in her Catholic faith, despite my earnest attempts to guide her otherwise. Father Rogers was on the verge of persuading her, but our new parish priest has unfortunately managed to unravel much of that progress in a single sermon," Mary admitted, weariness creeping into her voice.

"He holds firm convictions," Paul said softly. "I agree the Book of Sports needed revising, and pagan elements should be purged. But banning all sports echoes the Pharisees, who burdened worship with rigid tradition. Jesus showed us that wasn't the way."

Mary sighed, lines of worry etched on her face. "That's only the beginning. He'll target Irene, both for her Catholic faith and because she's in my service. I feel helpless to protect her."

"The best course," Paul suggested, "is to persuade her to attend church, to endure the services. It creates legal complications for anyone seeking to persecute her. While some may be apathetic, he clearly leads the Puritans in Chipping Sodbury—who now dominate the parish—toward renewed anti-Catholic fervour and further reforms. She is truly in danger. I would strongly advise her to consider a move, find a safer haven."

Mary pondered his words, a tumult of dread and determination swirling within her. She recognised the seriousness of the situation, and the imperative for decisive action weighed heavily on her.

"I must leave; I'm tasked with reviewing the parish records, tracking down unexplained absences – my own nephew included. I should have sailed to the New World with Father Rogers when I had the chance," Paul said, frustration clear in his voice. "Stormy times are upon us," she said softly. "We must each take up our cross, for the Church shall need steadfast men such as you, Paul." Her hand came to rest briefly upon his shoulder, and in that simple touch, a quiet spark passed between them.

before she quickly withdrew her hand, noticing John approaching.

"Ah, Mary! And Paul, how good to see you!" John greeted with forced cheer. "We should return home and continue our meditations, my dear," he added, a sharp edge beneath his jovial tone.

"God's blessings," Paul said, and strode away quickly.

"What did Paul want?" John asked, suspicion colouring his voice.

"He was warning us of trouble to come. I'll explain when we're safe inside. Let's go home," she urged, her voice firm.

Benjamin knelt within the inner ward of Berkeley Castle. Around him, on the green, the officers' tents stood in hasty rows, their canvas walls fluttering softly in the chill breeze that wound its way through the ancient stone enclosure. Beyond, the higher-ranking men—those judged worthy of the privilege—were lodged within the castle itself, their voices carrying now and then from the battlements above.

His hands moved with practised ease, meticulously scrubbing grime from William's armour, ever mindful of his exacting standards and his recent rebuke for falling short. Following William's instructions precisely, Benjamin sparingly applied small dabs of linseed oil, buffing it into the blued steel with a cloth only after he was certain all traces of mud, grime, and gunpowder residue were gone.

Next to the armour, William's disassembled pistols lay neatly arranged on worn leather. Benjamin carefully cleaned their firing mechanisms, paying close attention to the Iron Pyrite – the hard, gold-like material that, when struck against the wheel, created the essential spark. He knew it was becoming increasingly difficult to source in England, adding to the already considerable expense of owning a wheel-lock pistol. His precise movements, honed by weeks of repetition, transformed the once daunting task into a strangely comforting routine.

Only weeks ago, Benjamin had been utterly spellbound by Berkeley Castle. It was his first time setting foot inside such a place, and he had been overwhelmed by the sheer scale of the ancient fortress—the weight of its history, the grandeur of its soaring walls, and the majesty of its sweeping grounds. The stone ramparts seemed to rise endlessly into the sky, while the lush, green landscape unfurled like a verdant tapestry beneath them. Everywhere he looked, the castle whispered of ages past, its very stones steeped in stories and secrets long buried.

 Every aspect of the castle filled him with a profound sense of awe and wonder. He had eagerly spent his free moments exploring the ramparts, lost in imagining the fierce battles fought and the countless lives lived within its sturdy walls, picturing the shining knights of old who once called it home.

Now, however, the grandeur faded, replaced by the mundane reality of military life. The castle was no longer a historical monument but simply the backdrop to his daily tasks, the place where he cleaned armour, polished boots, and waited for William's next command. The ordinary had settled in, dulling the initial shine of excitement.

The morning had been another gruelling round of drills and practice. The horses, at least, had become accustomed to the jarring cacophony of musket fire. This was occasionally punctuated by the louder boom of one of the castle's small falcon cannons—drawn from its arsenal for training purposes. However, these cannon blasts were brief and infrequent, a result of the relatively scant supply of powder they had available.

Both Ralph and Samson filled Benjamin with pride—each had adapted admirably to the demands placed upon them, showing both courage and steadiness. He had seen little of Miller, as Sir Redmain seldom drilled with the troop, leaving that responsibility largely to William, who had become their de facto commander. Benjamin recalled overhearing William advising Sir Redmain to begin practising in the cuirass he intended to wear in battle, so that both he and his mounts could grow accustomed to the weight. But Sir Redmain had waved him off, preferring to spend his days dining with the Berkeley's or galloping off on hunts, rather than preparing for war.

The force at the Castle had grown to about three hundred men, half of them cavalry. Divided into three smaller troops—a necessary compromise to grant command to those who raised them—the cavalry included one company of Dragoons. The remaining Harquebusiers now proudly styled themselves "Cavaliers." This term, once a slur directed at flamboyant Royalist cavalry—their long hair, waxed moustaches, and elaborate attire ripe for ridicule—had become a badge of honour, representing their style and chivalric ideals.

The remaining one hundred and fifty footmen were a motley mix of pikemen, billmen, and musketeers, a largely unarmoured force with wildly varying attire and weaponry. Many lacked even helmets. These raw recruits – largely local volunteers and tenants of the gentry – presented a new training challenge. They were forced to adapt their tactics for integrating pike and musketeers, a process that ultimately benefited them all.

A messenger from the king had finally reached them, captains and lieutenants convening hastily in the castle's great hall to discuss its contents.

Benjamin winced as he caught his finger on a burr, a tiny drop of blood appearing on William's aptly named battle sword—a crude-looking weapon with a basket hilt and a broad blade sharpened on both sides. William had expressed his preference for this over a back blade that was sharpened on only one side, noting, however, that many in the troop carried such variations. Benjamin began honing the blade with a wet stone, ensuring it remained razor-sharp and battle-ready. When on foot, William preferred his more elegant rapier, its hilt and blade, a delicate work of art yet equally deadly weapon in the right hands.

At that moment, Owen peered into the tent. "Benjamin, William wishes for you to attend him in the great hall. Do take his diary with you; he will likely want to take notes," he instructed, gesturing toward the small brown book that William seldom set down.

Having placed the weapons into William's wooden storage chest, Benjamin retrieved the diary and Portable Case containing his ink and Quill Pen before proceeding across the courtyard, adeptly sidestepping tent pegs while exchanging greetings with the other grooms and servants of the officers, all of whom were diligently engaged in their respective tasks of cooking, cleaning, and mending equipment.

The weather was relatively warm but overcast, and Benjamin felt the light patter of raindrops as yet another brief shower descended on Berkeley. He tucked William's diary under his coat for protection. Upon reaching the entrance to the great hall, flanked by two heavily armoured men bearing halberds and adorned in the red and white livery of the Berkeley retainers, they parted to allow Benjamin passage, recognising him readily.

Stepping into the great hall, Benjamin felt dwarfed. Even Little Sodbury's main hall paled in comparison to Berkeley's immense space and ornate architecture, with its lofty ceilings supported by massive oak beams. Tapestries depicting kings and horses adorned the walls, while stained-glass windows blazed with heraldry. At the head of a long table sat Baron Berkeley. The Baron, a man of middling age with a round, affable face, was dressed in a flamboyant, crimson velvet ensemble of the latest fashion. Berkeley called for silence, and the lively chatter faded into calm. Seizing the moment, Benjamin presented William with his daily correspondence and writing case before retreating to his place among the other servants at the side of the hall.

As Benjamin surveyed the room, he noted the familiar face of Thomas Smyth beside William. Having arrived with a Company of dragoons that he had successfully raised and outfitted with Matchlock muskets and carbines he had imported from the continent, Thomas, like many present, was relatively inexperienced in military affairs. His Lieutenant, the loyal servant Matthews, had also become someone with whom Benjamin had exchanged a few words. Both men, however, possessed the humility to seek guidance and had been drilling diligently with the other troops, achieving a commendable level of competence—a fact noted by William one evening during a conversation with Owen.

On the first day of drills, Thomas made the unfortunate choice of mounting Micky—a sensitive grey gelding the Akins' had traded for Castilio the previous year. Micky was a horse of strong opinions and little hesitation in expressing them. The moment musket fire cracked through the air, he took one look at the chaos and promptly decided a swift and elegant departure was the best course of action. With a snort and a leap, he bolted, kicking up a cloud of dust and a chorus of laughter as Thomas clung on for dear life, his dignity flapping behind him like a forgotten cloak —much to amusement of his troop.

After a comical blast across the field, during which Thomas looked like a flustered knight battling a dragon, he finally wrestled Micky under control. Despite the initial struggle, they covered ground quickly. Returning to the group with a sheepish grin, Thomas announced, "From now on, Micky is my esteemed travel companion—a pack horse, perhaps! Who needs a steed that runs away when you can have a supply carrier? He'll be the finest looking pack horse in the county!" This brought a roar of laughter from the men.

"Is it too late for a refund" he quipped when passing by Benjamin, giving him a knowing wink.

His light-hearted banter and quick wit had the troop chuckling, but he wasn't the only one experiencing the antics of a spooked steed that day; several horses were skittish, bolting or becoming unsettled at the unfamiliar sounds and sights of the mock battle they attempted to replicate.

Benjamin had anticipated some queries regarding his presence from Thomas Smyth, knowing his father's reputation all too well; it was unlikely he would have readily given his consent for such ventures. However, Thomas seemed perfectly content to bask in the camaraderie and relish the sight of familiar faces around him.

Sir Thomas Berkeley, William's future father-in-law and captain of the other troop of Cavalier gentlemen volunteers, stood nearby, making William acutely aware of himself.

"We have received orders from His Majesty—may God preserve him," Baron Berkeley announced, his voice grave and carrying across the assembly. "Four days ago, the King raised his standard in Nottingham. Gentlemen, we are now officially at war with the rebellious Parliamentarian faction." A ripple of hushed conversation spread through the officers.

"His Majesty requests we dispatch our gathered forces to Worcester. Our task is to help gather then escort silver plate and other vital supplies for the war effort to a designated location. He will communicate our final destination and further mission details upon our arrival in Worcester." The Baron laid the letter on the table, his gaze sweeping the room. "Questions?"

William raised his hand. "Yes, Lieutenant Stephens," Baron Berkeley acknowledged.

"Worcester is approximately a day's ride with our wagons in tow," William stated. "My scouts have detected riders observing the castle, potentially indicating a nearby enemy force. What garrison should remain to secure this castle?"

he inquired respectfully, acknowledging Berkeley's seniority.

"I would propose we keep the foot soldiers here, along with perhaps half a troop of horse, to maintain a striking ability and assist with foraging for supplies," the Baron suggested, receiving nods of agreement around the room.

Sir Redmain cleared his throat. "I would like to take my troop to Worcester, if I may."

"As would I," Sir Thomas Berkeley echoed, both eager to avoid having their troops split and to seize the opportunity to link up with the King and his army in this, their first mission of this Civil war.

"I am prepared to divide my dragoons and place half of them under your command, Baron Berkeley," suggested Thomas Smyth, deftly gauging the atmosphere and anticipating that such a proposal would meet with approval.

"Very well, that sounds quite straightforward," the Baron replied, a playful smile illuminating his features. "I would ask Sir Thomas to take charge of the mission, and may God grant you, His protection."

Sir Redmain's countenance darkened, and he appeared ready to protest. Benjamin noted this but then observed him rein in his objection.

The Baron continued, "However, I must kindly request that the officers responsible for the men remaining here, instil a bit more discipline among their troops. I have noted venison upon their campfires far too frequently; the deer park at this estate has not been so ravaged since the days of Queen Elizabeth. Her hunting expeditions nearly drove the deer into hiding."

A sly smile danced upon his lips as he continued, "I can almost envision the poor creatures, whispering to one another, 'Not again! Here comes that regal huntress with her far-too-keen aim!'" Polite Laughter erupted around the table, the officers thoroughly entertained by the Baron's light-hearted commentary on their men's culinary indiscretions.

As wine was brought forth by the Berkeley servants, glasses were filled to the brim.

"A toast to our beloved King Charles — and may peace soon be restored to our realm!" the Baron proclaimed, lifting his glass high. Murmurs of agreement rippled about the room, several voices taking it up in echo: "To King Charles."

Sir Redmain then added "And may the Earls of Essex soldiers be as loyal as his wife" this vulgar remark did get a laugh from a few, it was long rumoured he was a cuckold, and word had just reached them that the Earl was to be the Rebel armies' commander.

After only a single glass, William excused himself from the meeting as soon as it was deemed polite to do so, with Benjamin trailing behind him.

"We have much to prepare," William said firmly. "Fetch Ralph and bring Owen's horse. I'll look in on the scouts myself. See that everything is packed—save my tent, for I'll need it tonight. Leave the buff coat out, but have my armour ready. And fetch the item from the castle smithy," he added, passing over a few coins. "Here—this will cover it."

The piece in question was the aptly named secrete—a concealed steel cap fitted within a hat—offering light yet serviceable protection while preserving a gentleman's proper silhouette. It was far cooler than a helmet and allowed better sight of the field. Following Sir Thomas Berkeley's counsel, William had ordered one made for himself.

"We depart at dawn," he concluded, his tone calm but resolute.

Chapter 45
Sunday, September 4th

On this splendid Sunday morning, John Stephens and his daughter, Jane, engaged in a spirited game of lawn bowls in the garden of their estate. The sun shone brightly overhead, casting a golden glow across the manicured lawn, where the vibrant green contrasted strikingly with the clear blue sky. Beyond them, the wooded vale of the Severn stretched into the distance, a sweeping, majestic backdrop to the tranquil scene.

Having just returned from church, John was eager to enjoy some light-hearted time with Jane. Yet beneath his cheerful manner lay a quiet concern—for he had lately observed a shadow in her mood, a lingering melancholy. As they played, he hoped gently to draw her out, to understand what had troubled her so.

As they played, the cheerful sounds of rolling bowls and laughter filled the air. John, embodying the role of a loving father, teased Jane with playful jests, attempting to elicit a smile from her fair face. "Careful now, my dear! I do believe I have the bowl here to win the day!" he expressed with mock bravado, prompting a light-hearted retort from Jane that sparked further banter between them, the bond of their affection evident in every playful exchange.

"I thought sports were banned on a Sunday, by Father Foster" Jane noted

"Well, I won't tell him, if you don't" John winked

Her laughter drew a chuckle from her father. "That's better, my darling," John said warmly. "It gladdens my heart to see you smile—it always has. You've a gift for brightening even the darkest day."

"It is good to smile," Jane replied, eyes sparkling. "Perhaps we should play as we used to."

With that, she cast her bowl, watching it roll true. "Ha! Victory is mine, Poppa!" she cried, clapping her hands in delight and teasing him with triumphant laughter.

Meanwhile, Mistress Mary Stephens observed from her elevated position within the manor, peering through the window with a contemplative gaze. She was seeking solace after enduring yet another vitriolic sermon delivered by Father Foster. His inflammatory rhetoric had left her feeling disheartened and frustrated, a stark contrast to the joyful scene unfolding in the garden. Though she longed to join the delightful game, the toll of recent experiences lingered in her heart.

As father and daughter revelled in their game, the morning sun continued to shine upon them, casting long shadows as it climbed higher in the sky. Suddenly, Mary's attention was drawn to a commotion at the far end of the long private pathway, leading up to their estate. From her vantage point, she discerned three figures approaching, one of whom appeared to be struggling and was supported by the other two. Concerned, Mary called out, "Mr. Cropper, please go down to investigate the situation. I fear something may be amiss." With a nod of understanding, he hastened away from his duties, eager to ascertain the arrival of the unusual guests.

Mary's heart raced with a mixture of curiosity and apprehension as she watched Mr. Cropper make his way toward the figures approaching along the private pathway. The once tranquil ambience of the garden was now tinged with uncertainty. As her eyes fixed on the trio, she
quickly recognised the familiar faces of Tim Jones and Irene, struggling to support a battered and dishevelled Glen. Mr. Cropper stepped forward without hesitation, moving to Irene's side to help steady her as they made

their way toward the servants' entrance at the side of the house.

Once inside, they gently eased Glen into one of the chairs around the servants' dining table. His body sagged with exhaustion, blood and grime crusting his torn clothes. Mary hurried in, her maternal instincts stirring at the sight. She approached swiftly, her voice tight with concern.

"What happened?" she asked, eyes fixed on Glen's face—distorted with cuts, swelling, and vivid bruises. Tim, too, showed signs of violence: a darkened eye, puffed and purple, spoke of a heavy blow.

"Can we speak somewhere Mistress?" Irene asked Mary urgently, her eyes wide with distress as Ruth and another servant rushed over, ready to tend to their wounds as best they could.

Mary nodded swiftly, guiding Irene and Tim into the main hall where they could speak in privacy, away from the bustle of the servants' quarters. Just as they entered, John appeared from the corridor, his brow furrowed with concern, drawn by the unexpected commotion that had disturbed the calm of the morning.

Irene Jones recounted her harrowing experience, her voice trembling with the weight of memory. "I was summoned to Father Foster's office alone to discuss the fines," she whispered, hands clenched tightly in her lap as if to hold herself together. "He gave me a predatory look, then said, 'The Devil does put his spawn into fine vessels.' His words hissed like a serpent's strike, and the way he looked at me —all the insinuation—made my skin crawl. And then, his hand brushed against me in a way that sent a shiver, not just of cold but of something far worse, down my spine. I felt… violated."

John's jaw tightened, his knuckles turning white as he gripped the edge of the table. Mary's breath hitched, her heart pounding as a cold dread seeped into her core, choking her with repulsion.

Irene's voice faltered, but she pressed on. "He then gave me an ultimatum," she said, voice barely steadying. "The fines were far beyond what we could afford. Or—" she hesitated, voice trembling—"he suggested we could come to 'an arrangement.' The look in his eyes—as he leered at my body —made the implication clear. A vile promise hanging between us. Refuse, he hinted, and there would be… consequences."

Irene paused, a tremor running through her. "Stunned and frightened, I slapped the priest – the touch of his skin still burns – and ran from his office," she confessed, tears welling. "I didn't want to burden Glen with it, afraid of what he might do, so we quietly started home, but I noticed a man was following us his face concealed by a hood" she paused putting her hand over her mouth as if recounting the story was making her relive the horror.

"We kept on down the path," Irene began, her voice trembling. "I believe Tim and Glen saw him too, and we quickened our pace. But as we neared home, two brutish men sprang from the hedgerow, their faces hidden behind crude cloth masks.

"They struck Tim down with horrifying ease—one blow, and he collapsed," she whispered, barely audible. "Then one of them seized me, his filthy hand clamped over my mouth, choking off my screams. The other two set upon Glen. I could do nothing… only watch as they beat him down. He tried to fight them, but—God help us—they kicked him, again and again. At least ten times before they fled, leaving us bloodied and broken on the path."

A heavy silence descended upon the room as the weight of

Irene's harrowing account sank in. John clenched his fists, unable to restrain his rising anger, while Mary felt a tumult of fear and outrage swelling within her. The tranquil Sunday they had hoped to enjoy had been irrevocably shattered, leaving them all to confront the unsettling ramifications of this violent encounter.

"To hell with these damned Fosters!" John erupted, his voice trembling with fury. "They keep finding new ways to attack us and our friends. I've always thought that priest had evil shining in his eyes."

Just then, Jane appeared at the doorway, her innocent face filled with concern. "Father, what's going on?" she asked softly.

John quickly turned, effortfully masking his agitation with a forced calm. "Nothing for you to worry about, my dear," he said, trying to sound reassuring. "Please go to your room."

Unbeknownst to him, Mary sensed his desire to shield Jane from the harsh truths—especially now, as she had finally begun to shake off her recent gloom.

"Do as your father says, and I'll come see you shortly," Mary said gently, her voice calm and soothing. Jane nodded, worry clouding her features as she left the room, her gaze lingering on Tim's bruised face. A heavy silence settled in her wake; the family left to grapple with the weight of what had been revealed—and the uncertain consequences that now loomed.

"We have a visit from one of these new committees Parliament has set up to govern, on the nineteenth. Perhaps I'll ask them what they are doing about safety," John remarked sarcastically.

"Do you think we should write to Bishop Banks about this? It might be wise to consult Paul to determine the best course of action in pursuing justice," Mary suggested.

John shook his head slightly. "No disrespect intended here, but it will ultimately be the word of a Catholic woman against that of an ordained priest from a rich and well-connected family. Regrettably, this will not bode well for us. The thugs, very likely affiliated with the Foster family, will simply be dismissed as common muggers," he said, a note of defeat seeping into his voice.

"We must resist this!" Mary declared, her voice sharp with conviction. "Has our country truly fallen so far that such injustice and cruelty go unpunished? John, you've already given up. Show some spine!" Almost immediately, she hesitated, the weight of her words spilling out before she could second-guess herself.

"What would you have me do, Mary?" John responded, his voice heavy with weariness. "Confront the priest? We're already facing trouble in the days ahead—who knows what these Parliamentarians will throw at us? The tenants have informed me they've all been questioned about the Royalists' comings and goings."

Irene spoke softly, meekly. "I apologise for causing you trouble, Master Stephens."

"Don't apologise," Mary said gently, her tone softening. "You did the right thing, Irene. Now, go and get something to eat and drink. Head down to the kitchen—the cook will look after you. I'll fetch Paul Akins; his medical training might help Glen more than we can right now."

John shot her a disapproving look, frustration plain on his face. "It seems I'm of no use here. Perhaps I should seek out Paul Akins—surely he has all the answers, Mary." With a tight sigh, he turned and strode away, his attempt at restraint undone by the tension written clearly across his features.

Benjamin carefully fed Ralph the last of the grain he'd managed to scavenge, topping off the hay ration with quiet devotion. A gnawing concern lingered in his mind—Ralph had grown noticeably leaner over the past weeks, the outline of his ribcage beginning to show. Their recent travels had not been overly taxing, and apart from the occasional scouting mission with William, they'd enjoyed relative rest since heading north. Yet Ralph seemed to lack the resilience of Samson, who adapted to the shifting pace like a seasoned soldier, thriving amid change.

In the days following their arrival in Worcester, finding suitable lodgings proved no easy task—compounded by the sudden influx of Royalists streaming into the city. With Gloucester firmly declared for Parliament, and whispers that even Bristol's tenuous neutrality was tipping toward the rebels, many had fled in search of safety and solidarity behind Worcester's Royalist lines. The city, already straining under the weight of its own, now groaned with the press of newcomers, making every effort to settle a challenge.

However, fortune smiled upon them, and they eventually located a cosy Inn with stables, conveniently situated near Sidbury Gate on the vibrant southern edge of the city across the road from St Peters church. The Inn keeper and his wife were lovely hospitable people, the wife popping Benjamin the odd apple to feed the horses and sharing their table for evening meals as well supplying them with ample supply of this local drink called perry, made from the abundance of pear trees in the area. The local militia, fervent supporters of the King, greeted the sight of Royalist horses with apparent enthusiasm, effectively dispelling the tension they had experienced during their somewhat awkward arrival, dominated by a few uneasy moments at the gates.

The Worcester population rallied in support of the Royalist cause, fuelled by camaraderie. In response to rising tensions, men and women worked tirelessly to strengthen the city's defences, patching and reinforcing crumbling walls, ditches, and earthworks in preparation for the looming conflict.

Suddenly, an uproar erupted from the gate, watchmen announcing an approaching column. Intrigued, Benjamin hurried outside to find William and Owen deep in conversation with the militia captain.

"What's happening?" Benjamin asked, curious.

"Sir Byron's column from Oxford – the one we've been expecting!" William replied, his face lighting up. "Come, let's see!"

Climbing to the top of the gate, Benjamin gaped at the grand procession: riders, wagons, and foot stretching into a long line down the road, bright flags fluttering in the overcast September air.

"So many!" Benjamin exclaimed.

William surveyed the scene with a calculating eye. "Just shy of five hundred, I'd judge—hard to tell with the wagons crowding the line," he said at last. Then he turned to his men. "Benjamin, fetch Sir Berkeley, if you please. And Owen—find Sir Redmain, or he'll take offence at being left out."

Owen shot William a wry smile, well aware of the delicate task of soothing the knight's pride. With a brief nod, he and Benjamin set off at once to carry out their orders.

Nearly an hour passed before the entire column entered the city, congesting roadways with wagons, horses, and soldiers that spilled onto the green next to St. Mary's Cathedral, despite the clergy's haranguing protests. Benjamin scratched his head, wondering where they would all find shelter. The small city of six thousand already strained to house them, with dwindling food supplies. The Quartering Act forced citizens to house soldiers, issuing promissory notes for reimbursement, but necessities were inflating each day, a brutal lesson in supply and demand.

Benjamin and William headed to the guild hall, their headquarters in the city's heart, where officers and officials gathered to discuss urgent matters.

Upon arrival, Benjamin caught sight of Sir Byron—dishevelled, his long dark hair clinging to his face. His sharp nose and narrow brow contrasted with his otherwise noble bearing, his expression marked by fatigue and grim resolve.

Inside the Guildhall, the air buzzed with low conversation and the rustle of parchment as officers and clerks gathered. Sir Byron stepped forward, commanding the room with a raised hand.

"Gentlemen," he began, his voice steady and unadorned, "I have summoned you to speak plainly. A substantial force is closing in behind us—my scouts place their number between thirteen and fifteen thousand, with four to five thousand cavalry."

Benjamin's eyes widened at the figure. He glanced at William, who remained composed, listening with silent focus.

"We were forced to leave Oxford some five days past. By God's grace, we secured much of the university's silver plate and other generous donations, along with powder, shot, and horses. The rebels, distracted by their zeal for desecrating churches, have overextended themselves, allowing us to slip through—though not without a few skirmishes. It is a miracle we've come this far—praise be to God!"

He paused to take a sip of water; his voice strained from exertion.

"We have come this far, but after surveying your fortifications, I fear we cannot stand against such a formidable enemy with our meagre numbers."

A stir rippled through the officers as chatter and conversation erupted.

"Silence!" one of Sir Byron's brothers shouted, cutting through the commotion.

"Messengers from His Majesty inform me that the King now makes for Shrewsbury," Sir Byron announced gravely. "We must at once gather all available resources, collect what contributions may be rendered to the war effort, and stand ready to convey these provisions to His Majesty—once my courier returns with confirmation of his precise movements. I have also petitioned the King to dispatch an additional escort to bolster our party."

He paused, his shoulders heavy with fatigue. "Rest assured, I shall leave a contingent of men to reinforce this position. Yet you must prepare yourselves for the possibility of a siege—at least until the King's army is able to meet this rebel force in open battle."

"Do we have any notion of the size of the King's forces accompanying him?" inquired the city's lieutenant colonel of militia, concern lacing his voice.

"I lack that information, nor would I care to speculate until my messenger returns," Byron replied, his resolve unyielding.

"Who will be remaining, and who will be departing?" queried Sir Redmain, his brow furrowed with anxiety.

"I shall require all available Horse after some recruits joined us in Oxford I have some two hundred horse half Dragoons. The infantry I command will remain here to strengthen your valiant militia. However, it is imperative that these supplies reach the King. Is there any map of the area that I might review?" Sir Byron demanded.

A clerk promptly approached, presenting a detailed map of the city and its surroundings. Sir Byron scrutinised the map intently, his finger tracing its contours while the senior officers mirrored his focus.

"We must deploy pickets here, at Lower Wick. Is that a bridge?" he inquired, pointing decisively at the map.

A local militia captain responded, "Yes, that is known as Powick Bridge, sir."

"Very well. We must station a holding force there to maintain vigilance and guard against any flanking manoeuvre," he commanded.

Sir Thomas Berkeley interjected, "I can dispatch our one hundred and twenty-five horsemen to stand guard there, we have come from Berkeley castle with orders to meet you here to bolster your escort, we know the terrain well, having scouted the area these past few weeks," he offered eagerly.

"Excellent. Ensure scouts are dispatched further afield to report any signs of the enemy. We must also watch for the Gloucester trained bands from the south, as they've turned rebel. We cannot risk being cut off; we must prepare and strengthen defences. I want every able-bodied person at work," Sir Byron insisted, his authoritative voice guiding their course of action amid the looming crisis.

Standing beside William, Thomas Smyth remarked, "It appears we will be departing soon."

"Yes, we need to pack all our kits and secure them in wag-ons, prepared for a swift exit. I gather Sir Byron does not wish to linger here any longer than he needs to for fear of being trapped," William replied, stroking his beard thoughtfully.

"What of this city? If the reports are true, it seems the rebels have little regard for the people's welfare," Thomas remarked, having quickly grown fond of Worcester's loyal and hospitable citizens. "With God's grace, they need only hold out until the King arrives with his forces. The rebels might reconsider a siege if they perceive a threat from the King's army," William replied, offering a reassuring smile to the worried Thomas Smyth. "We should attend to our duties."

Chapter 47
Investigations and Sequestration, 19th September 1642

In the pale light of morning, Little Sodbury stirred to life. Birds trilled in the hedgerows as sunlight spilled across thatched roofs and dew-pearled fields. Yet beneath the quiet calm lay a shadow of foreboding—for this day was unlike any other. Agents of the so-called Committee of Safety were expected at Little Sodbury Manor, come to inquire into accusations that the house had sheltered a renegade troop from Gloucester County in defiance of Parliament's summons.

In the stone manor, John Stephens and Mistress Mary Stephens shared uneasy looks during breakfast. Whispers of impending doom circulated through the village, growing more alarming with each telling. A visit from the Committee was a grave matter; rumours painted them as targeting suspected Royalists, and gossip suggested fines or even property confiscation could follow.

"John, where is that new solicitor you appointed? He should have been here by now," Mary said, her voice tinged with fear.

"I know, my dear. Mr. Atwood is cutting it damn fine indeed. I hope his legal advice is better than his timekeeping." John tapped his foot impatiently.

"What about your brother? I recall tales he was an MP. What of your family? Might they hold some sway with that pack of wolves running Parliament?" Mary asked, a hint of desperation creeping into her voice.

John Stephens sighed, the sound thick with resignation, and raked a hand through his already dishevelled hair. "Henry is no comfort; he'd sooner hasten our demise, bearing me no affection, nor the rest of family. I cannot believe Henry would align himself with our King, he will be one of the first to declare for Parliament if I'm any judge of his beliefs. Just as William was quick to declare for the King, so too must we make ready—the storm gathers swiftly," John said grimly. "These committees are but the beginning —omens of what's to come. Mark my words, more ordinances will follow, each crafted to crush those who stand loyal to the Crown."

Outside, the growing sound of hooves on gravel broke the hush of the morning, the clatter of metal ringing sharply through the still air. John crossed to the window, his face darkening as he looked out. His voice was tight with restrained fury. "Of course... it would be him."

"Who is it?" Mary asked, though the sinking feeling in her chest had already betrayed the answer.

"Richard Foster—and his wretched brood. Who else would come to gloat at our doorstep?"

A small detachment of Parliamentary horse trailed just behind, among them were his sons—Samuel, a hulking brute, and younger Saul, whose smooth face betrayed his youth amid the grim task the Stephens feared they had come to execute. John's jaw clenched as he faced his enemy.

They rode in with the arrogance of men who believed the land already theirs, heads held high, the smugness of presumed victory carved into their expressions. It was not just a visit—it was a declaration. Retribution had come, and they meant for the whole household to feel its weight.

The air grew heavy, and a long, sombre shadow seemed to fall over the Manor.

As they approached the main entrance to the Manor, John took a deep breath, steeling himself for the impending confrontation. He opened the door to find Richard Foster dismounting, his expression a blend of dispassion and authority that brooked no resistance.

"John Stephen Esquire," Richard called, his voice resonating with the weight of his office, "we are here under the authority of Parliament to carry out an investigation into your actions against the state. Allegations have been made regarding your allegiance to the Kings nefarious advisors, and you aiding and abetting a troop county horse who have deserted their post."

John felt his chest tighten as he stepped forward, rebuffing the accusation. "We are loyal subjects, Richard! My family's loyalty to the crown should be a matter of honour, not a crime this is a sham of an investigation if I ever saw one, especially with someone so biased as you leading it."

Richard, undeterred, motioned to the soldiers behind him. "Your son, William, serves the King's evil advisors as a Lieutenant in his army of rogues—a position of treason against the Parliament and the people of England. An investigation has been requested, and we are here to carry out a search and take stock of your movable goods. You must comply; resistance will be taken as an admission of guilt, though it seems you do not deny the accusation. Richard raised his eyebrows at John, who did not take the bait.

"Treason cannot go unpunished; I am merely the member of the committee, who has the privilege of informing you." Richard couldn't conceal his pleasure, a wide smile spreading across his smug features like a cat that has found cream.

Mistress Mary stepped forward, her composure faltering. "You cannot condemn us based on our son's choices. What evidence do you have? I demand to see it. We have not aided any traitor's cause. Show us your proof, you Villain! Any such search is unlawful," she said vehemently.

"Enough, John, control your wife's tongue. Know your place Woman," Richard barked, his voice sinister, his serious and formal demeanour returning. "You would do well to remember that loyalty to a monarch who defies the will of the people is treason most foul. Your actions have consequences, and the Committee will soon have the power to halt anyone wishing to aid the King's wicked advisors."

Richard produced an official-looking document, waving it for a moment. He then turned to the troopers. "Search the premises. I want accounts, bills, and any correspondence. Make sure you take a record of all sellable goods, especially any silver or gold plate and jewellery," Richard commanded.

The soldiers now dismounted, surged into the manor with brutal efficiency, slamming the doors open and shoving John aside as Richard strode in, his voice booming through the entrance. John and Mary, forced to retreat, found themselves backing into the great hall, while the troopers fanned out, their heavy hands already at work searching the manor.

"You may not sell or move any of the listed goods until after the finding of this investigation, otherwise you will be charged with royalist sympathies and delinquencies. This includes any horses, funds, and properties that may further assist the King's cause." Said Richard Foster

Tears welled in Mary's eyes as the troopers ransacked their home with callous disregard. "This is an outrage! We've done nothing wrong!" she said emotion choking her words

Mr. Cropper, his face etched with fear, lingered near the library door. As the troopers advanced, he stepped forward, a futile attempt to block their way. A brutish trooper shoved him against the wood panelling, pinning him. "Out of the way, you old goat," the trooper sneered, his helmeted face close to Mr. Cropper's. "Just try something and see what happens," he growled, "lead us to the family accounts and silver, or face the consequences."

Mr. Cropper, his spirit quite broken, nodded meekly and allowed himself to be led into the house library, behind which lay John's private study—now threatened with exposure, along with the estate's accounts. Meanwhile, Samuel and Saul entered the hallway; Samuel mounted the stairs to the upper floor, his brother close upon his heels.

John's fists clenched, a storm of anger, despair, and injustice roiling within him. "Is this what this country has become, when a gentleman must stand idly by while his home is defiled?" he cried out.

A corporal spun around, levelling a pistol at John just as he instinctively reached for the rapier at his side. Mary's heart seized with terror. Seeing the danger, John immediately raised his hands a gesture of submission.

Richard's expression hardened as he strode into the great hall—a place steeped in stories he'd heard since childhood. Tales of how the Welch family had taken this grand house from his rightful Foster line, rewarded with lands and title for their service to the Tudor cause generations ago. Now, standing beneath the high-beamed ceiling, surrounded by portraits of Welch ancestors, Richard's eyes gleamed with a cold, vindictive satisfaction. A twisted sense of justice stirred within him, as though he were reclaiming something unjustly taken.

"Loyalty has its price, John. My ancestors backed the wrong king. Consider your son's actions—William fights for a king who betrays his people. When reckoning comes, expect no mercy. This time, the Fosters will be on the winning side."

Richard's gaze swept the room, defiant against the Welches' portraits staring down at him. "Generations tried and failed to reclaim this place. I will be the one to bring justice," he murmured, as his trooper's filed past, loading papers from the study into saddlebags outside.

Meanwhile, in another part of the manor, Saul Foster lingered, torn by the conflict unfolding around him as he observed the devastation wrought by his father's orders. Troopers began a search for the private chambers of the house, looking for silver, jewellery, and any other valuables. One of their companions, not wearing a buff coat or bearing arms, had a clerical look about him and was writing down a list of items, irritation visible at the troopers' bullish approach, which was making his job harder than it needed to be.

Standing on the upper landing, Samuel glanced back at Saul. "What troubles you, brother?" he asked, his bent nose less pronounced since his recent encounter with William in Chipping Sodbury.

"This feels wrong," Saul replied, emotions shifting across his face.

"Silence, you whelp! This is what we've been working towards. This is our birthright, justice at last. Once Parliament pushes through the new laws, this place will be confiscated and sold to raise funds for the war effort, and we will finally reclaim what was stolen from us," Samuel declared, his voice ringing with triumph.

At that moment, Jane Stephens emerged from her bedchamber, her face a mask of terror and disbelief. "What is the meaning of this?" she cried out bravely.

Samuel's smile twisted with grim delight as he stalked toward her, roughly seizing her arm. "Unhand the Mistress! What are you doing?" Saul retorted, his voice laced with indignation.

Jane let out a scream, unaccustomed to such treatment.

"Silence, you whore!" Samuel snapped crudely.

Just then, Ruth appeared in the hallway, rushing to Jane's defence and thrusting herself between them.

"Ah—speak of whores, and here comes our Ruth," Samuel sneered, batting her aside with his free arm. His shove sent her sprawling to the floor, skirts tangling beneath her.

"Stay down," he growled, menace thick in his voice, "or you'll fare worse yet."

The commotion above carried faintly into the great hall below. "What's happening up there?" John called, alarm rising in his tone as the echoes of struggle reached him.

"It's Jane!" Mary cried, horror twisting her features, tears blurring her vision. In the chaos, she had forgotten her own daughter.

"Corporal, fetch Mistress Jane Stephens — and see that she comes to no harm," Richard commanded.

The trooper who had been levelling his piece at John gave a curt nod, slid the weapon back beneath his belt, and hastened up the stairs to carry out the order.

"She won't be harmed; I give you my word on that," Richard asserted, his tone resolute.

"Your word means nothing," Mary retorted defiantly finding her steel once more.

"Oh, but it does. I always keep my promises, Mistress Mary," he replied, a smug smile twisting his lips. "I told your husband I'd have this manor, one way or another. You had a chance to sell, but you rebuffed my generous offer. The Welch arrogance clearly runs in your veins, just like your sister's." A glimmer of something dark passed over his face. "But as I promised your husband, here I stand and mark my words, it's only a matter of time before this place is mine."

Richard approached the family coat of arms displayed above the fireplace, tracing its intricate design with his fingers. "Very soon, the Fosters will replace this crest I swear to the almighty," he declared, his voice laced with satisfaction.

Meanwhile, as the corporal reached the top of the staircase, he found Samuel gripping Jane tightly, one hand clamped over her mouth. Her struggles were no match for his strength. A nervous-looking clerk slipped past, eager to distance himself from the unfolding scene.

"Captain, your father ordered me to bring Mistress Jane to him—unharmed," the corporal said, catching sight of Ruth's sprawled figure nearby, her pretty features now twisted with fury.

Samuel leaned in close to Jane, a predatory gleam in his eyes, the grotesque roughness of his face standing in stark contrast to her unblemished beauty. She looked at him with both revulsion and terror.

"Stop it, Samuel," Saul urged, pressing forward. "Let me take her to Father."

"Not so fast, my lovely," Samuel leered, yanking her close and sniffing her neck like an animal. "A fine creature you are. Next time we meet, I hope we have more time to get better acquainted," he murmured, his foul breath hot against her skin.

"Come on, I'll take you downstairs," Saul said firmly, stepping between his brother and the frozen Jane, forcing Samuel back. Noticing her fear, he slipped an arm around her shoulders and guided her steadily down the staircase, his presence a quiet anchor amid the rising panic.

Samuel spun toward Ruth. "Oh no—don't leave me with him!" she cried, her voice sharp with terror as Samuel advanced, but Saul held Jane close, urging her onward down the staircase.

A sudden, panicked shout rang from the courtyard. One of the troopers tending the horses bellowed, "A mob's coming up the private path!"

Mary rushed to the window, heart hammering. A crowd of forty or fifty villagers surged forward at a jog, voices raised in fierce, unified chant: "Stephens! Justice!" At their head was Paul and Stephen Akins, flanked by villagers brandishing fisted, their determination unmistakable.

Among them, Tim the stable hand, Irene, and the limping but unyielding Glen Jones, now part of the rising tide.

"It appears we have stirred up trouble, sir," a voice trembled beside her. It was the clerk who had joined her at the window, his voice laden with dread. "It may be wise for us to withdraw. Our mandate was merely to serve the notice of investigation and to take inventory of the goods, which we have completed—rather uncouthly, I may add," the clerk said to Richard Foster, his sharp tone reproving.

"It is Paul and the tenants!" Mary exclaimed, turning to John, bewilderment etched deeply on her face as she registered the storm of emotions washing over him. Yet, as the glimmers of retreating intruders caught her eye, she called out to Richard in a mocking tone, "you go so soon?" Richard's expression had shifted from arrogance to concern, a flash of sudden uncertainty crossing his face.

"Fear not, we shall return," Richard retorted, offering a smug bow fraught with bravado, though a glimpse of trepidation betrayed him.

At that moment, Saul entered the room, his face ashen. He ushered Jane gently inside, and she seemed to awaken from a nightmare, rushing into her mother's arms with desperation. "Mother! They were rough with me!" Her voice trembled, the raw fear of their earlier plight hanging heavily in the air.

Just then, Samuel appeared at the hall's entrance, a figure of menace. With a cruel shove, he sent Ruth sprawling once again this time onto the floor of the great hall. Disdain filled his eyes as she scrambled, trying to salvage her torn dress, silent tears streaming down her face. A cruel smile twisted his lips before he turned and fled out of the hall towards the private pathway, where their horses awaited, leaving Ruth in disarray.

Saul, in a moment of sincere remorse, glanced at Mary. "I am truly sorry about this, it was ill done forgive me," he mumbled meekly.

Mary met his gaze, her face etched with distress and horror, her mind racing with grim possibilities. The weight of it all was nearly unbearable. She turned to find John, hands clenched around his sword's hilt, staring at the younger Foster with unfiltered hatred—his grip trembling with rage. In a flash, Saul bolted, fleeing the searing fury in John's eyes.

John's anger, stoked by insult and outrage, now burned beyond reason. Mary, busy tending to Ruth and Jane, cried out, "John, wait! It's over!"

Ignoring her pleas, John strode purposefully into the courtyard like a man possessed, adrenaline surging through his veins. He sought the mounted troopers and Richard, only to find them poised to burst forth against the formidable wall of bodies obstructing their path—a human barricade teeming with resolve.

At the top of his lungs, he bellowed, **"Richard Foster, I challenge thee to a duel, to settle this matter once and for all!"** His voice sliced through the fervent air, charged with a righteous fury that echoed his desperation. He un-sheathed his rapier, the blade glistening ominously in the light, roaring, "**A duel, God damn you!**" The final word erupted from his lips like a war cry, resonating with fierce defiance, scarcely ten paces from the stunned Richard, for once stuck for words.

Driven by a reckless impulse, Samuel drew his loaded pistol from the saddle holster in a heartbeat, cocking it in one swift motion. He levelled the weapon squarely at John. A sharp crack echoed through the courtyard as he fired, the shot sound reverberating off the walls like a death knell. The ball struck John's torso with brutal force, stealing his breath and strength. He staggered backward, collapsing to the ground with a heavy thud and a metallic clang as his sword fell from his hand. Bewilderment and shock washed over his face as he gazed up at the sky, the brilliance of the day dimming around him, the world narrowing to Jane's piercing scream.

Mary, too late to stop it, stood frozen—her heart splintered by the brutality before her. "John, my love," she whispered, voice trembling.

"Poppa!" Jane cried, her wail piercing the chaos. "No! Help him—please, God, someone help him!" She thrashed in Mary's arms, sobbing, desperate to reach him.

Mary held her tight, torn between protecting her daughter from the lingering danger and running to her husband, who lay bleeding on the ground before them.

"You fool!" Richard roared at his son, disbelief and fury intermingling in his voice, reverberating through the pandemonium.

Hearing Jane's screams, John whispered, barely audible, "Jane, my love… my light. I'm sorry."

His voice was lost in the chaos. He tried to move, to reach for her, but only his fingers twitched—feeble and trembling. The light in his eyes faded, replaced by hollow stillness. A single tear traced his cheek, disappearing into the crimson bloom spreading across his chest, seeping into the cold, unyielding earth.

The mob, once a chorus of protest, now seethed with a rage at what they had just witnessed, surging toward the horsemen, their cries of "murderers! Murderers!" ripping through the air. The parliamentary troopers, facing the fury of an unarmed but enraged crowd, spurred their mounts forward, relentlessly forcing a path through the throng, lashing out with the hilts and flats of their drawn swords. Villagers were knocked to the ground by the frantic horses, and the air filled with the sickening sounds of bone meeting steel and desperate cries as the troopers ruthlessly cleared a path, then bolted down the private path, fleeing the storm they had unleashed.

Chapter 48
The Prince, 22nd September

William urged Samson into a trot toward Worcester Bridge, eager to report to Sir Thomas Berkeley after his scouting mission. He was accompanied by Corporal Jones, now acting as his escort, the only remaining member of the detachment of five troopers. The others had peeled off to rejoin the main troop stationed near Powick Bridge, where the ill-tempered Sir Redmain was undoubtedly lamenting the lack of Worcester's comforts.

As they navigated the path, William passed by the construction underway of what promised to be impressive defensive earthworks lining the western bank of the main bridge which would be Byron's route out of the city when the time came—these formidable mounds of earth forwarded enhanced protection against potential threats of artillery the city would likely face if under siege. The sight of the beginnings of these fortifications in preparation for the challenges ahead made William's mind cast back to the horrors he had witnessed on the continent, where sieges and skirmishes had become a part of normally life.

As he drew near the fortified gatehouse of the splendid six-arched medieval stone bridge spanning the Severn, William inclined his head to the watchmen posted there. He could not fail to mark the unease in their glances — a quiet yet telling reminder of the conflict gathering on the horizon, shadowing them all.

The streets bustled with activity—wagons creaked under heavy loads as stern-faced soldiers stood guard and labourers worked tirelessly to load provisions. It was a chaotic ballet of commerce and military preparation: quartermasters barked orders, directing efficient packing and chastising any sloppiness. Those who faltered were made to unload and start again, as the wagons groaned beneath the weight of supplies in every shape and size.

William considered the logistics, calculating how quickly they could move with such a heavily laden wagon train. The sheer volume of provisions—and the valuable cargo from Oxford—was essential, yet it posed a serious burden, one that could cripple their mobility if a swift retreat became necessary.

As they neared the Guildhall, a troop of elegantly dressed cavaliers came into view, their finely tailored garments catching the fading autumn light. Two guidons fluttered in the mild evening breeze—one royal, the other quartered with golden lions in two sections and a light blue and white chequered pattern in the others. It was a striking scene, the vibrant colours of their attire vivid against the encroaching twilight. Yet their horses told a different tale —flanks lathered with sweat, sides heaving—clear signs of a ride pushed to its limits.

William's heart quickened as they drew nearer. First he spotted the familiar guidon, then the silhouette of the lead rider—and a surge of recognition lit his face. As the cavalier came into full view, a wide smile broke across William's face. It was none other than Prince Maurice.

The Prince's presence commanded attention. His fair complexion contrasted sharply with the dark waves of hair spilling from beneath a broad, plumed hat. He carried a vivid blend of youthful energy and noble gravity that set him apart.

His dark eyes were both warm and piercing, alive with quiet intelligence. A newly grown, neatly trimmed moustache lent further refinement to his distinguished features, enhancing the effortless charisma and easy company that William had always admired and enjoyed.

As Prince Maurice turned to acknowledge the approaching pair, his face broke into a broad smile, radiant with the warmth and joy reserved for a long-absent friend. He wore a finely tailored buff coat, richly embroidered with intricate patterns woven in gleaming gold thread that caught the mellow light. The garment conveyed effortless majesty, tempered by the disciplined bearing of a child shaped by war.

"By the grace of God! It is my most esteemed friend, William Stephens!" he declared, his accented English resonant with heartfelt joy. With a graceful flourish, he urged his sleek, black gelding forward. As they came abreast, the two men embraced with soldierly vigour—a wordless bond of enduring loyalty, unencumbered by formality or courtly affectation.

"It affords me great joy to see you, my Prince," William replied earnestly, the affection threading through his voice palpable.

"Ah! I see that you are accompanied by your steadfast companion, ja, Owen?" Maurice continued, offering a nod of familiarity that enveloped the moment in a cocoon of warmth. Owen beamed with delight, clearly honoured by the Prince's remembrance; his chest swelled with pride as he acknowledged the royal greeting.

The trio engaged in light-hearted banter, momentarily casting aside the weighty duties and grim concerns of war, as the autumn dusk softened the world around them.

William could not help but observe that some among the Prince's high-born companions regarded them with thinly veiled impatience. Two conversed in French—measured in tone, though not so guarded as to escape his notice. More than one countenance bore the faintest trace of disdain, their expressions betraying disapproval at the Prince's easy familiarity with two soldiers whom they, no doubt, considered far beneath the dignity of their exalted station.

Prince Maurice, ever perceptive, caught William's glance and smiled wryly. "Do not fear zem, dear William. My uncle's nobles—ach, they are an exceedingly prickly breed. Raised in peace and plenty, ja? they become most unreasonably vexed over matters of ze most trifling sort." He clapped a gloved hand on William's shoulder. "Now, I must speak with Sir Byron—might I prevail upon you to escort me?"

"Gladly. I must also report to my commanding officer, Sir Thomas Berkeley, who presently occupies that makeshift command post yonder," William replied with a conspiratorial wink. "It would not do to keep him waiting—he is, after all, my future father-in-law."

"Ach, I never thought I'd live to see the day!" the Prince chuckled. "Tired of tavern wenches at last? Congratulations. She must be a remarkable Lady to have settled your roving heart, mein Lieber Freund. It seems we have much to discuss—later. First, to business."

With that, they turned toward the Command Centre, the air between them charged with equal parts duty and camaraderie.

"Please follow me your grace "William said with a slight bow.

"Very well, please guide us onward" the Prince replied beckoning on his entourage.

In the torch-lit great hall, its beams draped with banners, William delivered his report of Horse sighted across the River Severn—on the eastern bank near the Teme's confluence—moving southward toward the Upton crossing. He had long urged the slighting of the bridge in earlier councils, though his counsel had been overruled. Dense undergrowth obscured the enemy's numbers, making it impossible to gauge their strength or allegiance with certainty. He relayed these findings to the gathered officers, including Sir John Byron and Sir Thomas Berkeley, though their attention was elsewhere—drawn instead by the arrival of Prince Maurice, whose thoughts were fixed on reinforcements and the urgent need to advance swiftly.

Despite his youth, the Prince, both resplendent and weary from their arduous ride from Bewdley, commanded immediate respect. He announced that they had pressed forward with great determination, riding through the night in stretches. He informed the assembly that his brother and his forces were positioned to the north-west, roughly three hours' ride away, a deliberate choice not to overcrowd Worcester. With a confident air, he continued, explaining that Prince Rupert and his contingent of approximately seven hundred horsemen would serve as a rearguard for Byron's column. The mention of Rupert's name rippled through the assembly, the prospect of such reinforcements sparking murmurs of approval.

A meticulously detailed map lay spread across a polished wooden table, and Maurice gestured for William to approach. "Is that the bridge you mentioned?" he inquired, pointing decisively at the map.

"Yes, my Prince, here is the bridge at Upton, where the force we spotted could cross," William replied, pointing steadily to the two bridges on the map. "It is about a ten-mile ride from there to this—Powick Bridge, which lies three miles south-west of the city." His tone was measured yet resolute. "We have three troops of horse posted near Powick, but they are insufficient to withstand a determined enemy push. The men are encamped in the fields of Lower Wick, screened by trees and thick hedgerows. Orders are strict—no campfires, no signals—nothing to betray their presence."

Sir Byron interjected, his voice firm and edged with authority, betraying a hint of irritation at the prince's deference to a mere lieutenant. "I stationed them there to block any attempt at encirclement and to safeguard the route to our king. It is a calculated risk—but a necessary one. Still, the force won't hold if the Gloucester trained bands appear from that direction."

"I will send a messenger forthwith, my bruder," the Prince declared with authority. "He shall advance our forces to Wick Fields, ja, approaching at an angle to conceal our strength should the enemy dispatch scouts." He pointed at the map, tracing the roadways that would facilitate this manoeuvre. "He will depart at first light and should arrive just before midday." His determination was unmistakable in his tone. "Where did you see these horsemen, William?"

"It was about here," William replied, pointing. "We rode some four miles south of the village. Realistically, Upton remains the only viable crossing—they could well be across by now and on their way to Powick. We did not linger, cantering back swiftly to avoid alerting them to our presence. It is difficult to gauge their numbers—perhaps a few hundred. They may represent the vanguard or rear-guard of a larger force."

Suddenly, the door burst open, and a well-dressed officer hurried into the room, his brow glistening with sweat from exertion. "Forgive the interruption, sirs!" he panted, breathless. "Not half an hour past, a small band of horse-men approached the Sidbury Gate. When challenged, they called out, asking where our loyalties lay. Upon declaring ourselves for the King, they turned tail and rode off at speed."

He paused, drawing a deep breath before continuing. "A few minutes later, another rider arrived—this one claiming to be a defector. He gave himself up at the gate without resistance. Says he rides ahead of a large Rebel force that is making its way here." His words hung heavily in the air, as the men processed this revelation.

"Send him in," the Prince said at once, his tone calm but sharpened with urgency.

Two burly sergeants pushed forward a soldier whose long boots marked him as cavalry. His bearing was that of a gentleman, though he looked dishevelled, tired, and grimy from hard riding. Before he could speak, the Prince's voice cut sharply across the room. "What is the size of the force, and what does it make up?" Prince Maurice asked the man in his direct manner.

"Umm, it's hard to say; over ten thousand, my lords. Their forces are rather strung out, foraging for supplies. They have committed ungodly defilement of churches and treated the common folk most poorly," he said.

"What do you expect from those willing to fight against their anointed King? Is that why you've defected? What is your name?" the Prince replied.

"James Hargrave, my lord. My father is a wealthy merchant in London and compelled me to take up arms in Essex's army. Yet I had my misgivings—and after witnessing the conduct of certain radicals among their ranks, I felt honour-bound to depart and offer my service to the King. I only hope I may be forgiven." He bowed deeply, the weight of shame plain upon him.

"Das is good to hear. Can you share any additional information? How far away are they, for example?"

"A substantial force of cavalry passed me on the road, my lords. At first, I feared I was being pursued, but I managed to conceal myself—and my horse—in an abandoned barn. There may have been as many as a thousand, though I cannot say with certainty. I remained hidden for some time before following their trail, which veered south just short of Worcester. A portion of their rearguard lingered for a while, and I saw them turned away at the gate. It was then

I seized the chance to throw myself upon your mercy—and offer my service," Mr. Hargrave said, his sincerity unmistakable.

The Prince rubbed his thin moustache in contemplation. "That will be the horse you observed, William."

"We must be ready to depart at first light—see that all preparations are made," Sir Byron instructed the assembled officers, his tone firm, though tinged with a hint of strain. The presence of the Prince seemed to unsettle him, throwing the usual chain of command slightly off balance as he sought to reassert his authority.

The Prince stepped closer to Sir Byron and spoke in a low voice, careful that the defector would not overhear. "I think we should await my bruder's arrival. If we march at dawn and this host falls upon our rear, the convoy will be sorely exposed—particularly if their numbers match or exceed our own."

"Respectfully your grace, whilst I agree, the longer we stay here the greater the chances of Essex army falling on Worcester. Have you seen the walls? The efforts to repair and improve have been aboral, however as soon as the cannons come to bare, they won't last long" Sir Byron said

"Yes, I have inspected some of the walls, but it will take time for Essex army, even when they are at the walls, to set up their cannon to break down these defences; ample time for us to get away, but for now make all preparation and let it be known we are leaving at first light" The Prince said quietly before making his way back over to William and the map.

"Very well, Your Grace—but the King has entrusted me with the duty of returning this plate to him, and this remains my command. Nonetheless, I shall await your brother's arrival," Sir Byron replied, his tone laced with thinly veiled irritation. Without another word, he turned and began issuing orders to the officers, who promptly hurried off to relay them to their respective units.

"Your Sir Byron seems quite tense, does he not?" Maurice whispered to William, noting the noticeable fluster in Sir Byron's demeanour.

"He is simply eager to deliver this Convoy to the King. He is a solid commander, one of the more competent ones," William replied in a hush.

The Prince raised his eyebrows, a knowing look passing between them, with William subtly implying that the calibre of their officers was somewhat wanting.

Lowering his voice to almost a whisper, the Prince said to William, ""My bruder, he seeks a fight with the rebels. Once Sir Byron's convoy is safely on its way to my uncle, he will look for any chance to engage. We must reinforce that bridge as soon as my brother arrives; it is a perfect place to confront this force."

"When we dispatch a massager to my bruder, get a second to go to your troops at the bridge to stay on alert," the Prince continued, still keeping his tone low

"No need your grace. I have sent most of my scouting party back with the news and that instruction already" William said.

"Very Good, William." The Prince turned, raising his voice so all could hear "Well done, Mr. Hargrave; you serve your king admirably this day. I will have you brought to me later for further conversation, after you have had a bite to eat and a chance to freshen up. But until then, these two men will keep you company. I hope you understand, ja?" the Prince said smoothly, gesturing for the guards to escort him away. Once they were gone, the Prince turned to Sir Byron once more.

"Sir Byron, do you have anyone up in that fine-looking cathedral that dominates this beautiful city skyline? I would say its aspect overlooks the southern approaches well, ja? Looking at this map?" the Prince asked.

"Umm well, no" Byron replied awkwardly "The acting Dean has objected to us posting soldiers there. They are rather unhappy of our use of their college green and the mess we have made of it." Sir Byron's reasoning sounded a little feeble.

"Tell the acting Dean this is the King's will—and do not take nein for an answer. Post lookouts to watch toward Powick at first light and report directly to me, if you would, Sir Byron," the Prince added.

Byron paused before replying, as though suppressing his instinctive reaction to the young foreign Prince's assertiveness. "I shall have men posted there and ensure their findings are relayed to you, Your Grace." He beckoned one of his brothers and whispered instructions into his ear.

As the room fell into conversation, the officers and men set off to ensure the garrison was on full alert; the Essex army was drawing near.

The Prince turned once more to William. "We have much to catch up on, ja. Let us find a room, perhaps a glass of wine to wash down some bread and cheese. I am very famished. We can discuss the situation in the south-west of my uncle's realm, and perhaps you can introduce me to your future father-in-law," he said with a warm smile. A servant, who was within earshot, dashed off to fulfil his wishes.

William stood pondering, stroking his chin in contemplation.

"Ach, I know that look, William. Pray, tell me, vat are you thinking?" The Prince said, excitement in his tone.

"I think I have an idea; it might be risky" William said with a glint in his eye.

"I like the sound of it already, mein alter Freund," the Prince replied.

*   *   *

Benjamin heard more shouts, the sound of hurried footsteps, and the clinking of armour as soldiers rushed to the city wall outside once more. The commotion and excitement permeated the stables, unsettling the horses, who paced restlessly in their stalls, clearly distressed by their confinement.

With a sense of urgency, Benjamin set about calming the restless horses, achieving only modest success amid the rising cacophony outside. Just then, Owen appeared through the main stable doors, leading his heavily built piebald horse—perhaps a touch too agricultural for Benjamin's refined taste in horses, but sturdy and strong enough to bear the weight of a man like Owen. Unlike his more spirited equine companions, this beast seemed far too weary to display any excitement as it joined the others in the stable. Owen guided it to its stall, conveniently located next to Ralph's, the familiar surroundings providing a sense of comfort amidst the excitement outside.

"What's happening?" Benjamin inquired; with concern.

"There is news that the Parliamentary army is nearby moving up on us from the east," Owen replied matter-of-factly, the weariness of his long day evident in his voice.

"Really? How big an army?" Benjamin asked, his eyes wide with surprise.

"I don't know, lad. Did you manage to finalise that deal on that pack horse? William's keen we have one. He shouldn't have sold the one we had from London" Owen said, abruptly changing the subject.

"It was a hard bargain, but he is now in Samson's stable yonder. Master William's kit is ready, all set to load once we are prepared to depart. I wasn't certain whether Master William would return or if he intended to camp at the bridge with the troop," Benjamin responded.

"We all leave at first light to rejoin the troop. William's presently occupied with Prince Maurice, but he'll be keen to return—you know how he dislikes leaving the men under Sir Redmain's sole command for long."

They shared a knowing glance, until Benjamin's eyes widened.

"Did you say the Prince is here?" Excitement lit his handsome features.

"He surely is, lad—and his elder brother, Rupert, is close by with a formidable force of cavalry. They know their business, but keep that close—word mustn't get out. They'll join our lads come morning, and we're to serve as rearguard for the wagon column. Best get what rest we can. Tomorrow will be a long day."

Owen's gentle tone steadied Benjamin; he had come to rely on the older man's calm, finding comfort in his unshaken composure.

"I'll try," Benjamin said, though concern still troubled him. "But… do you think the Rebels will attack?"

"I don't believe they will. The fortifications, even in the state they are in, will require siege equipment, and a night assault demands careful planning and ample preparation, and are often costly in lives, so therefore, it is quite unlikely lad," Owen remarked as he settled into a corner of the Inn's stables. "However, to be prudent, we should snatch some sleep here, so we can make a quick exit if necessary." He winked at Benjamin before allowing his eyes to drift closed.

"Will I need to go into battle?" Benjamin asked, a hint of anxiety creeping into his voice.

"No, lad. Just stay with the baggage and the spare horses. Will made a promise to his father to keep you safe, honouring the friendship he bears your family," Owen replied, closing his eyes once more.

"Are you afraid of facing battle?" Benjamin inquired, curiosity getting the better of him.

"Yes," Owen admitted, his tone clipped. "Now let me sleep, boy. Please, refrain from asking so many questions." Fatigue seeped into his voice, momentarily overshadowing his usual patience and benevolence.

Sleep eluded Benjamin. A brief but heavy downpour of rain punctuated his restless thoughts, making him glad of the shelter of the stable, his mind racing with the day's events: the impending peril, the excitement of potentially meeting two Princes, and the uncertainties of tomorrow. He struggled to calm his turbulent thoughts, lacking Owen Jones's innate ability to sleep anywhere, any time – a skill Owen claimed as the hallmark of a true veteran.

Chapter 49
The Escape, 23rd September 1642

The first light of dawn crept into the humble confines of the Worcester Inn's stables, casting a soft glow over the resting horses and scattered hay, its dust hanging lazily in the still air. Benjamin busied himself with loading the packhorse with William's gear, while the faint stirrings of the waking city drifted in from outside. The air was brisk, laced with the scent of damp earth and straw, as he worked diligently in the half-light, ensuring the stables were left as tidy as they had found them.

Just then, William appeared, urgency written plainly across his face. "Benjamin, we must make haste! Rouse Owen from his slumber—I want to rejoin our troop without delay."

"I wasn't sure what you wanted to wear today," Benjamin replied, a hint of fluster in his voice as he fumbled with the straps of a saddlebag.

"Umm, nothing too heavy," he began, then paused. "Actually," he continued, "bring my back and breastplate, helmet too, if you would. Load the rest, but I'll take my bridle hand gauntlet as well." William didn't trust such valuable equipment to the troops' carts now with the camp near the bridge.

With a teasing grin, William nudged Owen awake with a light kick to his side. Momentarily groggy, Owen mumbled something and nodded off again—until a firmer prod made him spring up with a start.

"Sorry, Will!" he blurted, hastily gathering his belongings. "You should've woke me up," he grumbled in Benjamin's direction.

"You looked like you needed the rest," Benjamin replied with a cheeky grin. "Trust me, I nearly did—what with your snoring rattling the rafters."

Owen, now fully alert, shook off the last of his drowsiness with impressive speed and busied himself with getting his kit together.

Among Owen's gear was his imposing one-handed pole-axe, which he inspected with quiet admiration before strapping it securely to his saddle. Its deadly-looking head caught the dull gleam of early morning light as he set about donning his plain, munition-grade back and breast-plate, along with a simple three-barred pot helm. Unlike William's carefully blued armour, Owen had his kit blackened at a local smithy with oil—a rougher method, but one that offered comparable protection against rust and rendered him less conspicuous while scouting.

"The word is we're to leave at first light, but the Prince wants to wait for his brother's arrival—and for clearer news of where that force of Rebel horse might be. Still, the convoy must be ready to depart at a moment's notice, so Sir Byron is getting it formed up, ready to cross west, over Worcester's bridge as soon as he receives word from the Princes," William explained.

As if on cue, the noise of creaking carts and the clatter of hooves echoed through the dimly lit stables, belying their attempts at discretion. The bustle of the Inn and the preparations for departure stirred the horses, once more.

Now fully outfitted in back and breastplate, his bridle gauntlet darkly blued yet gleaming from Benjamin's care-ful polishing, William stood as Benjamin tied a red silk sash around his waist—the only clear mark of allegiance should they go into combat. The rebels, by all accounts, wore light russet in Essex's colours, while the King's men bore the red.

With the prospect of action before them, William set his prized helmet upon his head—a gift from the Prince himself, and by far the most notable piece of his otherwise modest kit—cutting a figure every inch the seasoned soldier.

He drew his basket-hilt sword and ran a careful thumb along the edge, testing its keenness, ensuring it was ready for whatever the day might bring. "You grow more adept with each passing week," he said, his eye falling approvingly upon his pair of fine wheel-lock pistols, their steel gleaming as brightly as the armour Benjamin had so diligently burnished.

At such unexpected praise, rare as it was, Benjamin's face lit with quiet pride, a welcome warmth rising amidst the morning's taut expectancy.

"I shall ride Ralph today," William continued. "I'll need fresh legs if the day turns hard. Samson is tethered outside—you'll take him. Keep close to the pack horse, and fall in with the baggage train when it moves out. We shan't be far behind, God willing."

He gave Benjamin a firm pat on the shoulder, sensing the lad's restless energy—and his silent worry for his beloved Ralph—as they made ready to meet whatever the uncertain day would bring.

As they made their way, bidding a quiet farewell to the kindly Innkeepers, they ventured through the congested streets toward the guild hall, where the Prince and his small escort of nobles awaited them. The animosity directed toward William had shown no signs of abating, particularly after the Prince chose to spend the evening reminiscing with his old friend and had even granted him a much-coveted room for the night, allowing for a few precious hours of rest before the day's duties.

"Our Mr. Hargrave is en route with his orders—he seems eager for redemption. Arrangements are in place with Berkeley," Prince Maurice said with a smile, winking at William. A knowing look passed between them, further piquing the curiosity of their noble companions.

Crossing the Bridge Gate, they passed soldiers hollow-eyed with fatigue after a long night on watch, fearing a rebel assault from the east. The strain etched on their faces spoke to the tension gripping the city. Soon, the three troops of cavalry stationed there—along with the remnants of Sir Byron's horse—would depart with the baggage train.

A wave of anxiety swept over Benjamin as he fidgeted with his reins, bracing for whatever lay beyond the safety of the walls. Yet beneath the nerves, a thrill stirred in him: they were riding to join the King's main army. The thought of marching beside a Royal Prince still left him in awe. If only Jane could see me now... and her mother, Mistress Mary, he mused.

As the party ventured forth down the old road and onto the lower Wick Fields, nestled by trees and hedges, they were greeted by the sight of their own troop busily dismantling their camp. To the west, cresting the distant rise, a strong body of horse came into view, banners and guidons borne high. William could just make out the colours of the House of Wittelsbach among them, the flags snapping in the wind, while the red sashes knotted at their waists marked them beyond doubt as Prince Rupert's seven hundred horse, come up in reinforcement.

"Ha! My bruder was never one to linger—they have made fine speed to reach us," the Prince remarked, as they approached from the direction given in his message. The affection he bore his elder brother was plain to see.

Upon entering the camp, William was met by a decidedly irate Sir Redmain, who came striding towards him with a face carved in displeasure. Meanwhile, the Prince and his attendants remained engrossed in earnest conference, their eyes sweeping the ground about them with a soldier's keen regard for the lay of the land.

"Where have you been?" Sir Redmain barked, cutting off William before he could respond, "You were meant to relieve me last night after you made your report!"

"My apologies, I was…" William began, but before he could explain further, Sir Redmain interrupted again, pointing his finger at William.

"I didn't get a wink of sleep out here, it hammered down with rain at one point and it was freezing throughout the night and with no fires!" He shuddered, visibly reinforcing the harshness of his circumstances.

Eager to shift the subject, as a wave of embarrassment crept up his spine at being chastised in the Prince's earshot, William took the opportunity to steer the conversation toward duty. "My apologies, Sir. Have the scouts reported back yet?" he inquired, maintaining a steady voice despite the notable unease.

"No, they have not," Sir Redmain snapped, irritation coursing through his words like a current.

"Then we ought to send a party out to search for them," William replied, concern for his men evident in his earnest expression.

"They haven't returned because I dispatched no one—we are leaving!" Sir Redmain laughed derisively, as if William's suggestion was the folly of a dullard.

William stared back in bewilderment, disbelief washing over him. Just then, Prince Maurice trotted his horse over, his authoritative presence magnifying the seriousness of the situation.

"Did I hear you say we have no scouts watching for the enemy?" he interjected, his tone brisk and uncompromising.

Dressed in his splendid buff coat and mounted on a striking black charger—a clear emblem of his noble stature—Prince Maurice's commanding presence gave Sir Redmain pause, a spark of recognition crossing his face.

"This is Prince Maurice, Your Grace. And this is Sir Redmain, captain of my troop," William said diplomatically, masking his growing contempt. For his family's sake—and for his poor sister, who would one day have to endure this odious man as a father-in-law—he kept his tone civil.

Sir Redmain offered a hurried, somewhat awkward bow, his expression tinged with embarrassment as he looked up at the mounted Prince.

"We have met before, Your Grace—during your former visit to your uncle, some years past. I gave generously to the collection raised in support of your family's cause to reclaim the Palatinate."

"That would have been my elder bruders, not I," the Prince replied. His gaze—sharp as a falcon's—did not waver. "Now, can you answer my question, Sir Redmain?"

"Yes—I mean, no… Your Grace, I have no scouts presently abroad, but I can dispatch some forthwith," Sir Redmain stammered, his hands fluttering in nervous agitation, plainly taken aback. "I have a few dragoons set to watch the bridge—they'll give warning should any force advance from that quarter."

He gestured toward the thick line of trees and hedgerows that bordered the road, hiding from view the stout stone bridge beyond.

"A few dragoons, sir? We know a sizeable force of enemy horse was on the far bank of the Severn. We must determine whether they've crossed to this side." The Prince's tone sharpened. "Send a couple of men—quietly—across the bridge to confirm what I suspect."

He paused, his irritation plain at the man's want of initiative.

"I believe we shall find our foes in zat village," the Prince said, his accented words cutting through the morning air. "Any soldier worth his salt would make use of zat church tower." He gestured toward the distance, where the crenellated roof of St Peter's Church at Powick rose just visible above the trees. "And if that be so, Sir Redmain, then they already know you are here."

With a sudden urgency, he turned his horse. "I must speak vid my bruder at once!" He cantered off, his escort riding close behind.

Meanwhile, Benjamin, coming up slightly behind, keeping a respectable distance with Owen and the pack horse, couldn't stifle a soft chuckle at Sir Redmain's flustered demeanour. The usually stoic captain wore a look of exasperation that bordered on comical, prompting Owen to flash a broad grin, sharing in the humour of the moment. "Best you make your way to the wagons shortly, lad," he suggested, gesturing at the wagons being loaded with some of the final items.

Just then, the echoes of distant musket fire shattered the semblance of calm, cutting through the air with an urgency that commanded their full attention. They all turned instinctively, their expressions betraying a mixture of concern and wariness as they strained to pinpoint the source of the sounds.

With keen ears, Benjamin quickly discerned that the musket fire emanated from the east, towards the city; the cacophony heralding the brewing conflict.

"They are attacking the city," Benjamin said, his thoughts briefly drifting to the kind Innkeepers they had left behind.

More volleys of musket fire echoed in rapid succession carrying faintly in the distance, each report stirring a rising tension among the assembled soldiers who stood silent, all straining to hear, making the imminent danger feel all too real.

"Get on with it!" Owen's voice boomed, shattering their stupor. The air—once alive with the sounds of morning bustle and easy talk—now crackled with the raw edge of anticipation.

"We need these wagons packed and back with the main convoy!" he barked, his gaze fixed upon the troopers labouring to load their gear into the carts—far too slowly for his liking. Beyond them, the long column waited in Worcester, ready for the word to move. The urgency in Owen's tone rang through the camp, a sharp reminder that every moment lost might cost them dear.

The musket fire had fallen silent as suddenly as it had begun, and the stillness that followed was heavier than the noise.
Turning to William, Owen said, "Shall I send someone into the city to find out what's going on?"

"No need to worry about that Owen, but if you go and find Sir Berkeley and bring him here, I will bring you up to speed" William ordered.

Some time passed before Thomas Smyth—captain of a Company of dragoons, now restored to full strength thanks to Sir Byron, who had given him the remnants of a unit mauled in an earlier encounter before reaching Oxford—rode up from the direction of the bridge. At his side came a small escort, among them his ever-faithful servant, Matthew.

"William!" he called, concern in his voice. "Do you know what's afoot?"

"It's nothing to fret over," William replied evenly.

"We've no sight of the enemy at the bridge," Smyth reported. "We are about to send scouts across, though a pair of villagers from the south bank claim the foe lies yonder In Powick village itself. We have also taken a few men come down from the city, who confessed to having gone over to see them. They say the enemy is in strength, but would speak no further."

He hesitated, his brow furrowed. "What would you have me do with them?"

"See that no one crosses the Powick bridge from Worcester—forthwith," William said, his tone leaving no room for question. "We'll have no word carried about Prince Rupert's force; there are those in the city who are not the King's friends."

Sir Redmain, still reeling from the swift turn of events, turned to William with uncertainty in his voice. "Perhaps it was best we join the column as guards," he suggested, his nerves plainly frayed. "That is our charge, after all."

"I believe it's best, Sir, that we wait for the Princes to give us our orders; they are approaching," William asserted, his tone failing to mask his growing irritation.

Then, from the direction of Upper Wick, a formidable sight emerged: some seven hundred Royalist horsemen—a diverse mix of Cavaliers, both young and old. Their guidons fluttered in the breeze as they rode, many wearing a motley array of helmets and broad-brimmed hats. Though few bore armour, their strong buff coats—varying in cut and quality—spoke of a force prepared to move fast and strike hard.

Some carried ornate pistols, while others had longer carbines protruding from saddle holsters, complemented by an array of resplendent sword hilts visible on their belts suspended from baldrics, which jingled as they rode. The horses varied in shape and size, but most were of very fine hunter stock, solid yet athletic; well ridden by gentlemen accustomed to such quality steeds, a detail noted by Benjamin as he felt a tug of reluctance to leave his troop behind amidst such excitement.

Approaching in a long column, they skirted the edge of the tree line bordering the Wick fields. At the forefront of this valiant formation rode Prince Maurice, now accompanied by a taller, leaner figure, dressed in sumptuous attire that spoke both of noble lineage and impeccable style. This was Prince Rupert, bearing a striking resemblance to his brother. Slightly out of place, a powerful and athletic white dog of an unfamiliar breed bounded ahead, its enthusiastic bark confirming its canine nature as it darted through the ranks.

Without preamble, Prince Rupert gave his command. "Maurice, order a few companies of dragoons to take position in the tree line overlooking the road from the bridge. If the enemy crosses, tell them to hold their fire until a substantial force is over this side—then strike. We'll ride swiftly to support and all being well, catch the devils by surprise."

He surveyed the terrain with a practised eye, taking in the lay of the land and the readiness of the men. "Who commands these soldiers?" he asked, his tone imperious.

"That would be I, Your Grace," replied Sir Redmain, stepping forward and offering a deep bow.

"You are now under my command," Rupert said with calm authority. "Join mein men on ze top fields over zere. Keep your guidons lowered und no trumpeters until I give the word. Stay to ze tree line as much as possible we must try and conceal our true strength."

Just then, Sir Thomas Berkeley appeared with Owen, riding up from the direction of the city.

"God blessing on, Your Graces and sirs. I encountered Corporal Jones en route with a report: the garrison discharged volleys as ordered, and the men now posted in the cathedral have sighted a considerable number of cavalry on the far bank near the village of Powick. It's difficult to gauge their numbers, given the tree cover and foliage but perhaps as many as a thousand," Sir Thomas reported, his gaze narrowed in thought. "However, Sir Byron is with the convoy and requests if the column may depart."

Sir Redmain, pompously standing by the elevated company of both Princes and several recognised nobles, interjected grandly, "These are His Highness, Prince Rupert, and his brother, Prince Maurice, who have just informed us that we are now under their command."

Sir Thomas Berkeley responded with a respectful bow toward the Princes, comically tipping his hat to reveal a metal cap hidden beneath, before settling it back atop his head. "It would be an honour to serve under you, Your Graces. I had the pleasure of meeting His Grace Prince Maurice last night—thank you, Sir Redmain, for the reintroduction." A faint, sardonic smile touched his lips.

Prince Rupert offered a slight nod. "I shall have mein men rest for a while, und keep a low profile. Ve have been riding hard." He paused. "I would like to have zat column stay put for now. Please relay my regards to Sir Byron, und tell him ze departure will be at ten o'clock tonight – unless I tell him otherwise. Ze cover of darkness will be our last resort." He paused in contemplation, a smile crossing his handsome face.

"I want those rebels to cross ze bridge," Prince Rupert said, a predatory glint in his eyes. "So ve can give Zim a proper thrashing! Ze ground is favourable for us here, und we must remove them as a threat before ve move."

The assembled officers replied in unison, "Yes, Your Highness," smiles spreading among them—though Sir Redmain seemed less enthusiastic, his usual bravado faltering at the prospect of a real fight.

"Bruder, mein Lieber Freund," he said, pressing his hand onto William's shoulder. "Lieutenant Stephens here assures me the muskets will signal, and our messengers' tale will be reinforced with our foes over the bridge. God willing, they will attack when we let a second volley fly." Prince Maurice spoke with enthusiastic conviction.

"A risky and daring plan, Lieutenant — and luckily, I like it!" Prince Rupert exclaimed, punctuating his words with an exuberant slap of his thigh, his broad smile infectious.

"A more cautious commander might choose to slip away quietly in the shadows," he added, casting a pointed glance toward some of his noble companions, before leaning forward with a mischievous grin, plainly savouring the thrill of the gamble.

"But it is time we put zese rebels back in zeir place! I do believe you and I will get along very well. My bruder holds you in high regard, und I trust him implicitly." With that, Rupert gave his brother a jovial punch on his arm.

William noted how Maurice took pride in his brother's words, his demeanour shifting to that of a willing subordinate—glad, it seemed, to slip comfortably beneath Rupert's wing, happy to let him take the lead.

As their discourse drew to a close, several senior officers gathered—Commissary Wilmot, Sir Charles Lucas, and Sir Richard Crane, captain of Prince Rupert's Lifeguard—all eager to see the plan set in motion and no less ardent for action than the Prince himself. Standing somewhat apart was Lord Digby, a more restrained figure, his countenance marked by disapproval, then pompously demanded to be taken to Sir Byron and to inspect the column.

The deserter, one Mr Hargrave's bore a forged order and had slipped away just before dawn to follow the trail of the rebel forces. Disguised as a messenger from Essex's army, he carried instructions bidding them advance upon Worcester by way of Powick Bridge, with intent to encircle the city. They were to act only upon hearing a second volley of musket fire—the first to mark the arrival of their vanguard to the east of the city, the second to signal that the assault was begun.

Prince Maurice would dispatch a messenger to the city to signal a second volley—this would serve as the lure to draw the Rebel horse across, leading them straight into the trap.

Prince Rupert wished to grant his horses and men a brief rest, while also allowing the defector ample time to deliver the false orders to the enemy commander. If all went according to plan, they would spring the ambush and crush the enemy cavalry—securing for the King a decisive first victory.

Carefully, Thomas Smyth retraced his steps toward the bridge with reinforcements, taking pains to maintain a low profile. Nearby, the remaining soldiers dismounted in Wickfield, their movements slow and deliberate. They loosened saddle girths beneath the scattered hawthorn trees, seeking the dappled shade and meagre concealment from the warm, relentless sun that had quickly dried the wet ground. Allowing their horses to graze in small, quiet groups, some soldiers took long drinks from their water flasks, while others led their mounts to the river. They kept their voices low, exchanging hushed words and glances, never straying far from their steeds or disturbing the stillness of the field.

The atmosphere gradually grew relaxed and congenial as the hours slipped by. Midday came and went, yet there was still no sign of movement across the bridge. As the supply wagons—laden with tents and baggage—began to make their way north, returning to the city to join the column poised to depart at the Prince's command, Benjamin approached William.

William remounted Ralph, who was fresh and well-rested. From the saddle, he surveyed the gentle slope stretching across the fields, eyes scanning the distance for any sign of movement. William felt restless wishing to sound the second volley.

"I am setting off now, Master Stephens," Benjamin announced, nudging Samson forward to join him.

Ralph and Samson turned toward one another, noses gently nudging as they relished the moment, having forged a special bond over the years spent as paddock companions; it was as if they were bidding a fond farewell to each other.

Benjamin affectionately patted Ralph's neck, taking pleasure in witnessing their interaction. William's face reflected surprise as he was jolted from his reverie, suddenly realising that Benjamin was bidding farewell to Ralph just as much as he was to him.

"We will be right behind you, Benjamin. There is nothing to fear," he reassured him, sensing Benjamin's reluctance to leave Ralph behind.

"May God grant that to be true. Look after him, Ralph," Benjamin replied with a smile, giving his equine companion another gentle pat.

"Off with you now, lad. Tend to Samson and that pack horse, and we shall see you soon," William urged him more warmly than his usual commands.

With a determined kick, Benjamin urged Samson forward, unwilling to look back as emotions swelled within him, threatening to spill over. He was determined not to embarrass himself before William and the troop as he joined the small procession of baggage wagons trudging along the path toward the city.

William smiled faintly, his thoughts turning homeward. From his saddlebag he drew a small locket—his father's gift—and opened it to the delicate miniatures of his mother and sister. For a moment, their familiar faces brought a quiet comfort. Then he closed the clasp and slipped it back into its place, forcing his thoughts to the present—to the tremor of anticipation, and the heavy weight of his plan, at once a thrill and a burden upon his shoulders.

Benjamin fell into step with their troop's quartermaster, a grizzled, weathered man whose competence was obvious. He was skilfully manoeuvring a wagon, a stern yet astute figure. Benjamin realised, surprised, that he was Sir Redmain's steward. A smile crossed Benjamin's face – he reminded him of Mr. Cropper, cut from the same cloth.

The two miles passed slowly, with frequent stops as wagons were bogged down in ruts. They passed a small group of horsemen heading towards Powick Bridge. "That was Sir Byron, lad," the wagon master remarked to Benjamin. "He looks none too pleased," Benjamin remarked, noting the man's clearly vexed expression as he stood flanked by one of the nobles who had arrived with Prince Rupert.

As he walked beside the wagon, leading his packhorse, Benjamin savoured the last of the warmth before winter's chill. His thoughts drifted to Fairfield Farm, to friends and family. He ached for his sister and, surprisingly, even for his father – a man whose constant criticism had bred resentment. Now, Benjamin simply regretted never saying goodbye.

His thoughts, unbidden, turned to Jane – a memory he'd tried to avoid. The recollection brought a shudder of pain, mirroring the growing unease in his stomach as distant musket fire cracked through the air. A wave of nausea washed over him, battling the urge to turn back. Another volley of musket fire then erupted as Worcester Bridge came into view, perhaps the second signal he'd overheard the prince discussing.

"We must keep moving, lad," the quartermaster said gruffly, flicking his reins to urge the wagon horse forward, almost as if he could read the turmoil within Benjamin's mind. "They have their duties, and we have ours. Sometimes it is harder not being there to help our friends when they need us, but our duty is no less important."

Another round of musket fire echoed, more sporadic this time, but it seemed to be coming from behind rather than towards the city. Benjamin offered a silent prayer to God before earnestly saying aloud, "Please keep them all safe."

Chapter 50
The Fight at Powick Bridge, 23ʳᵈ September 1642

Fierce musket fire erupted from the direction of the bridge, sending plumes of smoke billowing into the distance carried by the breeze.

"To arms! To arms!" the corporals bellowed, and trumpets blared, prompting the men to spring to their feet and rush to their horses.

The two princes swiftly mounted, commanding their Colonels to form the regiments into three ranks. The order cascaded down the line: Colonels to Captains, Captains to Lieutenants, to Cornets waving bright guidons as rallying points. Trumpeters blared the calls, corporals shouting and cajoling their men into long, ordered lines.

Prince Maurice trotted over to William, who was diligently guiding his troop into position with the commanding assistance of Owen's resonant voice. The sight of Sir Redmain struggling to mount the tall frame of Miller was both amusing and exasperating, as he appeared almost helpless amid the ensuing chaos.

"William, they must have sought to cross before the second signal—or else mistook those wagons for part of the convoy departing," Maurice said, a wry smile curling his lips as he savoured the prospect of battle. "Either way, my bruder will have his wish."

"I vant your troop to serve as my Lifeguard," he added, giving his companion a friendly punch on the shoulder. "I vant you by my side—and him as well!" He nodded toward Owen, who stood nearby with his horseman's pole-axe resting on one broad shoulder, bellowing for the men to make haste.

"It would be an honour, Your Grace," William replied, a glint of nostalgia in his eye. "To ride beside you again—like old times. Only keep those musket balls from finding me, eh?" he added with a grin, the jest easing the tautness between them.

"Someone, for the love of God, give me a leg up!" Sir Redmain shouted, his face growing redder with each passing moment as he struggled to reach the stirrup, hopping along as Miller slowly moved off. Amidst the commotion, Sir Redmain's flailing attempts rendered him utterly hapless.

To the amusement of the Prince and William, a nearby soldier quipped, "God help us if all of the King's knights are like this one," eliciting laughter from the men within earshot—a gibe that Sir Redmain, singularly focused on his mounting predicament, seemed not notice.

Turning to survey the slight dip of the ground, the intermittent but foreboding murmurs of musket fire filled the air. A mere handful of horsemen emerged from the tree-lined track leading off the bridge, their mounts gripped by obvious panic. The steeds, eyes wide and wild, bolted forward, hooves churning the earth. The riders, struggling to maintain control, grasped at the reins in vain, their bodies pitching and swaying as they desperately fought to stay mounted.

The disarray provoked a chorus of jeers and taunts from the ranks of the onlooking Royalist Cavaliers, who were now drawn up in a formidable line, ready for action in impressive speed. Their own horses, magnificent steeds, pawed impatiently at the ground, sensing the nervous energy of their riders. The animals tossed their heads, their powerful necks arching, as if eager to unleash their pent-up energy upon the approaching foe, adrenalin flowing though horse and rider alike.

A line of horsemen spilled into the open field as the tree line and hedges receded. Wearing russet or tawny sashes in the Earl of Essex's colours and clad in varied Harquebusier armour—mostly back and breastplates with lobster-tail helmets—they cantered up the track, enduring the dragoons' fire. Encircling the tree line, they prepared a rear assault, aiming to strike back against the dismounted enemy concealed behind the foliage, their trumpeter blaring orders.

William's attention snapped to the lead Parliamentarian officer, who now gestured frantically toward the crest of the rise, the whites of his eyes flashing with stark terror. There, a long, unwavering line of Royalist horsemen stood in good order poised to strike. The officer's shouted commands were swallowed by the din, his men merely clumping together in a disorganised, terrified mass.

Prince Rupert rode along the Royalist line, radiating infectious energy. "Draw your swords!" he roared, his Germanic voice tinged with a Dutch accent. "Ve will meet these scoundrels with steel! A canter charge—our battle cry will be so fierce, they'll flee like the rabble they are, for ze King!" His rallying cry sparked cheers, his command crackling with urgent fire. "Now, we charge!"

Though unconventional—William's time with the Swedish cavalry had taught him a steady trot, formed in by a tight formation, knee to knee and a final canter charge—Prince Rupert's rapid approach, however, given the short distance, would capitalise on the disorder among the rebels William could see.

William felt a thrill of nervous excitement, the Prince's energy stirring his blood. "For the King!" he roared, joining the swelling cheer.

Without hesitation, Rupert spurred his magnificent grey into a controlled canter, guiding him gracefully down the slope. His lifeguard, composed of senior nobles, followed instantly. William and his troop surged forward, while even the previously unhorsed Sir Redmain, sword raised high, rallied the men with a cry of "The Second Sons!" His shout mingled with the rising war cries of "For the King!" as the three ranks thundered toward the enemy.

Forward they charged, trumpets blaring. The slight decline, not quite a hill, lent them extra momentum. Hooves kicked up chunks of earth, the ground vibrating with a rhythmic beat, light flashing off polished blades.

William focused intently ahead, the thrill of the charge coursing through him. The Rebel cavalry, still struggling to form, now presented a disordered block about six rows deep—a crude, disjointed imitation of some of the Dutch manual William had read. Panic spread through their ranks as musket shots cracked behind them, a sign that Smyth and his Dragoons were firing into their formations from the rear.

The Parliamentary horsemen, heeding their officers' orders, reached for carbines and pistols. In that instant, time seemed to slow, anticipation pressing down like a weight. William's senses sharpened—every detail etched in stark clarity. Metal glinted, officers' faces tightened with urgency, and in the distance, treetops swayed in a silent breeze that whispered of the coming clash.

As the Rebels levelled their carbines, the air thrummed with taut, electric tension. Then—ragged thunder split the silence—flashes of orange spat from their line, smoke curling skyward like coiling serpents, briefly swallowing the field. The acrid haze billowed outward, its first breath a sharp, sulphurous sting that burned the nostrils and clawed at the throat, laced with a faint metallic tang. William held his breath against the choking cloud, muscles taut, eyes darting left to Prince Maurice, then right to Owen, who lagged under the lumbering gait of his heavy mount—yet both were miraculously untouched.

Adrenaline burned through William's veins. Ahead, an officer loomed—wild-eyed, desperate—fumbling for his sword after firing his pistol. His frantic motions reeked of fear, and William was closing fast.

In that charged moment, every heartbeat resonated like a drum, a testament to the fierce clash about to unfold. Pointing Ralph just to the left of his target so he would force a gap between the officer and his livered trumpeter. Feeling a sense of relief that he wasn't hit, squeezing Ralph's flanks, he urged the gelding onward, crashing into the Rebel forces amid the horrific cacophony of men and horses.

William's opponent was to his right, blade only half-drawn —too late. With a slight shift of his arm, William's sword found its mark, shearing through the man's neck. The momentum of his charge carried the stroke clean through; a single, merciless sweep.

William crashed through the gap in their ragged formation, his sword slicing through the next rider as if cleaving butter, gore splashing onto comrades to his rear, their faces etched with shock and horror. Simultaneously defending against a trooper to his left, William parried a cut, using his horse's weight to batter his way through. Ralph delivered a flying kick to an attacker attempting to wheel around to their rear, warding him off as the Royalist assault ripped through the enemy ranks, buckling the formation as many reeled away from the fierce onslaught.

In that instant, Prince Maurice drove the point of his rapier cleanly into the gap of a trooper's helmet—the man had just struck at William, his blow glancing off the basket hilt with a jarring shock that numbed William's arm. The steel was notched and dented, yet it held. The Prince's thrust snapped the attacker's head back with a sharp cry, and Maurice pressed on gallantly into the melee.

To William's right, Owen made his presence known—his pole-axe fell with bone-splintering force upon a man's shoulder, felling him where he sat. The rebel's sword slipped from his grasp as he wheeled his mount about, desperate to flee the maelstrom.

Steel clashed, men cried out, and horses screamed, all lost in battle's fury. The fight balanced on a knife's edge— valour against chaos, life against death. William pressed on, shutting out the carnage as horse and rider whirled in a deadly dance. Instinct took over: kill or be killed. The ground shook under pounding hooves, mud and powder-thick air closing in around him.

William guided Ralph with practised ease, the gelding un-fazed, ears pinned, answering each command with un-wavering courage. Weaving through the chaos of friend and foe, he took glancing blows and jolts, silently grateful for the steel that turned them aside. His sword—once sil-ver, now streaked with crimson—struck with measured precision, slipping through gaps in guard and armour. In that moment, he was the King's vengeance made flesh, cutting down all who defied the sovereign's right. A fevered frenzy gripped him, instinct and muscle memory driving his hand more than conscious thought.

Through the roiling press of men and horses, he caught sight of Prince Maurice—a beacon of defiance amid the maelstrom. His hair streamed behind him like a battle standard as he turned aside a cut at his flank with effortless grace, then drove his blade home in a fierce riposte. The rebel horseman gave a strangled gasp, sagged in the saddle, and tumbled to the churned earth below.

The Parliamentarian force began to fracture under the relentless onslaught, their formation splintering as the more numerous Royalist horse swept around them. The extended Royalist line wrapped them in a deadly embrace, giving the illusion that horsemen were coming from every direction. Those Parliamentarians advancing from the bridge turned in alarm, urging their troopers to retreat—choosing flight over fight.

Many were jammed fast upon the narrow bridge, no more than two or three able to pass abreast, while those on the footway found themselves unable either to advance or to fight. Trapped and exposed, they became easy marks for musket and carbine fire from the trees and hedgerows. In desperation they loosed blind shots into the foliage — a futile show of defiance — shouting for their comrades still upon the bridge to fall back.

A group of valiant Rebel officers formed a desperate shield around their guidons and colours as Royalist cavalry closed in, determined to take them as prizes. But the fight wasn't completely one-sided. The better-armoured Parliamentarians showed fortitude, enduring hard blows and holding their ground against the better-mounted Royalists.

However, what the Royalists lacked in protection, they more than compensated for with horsemanship and agility. They expertly maneuverer their less encumbered, better-trained steeds after the initial charge, and as the battle dissolved into a swirling melee, the resolve and spirit of the beleaguered Parliamentarians began to wane as they realised the tide had turned decisively against them.

William's gaze swept the battlefield and settled on Prince Rupert, who was locked on the officers shouting desperate orders to safeguard their flags and guidons. Panic had begun to spread through their ranks faster than the Royalist advance.

Rupert's lifeguard struggled to keep pace with his furious energy as he drove forward to shatter the last pockets of resistance. A challenge to protect, he surged ahead, his voice a clarion call that spurred others to follow. Matching his brother's fervour, Prince Maurice galloped to be alongside him—a magnificent display of royal courage, determined to crush the rebels' final resolve.

"Follow me! Protect the Princes!" William shouted to his troop the second son's trumpeter, sounding the notes of command.

"Seize ze flag!" Prince Maurice bellowed, his voice cutting through the din of battle as he fought to rally support amid the chaos. He kicked his horse on toward a cluster of enemy officers guarding several red guidons—standards held high in a fading attempt to inspire their wavering men. The nearest banner was crimson, bearing the image of an armoured arm and the Latin motto Vincere Spero —"Hope to Conquer."

Not today, William thought, spurring Ralph forward as a surge of resolve coursed through him. With practised ease, he shifted his sword to his left hand—the one upon the bridle—letting the blade rest lightly against his tall riding boot as he drew a wheel-lock pistol. Pressing his heel to Ralph's flank, as Benjamin had once instructed, he brought the horse into a travers—that graceful sideways motion wherein the horse's forehand remains forward while the hindquarters slip inward at an angle. The controlled shift turned both man and mount half-across the line of attack, offering a steadier seat and a clear line of fire ahead.

Taking careful aim, William levelled the pistol at a trooper charging toward the Prince's exposed flank. The shot cracked out true—yet instead of striking the man he intended, the ball hit his—horse. The beast reared in a panic, unseating its rider and sending him crashing hard to the ground. The thrashing horse, wild with fear, blocked the path and delayed any other would-be attackers.

Pressing onward, William hurled his spent pistol into the seething mass of enemy horsemen, watching it vanish amid the chaos. Seizing his sword once more in his right hand, he drove forward toward Prince Maurice, the roar of battle swelling and closing in around him.

The Prince fought fiercely, striking into the enemy ranks with unflinching resolve. A rebel blade glanced off the underside of his chin, drawing blood as he jerked his head back instinctively to avoid a deeper cut.

In that instant, his elegantly crafted rapier found its mark, thrusting deftly into the unguarded armpit of his assailant, driving deep. The man yelped in pain and released his reins.

One of the French gentlemen from Maurice's entourage, witnessing the fray, spurred his horse forward to aid the Prince. Shouting curses in French, he swept his blade in a swift arc across the neck of the Prince's opponent, silencing his cries in a grim yet efficient fashion.

From the corner of his eye, William caught a blur of motion—Owen, charging forward like an unstoppable force of nature. The clash of his pole-axe against a breastplate rang out over the din, sending an unfortunate rider sprawling, the clatter of armour swallowed by the chaos of battle.

Urging Ralph forward, William pressed through the throng, striving to reach the Prince's side as he forced his way into the press. Owen closed in beside him, and together they fought with ruthless precision—blade and axe working in deadly harmony as they hacked, parried, and struck down their foes.

"Watch out, Colonel Sandy!" bellowed a robust officer in a thick Scottish accent, urgency sharp in his voice—but the warning came too late.

Owen's pole-axe crashed into the colonel's chest, the head biting deep into his breastplate. The blow landed true, leaving a jagged dent—but the finely forged armour held, sparing the man a mortal wound.

Undeterred, Owen pressed on, carried forward by his horse's momentum. With a practised wrench, he freed his axe and turned it on a nearby cornet bearing one of the standards. The pole-axe struck squarely in the cornet's face, and the banner wavered.

Without pause, Owen seized the flag from the dying man's grasp like a lion claiming its prey.

In the final throes of the contest, the winded Parliament-arian colonel, driven by desperation, lunged forward with renewed ferocity, swinging his blade at Prince Maurice. The backhanded cut grazed the Prince's left arm as he battled another foe, forcing him to momentarily lose his grip on the reins.

The fine thick leather of his buff coat held firm—the blow failed to cut through, but the force of it made Maurice recoil, flinching as he turned a wary eye toward his assailant.

The colonel, seething with rage, drew back for a second swing, channelling all his strength into a fatal blow. His

face twisted in grim triumph at Prince Maurice's momentary helplessness.

But William, poised and resolute, had already drawn his
second pistol. He took aim, measuring the distance—less
than two meters, yet far from certain. Holding his breath,
he squeezed the trigger.

The mechanism of his wheel-lock sparked, and a shot rang
out. For a tense, agonising moment, the rebel officer vanished behind a plume of powder smoke. William held his
breath, frozen, anticipation surging through him.

Then the smoke cleared.

The ball had found its mark. The officer's horse now stood
riderless, its master sprawled lifeless beneath its hooves,
trampled amidst the circling tumult. A groan rose from the
rebel ranks at the sight of their fallen colonel. Panic followed—what had been a stout last stand dissolved into
chaos as the men broke and fled in disorder, their courage
spent.

Seizing the moment, the Frenchman wheeled his mount
and charged toward the Scottish officer who had given the
alarm—blade high, eyes alight with fury.

Prince Maurice cast a glance toward William, acknowledging him with a brief smile of gratitude and a nod of the
head, though a wince betrayed the pain in his wounded
arm. William, not wishing to lose another precious pistol
to the melee, swiftly returned the still-smoking wheel-lock
to its holster, a wave of relief washing over him as he saw
the field now firmly turning in their favour.

"We Yield! We surrender!" bellowed the Scottish officer,
his voice pleading and desperate. A deep cut marred his
shoulder, bleeding profusely as he struggled to escape his

French attacker. "I surrender!" he cried, discarding his weapon along with a cadre of his troopers, none wishing to meet a gruesome end. Soon, he and his comrades were captured by the victorious Royalists, the tide of fighting irrevocably shifted to a route and hunt.

With unyielding spirit, Prince Rupert spurred his steed onward, a fierce glint in his eye as he pursued the fleeing rebels toward the distant bridge. Behind him, Prince Maurice—weary but resolute—pressed forward, riding with greater caution as he nursed his wounds.

Meanwhile, William called out to Owen, instructing him to secure the captured guidons. His gaze flicked to Owen's horse, its sides heaving like great bellows as it struggled to catch its breath, staggering under the strain of the brief but brutal engagement.

As William urged Ralph around the bend in pursuit of the Princes, he noted with relief that his own mount remained responsive and full of vigour. But the scene ahead was chaos.

The rebel cavalry, routed and in panic, scrambled toward the bridge. To find the crossing choked with men and horses, the way forward blocked and perilously exposed. From the hedgerows beyond, Royalist dragoons continued to pour musket fire into the fleeing ranks.

In their desperation, the Parliamentarian horse, burdened with armour and gear, were driven into the river, swollen from recent rainfall, the waters rising to their mounts' bellies and bogging each step. Hooves churned the soft riverbed, slipping and flailing, while the steep, foliage-slicked banks turned every landing into a scramble. All the while, pursuing Royalists fired pistols and carbines. Some horses lost their footing, throwing riders into the cold, surging water; others pressed onward, men clinging desperately to flanks and reins as the current tugged at them. The air rang with the thunder of shots, sparks flying from discharged weapons, adding terror to every splash and struggle. Yet most made the far bank, hauling themselves up the slope and racing across the fields beyond. The pursuit was relentless but brief; the rout complete.

Yet William's keen eye caught sight of a small force of enemy dragoons still in good order on the far side of the bridge. Hastily, they adjusted their disciplined formation, forming a defensive line ready to unleash volleys of death upon any pursuers wearing the King's red.

"Your Grace, look!" William exclaimed, urgency lacing his voice as he drew the attention of both Princes, his heart pounding at the looming threat.

As if reading William's mind, Prince Rupert shouted, "Do not charge over the bridge!" His commanding tone cut through the din. "Recall the men; the enemy is in full retreat. The day is ours!" His words vibrated with the thrill of imminent victory.

Yet within the ranks of several Royalist troops, a fervour ignited. Their blood surged with the heat of battle, awakening a primal instinct that drowned out the calls of their leaders and strained sounds of the breathless trumpets desperately sounding the recall.

In reckless zeal, some charged after the fleeing rebels across the bridge.

William watched their folly a moment longer before turning his horse with grim resolve. Guilt tugged at him—he had helped shape this encounter, and now had more faces to haunt his dreams. But a swift, decisive victory was the only path to peace. The sooner the rebellion ended, the fewer lives would be lost. He prayed to God that this day would mark the beginning of its end.

He shifted his focus to rounding up any prisoners he could find. His troops rallied to his commands in good order and obedience to his proud relief, their voices rising in fervent cheer: "God save the King, God save the Second Sons!" Owen now waved the captured guidon triumphantly to the elation of their men.

From the thicket emerged the powder-marked figure of Thomas Smyth, accompanied by Matthew with a good number of his men, all their ammunition now expended, his men eager to scavenge from the fallen. "We did it, William! We won!" he proclaimed, his enthusiasm radiating the exuberance of one newly acquainted with the throes of battle and celebrating their survival. Yet, as he surveyed the scene, a heavy weight of awareness muted his celebratory demeanour.

His gaze fell upon the carnage—the lifeless bodies of both horses and men strewn about, some still alive but grievously injured, crying out for God or their mothers, or simply groaning incoherently. The triumph that had lit up his face faded into a grim understanding, twisting into a look of profound disgust. The harsh reality of victory weighed heavily upon him, casting a shadow over his kind soul, dispelling all traces of jubilation amid the haunting scene.

"May God forgive us for the sins we commit this day," Thomas Smyth declared, looking up at the sky to divert his gaze from the brutal truth of war.

A cheer reverberated through the Nag's Head, a lively Shrewsbury tavern whose low, beamed ceiling was thick with the mingled scents of wood smoke, pipe tobacco, ale, and unwashed bodies. The atmosphere crackled with jubilation as ballads and jaunty lute tunes intertwined with boisterous banter and high-spirited conversations. The crackling hearth, its fire battling the encroaching chill of the bitter October evening, cast a shimmering glow across the room, illuminating the flushed faces of the merry patrons. The "Second Sons" – a title they now wore with pride – clinked their tankards of frothy ale and beer, offering loud toasts to their King, their Royalist exuberance tangible in the smoky air.

Owen Jones raised his tankard high, drinking deeply from the barley beer that the pub served, a brew that had quickly become the favoured libation among their troop. The rich, malty flavour was a comforting companion to the vibrant camaraderie enveloping the room.

"Is William coming this evening?" Benjamin inquired; his brow slightly furrowed as he scanned the crowd for his friend.

Owen chuckled, mischief glinting in his eyes. "I daresay he wishes he could join us—but alas, he's holed up in the castle again tonight with Prince Maurice and his officers. Likely enduring Sir Redmain's latest tale of how he single-handedly drove the Parliamentarians into the river," he guffawed, his mirth contagious.

The mere mention of Sir Redmain drew a ripple of laughter. "Once Sir Leg Up finally managed to mount his horse!" one trooper shouted.

"Here's to our glorious captain, Sir Leg Up!" another bellowed.

The room erupted in uproarious laughter as the revellers raised their tankards. "To Sir Leg Up!" they chorused, and even Owen joined the toast.

The camaraderie inside the Nag's Head had reached a fever pitch, fuelled by the recent victory at Powick Bridge. Their troop, proud participants in that clash, now enjoyed coveted bragging rights within the swelling ranks of the King's army. Though weeks had passed since that first substantial engagement, it was celebrated—and embellished—anew with every retelling, Owen's hearty laughter rising above the din in testament to their shared triumph.

As tales of valour and bold endeavour filled the smoky air, the bonds of brotherhood were renewed over brimming tankards and loud, good-natured toasts. Amid the laughter and din, the patrons of the Nag's Head found solace and unity—rejoicing in their victory and hungering for the glories yet to come. A warm glow of shared ambition lingered about them, like firelight on polished steel, as they awaited the next chapter of their adventure.

"I think I shall head up to the castle stables, to check on the horses," Benjamin said, his earlier enthusiasm tempered by weariness.

"Lad, the horses will do well enough without thee," Owen replied with a knowing smile. "Take thy ease and savour the night. Even years hence, you'll remember such an evening—bright as any hearth-fire in winter."

His gaze drifted then to a buxom, fair-haired lass whose cheeks glowed like ripe apples, and whose arms looked strong enough to hoist a cask, let alone two tankards. She moved through the throng with practised ease, deftly elbowing aside the overbold and slipping clear of wandering hands. Her apron bore the stains of many a spilled ale, yet the quick sparkle in her eye made plain that any man who tried her patience might wear his drink rather than taste it.

Benjamin, lost in thought about his horse, was oblivious to much else. Ralph had emerged from the fray with only a few light marks and scratches—an outcome for which Benjamin was exceedingly grateful. Yet since the battle, Ralph had seemed off, not quite himself.

The horse now showed new quirks: weaving restlessly in the stall and laying his ears back at all who came near— save Benjamin, at whom he still softened. Yet there was brighter news. Thanks to the ample stores of grain and haylage furnished by the Royal Quartermaster—a mark of the King's favour for their triumph at Powick Bridge and the capture of an enemy standard by Corporal Owen, one of many taken by Prince Rupert's men—Ralph's feed was finer than ever.

He had begun to fill out once more, the gauntness easing from his great ribs, and a healthier flesh covering them at last. Benjamin hoped to keep him so, though the sudden turn to cold weather promised to make that a hard battle in the weeks to come.

Benjamin was pleased that Miller returned safe and sound from the action, being Sir Redmain's mount that day, alongside the rest of their cavalry troop. Remarkably, only two injuries had been reported in their troop: one soldier sustained a cut to his shoulder, and the farrier suffered a broken leg from a fall. Royalist losses on the whole were estimated at around thirty-five men in total, with over double that number sustaining various wounds, including injuries to Prince Maurice and Sir Henry Willmott, one of the nobles forming Rupert's lifeguard that day, though thankfully neither were serious and both men where convalescing at the castle.

To William's frustration, most losses came from those who pressed the bridge after Prince Rupert had ordered a recall. Some resolute Rebel dragoons mounted a disciplined rearguard action before withdrawing, delivering a few deadly volleys in the process. In contrast, total Rebel losses were reported at around sixty on the field, with perhaps a handful more falling while attempting to flee in desperation across the river.

The Royalists had taken around fifty prisoners, some of whom succumbed to their wounds and were left in Worcester for burial, while others were taken on the journey to Shrewsbury. Colonel Sandy was left in Worcester, the doctor giving him little chance of survival. Owen, for capturing a standard, was gifted a fine, stocky horse from the best mounts taken by Prince Rupert himself, which they aptly renamed Powick – a considerable upgrade from Owen's old mount, even Owen admitted. After seeing the effect on Thomas Smyth's usually high spirits, Benjamin felt fortunate not to have witnessed the combat first-hand and was grateful to God that his friends and their horses had emerged largely unscathed.

The clash, though fierce, lasted less than half an hour. Judging Worcester indefensible despite its hurried repairs, Prince Rupert led the bulk of the cavalry north—Sir Berkeley and his troop among them. Behind them came infantry unwilling to remain and face Essex's advancing forces, no doubt eager to avenge their reverse at the bridge.

Beneath a torrential downpour that quickly turned the tracks to thick mud, Prince Maurice, the Second Sons, and Smyth's dragoons joined the convoy escorting the wagons to Shrewsbury. The lightly wounded, and most of the prisoners were taken along to join the King's growing army gathering there.

The victory had emboldened many, and the convoy delivered the King much-needed funds to pay his troops. At the same time, Parliament's heavy-handed persecution of suspected Royalists seemed to be backfiring, driving the undecided into the King's camp.

A sudden chill swept through the tavern as the door swung open, admitting two hooded figures. The gust of cold air carried with it a reminder of the hard winter pressing ever closer. They spoke briefly with the Innkeeper, who soon nodded toward Benjamin and Owen. Though Owen had downed several tankards in rapid succession, his eyes were still keen enough to catch the exchange.

The two figures approached their table, drawing back their hoods at the last moment. To Benjamin's astonishment, it was his friend Thomas Ward, accompanied by his father, Stephen

Akins—and Thomas beside him. Both looked weary, their faces drawn and pale with care.

"Father!" Benjamin exclaimed, his heart leaping to his throat—half fearful of his father's judgement over his elopement, half astonished they had found him at all.

"How came you both to be here?" he asked.

Thomas stepped forward first, a broad smile breaking through his weariness as he clasped his friend in a firm embrace, while Owen offered Mr. Akins a courteous bow and greeting in the manner due his senior.

Benjamin stepping back to face his father bowing his head slightly, bracing for a scolding. "I'm sorry, Father, for leaving without your permission!"

Stephen's stern face softened. "I'm just glad you're safe,

my foolish boy" he embraced his son. "Praise God, we heard whispers of battle from villages on our way to Worcester—of Parliamentary horsemen in panicked retreat—but then we were told the city was under Parliament's control."

"We've heard all manner of nonsense," Owen said. "Some claim Sir Willmott's dead—but you'll find him alive and well, drinking with the Prince in the castle tonight. Rebels spin any lie to mask their shame. Truth is, we gave them a good hiding at that bridge. It was tactical withdrawal, as we call it," he added with pride.

"I see. Well, it's a relief we made it here," Stephen replied.

"We evaded Parliamentary patrols around Worcester; apparently, they've been hanging traitors. Some say it's the Royalists who lost the day and are spreading rumours that the King's men retreated. But it's been quite an adventure!" Thomas added, though his tone lacked his usual excitement.

Benjamin's thoughts drifted to the kind Worcester Innkeeper and his wife, concerned about their fate under the rebel's occupation, after their kind assistance. He also pondered the defector, entrusted with delivering false orders to lure the Parliamentary horsemen to the bridge.

Stephen's formal, austere manner returned. "I bear news for Master Thomas Smyth. A letter of his found its way to me, advising of your departure from Berkeley Castle toward Worcester. I must tell you—Bristol is said to be on the brink of declaring for Parliament, if the rumours prove true. Bath's trained bands have already done so, and word has it the navy now sails under Parliament's command. Worse still, several of Master Smyth's own ships have been seized—one laden with arms and blades newly arrived from the Continent. Parliament now demands that he present himself in London forthwith."

"That's terrible news, the last thing Thomas Smyth needs right now is more bad news; he's been very downcast since the fight at the bridge," Benjamin exclaimed.

"We have fared but little better, son. All our riding horses are gone, even the mares, and poor old Duke and Bob. Most were seized by the Parliament's men, though Castilio was spared, being ridden by Thomas when they came. Your sister and Uncle Paul are well—God be praised. Yet I must speak with William, and that without delay."

"Is this because of me, Father, for joining the Royalists, I mean?" Benjamin asked, concern knitting his brow.

"No, my son," Stephen replied, his voice weighed down with troubling news. "It's the result of our efforts to drive away some Parliamentary officials who were ransacking the manor, searching for evidence to condemn the Stephens for aiding the King. The entire village of Little Sodbury has suffered the consequences in one way or another." Benjamin could sense his father was holding something back.

Benjamin's mind shot straight to Jane, a pang of fear clutching at his heart. That familiar, sickening feeling, the unwavering love he felt, would it ever lessen? Would he always be **bridled by loyalty** for her, and weighed down with these intense emotions?

A sharp edge entered Owen's voice. "Have they taken Little Sodbury Manor, then?" he asked, concern etched across his features, tightening the lines around his mouth. "How is the household? My father and brother Tim; are they alright? And Irene...is she okay?" He pressed, urgency tightening every muscle in his huge frame.

"They were fine when we left them, Owen, and the Stephens still hold residency of the Manor for the time being," Stephen said, placing a reassuring hand on Owen's large shoulder. "I wish that was the only ill tiding I bore," Stephen Akins added, his expression turning grave. "But I need to relay this information to William first, and in person."

"Are you both staying?" Benjamin asked, dragging his mind away from his concerns for Jane, his voice laced with hope.

"Lad, we have little left to lose. We can't bounce back at the stud farm without Thomas Smyth's help, and his fate is now locked up in this ungodly contest between fellow Englishmen. It appears you must pick a side in this madness, so I intend on fighting for the King for what I can offer and hope we can bring a swift end to this unfolding tragedy, despite the odds seeming stacked against his grace," Stephen Akins said sincerely.

"It will be an honour to have you, Mr. Akins. I'll get you some kit at a good rate; we have some spares that might fit. I'm sure we can get you into our troop, although our ranks have swelled to sixty now, I'll see what we can do," Owen said, now clapping Stephen on the shoulder. "I will speak to Mr. Smyth and then look to our positions, thank you, Owen. But if I may, I must speak with William," Stephen Akins requested.

"Yes, of course. I shall escort you to William now," Owen offered, observing that the normally cheerful and fun-loving Thomas Ward's demeanour now mirrored that of Benjamin's father—a dark shadow had settled upon his features. Owen and Benjamin exchanged worried glances, the carefree atmosphere that had once filled the room dissipating into an ominous void. This night would certainly leave an indelible mark on Benjamin's memory.

Author's Note & Disclaimer

This work is a work of fiction, inspired by real events and historical figures from the seventeenth century. While every effort has been made to reflect the customs, politics, and spirit of the age, certain characters, events, and details have been altered, condensed, or reimagined for the purposes of storytelling.

Many of the persons depicted herein are entirely fictional; others are loosely based upon historical figures whose actions, words, or fates have been adapted to serve the narrative. Any historical inaccuracies are the result of the author's own oversight.

By way of example: **Thomas Smyth**, a fabulously wealthy merchant and supporter of the Royalist cause, was indeed a real person who resided at **Ashton Court** and died of illness on **2 October 1642 in Cardiff**. His involvement in the events of this book, however, is entirely fictional. Likewise, enterprises such as high-end horse breeding were not commonplace in England at this time; the Akins' family's trade in this regard would have been highly unusual and only feasible through the patronage of a man such as Smyth, as imagined in this story.

This book should therefore be read as a work of **imaginative reconstruction**, rather than a strict historical record.

Brindle Books Ltd

We hope that you have enjoyed this book. To find out more about Brindle Books Ltd, including news of new releases, please visit our website:

https://www.brindlebooks.co.uk

There is a contact page on the website, should you have any queries, and you can let us know if you would like email updates of news and new releases. We promise that we won't spam you with lots of sales emails, and we will never sell or give your contact details to any third party.

If you purchased this book online, please consider leaving an honest review on the site from which you purchased it. Your feedback is important to us, and may influence future releases from our company.